Crush in the Cascades

THE RACE FOR RICHES OR ROMANCE

LISA S. GAYLE

Crush in the Cascades

LISA S. GAYLE

THE RACE FOR RICHES OR ROMANCE

Cover design by Yummy Book Covers

For my family, who loves the outdoors

One

A high-pitched woman's voice carried across the grassy clearing. "You're taking my suitcase *away*?"

Cooper scrunched his brows at the piercing sound. When his eyes found her, he chuckled. She wore an elegant, orangish-red cocktail dress. Satin strips of sheer fabric danced in the light breeze and sparkled in unison with the reflective ripples on the lake water.

"Why can't I have my own things?" she continued. "Most of my clothes are for running, and this is an *athletic* competition."

A personal assistant reached for her light pink case. "Miss Amity, please," the man replied. "I don't make the rules."

Cooper extended his arm, pressing up on the silver nozzle of the water cooler, and froze. Closing his eyes, he let a disbelieving groan escape his throat as he made the connection. Amity was his partner for the first leg of the race. Fifteen minutes ago, an assistant director asked the men to draw straws—and dammit to hell—he'd drawn hers.

She likely didn't know. The assistant had been firm about the men keeping it to themselves, probably to increase the drama in the opening scene. No big surprise there. When he'd signed up for the show, he knew they'd milk the drama. He hated shows like this, but he needed the money—he *badly* needed the money.

Cold water splashed over his fingers, and Cooper quickly pushed the nozzle down, shaking off the excess drops. He frowned at the unnecessary presence of a water cooler in the great outdoors while taking a long swig from his Nalgene bottle.

Amity left the group camp, attempting to hoist her heavy, red Kelty backpack across her bare-skinned shoulder, and wobbled across the uneven meadow toward the lake. If this woman were someone else's partner, he'd have laughed—but the joke was on him.

He sighed, watching her heel twist sideways in a dirt hole, and chuckled in surprise when she somehow pulled her foot up without injury. From California, he'd guess. After taking numerous clients on tours, he could predict almost instantly their home state.

With a gust of wind, her long, flimsy dress swirled around her tan legs, fully revealing a three-inch pair of black strappy, open-toed high heels. All he could do was stare with his mouth hanging open. Who wore open-toed heels on an action-adventure show? And then did absolutely nothing to resolve the situation? He would *not* let her take him down, even if he had to drag her across the finish line. Even now, the woman could take off the heels if she knew what was in her pack.

Their pre-equipped Kelty backpacks were full of Cooper's favorite gear. He'd already gone through every item in his pack in gory detail, memorizing the contents, and was pleasantly surprised. Their packs contained hardcore backpacking gear and two sets of clothes that fitted accordingly. Almost every item he'd bring on a tour was in there, minus some of the emergency equipment like fire blankets and tourniquets. He assumed those items were fully stocked by the show's medical team. If a situation like that occurred, the show's crew would handle it, which was a nice change for him and less to carry.

Before he'd been paired with the out-of-place woman, Cooper couldn't believe his good luck. The show's contract hadn't specified what type of athletic competition they'd be doing, and he'd landed exactly in his element. If he were home, he'd be prepping for his next Rocky Mountain tour, packing the gear himself to equip the group, then home three days later with a lager in hand, watching the Broncos. His golden retriever, Jax, would be curled up by his feet after taking a long walk in the woods with him around his cabin. He let out his breath and tried to focus. Win the cash and get out—that was the goal—then he could go home.

Cooper glanced across Sparks Lake at the patchy, snow-topped peaks in the distance. Of all the places to be stuck on a train-wreck show vying for cash, Oregon was perfection—trails, evergreen trees, lakes and rivers, and a set of mountains that made a man want to be lost for days in the wilderness. It was greener than the Colorado mountain areas. More under-brush and fewer rocks, probably due to all the rain in Oregon, but the summer weather seemed decent and warmer than back home. Nights would be cold but tolerable.

The main director asked them to line up. As instructed, Cooper planted his feet on one of the many mats structurally laid out along the lakefront grass. For ten minutes, the camera crews adjusted the lenses, lighting, and sound. He rocked back and forth and scraped his hand across his face a dozen times, forcibly holding his feet in place. It would be a long three weeks if they had to do this before every scene.

The male contestants stood in a row facing the women.

3

Alex Bandon, the show's host, moved into place at a center platform, standing at the head point, while the two rows of contestants fanned out at an angle from him. The crews adjusted the cameras, so the lenses captured Bandon in front of the picture-perfect lake with the Cascade Mountains silhouetted in the distance. Not bad. If Cooper had to suffer through that job, he'd go for that angle, but looking like a Men's Wearhouse model, Bandon's flashy suit and styled, dark-brown hair killed the shot. You couldn't pay him to go there. Well, maybe you could, Cooper reminded himself. There was very little he wouldn't do to win this money.

"Okay, contestants," Alex Bandon boomed out in an energetic voice. The host was one of those peppy types, which didn't bother Cooper since he was used to it, as his best friend, Dominic, was like that as well. He and Dominic ran Rocky Mountain Inspiration, their tour company, and were in each other's space multiple days a week.

Moving his hands with animated, screen-worthy gestures, the host continued, "Given that this is the first season, we will discuss the show's basic premise live on camera so the audience can see your reactions. However, before we start, I must remind you about two critical rules that, if broken, will result in your immediate removal from this competition."

Alex Bandon eyed them all with a serious look. "First, you cannot physically harm another contestant in such a way that they can no longer compete. We see and hear everything. The cameras will always be rolling, so we *will* catch it."

A commotion occurred behind them when a large camera toppled from a stand into the grassy dirt. Several contestants, both male and female, yelped in surprise. What did these people think? That a bear was jumping out at them?

Cooper watched what looked like the head of the film crew run over and rant at his team about how to set up equipment on uneven terrain. Bandon clapped his hands together, drawing their attention back to him like he was ready to get the show rolling. So was Cooper. He didn't want to hear any more rules unless they were about the competitive challenges. Though he knew safety rules were crucial, he hated that anyone would need to be reminded of basic respect.

The host continued, "With that out of the way, let's get on with—"

"I'm sorry," Amity interrupted, raising one hand like she was in a kindergarten classroom while the other remained wrapped around her torso. Her voice shook as she asked, "What's the second rule?"

Was she nervous or cold? Perhaps both. Any woman who wore a dress without a cover-up deserved to be cold, but still, Cooper felt a slight twinge of concern for her, like he should run across the divide between the men and women and pass her his sweatshirt. He shook his head to clear it. Why help a woman that didn't belong? Better that she learned her lesson and wimped out early on. Besides, he'd need his extra layer when they got higher in elevation.

Amity moved her hand, which he now realized had fingernails painted with bright purple polish, above her eyes to block the sun as she continued to address the host. "You said there were two rules."

And Cooper gawked at her, adjusting his tattered baseball cap with a whole new level of astonishment hitting him full force. This woman had no sunglasses, no hat, and of course no jacket, yet she somehow made time to paint her fingernails and put her streaky brown hair up in some sort of twisty updo; and based on the silky, flawless skin of her uncovered shoulders, she'd be crying after the first mosquito bite.

"Oh yes," Bandon responded. "Thank you, Miss Amity. Got sidetracked by the commotion with the cameras. Although this was in the contract, it's vital we are all on the same page. Any romantic encounters must be consensual."

Cooper closed his eyes, letting out a pained groan. Since he didn't read all fifty pages of the contract, he had this coming, but still, he did not sign up to be a playboy, gigolo, or whatever. No way anyone was filming him having sex on television while he competed for money. He didn't even want to make out. If he wanted that, he'd go to a bar and find a woman looking for the same unattached one night of hot sex as him— privately—not a broadcast on national television.

Complication, social media, and expectations—they all gave him a panic attack. That's why he wasn't on social media, just his business, but somehow, he didn't think that mattered. He'd probably have people join his tours, thinking he'd give them *more* than a backpacking experience. Thankfully, this was an action-adventure show, and he assumed the rules were just a precaution, given that the contestants would be isolated in tents and on trails together.

Alex Bandon pointed at the head director, a middle-aged woman with raven black hair and an office-ready pantsuit, who he thought had asked to be called by her last name, McKenzie. That he could understand—he went by his last name as well—but business clothes in the middle of nowhere? These show people missed their own memo. Or, more than likely, most of them would be flown in by helicopter from their five-star hotels in Bend to monitor the daytime scenes and, therefore, could dress however they wanted.

"Ready when you are," Bandon said to McKenzie.

McKenzie led the crews and counted down for the official show to begin. "…3…2…1."

Bandon turned to face the camera directly in front of him. "Welcome to the first season of *The Race for Riches or Romance*, a new, action-packed reality TV series—"

Cooper's muscles tightened. What the hell? Okay, the rules

were *not* just a precaution. After taking a deep breath, he tugged on his sweatshirt collar. He'd signed up for an action-adventure show—not a damn romance. Cooper almost raised his hand like Amity had to ask if fake romantic encounters were required to win. He'd seen that on other shows—on the romance shows that people *willingly* signed up for.

"You are the first twenty—" Bandon continued, but Cooper temporarily tuned him out.

The contract said to be ready for surprises. We guarantee physical challenges and much, much more, he remembered reading. A woman was not the *more* he had in mind. How stupid could he be? Of course there would be a romance angle. These reality TV watchers ate that stuff up. He knew—his sister, Hannah, was one of them. She was addicted to the screen every time one of these dumb shows came on.

When Cooper told his sister that he was going on an action-adventure reality show, she'd jumped up screaming, "I can't believe it. That's awesome and *so* not you." Without taking a breath, she'd continued, "Why? You hate those shows. I should go in your place, dummy." Then she giggled and hugged him. "Oh well, put in a good word for me."

"No way. You're too young," Cooper had said to her. His sister was only twenty-four, four years younger than him, and he'd never let anyone hurt her. He'd hated every one of her boyfriends to date—probably a normal reaction for a big brother. "Not a chance," he'd continued. "Reality TV messes people up."

"Then why? Oh…" Hannah had said when she'd realized. "I know why. *Win*," she added fiercely. "Win, so you can help them."

Cooper tried to force his mind to the present as the host continued. "—first season will be full of constant challenges, testing your athletic limits—"

Athletic ability wasn't a concern, Cooper thought, tuning

Alex Bandon out again, but romance? That was another story. Every muscle in his body remained tense, which was not a great way to start a challenge. Maybe if he worked the problem through in his mind, he could relax.

Would he quit the show if a relationship were required? Probably not. Would he lie to get the money—even if he was supposed to claim he was in love at the end? Maybe so. None of the people on reality TV shows stayed together anyway. Every time he'd said that to Hannah, she listed a dozen couples that she claimed were together, to which Cooper nodded placatingly but didn't really believe. These shows were all about fake drama and real money.

"—two million is up for grabs, divided evenly at one million for each contestant in the winning pair—" Speaking of money, pay attention, he thought, but the host's chipper rambling droned on.

Cooper wasn't against love. He could appreciate a good relationship. His parents were happily married, and he'd always envied that Dominic had someone to return home to after their tours. But so far, he couldn't find a woman who understood his need for space. Multi-day backpacking trips and a permanent relationship did not seem to go well together. Regardless, real love could not be found on a television show, no matter what Hannah thought.

Hannah was too kind to understand big city vultures. He saw them on his tours a couple of times a month, trying to find serene locations that they could brag about having visited. Usually, they focused on the perfect selfie shot and how many bottles of fine wine Cooper could carry into the wilderness for them. Those types were outnumbered, though, by incredible, down-to-earth people looking for a genuine adventure in the outdoors.

Cooper looked across at the women who were lined up facing him. Of the ten females, maybe two looked like they were dressed for the rugged outdoors. All of them had athletic figures, whether slender or built. He eyed a petite woman that was fourth in line with North Face hiking clothes and long dark hair. Then, tenth in line was a tall woman with camo gear and short, bleach-blonde, spiky hair. Both women appeared to be ready to hike down a trail. He'd listen for their names.

Sure enough, moments later, they went down the line announcing the women's names. The North Face girl was Kim, and the camo girl was Bria. He'd shoot for finding a way to be one of their partners.

Cooper glared at Amity. Surely, he wouldn't be stuck with her the whole race. Seventh in line among the women, she was slightly diagonal across from him as he stood fifth among the men. Still looking cold and uncomfortable, she hugged her arms around her waist, exposing a silver bracelet that sparkled on her wrist with all kinds of charms hanging off of it. A pissed-off frown was now etched across her oval, makeup-covered face, framed by a few loose, wispy strands of hair that seemed to have escaped from her tight updo. Why the frown? Perhaps she was still upset about her confiscated belongings?

He scanned up and down her frame, his eyes settling on her feet. Her heels were now driving down into the soft dirt like stakes from a tent. If he remained partners with her, the heels might come in handy—to use as a tool for outdoor survival, he tried to convince himself, though she did look good in them. He blinked his eyes in surprise at his attraction —to what?

Amity was pretty in a cute sort of way, but, as he'd already promised himself, he would not stick his tongue down some woman's throat for America's entertainment—and certainly not Amity's throat. High-class elegance with complicated hairdos and expensive dresses equaled trouble. A woman like her wanted a man with money, not a down-to-earth guy like him that liked to go out and do regular things.

A shocking pulse went through his body as he continued to stare at her. His breathing accelerated as he realized his attraction to her had been masked by his initial irritation of being paired with a liability. She was *exactly* the type of woman he avoided.

Dragging his eyes away from her, he analyzed the men instead. There was a nice mix of different types of people. A few were guys in formal gear that would be perfect for Amity. He'd let one of them vie for her, and hopefully, that would save him from getting duped.

Cooper jerked to attention as Alex Bandon pointed to each of the men and listed their names, causing him to flinch as the host announced his first name on what would become national television.

"Now it's time to describe the race," Bandon broadcasted, his deep voice carrying across the open field as he faced the towering camera. Better not be more pointless romance garbage, Cooper thought, watching the host fan his hand across the sky, presumably showing the television audience an introduction to their surroundings. "The race will alternate between wilderness skill challenges and trail challenges in the picturesque Oregon Cascade Mountains."

Now Bandon was talking—this Cooper could do. Maybe the romance angle was just to keep viewers watching, sappily hoping that some fool would start a ratings-catching fling. Not him. Cooper wasn't here to date women, whether they were his type or not.

"The last team to complete a challenge for each leg of the race will be eliminated," Bandon bellowed out, sounding just like that sap of a host from *The Amazing Race*. "Losing teams will start the next leg of the race with a time penalty, in five-minute increments based on where they finished in the previous leg. For instance, first place gets a five-minute head start from the second-place team, and so on. Winning teams will get to choose a new partner for each leg, schoolyard-pick style, and teams will remain male-female." Bandon eyed them all carefully. "This is more than just a show about money."

Cooper tilted his head up. What was this? Choose a new partner? That right there was the most important reason to come in first. He'd watch the women like a professional recruit during the challenges and do everything in his power to choose a woman who had outdoor skills. If he could pick now, Kim or Bria, but he may learn over time that other women were an equal or better choice.

"You will," Bandon continued, "only have the supplies in your pack and on your person during the competition."

Cooper grinned, thinking of how Amity had on her useless dress and spiky heels. He couldn't deny his physical attraction to her, but he knew it would end there. Though they had two other outfits in their pack, a heavy coat, and a set of trail running shoes, she'd pay somewhere along the line for having no backup clothes.

Nature had a way of throwing surprises at you—rain, wind, bugs, sun—the elements always beat down the unprepared. As long as it didn't cost him the first leg of the race, he found it humorous. A film crew could fly her out in an emergency chopper if she got herself into too dangerous of a situation.

Bandon moved on to have the guys announce the partners they'd drawn and answer questions. When it was Cooper's turn, he didn't see any point in holding back his opinion. Honesty would alert the other women that he meant business, and hopefully, he'd attract a new partner.

"Easton," Bandon said.

Cooper flinched.

"For the first leg, you drew?"

"I go by my last name, Cooper." With a tight frown, he looked at the seventh woman in line. "And I drew Amity."

"Very well, Cooper then," Bandon said, his pleasant voice contradicting Cooper's mood. "Are you happy with your selection?"

"No, Bandon, I'm not." Cooper gazed at the host. "Any chance I can choose a different partner?"

Two

Amity's mouth dropped open. Who did this guy think he was?

"I go by Alex." The host smiled, looking at Easton Cooper as if he were amused. "Out of curiosity, who *would* you select as a partner?"

"Kim or Bria," the Easton guy said with a nod before adding, "Alex," acknowledging the host's request to call him by his first name.

Kim smiled shyly, and Bria did a little fist pump.

"What do you think about that, Miss Amity?" Alex asked her.

Amity looked at Alex Bandon with distaste. Why was he taking Easton's side? And she would make it a point to call him Easton after seeing him flinch at the name. She would *never* call him Cooper.

"I think I'm sick of everyone calling me Miss," Amity spat, clenching her arms tighter around her waist, "and if that jerk wants a different partner, then you should give him one."

Alex laughed, a buoyant flowing vibration that slowly faded into a warm smile. Though normally she might appreciate such an energetic guy, she pinched her lips tighter, not liking the host's amusement at her expense.

"Forgive me, Amity," Alex said respectfully. "I thought you went by Miss after hearing the directors call you that. And unfortunately, both you and Cooper are stuck with one another for the first leg of the race. I encourage you to win so you can choose a different partner for the second leg."

"I intend to," Amity mumbled, fully aware that three cameras were zoomed in on her glowering face.

Amity had analyzed the row of men during Alex's introductory spiel, and honestly, she'd passed right over Easton Cooper in her initial assessment of partners, even though he stood boldly in the middle like he belonged there. Maybe he did, and that had Amity clenching her fingers until her newly polished nails dug into her soft skin. Scowling, she noticed a meddlesome camerawoman capture her every look. Amity quickly twisted her features into what she hoped was an indifferent mask as the lens zoomed in, but her eyes began to water, so she gave up. There was no helping it—she couldn't hide her emotions.

She let out a puff of air, releasing her fists and flexing her fingers. Perhaps it would distract her if she did a more detailed scan of the men? A few looked promising, but before she could really consider her options, Easton's assessing eyes locked onto hers. She scrunched her nose up—any man was better than him. With a cynical grin plastered on his scruffy face, his eyes switched between her dress and heels like he thought she was a joke. Could you hate someone after only hearing them say a handful of words?

She wanted to flip him the bird and thought, why not? They couldn't air that, could they? So she did, and he chuckled quietly. She cocked her head to the side, deciding to look him over more closely—know your competition, right? He certainly wasn't going to be an ally.

14

Easton stood in a carefree pose, his long arms and legs reminding her of a limber tree. His lean build was topped with scraggly, dark brown hair that poked out from around the sides of a faded blue baseball cap. It looked like the barber had cut at random. Maybe he'd done it himself with sheers, she thought, flashing him a derisive smile that suddenly had him shifting around on his tiny mat and staring at the grass in front of him. Interesting. Did he really want to give her the advantage of surveying him unabashed? She'd take it.

Her eyes raked across his torso, noting his discolored, ratty green sweatshirt before traveling down south to discover tan hiking pants with zipper compartments all over them. Her cheeks tingled with a blush as she tried not to focus on his groin, forcing her eyes back up to read the worn letters on his sweatshirt—Rocky Mountain National Park. That figures, she thought—a mountain bum.

He looked like one of those relaxed guys that took nothing in life too seriously, but his determination to find a different partner told her otherwise. Amity could sense that he wanted to win. Although maybe that meant they'd survive the first leg, it was insulting that he didn't think she had anything to offer. Amity *would* find someone who wanted her as a partner.

The show's official title had surprised her—*The Race for Riches or Romance*. Though Amity hadn't really come with either of those goals in mind, both would be nice. Money, of course—who didn't want a million dollars? And a guy? She'd like one of those too, but the *or* in the title was tricky. Really, how could anyone on the show make them choose? She shrugged. Just in case, she'd try for both—the money and the guy—and hope for one.

Amity scratched her cheek, suppressing a laugh, while trying to imagine a guy in this lineup that would cause her to say, 'Why yes, Alex, I'd rather have the guy.' But maybe? After all, she'd been unsuccessful in finding a man back home with her long hours and repetitive routine. Why not find one while on vacation? Perhaps it would lead to something like the kind of love her parents had—the solid selfless kind. She needed someone who cared more about her than his own selfish agenda, and a man like that was *exceedingly* hard to find, especially with a million dollars at stake.

But she'd never find him if she didn't try. She jutted out her chin, her eyes re-scanning the row. After a few moments of examining the men like contestants on *The Dating Game*, Amity brushed her hand across her forehead, pressing her palm against her aching temple. Who found a guy like this? Like a desperate, juvenile manhunter? A soft sigh escaped her throat before she decided—don't give up! If she kept overanalyzing every opportunity, then she'd be alone forever.

From a glance, Easton Cooper appeared to be one of three that looked like the backcountry-outdoors type. She'd avoid those guys. If they were anything like Easton, then they were not for her. She kept scanning. There was a guy near the host that looked like the tattoo-motorcycle type—also not her style. Then there were a couple of overdressed men in suits, looking all fancied up. Although extremely judgmental of her, especially given her own inadvisable attire, she'd avoid them as well.

Perhaps Miles? He'd drawn her gaze instantly, as she'd had to casually keep rolling her eyes down the line to keep from visibly drooling over him. Wearing a blue button-up shirt and khaki pants, he stood second in line with black hair, pale skin, and a proper posture. He'd burn in Palm Springs, but there was always sunscreen. Then, fourth in line, next to Easton Cooper, stood the equally drool-worthy Isaac—a dark-skinned, very tall guy with casual jeans and a basketball jersey, looking athletic in a team sport sort of way.

Amity leaned forward and peeked down the row in both directions to analyze the other women, and her chest tightened. What guy *would* choose her in her preposterous clothes? She'd never have worn them if she'd known they were diving right into an athletic competition. The casting director said to arrive for an opening scene at an undisclosed location and dress for the occasion. Based on those words, she'd assumed a formal event, so she'd dressed accordingly. Now, she understood the sly director's plan—a bunch of mixed-up drama.

Amity allowed the blood to rush to her cheeks and envisioned herself in casual clothes. It didn't help. Even a simple glance at the well-suited contestants caused her pulse to re-spike, so she stared at the foreign trees and daunting mountains instead. No wonder they'd taken away her accessories and over-packed suitcase full of clothes. Most of her things were absurdly unnecessary and too heavy to carry down a trail. Still, she'd been looking forward to wearing those cute Lululemon leggings and the set's matching sports bra. She'd never worn the expensive brand before.

But if their goal was to equalize the contestants and throw them off by stripping away their comfort items, she had a little secret. During the personal assistant's incessant nagging, she'd stuck her smallest makeup bag in the side of her underwear, and it was on her *person*—so she had lipstick, mascara, blush, brow tweezers, nail clippers, beauty scissors, a miniature hairbrush, and even a tiny bottle of sunscreen.

She knew how to spruce up with resourceful selections. Her mom, being the queen of girly-girl, taught her how to hunt for coupons and sales like the hawk circling above her searched and dove for prey. There was no way she'd have let that annoying PA minion seize the makeup bag she'd worked so hard to earn. Besides, wasn't that the point of being on television? To look good during all the drama? Well, to look good while competing anyway. She didn't really want to be involved in drama.

Her eyes followed the majestic, brown-and-whitesplotched hawk across the horizon while she surveyed the rest of her surroundings. All twenty contestants, including herself, were at some dirt-covered meadow lake campground at the base of several trails and roads that appeared to dive right into a green pine tree, bigfoot forest. Regardless of the terrain, if the competition was to get up or down a trail, she wasn't too worried. She could handle distance.

Amity brought her attention back to the show, twisting and straightening her spine to face the group as the camera crew circled around her like gnats. Casually, she bit her cheek and moved her arms across her chest, looking away from the intrusive lenses toward the chipper host. She felt a slight tickle on her hand, and her eyes darted down, spotting a black water bug on one of her gown's thin spaghetti straps. Or perhaps it was a mosquito?

She sucked in her breath and flicked the potential bloodsucker away with her index finger, reflexively protecting her skin and the satin strand. Her boss lent her the dress from a friend's boutique two stores down, and now she'd have to pay for it. There was no way 'the clothes on her back' were coming out of this in one piece. Not that a spindly insect could do anything overly harmful to the fabric when the hem was already covered in campground dust.

Amity wrinkled her nose, gently jostling the fabric while attempting to shake the dirt off the sheer blood-orange trim. The filth clung firmly, and her efforts made no difference. Her boss should have selected a cheaper dress, but how could they have known it would get ruined? She'd borrowed everything, including the new designer suitcase, intending to keep the price tags and return them good-as-new as agreed upon to the shop owner. Oh well, she thought, letting out her breath— she'd worry about it later.

Amity peered back up, taking in the clear blue sky and shooting her father a confident smile. 'I'm finally on an adventure,' she told him, and, 'I'm going to win so I can live our dream.' She brought her eyes down, and her pupils, again, annoyingly locked onto Easton's. A tingling flush filled her cheeks at his noticeable grin as his eyes skimmed down to glance at her shoulder, her dress hem, and then back up.

What? The bum was entertained by her perfectly *normal* reaction to a bug. He didn't care about being eaten alive? Nobody liked being a meal, she thought defensively. And her dress? Nobody liked being dirty either. Seriously, who wanted to camp in the woods? Truthfully, she'd hoped for a tropical beach or a cacti forest—somewhere warm like she was accustomed to—not Sasquatch territory, but it would have to do. She couldn't afford to be picky.

Amity refocused on Alex Bandon, trying to ignore the ratty sight of Easton Cooper and his wandering eyes. The dope was still assessing every woman in line like he was sizing up military recruits.

Alex continued, "As discussed, the race will alternate between skills challenges and trail distance runs—"

Her breath hitched, and she stood on her toes, attentively waiting for the host to continue. A few moments ago, Alex had said something about trail challenges but nothing about distance runs. Trail runs she could do. Heck, she'd take her heels off and run barefoot if she had to.

She smiled, feeling the comforting adrenaline rush that flowed through her veins just before she took off on a run. She was ready until Alex finished his sentence. "—and the first leg will be a skills challenge."

Her hands dropped to her sides, her warm buzz turning to ice. Well shoot! Hopefully, she made it through the first leg. She wasn't about to have any kind of all-expense-paid adventure if she didn't.

Three

Cooper's head popped up, an easy grin lighting up his face. A skills challenge was good news for him. He'd be able to complete the task on his own, whereas running a trail was not something he could do *for* Amity.

"Please, ladies," Alex announced, "go stand by your partners."

Amity fumbled toward him, tripping over the grassy knolls. She held her long, sheer dress up by fisting the delicate fabric, making quite the scene. The camera crew agreed, circling around her like she was, in fact, some big-time movie star. She probably loved that. Cooper didn't buy the sour look she had plastered on her dolled-up face. He smirked, raising a brow.

"*Don't* say a word," she hissed.

He chuckled.

"Now," Alex continued, motioning toward the tree line, "the first challenge will be completed by the ladies—"

Oh shit! He winced, peeking down at Amity, thinking she'd be smirking and taunting him, but instead, she gnawed on her lip, frozen, like a gerbil that had just been let out of its cage for the first time. That didn't make him feel better.

"What's wrong?" he whispered.

She brushed him off with a hand gesture, and although she'd released her teeth from her lip, she wrinkled her nose, squinting at the challenge stations lined up under the trees like they were from another planet.

"—with the men allowed to instruct and encourage their partners through the challenge. Communication will be paramount in every leg of this race."

Cooper would be instructing all right, and he hoped Amity would listen to every word he said.

Alex clapped his hands together. "Contestants, I will explain challenges and other aspects of the race as we go along. The film crew will decide which parts are shown. For instance, when I explain your next challenge, many of my words will be replaced by a visual representation for the television audience. Understood?"

Most contestants nodded, and Alex continued, "There are ten identical stone fire pits in the foliage under the trees. Each pit has a piece of twine above it, supported by two metal stakes on the sides. You must start your fire on the ground and let the flames burn through the twine. No lifting burning objects up to the twine by hand. Your team's flag will pop up when the fire fully burns through your twine. The first nine teams to complete the challenge will move on to the next leg of the race. There's a wooden bench for each male partner to sit on during the challenge.

"Men, you may talk to your partner, but you can't move off the bench or touch any objects. If you do, you'll incur a twenty-minute time penalty for each violation. Ladies are to start a fire in the pit using items in their own pack and from the forest. You can't touch another team's fire pit, throw things at it, etc. You'll draw colors for placement. No discussing the task until the countdown is complete."

Cooper knew where the flint was in his pack, so he'd be

able to tell Amity where to find it in hers. It would be the fastest way for them to get a fire started. Their packs didn't contain matches, but he'd discovered a magnifying glass they could use with the heat from the sun. Or they could try rubbing sticks together, but someone inexperienced had no prayer of creating enough friction to start a fire that way.

Alex offered a container to Amity, and she pulled a stick with a dark blue tip. Cooper swung his head around to search the trees for the blue station. Damn, right in the shade under a sizable grand fir. Using the magnifying glass to reflect the sun was out. Though he'd planned to use the flint, it didn't provide them with a great backup option.

After Alex announced for teams to find their stations, he and Amity grabbed their backpacks and walked over to their spot. Cooper threw his gray pack down and sat on the pine bench, baring his teeth. He'd been a bencher in high school football, and while he'd hated it then, he hated it even more right now. The wilderness was his varsity sport, and he shouldn't be benched.

He looked around for a distraction and quickly found it didn't help. Various camera crews were set up with perfect shots of all the action, ready to film them like a damn Hollywood soap opera. He let out a long-winded sigh, deciding he'd do his best to pretend they weren't there.

Amity stood on the side of the fire pit with her arms crossed, alternating between scrunching her features at the fire pit and scanning the underbrush for sticks. Not once had she glanced at her pack. Did she know how to start a fire without matches? It didn't matter, he decided. Either way, he'd instruct her. All he cared about was getting through the challenge. Beyond that, he didn't care what she did or didn't know.

Alex did an introductory talk for the cameras and counted down. "...3...2...1." And Amity took off for the trees before Cooper could get a word in.

"No," he shouted. "Wait."

She spun around, meeting his exasperated glare head-on. "What? Don't we need wood to burn?"

"Not yet." Cooper motioned for her to return, and thankfully she jogged back. "Open the small side pocket on your pack," he continued in a quiet tone that he hoped the other teams wouldn't overhear. "There's a flint inside."

"All the other teams are getting wood." Amity gestured one hand toward the forest while resting the other on her hip. "We're doing this *wrong*."

His shoulder blades tensed while his ears rang with the annoying echo of her whiny voice. "First," he said, trying to maintain an even tone, "you need to get the tools out that will start the fire. Then you can gather materials. It's an advantage to get the flint out now when the other teams can't see where it is. I'm probably the only one who knows." He darted his eyes around, assessing the other teams' progress while pointing at her feet. "And you need to change your shoes. They'll slow you down."

Amity's skin flushed a soft shade of pink. "I don't have any other shoes."

Closing his eyes, he took a long, deep breath, feeling his lungs expand, before letting the air out slowly. Twenty minutes, then he'd be done with her. "Trail shoes are also in your pack. Get the flint out first. I don't want the other teams to see where it is."

Amity glanced over her shoulder, eyeing the other contestants, hesitated, then shrugged and said, "Okay, I hope you're right." She quickly crouched down, fumbling through the small side pocket on her pack, and pulled out the flint, a pocketknife, and a handful of other items. She then shoved them all back into the pocket and continued searching.

Cooper threw his hands over his head, running them down the back of his baseball cap. "*What* are you doing?"

He'd had a few women like this in his tour groups before, and normally they expected him to just do everything for them. They didn't actually want to be on the tour. Some of them had seen that movie called *Wild* and thought they wanted to find themselves, but really, they didn't because none of them did the work themselves like Reese Witherspoon's character had. And others were being dragged along by a boyfriend or some other family member who also didn't have a clue, but he didn't mind—that was his job. He liked doing it, only right now he couldn't.

"Get the flint *out*." He pulled roughly on some wayward strands of his hair, poking out from around his cap. The resulting pain in his scalp was all that contained him from getting a twenty-minute penalty. "Why are you putting it back in?"

"Shut up, *Easton*, and tell me what a flint is!"

He flinched before his mind processed her absurd words. "Tell you what a flint…" He moved his hands down, covering his face, and grumbled between his fingers. "You're kidding." He couldn't even tell her not to call him Easton, he was so dumbstruck.

"What is it?" Amity shouted. "Explain now. We don't have time for this."

"You had it in your hand," Cooper said, spitting the words at her. He gestured toward her pack. "It's the little gray rectangle that looks like a block with the small scraping tool attached to it."

"No." She shook her head at him and laughed with her hand placed pretentiously on her hip. "There's no way a block can start a fire."

"Yes…it…does." He locked his muscles in place to keep from jumping off the bench. "This is what I do," he tried to explain. "Just listen, please."

"I'm sorry," she said, moving her hand off her hip to

motion her palm in his face, "but you don't know what you're talking about."

"You're kidding," he repeated, laughing in disbelief. "Fu —" he began to say but caught himself and yelled, "Fudge," to the trees instead. He would do his best not to curse with a woman present. "Okay, let's get something straight." He moved his head around her palm to glare menacingly into her eyes. "I'm not losing this competition, so please listen to every word I say and do *exactly* what I tell you." He pointed to the small pocket on her pack. "Get the small, gray rectangular block out of that pocket."

Amity glanced over her shoulder at the other teams again before whipping her head around and narrowing a set of magnetic brown eyes at him. She raised her chin defiantly, turned, and jogged off toward trees, her frame flailing as her heels twisted unevenly with each step. She looked ridiculous—and sexy as hell. He fisted his fingers, letting his anger out by knuckle-punching his other hand. What he wouldn't do to have an actual punching bag right now.

Unable to withhold a condescending tone, Cooper called after her, "What…are…you…doing?"

"Worst partner *ever*," he heard her grumble as her impractical, satin dress blew in the breeze. It looked like she was a model filming an advertisement for perfume with all the cameras trailing beside her. She yelled over her shoulder, "Like I said, you *don't* know what you're talking about."

Cooper wanted to shout back but decided to let her get started on the wood. He braced his hands behind his neck and inhaled deep breaths, like he was in one of his sister's yoga classes, while he stared fixedly at the dried brown pine needles by his feet. He knew better than to be harsh with women, but this woman didn't belong. She would unfairly send someone home by her lack of knowledge about the outdoors, and in a matter of minutes, it might be him.

He dislodged his hands and shook his head. It didn't matter if she belonged or not, he reminded himself. Deal with the situation. He'd learned that from being in the dangerous backcountry most of his life. She'd come back and realize she didn't know what to do, and then he'd try again. He scrubbed his fingertips across the scruffy stubble on his chin and stared at the fire pit, unable to watch the other teams until he got himself under control.

Amity came back a few minutes later, carrying a ridiculously small amount of wood in one hand and her heels in the other. She must have taken them off, finally realizing that either she couldn't walk straight in them, or she'd sprain an ankle. Either way, she now tiptoed around barefoot, gathering little twigs while hectically glancing at the other teams, who had twice as much wood.

"Ignore the other teams," he instructed. "Let me worry about them. Get both the flint and the pocketknife out in case the scraping tool is too hard for you to manage..."

But Amity ignored him, jogging back into the trees and bouncing off each step like sticks were jabbing into her bare skin, which of course, they were. Why wouldn't she listen to him?

On her way back, a satin ribbon from her long dress snagged on a downed tree limb. She quickly ripped it free and ran to dump the wood by the fire pit. She did care about winning, at least somewhat. Perhaps longevity on the show increased her chances of exposure?

"Where are the matches?" Amity asked, rushing out the words. "Which pocket?"

Cooper groaned. "There *aren't* matches. Why would I tell a woman like you to get a flint out if there were matches?"

He already knew that two other teams had started their fires, six were scraping magnesium off the flint and attempting to light theirs, one was still trying to find the flint in their pack, and then there was them. One of two teams on the path to total failure. And he could *not* lose.

"How would you know?" Amity looked over her shoulder. "We only just got our supplies…" Cooper saw the moment it dawned on her that he knew what he was talking about as she saw all the flints and knives in the hands of the other women. Her cheeks colored that glowing, subtle light pink shade before she let out a little huff of air and said, "Fine, you win."

She then crouched down, her bright-purple-polished toenails poking out from underneath the deep orange satin fabric of her dress, ill-suited amongst the brown dirt. After searching through the pocket, she finally pulled out the flint and pocketknife. "Tell me what to do, Easton."

He flinched. "It's Cooper."

The corner of her mouth lifted. "Is it?"

Cooper's lips twitched, and although he knew better than to react, he usually did. Evening out his features, he said, "Now, grab some dry pine needles off the ground and make a small pile in the center of the pit." She dashed off to do as he asked while he continued to talk, and dammit if he didn't feel overly gratified by her finally listening to him. "Take four or five tiny twigs and put them on top."

"And then the larger pieces of wood?" Amity asked.

"Not yet. You'll need to get a flame started first. The fire needs room to breathe."

Amity frowned but complied.

"Now open the pocketknife…no," he added calmly as he watched her fumble to try and pull out the blade. "You have to hold down the small safety button on the side." When she finally got the knife out, he continued, "Put your thumb on the backside of the knife and strike the blade down the side of the flint to strip off some magnesium."

"What?" Her hands shook. "Speak English, please."

"Start striking the blade on the side where the silver

magnesium…" Cooper watched her turn to look at the other teams so she could figure it out. More wasted time. He leaned forward and snapped his fingers by her ear. "No, focus on me."

"Easton," she said through her teeth. "Get your fingers away from my face before I cut them off with this knife. I need to see it done by someone else."

"By someone else?" Cooper shouted. "I live this stuff. All you have to do is listen to me." He locked his arms into place, using every ounce of his willpower to stay put. "You are *so* clueless about the outdoors."

The look Cooper received as she carefully lifted her eyes to meet his shut him up, but he returned the look. Yes, he'd over-reacted, spiked by her accurately cutting use of his first name paired with her inability to start the fire, but he couldn't help it. Something about her got painfully under his skin—and they were losing. If she only understood that he could not lose.

"Want a different partner, *Princess*?" Cooper asked with a cutting edge to his voice. "Good. Me too."

AFTER FIFTEEN MINUTES of trying to get a spark to light the less-than-magical magnesium and pine needles, Amity's arms shook while small, mascara-filled tears ran down her cheeks. Her fingers were raw and bleeding—she'd cut herself twice with the edge of the pocketknife. Magnesium was definitely not like the lighter fluid she'd seen people use at the barbecues she'd attended back home.

Now she looked like the princess Easton claimed her to be, breaking down in front of multiple cameras, as almost every person in the camera crew had moved over and zoomed in on them as their drama unfolded. They'd yelled at one another and panicked for ten minutes until she'd lost it and screamed that he was a know-it-all hillbilly. She'd be even more the villain as she stereotyped him on national television, while somehow, she figured that he'd look like a smart mountain hunk even though he'd stereotyped her as well. She *hated* him.

Over the past five minutes, he'd switched to pleading with her rather than insulting her, which had actually helped motivate her until she'd sliced her hand again. The medical crew moved in, and she shooed them away. She was tough enough to handle this. Her life definitely wasn't Cinderella balls with beautiful dresses, princes at midnight, glass slippers, and fancy hairdos, like she was sure everyone now believed. She sucked in her breath at the thought—fancy hairdos.

"Amity, pick up the flint," Easton continued in a desperate plea. "*Please* try again. Switch back to the scraping tool instead of the knife."

Amity grabbed the pocketknife with a renewed sense of spirit that had nothing to do with Easton Cooper. She began to unwind her silky hair from the intricate French twist she'd worked on all morning. The fragrance of an entire cheap bottle of hairspray fumed around her, mixing in with the heavy smell of smoke from the other teams' successfully lit campfires.

"What?" Easton yelled. "If I lose because you decided it was time for a fucking beauty pageant—"

Amity tuned out the rest. She closed her eyes and reminded herself that it would grow back. After a deep breath, she reopened her eyes, sawed off the bottom half of her beautiful, brown hair with the sharp blade, and threw the thin, hairspray-soaked strands in the fire pit on top of the pine needles.

Amity stole a quick glance at the other remaining team. The auburn-haired woman had a small flame, so she had to hurry. With determination, she grabbed the flint and struck the knife against the side of the stone again and again, ignoring the intense pain on her palms and fingers. The sparks flew brighter, like tiny fireworks, as she intensely focused. She knew that she *could* light her hair, and sure enough, the tiny pile flamed to life with a gross but ironically relieving burnt hair smell filling her nostrils. She grabbed a large handful of pine needles and gently added them, watching the flames grow.

"Wouldn't have thought of that," Easton said simply.

"I'm not surprised." Amity flashed him a look. "No woman could stand to live with you."

Without acknowledging her snappy response, Easton twisted around to analyze the redheaded woman and her tattoo-covered, muscularly built partner. "Amity, we can do this," he encouraged, the faith returning to his voice. "The other team hasn't collected enough wood. Put small twigs on now. You have to get more substantial fuel for the flames to burn high enough. That's it. Now bigger branches."

Amity watched her wad of hair disappear under the flames as she reached for a larger piece of wood, beyond grateful that she'd made the mistake of lighting her hair on fire in eighth grade. She'd joined track that year, and her appetite had increased tenfold. One morning, while making a batch of ched-dar-scrambled eggs on the gas stove, she'd brushed her hair across the burner, watching the silky strands flare up like a wildfire. She'd screamed and jumped around until she'd spotted her mom's flower vase, pouring the cloudy water over her head to douse the flames.

And the reason her hair lit up? Volumizing mousse! How was a fourteen-year-old supposed to know? At least her teenage boy-craze phase taught her a valuable life lesson on how low-cost haircare products and fire did *not* mix. She just never knew how valuable that lesson would be.

"Okay, good job, Amity," Easton encouraged, pulling her back to her task as she threw another two large pine branches across the growing flames.

Anxiously, she glanced at the redheaded woman's fire pit.

"No," Easton instructed. She wanted to slug him. He hadn't really been helpful. *Right* maybe, but not helpful. "Ignore her," he continued. "It's my job to worry. You need to focus."

Amity returned to fueling the fire. She eyed Easton when he clapped his hands, eagerly rubbing his palms together and rocking around. Though she understood it must be difficult to sit on a bench with no real control over the challenge, she still thought he was a terrible partner. Thankfully, she only had to remain cordial with him for a few more minutes.

"Another log," he encouraged. "Good. Blow on it again to give the fire some more air. Almost there. Another log now."

Amity listened to every word Easton said until the string burned clean through, and their blue flag popped up, signaling their completion of the task.

She couldn't even cheer, she was so depleted, but Easton jumped up and shouted, "Yes, thank god," raising his fist in the air and then punching it into his other hand. It reminded her of how men cheered for football touchdowns with their bro friends around the television. She shook her head and looked over at the remaining team. Their flame flickered close to the string but still hadn't burnt through. Remorse ran through her, and she tried to flush it out. Losses were part of the game.

The auburn-haired woman started crying, and the tattoo biker dude let out a bunch of swear words. She felt for him as he hadn't had a chance to actually participate. Alex Bandon announced the pair were eliminated and explained where they should go for their exit interviews. The host then turned to Amity and Easton, clarifying that they were free to go over to the group camp for dinner and interviews.

Without looking at Easton or even acknowledging their win, Amity grabbed her flint, knife, and heels, stuffing them into the top of her red pack. Still shaking and charged with adrenaline, she held her head high and walked toward camp, trying to maintain a small scrap of dignity even though she was starving, freezing in her flimsy dress, and in need of medical help for her chopped-up hands and feet.

She'd made it to the next leg of the race and could relax—as long as she never had to be anywhere near Easton Cooper *ever* again.

"Good job, Amity," she heard him say as she walked away.

Great! Kindness and sympathy didn't help. It was much easier to hate him. She swallowed through a lump in her throat, unable to respond without giving herself away—she didn't want him to see her cry again.

And the tears were coming. She hadn't had such a dramatic experience in her first twenty-five monotonous years of life. Her dad was right—life experiences were intensified by taking adventures and risks, but she couldn't decide—was her first real undertaking on this journey the fire-building challenge or being paired with Easton Cooper?

Four

Cooper rubbed his hand along his jaw, trying to release some of the tension from the most messed up thirty minutes of his life, watching Amity turn her back on him and limp off toward the campground. Good riddance, he thought with relief but also with an adjusted opinion of the woman. For all her focus on looks, she'd chopped her hair off without a second thought.

He was surprised she'd sacrifice her precious hair to stay on a show. It didn't add up, but then again, searching for the Hollywood spotlight was probably a rat race. At the very least, her motivation to succeed impressed him.

Cooper did actually know that certain types of hairsprays were flammable. During his sister's high school years, his mom had bickered incessantly with Hannah about being careful around the fire pit in the backyard. He just didn't think about it after ten years of lighting flints like a master woodsman. He had to give Amity some credit for thinking outside of the box.

Alex Bandon walked up to Cooper before he could head over to the group camp. The directors wanted to interview him right away, if possible, probably to capture him at his heightened irritation. It worked. His interview made him sound like an ungrateful prick because even after Amity had sliced off her hair to save them, he was still amped up.

Cooper rolled his arms in pinwheel-like circles, stretching his tense back muscles, as he strolled across the meadow, unable to get the mixed-up set of events out of his mind. Amity was doomed, and he wanted nothing more to do with her. She'd only make it one or, if she was lucky, two more legs. The woman couldn't cut off her hair to make it down a trail or pitch a tent, and in a matter of days, she'd likely have to do much more than that.

Yet unexplainably, he found himself searching for her when he arrived at camp. What a waste of energy, he thought, shaking his head while his eyes betrayed him, drifting until he spotted her by one of the campfires. She'd changed into wilderness-appropriate clothes from her pack, a dark purple, long-sleeved polyester shirt the color of plums and long black leggings provided by the show. The casual look suited her much better—or maybe it just suited him.

His feet, feeling disconnected from his brain, walked toward her, and as he approached, he noticed her hands were now all wrapped in bandages. A mystifying bout of anger coursed through his tense limbs. She shouldn't have gotten hurt. He would never have allowed it if he could have helped her. The damn directors seemed to be searching for ways to put the contestants at odds with one another. Of course, it *was* reality TV. He'd be having a conversation with Hannah when he returned home about the crap television she watched and what it did to real people.

Amity had somehow cut her hair along the bottom, improving the jagged mess she'd made of it during the challenge, so it was now an inch or two above shoulder length. She looked natural and unkempt but also feminine and put together at the same time. He squinted his eyes to study her soft features in the dim evening light and realized that she had freshly applied lipstick and blush. How? And why did he like it? She looked so ruggedly sexy he didn't even realize he'd made it to the campfire.

Four other contestants glanced tensely up at him as he asked her, "How in the hell did you get makeup on?"

As if he'd broken the law by speaking to her, Amity stared him down. The reflection of the flames bounced off her hypnotic brown eyes as a shot of desire went straight through his core. He noticed a cameraman crouch-walk over and point the lens at his face, but he didn't care. At this point, America would see him act like an astonished fool—he couldn't help himself.

"Easton," Amity began sharply. He flinched involuntarily, again giving away too much. Another set of feet scampered around. He noticed a camera held by a short woman with streaky blue-blonde hair focus in on Amity as she spoke. "As far as I'm concerned, I never intend to speak to you again unless I'm forced to do so to win a challenge. And even then, I will pick *anyone* but you. So get lost." She pointed across the camp. "There's another campfire over there."

Cooper shoved his hands into his pockets, pinching the nylon fabric between his fingers. He tried to remind his brain that she was everything a guy like him didn't need. Even if he did, which was not ever going to happen, a woman like her would get bored with him after the first night out. Local joints were not this woman's style.

"As you wish, Princess." Turning to leave, he added, "You know the chemicals in all that makeup attracts bears."

Amity wrinkled her nose up in disgust and flipped him the bird.

Cooper grinned as he turned to walk away, noticing her eyes dart to the trees. The Oregon Cascades didn't have that many bears. They existed, as did a few mountain lions, but it was rare for anything that dangerous to come near this many people—though he was sure she didn't know that.

Letting the air out of his lungs, Cooper grimaced at his stupidity for even speaking to her unnecessarily. He walked to the men's tent and threw his gear on the remaining cot, not caring in the slightest which one was his. He was used to being crammed into tents with other trail guides. As long as he didn't have to bunk with people like Amity, he'd be fine. He and his buddies only slept in the same tent as the tourists if there was a medical situation or something drastic like that, thank god.

After getting a bowl of chili from the crew, he headed for the second campfire and strategically chose a spot near Bria. She sat in a low-to-the-ground camping chair with her feet crossed out in front of her, staring at the flames, her spiky blonde hair still carrying a few protruding twigs from the fire challenge.

Bria's partner had been unhelpful during the challenge. He'd heard the clueless things the guy told her, like adding moss, which in reality would only smother the flames due to the lichen's wet, dense texture.

Bria looked up, scrutinizing him with her eyes, as he scooped a spoonful of beans covered in cheddar cheese and fragrant red onions into his mouth. He ate a few bites to appease his grumbling stomach before introducing himself to her. "Hey—"

"Cooper, right?" Bria interrupted.

He nodded, swiping a dangling string of melted cheese off his chin. "That's right."

"I gotta tell ya." Bria paused and rubbed her fingers across her lower lip. "I'm here to win. So if you wanna be my partner, like you said, then I wanna know that you're gonna give it your all."

Cooper knew his body looked lanky, but underneath his

sweatshirt and hiking pants were tight lean muscles. He didn't like to bulk up because it added weight to his rock climbs. "I'm here for the money, and that's it," he said. "I plan to win."

Bria eyed him carefully, perhaps deciding whether he was a true contender, before saying, "Then I'll pick you tomorrow, or you pick me. Depends on how these show people decide to pin us against each other. I guess if they let the guys pick first, we may not get a say since you came in next to last. You and Hollywood didn't exactly tear it up. Wouldn't pick ya if it wasn't the girl's fault."

Cooper smirked, realizing that Bria had a nickname for Amity too. He preferred Princess. Hollywood made him think of *Top Gun*, and Amity was far from a badass fighter pilot.

"Agreed," he replied.

Watching Bria's head turn, he spun around to follow her gaze. Dammit, Amity stomped off toward the women's tent. He let out an audible sigh, realizing she'd overheard Bria blame the fire challenge on her. While it had been Amity's fault that they'd nearly lost, she'd also been the one to make sure that they didn't.

Cooper placed his hands behind his head and looked up at the clear night sky, the Milky Way visible without any nearby light pollution. This was the lifestyle he enjoyed, minus the cameras, and he needed a woman who enjoyed it too. Not a high-maintenance, hot California girl. The sooner he got Amity out of his mind, the better.

AMITY LAY IN HER SUFFOCATING, ugly rust-orange sleeping bag on a springy cot staring at the mesh fabric of the women's group tent. A cool breeze surged through the zipper window as she peered out at the sparkly sky. The milky blur of the galaxy looked fake, just like the pictures she'd seen on her boss's computer screensaver.

As incredible as it was, being alone with only her thoughts in the quiet tent overwhelmed her. She liked white noise while she slept, like a low-volume TV show, cars whizzing by on the neighborhood streets, or at a minimum, a few crickets chirping. But here, there was almost no sound except the occasional snore or rustling sleeping bag of one of her competitors.

She swallowed, her dry, cold throat uncomfortably swollen from a combination of inhaling campfire smoke and dealing with the flood of emotional drama. She thought of the Bria woman's Hollywood comment. Because of her formal entrance and near failure at the fire challenge, now all the contestants thought she was an entitled, rich woman, which couldn't be further from the truth.

She brushed a tear away with her palm and thought of her father. He'd be proud she found a way to travel but disappointed she wasn't enjoying it. This adventure should have been with him—someone who loved and cared for her—not a bunch of strangers.

None of the contestants had been nice to her after the challenge. They'd all but ignored her during dinner as they'd maneuvered for placement, hoping to be chosen by a strong competitor the following day. She wanted to blame it on Easton Cooper—*wanted* to even though she knew she'd dug her own hole. Still, it wasn't fair that a cocky outdoorsman was handed an environment of his liking on a silver 'backpacking' platter—but that would be his downfall, she realized—he was too sure of himself.

Another small tear escaped and dripped onto her lumpy camping pillow. She hadn't cried much since her father died, learning during those long, lonely months that crying accomplished nothing, but out here, at the base of a mountain range, she felt like a little kid again. Her only hope was that the trail challenge tomorrow involved speed. Regardless of her male partner's pace, she knew that she could outrun every one of the women here, and that would get her and her new partner across the finish line.

Granted, her exhausting daily runs were not on trails, but she'd become an expert Palm Springs hurdler, lunging over curbsides and fences while sidestepping tiny lizards and beetles. She ran down stairwells and through parking lots, dodging tourists and prickly pears. She weaved through the garden and pool areas, skirting by hedges and water features —around anything and everything at the resorts.

It was her escape, her happy place, and to her advantage, she ran in the heat. Even with the elevation gain, these mild temperatures would be a breeze. Amity drew in a relaxing breath and smiled, wiping away the moisture on her cheeks. She could do this. In the morning, she'd show them all what Amity Rose was capable of. It was someone else's turn to cry.

Five

Cooper watched Amity step into line wearing a sleeveless, dark purple shirt and skintight, black exercise leggings. Were the producers trying to torture him? Hiking clothes on women were a total turn-on, and on Amity, they fit like a glove. Her highlighted-brown hair, pulled up into a messy ponytail with the newly frayed edges sticking out, appeared downright adorable.

Irritated with himself, he tipped his cap down to shield his eyes from the sun, and if he was being honest with himself from Amity, while he focused on the surrounding mountains in the distance—Mount Bachelor, The Three Sisters, and Broken Top—a set of five peaks in all with endless trails beckoning for him to hike in the heat of the perfect July sun; and he knew there were even more mountains in the Cascade Range waiting for him to discover.

On the bus ride over, he'd followed their progress on his GPS and phone until one of the director's assistants took his gadgets away. Keeping track of his location was a natural habit for him, and his tracking devices were the only items the crew took from him that put an uneasy feeling in his gut. But the assistant wasn't as stealthy as TSA. He'd easily tucked a compass from his backpack into his pants' side pocket, as he always did when his pack wasn't with him. A compass would come in handy, perhaps even become necessary along the trails out here.

The well-known Pacific Crest Trail wasn't far from their current location at Sparks Lake. He'd both read and dreamed about taking a month-long backpacking trip up the renowned route, but he'd not had the chance—though this was hardly the relaxing trip he wanted to take. He'd come back and enjoy it properly someday—all of it—and he'd bring any gadget he wanted. He couldn't deny that he loved the challenge of limited gear; he just didn't want anyone telling him what to do. Perhaps he'd feel better as they got farther away from places where these crafty directors could trap him.

Currently, they were only about forty miles from the Central Oregon town of Bend, where all the contestants had stayed the previous night in separate rooms with strict rules not to speak to one another. The directors wanted them to meet at the show's opening, so they weren't even allowed to leave their rooms. He'd paced in his hotel room for hours, desperately wanting to explore the town's craft breweries and mountain gear shops instead of ordering room service and staring out the window at the lucky people on the street—people who could move about freely and didn't have to stand on a damn mat.

Cooper snapped to the present as Alex Bandon stepped onto his hosting platform, still located in the same central spot as yesterday with a backdrop of Sparks Lake and the Cascades. Oregon was a nice change from the Colorado Rockies, where he and Dominic ran their trail tours together, but he missed Dominic. It was pure torture dealing with trail newbies without him.

Although if Dominic were here, Cooper would never hear the end of it regarding Amity. His best friend knew him too well. Countless times, Dominic told him he needed to find a woman with a little more spunk. His best friend thought he was too laid-back to spend his life with a woman that was exactly like him. Cooper grimaced as he fixed his eyes on Amity. Even though Amity was a pain, Dominic and his wife, Chelsea, would like her.

Bandon clapped his hands, drawing their attention. Thankfully, the host wore brown trail clothes today instead of a formal banquet suit. Cooper couldn't stand the showy look. Although fancy clothes reminded him that this wasn't real—it *was* a show—and exactly why he shouldn't be pining over a woman.

McKenzie, the impressively efficient head director, began the monotonous countdown before Alex's voice rang out, "Good morning, contestants. Today is our first trail challenge. The race will be on foot. You'll take the smaller detachable daypack off your larger pack. The smaller pack snaps off and is filled with quick energy snacks and a water bottle. Also included is a water purifier for pumping fresh, filtered water out of the streams and lakes. You will not be provided with water upfront, and if you fill your bottles from the cooler before the challenge begins, you must dump the contents out before the race starts—"

Smiling in amusement, Cooper watched Amity while she fumbled around, checking in the small pack for the listed items. At least she was finally paying attention to the contents in her pack. She'd learned something yesterday. He sighed, cursing at himself for caring.

With pinched brows, Bria studied him. If he wasn't careful, she'd think he had a thing for Amity. The problem was—he clearly did—and that had him spiraling into a panic, tugging on his shirt collar and gasping for air. These new clothes were supposed to be breathable, but the T-shirt they'd given him came uncomfortably close to his throat. He shuffled his feet, cooling the back of his neck by fanning his baseball cap. Get a grip, he told himself. He couldn't let a woman he barely knew get her fancy fingernails wrapped around any part of him.

"—time to choose partners," Alex continued. "Selection will begin with the woman in the first-place team followed by the man in the first-place team. We'll start with the winning team and go down to the last-place team. Once you're chosen, you're chosen, and you're required to race the leg with that person."

Cooper slammed his eyes shut. Any woman but Amity, he chanted in his head. Obviously because the woman was a liability in the outdoors—but the worst of it was this new obsession where he couldn't keep his eyes off of her, and a distraction would end him in this competition. Even now, he kept track of her in his peripheral vision like a damn body-guard. He wanted an 'Amity off' button in his brain. At least he had a decent chance to get away from her—he just needed Bria to come through.

The contestants began their selections, and Cooper listened intently. Some woman from the first-place team named Becky, with a honey-brown complexion and glossy black hair, chose Liam, the guy she'd won the challenge with. Cooper had passed right over Becky when he'd assessed contestants on the first day in her ripped jeans and casual sweater, not being able to guess her outdoor skills, though he realized now she must have some. He'd keep track of her.

And Liam was a threat. He'd been calm during the fire challenge and, based on his comments, knew his stuff. Cooper thought he'd heard someone say the guy came from Montana ranch country, which fit because he had tan, weathered skin, a muscular build, and one of those off-white, rodeo-looking cowboy hats. He'd even gripped it the way cowboys do in the movies when he'd plucked it off his sleeping bag this morning and set it on his head. The cowboy types didn't typically join his tours, so he knew less about Liam's potential skills than he'd like.

Liam and Becky locked gazes, already a power couple in Cooper's eyes. He grinned at Liam when the cowboy looked his way and was met with a tip of Liam's hat. Cooper snickered. Apparently, his constant scrutiny hadn't gone unnoticed—Liam was watching him too. Cooper tipped his ten-year-old baseball cap, watching Liam laugh in return. Friend or enemy? Most likely enemy.

But at this stage of the race, he had more pressing matters to worry about. Cooper looked at Bria for confirmation, watching her reactions as he waited for her turn. Since Becky selected Liam and both first-place contestants had a partner, it was on to the second-place team, then third place, and so on. Cooper took note of each contestant's reaction as they went down the list. When they reached fourth place, Bria said his name, and his tense muscles uncoiled.

Alex chimed in, "Cooper, how do you feel about being partners with Bria?"

He fastened on a smile. "I'm stoked. Bria and I are going to fly down the trail."

"Yeah," Bria cheered with what Cooper realized was her signature fist pump.

The selections continued. When a guy was up to choose a partner, Cooper's stomach knotted every time he had to watch Amity's hopeful face fall. Guilt settled uncomfortably in his gut, and again, he cursed it away. He didn't understand why he cared. Was it because he felt responsible for her fate after their disastrous first challenge?

A part of him wished he could choose her and allow himself to act on the unexplainable pull he felt toward her. It still pained him to look at her bandaged hands and, for some reason, feel like he was at fault for her injuries. Though she finally had on the trail shoes from her pack, he'd guess that her feet were hurting from the stick jabs yesterday and wound up in uncomfortably tight gauze.

Although, oddly enough, today, Amity didn't look rattled. Maybe because she was wearing appropriate gear? She glanced up, catching his gaze, and with a deep-set frown, shot him a fiery look. He didn't have a reason to stare, so her irritation was warranted. Abruptly turning her head away, she focused on the two men who remained without partners.

One was the guy from team seven that Kim, the other woman he initially wanted as a partner, had abandoned. Cooper thought his name was Miles, and he'd absolutely been the reason for Kim to come in seventh. During the fire-building challenge, Miles had instructed Kim that he'd seen another team locate the flint in the main part of their pack, so Kim had spent several precious moments looking for her flint in the wrong place. Rumors around the campfire were that he was a big-city corporate guy who worked out in an indoor gym. If so, the guy likely wouldn't have much experience in the wilderness.

He halfheartedly hoped that Miles did choose Amity so that she'd be eliminated and his weird obsession with her would be over. But when Alex Bandon asked for Miles to make his selection, and he did, in fact, choose Amity, a stinging pain twisted in his chest. Jealousy? Protectiveness? Did he even want to know?

Surprised expressions crossed the faces of most of the contestants at Miles' selection. Even the host seemed confused by it. Miles' other choice was a stronger-framed woman from the eighth-place team, and she looked fit.

"Miles," Alex inquired, his booming voice projecting out his words, "could you explain why you selected Amity for the trail race?"

Without hesitation, Miles responded, "Clara is too short and bulky for fast-paced running."

Amity sucked in a loud breath. She leaned forward and peeked over at Clara, who appeared shell-shocked within seconds of Miles' statement. "That's offensive," Amity shot back at Miles from across the line. "Don't be a jerk."

"Just telling it like it is," Miles said with a satisfied grin. "What's your problem, anyway? You should be more appreciative." In a harsh tone, he added, "You're lucky I even chose you."

Amity threw up her arms, fixing her eyes on the host. "Are there any decent guys on this show? Seriously, didn't you have hundreds of applicants? Because right now, Alex, I want to bury every guy here." She clenched her bandaged fists, adding, "Ugh," while kicking up some dirt. After her tantrum, she mouthed, "Ow," with a little pop of her lips, grasping her injured palms and turning away from the cameras.

A guttural groan escaped his throat, followed by an inconvenient testosterone rush. She shouldn't be in pain. He wouldn't allow it to happen again. Wait, what? Amity wasn't his responsibility, and on top of that, now he wanted to deck Miles? He wasn't an aggressive guy. It's like someone had passed him a love potion, and he'd lost control of his mind.

Cooper shuffled his feet, sucking for air while tugging on his uncomfortable shirt collar—maybe if he sliced the neckline with a knife, he could breathe. There was no denying his body's protective reaction was stirred by Amity, but for crying out loud, she didn't even really look like she needed protecting. Her fists were balled, regardless of the gauze, and she looked ready to pounce on Miles for his stupidity. She was proving to be a little spitfire, just the type his friends recommended for him—a woman who didn't hold her tongue when she was upset.

Clara stood still, pinching her bottom lip between her fingers. Perhaps to hold back tears? Miles was a piece of work. Cooper let out a frustrated sigh—he couldn't believe the guy.

Yes, Cooper had already been an ass during this competition too, but he would never insult a woman's genetics.

Alex's face hardened. "Man, I don't think you're doing yourself any favors in America's eyes here. Perhaps you should apologize to Clara?"

With a flippant shrug, a less-than-sincere tone drawled out of Miles' mouth. "Sorry, Clara, meant no offense."

"Clara," Alex probed, "anything to say to Miles?"

Clara removed her fingers from her lip and shook her head, clasping her hands out in front of her. "No, I'm just glad he's not my partner." She glanced sympathetically at Amity before looking at her default partner and added, "I think Dan and I will do well."

Dan nodded. "We'll take Miles out."

Amity looked down at the dirt, avoiding everyone's eyes. That meant the other teams would be rallying against her, too, just because she'd gotten stuck with a dick, and it might very well come down to Amity and Miles versus Clara and Dan at the finish line. His neck muscles tightened at the thought of Amity's elimination, his emotions and brain not seeing eye to eye. He felt like a damn teenager, yearning for the pretty girl that would never be his.

Cooper's mind kept running through thoughts that it shouldn't—like that Amity had a chance—and that *he* could help her. He flexed his fists and glared at her. His rebellious imagination, now tied in solid with his emotions, ran freely with dangerous delusions while he tried to flush them out. Why Amity? Why now? When he needed to focus on winning cash, not being partners with a woman who didn't belong.

"All right, now that you all have a partner," Alex blared out, "let's discuss the task. The first trail challenge is approximately thirteen miles."

No problem, Cooper thought. At speed on trails, he and Bria could probably average ten- to twelve-minute miles.

"A map will be handed to your team," Alex continued. "We'll have you start on Green Lakes Trail, which will flow into a few other trails and eventually take you to the Pacific Crest Trail, also known as the PCT. The PCT will be our route for most of the race. Be aware of other hikers in the area. No running over anyone on the trails. We don't have exclusive access to these routes." Alex did his signature hand clap to move things along. "Now, please go stand by your partners, and we'll take you to the trailhead."

Cooper's eyes roamed, and he let out a string of profanity. A few of the men eyed him warily. He shook his head to indicate nothing was wrong, but it was. He was pathetically unable to stop himself from tracking Amity. His eyes found her standing rigidly next to Miles with her arms wrapped tightly around her waist. He wanted to walk over to her, tuck her into his arms, and shield her from everyone, especially Miles. What an idiot move that would be—she'd instantly push him away, and rightfully so.

Cooper forced his eyes away, concentrating on Bria. "Do you have any experience running or hiking on trails?"

"Yep," Bria said as if expecting the question. "Basic training followed by active duty with the Army. Just finished four years of service. I'm taking military leave now. How about you, mountain man? I'm not going to find out you're some wuss after going outta my way to choose ya, I hope."

"Nah, I can hold my own. I spend about two hundred and sixty days a year on trails. We've got this made. Let's take first."

"Hell yeah." Bria clapped her hands together. She turned, looked at the other teams, and added, "Bring it, losers."

A laugh broke from his chest. Somehow Bria could already get away with things like that, and none of the contestants judged her for it. She had character—he'd give her that.

The show's crew bused them over to the base of the appropriate trail, explaining that this would be the last vehicle they saw for several days. Cooper hopped up from his seat, moving aside so that Bria could get off the bus first, and followed her down the aisle. He approached Amity, who was still in her cushy seat, hugging her pack, and gestured in front of him. "Ladies first?"

Amity leaned back. "No, you go ahead. I'll be passing you by on the trail soon anyway." With a sassy smirk, she added, "Ladies *first*, right?" and then gestured *him* forward.

Where had her sudden bout of confidence come from? He hardly had time to register his first hard-on for the most inadvisable female on earth before he relaxed his body and convinced himself that he'd gladly walk away from her.

Six

A mity stood in the shade under a towering evergreen tree and slung her daypack across her shoulders, snapping the straps in place, pleased that the crew would take her heavier backpack to the group camp for the night. With a lighter amount of weight, she'd cover the thirteen miles, equivalent to about a half marathon, in approximately two hours. It just depended on how fast Miles could run.

Could she get any bigger of a loser as a partner? Shockingly, Miles was even worse than Easton. It took true meanness to hurt a woman's feelings for no reason. If she could just win this leg, she'd choose whatever guy she wanted, and there was no greater motivation than that. After all, she'd come for an *enjoyable* adventure.

"So, you can do this?" Miles asked her, plopping down on a log under her tree, wearing a bright orange shirt so fluorescent it hurt her eyes. "I'm all about getting screen time. Attention is the goal. That's why I'm here, and yesterday, you and that Cooper guy made quite a scene." He scanned her frame. "But I also have to get into the next round while we're at it. I hope you're capable of putting one foot in front of the other."

Amity scoffed, rolling her eyes toward the sky. "You'll find out soon enough." After a pause, she couldn't help but ask, "Why were you such a dick to Clara? You'd already chosen me when you poked at her."

Miles shrugged and said, "Ratings," with a cocky half-grin forming across his polished features. "Stirring the pot will earn me screen time. I could care less if I piss her off." He shoved a bite of a granola bar into his mouth and grumbled words out while he chewed. "Don't need her on my side. The cameras barely followed the girl yesterday. She's dull. You, on the other hand," he added while angling his head toward her, "can bring me some ratings, and believe me, ratings I understand. Being a news broadcaster in New York is competitive."

"You're disgusting."

"Why?" Miles finished off his granola bar and slung his pack over his shoulder, eyeing the water cooler. "Do you claim to be here for some other reason? You're an attention magnet. Might as well be honest about your intentions."

Miles walked away, and Amity covered her face in her bandaged hands, heat prickling up her neck and across her cheeks. Is that how people perceived her? Surely, all adventures weren't like this. Nature and hiking were supposed to be about peace and solitude, maybe even finding yourself, not emotional headaches and physical pain.

Amity lifted her eyes to survey the trail, only to find Easton Cooper staring at her again, this time with a miffed look across his scruffy face. Why did he keep doing that? She wasn't his partner anymore. What could she possibly be doing to tick him off now? Oh well, she thought, turning away from him—she hoped whatever it was really ate at him. Pretty soon, she'd leave him in the dust, and he could take his flint and shove it up his tight butt.

Alex Bandon called for the first team to line up, and Amity stared longingly at Liam and Becky, knowing she'd have to wait out the five-minute-per-place team penalty.

While the first-place team walked to the line, Amity pondered when she and Miles would be allowed to leave since they didn't finish the fire-building challenge at the same time.

In sync with her thoughts, Alex announced to the cameras, "For clarification, your team starts with the lowest finishing team member from the previous round." Alex listed each team's starting place to clarify. A series of grumbles erupted from those that caught on as Alex continued listing teams down to the last-place finishers. "Amity finished in ninth and Miles in seventh; therefore, their team will start in ninth, as will Cooper and Bria, since Cooper finished ninth, even though Bria finished in fourth."

"*What?*" Bria swung her hands down, smacking her palms against her thighs. "Alex, you really gotta tell us these rules. That means me choosing Cooper here," she said, pointing at him with her thumb, "put me at a major disadvantage on this round."

Alex nodded with a pleasant, screen-worthy smile. "Well, Bria, aside from the contract guidelines, the rules can change at any moment."

"Great," Bria grumbled. "Real fair."

Even though Bria had insulted her with the Hollywood comment, Amity kind of liked her. To be fair, Amity had earned her entitled-brat-with-no-skills reputation. Maybe she was looking at things the wrong way. Perhaps her reputation was an advantage? This was a game, and she needed to wake up and play.

Amity walked over to her annoyingly good-looking partner, who was now strung out on a log by the water cooler, chewing on a pine needle while analyzing the competitors like a relaxed toad. She peered around nonchalantly, noting that all the contestants were thankfully watching the more threatening teams—well, every contestant except Easton Cooper anyway, but he didn't count. Amity released her breath, grateful that she wasn't a threat to these people yet.

"Miles." Amity bent down and whispered, "Let's play it cool all the way to the finish line. I don't want to draw attention to us. In fact, I want them all to forget we exist."

Miles let out a dubious laugh. "Sorry, *Miss* Amity. That's not what I'm here for."

Amity shook her head at him, ignoring his jab—this was only a game, she reminded herself. "No," she said softly, crouching down to move even closer, her lips just below his ear, "you're not understanding me. I'm a *really* fast runner."

Miles' gaze dropped to her mouth before shifting to her cleavage.

Amity pulled her sleeveless purple scoop neck up to her collarbone. With an irritated glower, she continued, "I should be able to beat every woman here up that trail. Since the guys have to wait for their female partner to cross the finish line, that puts us near first as long as you can outrun the women."

Miles grinned in amusement, then began to laugh. "You think you can run faster than me?"

"Yes." Amity nodded. "Faster than most of these men."

Miles continued to chuckle, but he slowly trailed off, a speculative look crossing his face. Something in her expression must have convinced him to believe her. Experience analyzing people while broadcasting the news, perhaps?

Miles massaged his fingertips along his perfectly groomed jaw. Now that Amity was up close to him, his facial hair seemed over-the-top ridiculous, obviously requiring a professional stylist to buzz the hairs along his cheek into a flawless crescent. "I'm listening," he said, encouraging her with a swirling motion of his hand. "Go on."

"I hope you're more than talk." Amity took note of Easton's rigid frown, standing stiff as a two-by-four in his dark green shirt and black running shorts. Everyone seemed to have been given different clothing styles and colors, his making him blend into the forest like a planted tree. She pivoted her head so he couldn't read her lips as she continued whispering to Miles. "Because to blow past everyone and win, I need you to run like hell so we can have the attention on us in an in-your-face type of way. *Attention*," she emphasized. "You'll get what you want. I promise."

At first, Miles simply crinkled his eyes, but then a mischievous grin slowly lit up his face. "All right, Amity." He bobbed his head a few times. "I'm on board. Seems like a decent idea. I could use some *positive* attention. Need to offset your jerk comment from earlier."

"You were a jerk."

"Yeah, well...ratings." Miles shrugged, still holding his annoying grin in place. "But I like your plan today. I need to balance things out."

Amity stiffened her gaze, wanting to give him a few choice words in response to his despicable plan for ratings, but a blur in the trees caught her eye. A large, black camera lens poked intrusively through the branches. Was there no privacy anywhere? With the cameras on one side of her and the contestants on the other, it was like being stuck in an outdoor elevator. Amity took a deep, calming breath. Did it really matter if the cameras heard her? Probably not—only alliances with the contestants mattered.

The camerawoman with the blue-streaked blonde hair poked through the branches and pursed her lips in annoyance like she hadn't caught all of their conversation. Good! Amity would love to be able to shock America with a first-place finish. She'd come across as weak to millions of people during the fire challenge and reversing that image would feel pretty damn good. She turned defiantly from the camera and gave Miles a solid high-five, making temporary, strategic friends with the enemy. She had a race to win.

COOPER'S BLOOD BOILED. He braced his hands behind his head, taking in some air. After Amity's high-five and mind-boggling whispers to Miles, he now fervently disliked the guy. Why was she suddenly acting chummy with him? Her lips were just inches above the guy's ear while he made disgusting attempts to look down her shirt. Cooper wanted to knock the guy out of the race; or, if he was being more truthful, knock the guy's head in with his fist. He strolled closer to the water cooler, refilling his bottle and splashing cold water down his feverish neck while he strained his ears to hear their conversation.

"So, we have a forty-minute time penalty," Amity continued in a hushed whisper, "and I'll be running well under ten-minute miles at the slowest on these trails, even with the uphill. I should be much faster, but worst case, that puts us at a hundred and thirty minutes to run thirteen miles, plus the forty-minute time penalty, which means we'll have to haul balls to overtake the other teams. I don't want to waste time stopping for water. We'd have to learn to pump it with that purifier thingy, and there's no reason for us to stop for water during a two-hour run. In this climate, we can run straight through. If we do that, first place is ours."

So Amity was talking strategy, not flirting. Cooper cracked a satisfied grin, letting out a few light chuckles. Within seconds, his pulse rate slowed, and his taut limbs relaxed.

Amity whipped her head around and jutted out her chin. "Problem, *Easton*?"

For the first time since fifth grade, he didn't flinch. "Nah, Princess," he said, walking over to an adjacent tree and placing his long arms behind his head. "Just listening to your plans. I'll believe it when I see it."

"Well, un-listen," Amity hissed. "I'm not your partner anymore."

"Thought you didn't care for Miles' behavior," Cooper drawled out, acting as though Miles wasn't standing beside her. "Now he's your pal?"

Bria, walking over to the water cooler, eyed him.

"Just surveying the competition," Cooper tried to assure her. "We'll be the last two teams to leave. Might as well get friendly."

"Yeah, sure." Bria's thin lips tightened. "Just be sure to focus when we're on the trail." Glaring Amity down, she added, "Why waste your breath?"

Amity shook her head and said, "Whatever," to Bria—not in a mean way but in a way that seemed to indicate she didn't care what Bria thought. She then turned away, facing the trees, and bent over to clutch her toes, stretching her hamstrings.

With Amity's back turned, Cooper shrugged in response to Bria.

Bria grumbled something to herself and filled her bottle with water before turning away and saying over her shoulder, "She's why you'll lose."

Cooper felt like the wind had gotten knocked out of him. He could *not* lose. Where was his head? Well, that wasn't hard to answer. He tore his eyes away from Amity's flexible legs just as a cameraman with a goatee crouch-waddled over to train a camera on him.

"Is this really the best drama around?" he asked, holding his hand in front of the lens. "The first-place team left, for god's sake. Isn't the actual race drama enough?"

Amity irritatingly whispered in Miles' ear again, and the two of them filled water bottles and walked to another section of trees. Per the rules, all of them would have to dump the water out before the trail run began, so he was pleased to see Amity hydrate as much as possible before then.

"Show's over," Cooper said tersely, addressing the camera.

"For now, anyway. Bria and I are going to kick some tail." He jumped up and jogged a few steps to catch up with her.

"Yeah, that's more like it." Bria fist-bumped Cooper's shoulder. "Yeah," she added again with a pumped-up nod.

Cooper stayed by the cooler while they waited, several feet away from where Amity had purposely distanced herself with Miles. He ignored his compulsion to look at her, finally doing the things he *should* be doing to win—drinking water, stretching his calves, and jogging to warm up. Every five minutes, another team took off, already gaining an unfair lead on them, but they'd catch up. Bria had no idea how badly he needed a million dollars. There was no way he'd let them cross the finish line in last place.

Seven

Amity lined up at the starting block with Miles to her left and Easton and Bria to her right. She could not shake Easton Cooper. Fortunately, after their little exchange, the cameras backed off and focused on the teams leaving the start line, but the attention still unsettled her.

Amity wasn't just getting recorded for her dramatic moments of action; the camera crew seemed to zoom in on every interaction between the two of them. Was it because Easton kept staring? Because she was positive that his glares were entirely competitive. He'd made his position on her quite clear. She peeked at him and pursed her lips. Oh well, their drama would end soon. There was no way either one of them would choose the other as a partner. In a few days, the directors would find someone else with a more invigorating story.

And, looking around, it seemed to Amity that it wouldn't take them long. The camera crew had been at it for forty minutes, bustling around the contestants as they got closer to their turns, placing recording equipment all over them. They even secured cameras to their shirts and backpacks. Amity pivoted to her side, tucking a loose wire into her pack.

Running uphill would be quite the challenge in and of itself without all the cameras and voice boxes strung to them. It was so distracting that before long, the countdown timer, a big digital display just to the side of the trail, ticked down the last minute before they could start.

"Miles," Amity said softly into his ear, "we have to pace ourselves. Just run behind me and keep up. I promise I know what I'm doing." She gnawed on the soft flesh inside of her cheek. "You *can* keep up with me, right?"

"What?" Miles asked sarcastically. "You think I can't outrun your boyfriend over there?"

Easton glared at Miles like he was an irritating bug that needed to be squashed before turning to focus on the trail ahead of him. Easton's earlier focus on her seemed to have shifted to an intense focus on the task, and she was grateful for it. It was time for her to do the same.

"Forget Easton and focus," she said. "Are you in shape?"

Miles patted one of his biceps. "Two hours a day in the gym, babe."

Amity rolled her eyes. Miles would do fine on this run, but if the trail runs got any harder, and she was certain they would, indoor workouts wouldn't be proper training for outdoor distance runs. Not that she was one to talk. She'd had no clue how to do a skills challenge thus far—so she reminded herself while doing a warm-up shuffle in her new shoes, this was her chance to prove herself.

The timer counted down, and suddenly with a loud beep, they were off. Amity started out at a pace somewhere between a seven- and eight-minute mile, thinking her initial assessment of pace was probably too slow to make up for their time penalty. Bria sprinted off in front of her with Easton on her heels. She could hear Easton telling Bria they wouldn't be able to maintain such a fast pace. No duh, she thought—at least the dope was smart.

The trail began in the forest, running parallel to a crystal-clear stream, with giant, thick-trunked pines towering over them, the type of which Amity couldn't identify. She wanted to ask Miles if he knew anything about the trees, flowers, or animals in the area, as her mind generally wandered while running, but she doubted Miles would know. Someone like Easton would, she thought, and immediately tried to erase him from her mind. She refused to ask Easton—he'd probably smirk and not tell her anyway.

"We can't hear your boyfriend or the Army chick anymore," Miles said after a few minutes. "We should speed up."

"I'm running just over seven-minute miles," Amity shouted over her shoulder. "There's likely no other woman in this race that can keep pace with that for thirteen miles. And don't call women chicks. It's insulting. *Bria* will gas out here in a few minutes, and she'll have to adjust her speed. Also, Easton is not my boyfriend. Stop being a dick."

Miles laughed through gasps of air. "That really doesn't sound better. You saying the chick will *gas* out."

Amity snorted. If she put her money on it, she'd bet Bria didn't mind blunt, accurate statements no matter how silly they sounded. But outright disrespect? Military discipline would be ingrained in her. Of course, Bria had called her Hollywood as a jab. Maybe nothing bothered Bria. Regardless, Miles was despicable and, so far, all talk. Amity hoped that he could keep pace with her for thirteen miles. Running on a treadmill was a joke compared to this.

The trail continued, winding gradually through the tall trees in unison with the stream. There wasn't much underbrush, just some small, scraggly bushes with green leaves and lots of pine needles covering the brown dirt. Surprisingly, the smell was her favorite part. She inhaled the aroma of a warm, fresh Christmas tree with every much-needed breath.

Her legs burned, and she welcomed the challenge of it.

Given the mountains she'd seen from the clearing this morning, they were headed up in elevation, and the trail was proving that true. A slight incline turned into an angled ascent that most people would find exhausting to even walk up, but Amity felt confident. She'd have to slow her pace to eight- or even nine-minute miles until the trail flattened out, but she'd slow less than the other teams.

Running outside was her salvation—it had been her escape since her father passed away and the one activity where all her troubles blew away with each new satisfying step, and right now, she felt as light as the crisp pine needles crunching beneath her feet. The trail shoes provided by the show were incredible—there weren't even words. She'd never had running shoes that weren't from a secondhand shop. Every pair she'd ever owned were profoundly molded to the annoying shape of someone else's foot. Maybe she'd get to keep them?

She glided up the trail like a perfectly-folded paper airplane—flawless, angled, and weightless. Even with her feet mummified in gauze. Even with the sting of the wounds from the pokes and scrapes of the sticks yesterday. A little pain on her feet or legs didn't bother her anyway. She'd run through injuries anywhere from billowy blisters while breaking in her used shoes to pulled muscles from mishaps like stepping wrong on a curb.

But chopping her hands up on a knife while trying to start a campfire like a cavewoman was another matter—especially with a burly caveman yelling at her.

Speaking of which, "Take that, Caveman," Amity yelled at Easton as she raced past him on a higher bank of the trail with Miles right behind her. Easton glanced at her, less shocked and more irritated than she'd expected. He'd probably heard Miles' ungraceful, pounding footsteps as they'd gained on him.

Amity peeked at Bria, who was already sucking wind and

struggling to even keep up with her new slower pace as they flew past. That surprised her. She'd expected Bria's long legs to propel her, but perhaps she wasn't conditioned for such a fast speed.

"Ignore them, Bria," Easton instructed. "They won't be able to keep that pace."

Ha! Easton didn't get it yet. He still thought her weak in every way. Amity couldn't wait to see his defeated, exhausted face at the finish line. Hiking and running were not anywhere near the same skill set. He may know trails and outdoor survival, but running consistently enough to be in good half-marathon shape was a different matter.

Another half-mile up the trail, they overtook Clara and Dan, who were also breathing hard and jogging so slow it was almost at pace with speed walking. The trail kept a consistent upward incline through the large pines. At times, they slowed to cross wooden bridges across the translucent stream. Amity peered down at the small stones glistening under the ripples as they crossed, wishing to dip her battered feet into the ice-cold water. With the days ahead of them, she'd likely get the chance many times along the trails, but there was no time for that now.

Though Amity knew they had almost no chance of being eliminated, she still meant to press on at a fast pace. If they could finish near first, then she could choose her next partner, and that meant everything to her. She'd be vulnerable at tomorrow's skills challenge and wanted to try for Liam as a partner. Scooping up the hunky cowboy who looked contra-dictorily sexy in his unprecedented trail clothes had occurred to her when she saw Liam and Becky walk to the start line. After seeing his incredible success at the fire challenge and Becky's instant selection of him as a partner for this leg, she knew he was a gem.

She'd never actually met a backcountry cowboy before, but

she liked the way he'd treated the women by the campfire—calling them ma'am and insisting they go first for breakfast this morning. Such a gentleman. Of course, Liam had avoided her, but who could blame him after the impression she'd left everyone on the first day?

An additional mile into the trail, they ran into another team. She'd expected to see the petite woman named Kim, whom Easton had boldly included in his list of acceptable candidates, and Kim's current partner, some mysterious-looking guy named Justin with bushy red hair and a full beard; but instead, they raced up behind a brown-haired team she knew nothing about. She hadn't even memorized their names. The woman, wearing a teal shirt, and the guy, wearing a mustard yellow one, jockeyed for position with them, trying to cut her and Miles off.

"Really?" Amity yelled in frustration, getting dust kicked in her face from their sloppy steps. "There's still about ten miles left, and you think blocking us matters right now?"

She backed off, running patiently behind the obstructive team for a few paces before the trail widened, and she and Miles raced past.

About four miles in, Amity checked behind her and saw beads of perspiration dripping down Miles' manicured face as he swatted at a bee trying to land on his sweat-soaked, fluorescent orange shirt. Each contestant seemed to have been provided with two polyester shirts and a heavy jacket in their own signature color chosen by the show's crew. Amity loved the deep purple color she'd been given, not that her clothing color mattered for a race. Still, the vibrant shade felt like home as her mom often filled vases full of purple irises courtesy of the resort complex florist where she worked.

"Dammit, bee," Miles yelled. "I'm not a flower." He coughed and gasped between breaths. "Amity, I need to slow for a bit."

She *could* rub it in, but she wanted to keep him motivated. His bravado and desire for drama were nowhere to be found when he sucked for air like a drowning man.

"No problem," Amity said. "We'll slow to nine- or ten-minute miles until we hit flat land. Looks like the trees are thinning out up ahead. I can see the sunlight shining through."

"Yeah, great," Miles rasped out. His focus now seemed to be entirely on putting one foot in front of the other.

Amity was breathing hard, too, but she'd learned to slow her own pace when necessary. Just as she'd suspected, Miles wasn't used to hills or real trails. Elevation was likely a factor as well. She could feel the lower oxygen levels here compared to back home in Palm Springs, but the cooler temperatures in the Oregon mountain range seemed to balance that out for her. The air in the forest was a crisp, fresh breeze compared to the oppressive desert heat—and that woody balsam fragrance was addictive—she couldn't wait for Christmastime now.

Envisioning opening a meager stack of presents wrapped in holiday ads that were scattered around their tree had her smiling and ticking down the miles. They usually decorated the plastic needles with homemade popcorn strands and a full ninety-nine-cent box of miniature candy canes. While only the lower half of the tree lights worked now, amazingly, they still blinked, though the remote seemed to be permanently stuck on the white-light setting.

When she was younger, she liked the multicolored lights, and fortunately, they still worked back then, but now she could care less—the tree lights could stay on white forever. They'd seen a few newer trees at Goodwill in recent months, but neither she nor her mom could bear to replace their first tree. Amity bought it with her dad, and when she and her mom put it up, it felt like she was still a little girl, and he was upstairs waiting for her to come and shake him awake to open presents.

"We haven't seen another team in a while," Miles said about five miles in, pulling her mind back to the race. "Should we speed up?"

"Can you?" Amity asked.

"Probably." He pointed up the trail. "Cool. Look at that."

In the distance, a round, sparkling blue-green lake, looking like a basin in a dirt hole, came into view with another surreal view of the mountains, which now felt much closer to them. A bright blue sky outlined their rough, snowy peaks, and as they got closer to the lake, an open meadow carrying an array of wildflowers—yellow, red, purple, and white—popped into view with patches of green grass along the stream that funneled into the lake. She'd never seen anything like it.

But the beauty of it all was offset by the contrary boxy, black equipment carried by the crew members. On the lakeside, there were three cameramen catching shots of two different teams, one drinking water from their bottles and another pumping water from the lake with that crazy contraption she'd seen in their packs. It looked like Justin, Kim, Sean, a blond, surfer-snowboarder-looking guy, and Jade, a beautiful woman with brown, curly hair and lustrous dark skin.

Amity's heart sank, her shoulders sagging while she trudged along. Were all the other women more appealing than her? Not just in looks, but in desirability as a partner? Who would Liam seek out? Who would Easton... Oh no—not him! A tingle went through her belly, and for some reason, her mind jumped to the moment when she'd had to jolt her gaze away from his zipper-compartment pants. Her already hot skin flushed, and when splotches appeared in her vision, she sharply drew in her breath.

As they neared the lake, Amity's patchy vision disappeared, and she regained control of her breathing. Somehow Miles didn't notice, probably due to his own exhaustion, and Amity vowed to have no more disorienting thoughts of Easton

Cooper. She blocked the sun with her hand, wishing she had on the designer sunglasses that she'd tucked in the netted side pocket of the pink suitcase she'd never even get to use, and saw yet another camera that looked like a Mars robot on a tripod capturing an ideal shot of them.

"Let's stop," Miles huffed out. "I need water."

"No way," Amity shouted over her shoulder. "We'll be in fifth place if we keep going. You're not going to die. Suck it up, *babe*."

Miles laughed, then coughed a few times, probably from the inexperience of sucking dry air in through his throat. "Don't speed up then, or I *will* die."

Around mile six, they ran along an open plain with continuous breathtaking views of the mountains off to their right. The dirty, rocky terrain was more familiar to her in every way, including the baking surge of heat. It was no problem for her. In fact, the arid blaze was an advantage. The other teams would be slowing down now, and if they hadn't already stopped for water at the lake, they'd be at one of the wildflower-surrounded streams along the way. Her mind drifted as the miles ticked by, her only craving a soothing foot soak every time they passed a pristine, rippling brook.

It was a perfect run on a perfect day. One she'd enjoy immensely if it wasn't for the fact that even after her unexpected mini panic attack, she *couldn't* keep Easton out of her mind. So after another mile flew by, she decided to stop trying. They obviously weren't interested in being partners, so why panic about him popping into her thoughts? Her mind probably went straight to his groin because she tried so hard not to think about him at all, a psychological reaction or something—it had to be—she wasn't even attracted to him.

She imagined he was sucking in some serious air about now. In a way, it served him right. He'd been so arrogant with his outdoor knowledge that being put in his place would be good for him. Speaking of place, where was he now? Did she want him eliminated? In her head, she thought yes, but in her heart, she wasn't so sure. There was something about him.

"Thinking about your boyfriend?" Miles' voice caused her to jump—she'd almost forgotten he was there.

"Miles, you're an idiot if you think I have any interest in Easton Cooper."

"I'd be an idiot if I didn't think that you did. It's pretty obvious." After a quiet moment, he added, "You know, I'm not really as big of a jerk as I let on earlier."

"I think you're a slimy worm for insulting Clara. If you shape up, then maybe I can tolerate you, but that's as far as we go."

"I can handle tolerate. I'd like to be on good terms with you for trail challenges. Look," Miles added suddenly, "two more teams ahead."

Out on the open plateau, there wasn't anywhere to hide. "I see them," Amity said. "They've been visible off and on for the last two minutes."

"Why didn't you say anything?"

"Because you need to focus on your feet, and this is as fast as I can pace you before you start overtly gasping for air."

"Make me gasp. Let's take them down."

"Okay, but remember, you asked for it."

Amity set her pace back to eight-minute miles and listened to Miles huff and groan behind her. She heard him say a string of unkind words followed by a pained explosion of, "How the fuck are you in this good of shape?"

Amity laughed at that one, but mostly she ignored him. Within a few minutes, they caught the two teams they'd spotted, slowly overtaking them and watching their shocked faces as they ran past. Soon, Amity estimated they'd hit about eleven miles.

The gauze on her hands loosened, and the pain increased

as the bandages rubbed roughly against her cuts. She cringed as sweat finally seeped inside the wounds, intensely stinging like hydrogen peroxide treatment. She'd forced the pain out of her mind all morning, and now, in the early afternoon, with exhaustion taking hold, she had to work harder to numb herself to it.

"Miles." She twisted her head to shout behind her. "Two miles left. Let's kick it."

Another groan, but she heard his pounding feet comply. She noted sunburn appearing on his pale arms and cheeks, but there wasn't much she could do about it. Her sunscreen was tucked in her larger pack near her notorious flint, though she wasn't sure she'd give it to him even if she could—he deserved a little pain. Too much time in the indoor offices and gyms, it seemed. She forced the concern out of her mind. Miles wouldn't be her partner soon anyway.

Another mile, and she saw the second-place team. Isaac, the tall, dark, athletic guy, and Cassie, a pale woman with long-braided, blonde pigtails—another very pretty woman with perfect features that made Amity self-conscious all over again. Burning past Cassie would make her feel better.

She tried to race past them with Miles behind her, but a blonde pigtail swung around and knocked her in the face, slowing her progress. "Ouch," Amity said, holding the spot on her face where the braid had smacked her. She blinked, temporarily losing her vision.

Amity heard a surprised "What?" squeak out of Cassie's mouth while she recovered. "Isaac, don't let them pass."

She and Miles jockeyed for position with them for a moment before Miles finally told them not to be a-holes. To which Amity sucked in a shocked breath and said to Cassie and Isaac, "I don't think that about either of you."

"Yeah, you do, Amity," Miles said between breaths. "Just

say what you're actually thinking to people. They *are* being a-holes."

Amity's skin flushed. She'd didn't want to make enemies, but what could she do? Defending herself further against Miles' comments would do nothing, so she sped up to a near sprint which finally left Cassie in the dust, and Isaac had to slow down with her accordingly. Cassie confirmed her dislike in more ways than just jealousy, but she still thought Isaac seemed nice and might make a great partner at some point.

They passed through a thicket of pines, and as they pushed their legs and lungs through the last mile, they could finally see two big red poles on the sides of the trail and the first-place team. Becky and Liam were only steps away from finishing. After a final sprint, Amity watched them take first just feet in front of her and Miles. Dang! Oh well, she thought with a gasp of air—second place was still a pretty sweet finish, especially with the huge time penalty they'd incurred. She'd take it and get herself a decent partner for the next leg.

Eight

Second place! Cooper couldn't believe it. How in the hell had Amity and that Miles bloke come in second place? Cooper crashed to the ground, heaving chestfuls of air while staring in shock at the scoreboard. Did they cheat?

And here he was with another close call. Any more of those, and he'd be gone. Another disadvantageous time penalty was in his future, and what woman would choose him this time around, knowing that it automatically meant a last-place start for her?

After two minutes of lying sprawled out in a sweaty heap on the grass like a moist slug, Cooper rolled over and, without being able to stop himself, looked around for Amity when instead he should be getting his distracted, lethargic butt up to find water and rehydrate.

He and Bria had no hope of staying in the race if they'd stopped at the lake or streams for water. His throat was so parched he'd probably sound like a frog if he tried to speak, and his calves were cramping up like someone was squeezing his muscles in a vise. Hydration would be key if they were expected to complete more trail runs over the coming days. He'd be the first to admit that running a trail and hiking it were not even close to the same thing. He was definitely an avid hiker and climber, but running—not so much.

Whereas Amity? All thirteen miles, he'd expected to come across her whining and crying in defeat; and as much as he wanted her out of the race so his strange fixation on her would be over, he was afraid that if he had discovered her, he wouldn't have been able to leave her on the trail defeated.

What a wake-up call, though, when it was him who was nearly defeated. He and Bria decided to pretend like they were in a military drill, and without their joint persistence, they'd be gone. They'd finished only a couple of minutes before Clara and Dan, who were now giving their exit interviews.

Everyone in this race was tough, including Clara and Dan, who'd almost had them beaten with their time advantage. The producers didn't throw together a group of lazy bums. This crowd was one hundred percent athletic, and they all had unique skills. One of the reasons Amity had been selected for the race was now very clear to him. She was a *really* damn good runner.

A smile parted his lips. Her plotting at the start line *was* much more than just talk. She'd known what she was doing, and damn if he didn't find that sexy as hell. Cooper had badly misjudged her. The way he'd treated her was inexcusable. His parents and sister would be ashamed of him, just as he was of himself. He owed her a heartfelt apology.

Scanning the area, he spotted her sitting on a clump of grass by the stream with her feet dangling in the water. She tilted her face toward the sky, basking in the afternoon sun with her eyes closed and her arms braced behind her. She'd changed out of her leggings and into the polyester hiking shorts that were in style for women these days. He hated how revealing they were when his sister and the flirty tourists wore them back home, but right now, he enjoyed the look immensely.

A small smile played on her lips as she reopened her eyes and began analyzing the wildflowers on the surrounding bank while splashing cool water over her calves. This was the first time he'd really been able to see her legs without the long flimsy dress or leggings obscuring them, and holy hell. They were the most incredible set he'd ever seen—defined and narrow, gleaming with a perfect California tan. Man, everything about her was gorgeous.

He caught her glance at him in return and flashed her the grin that he'd learned provoked unwanted attention from the tourists back home. This show had a romance angle, and she had his attention. If he got so soft on her that he didn't want her eliminated, then why try to stay away? Pursuing her would be fun, but only if she had any interest in him in return. Unlikely, after the stupidity of his words and actions, but he'd give it a try.

Amity scrunched up her features before whipping her head around to focus on the water, her short ponytail swishing with the movement. She didn't even look like she'd gone running— done up and not even sweaty, her face shining and lips sparkling in the sunlight.

She'd had time to cool down, change clothes, put makeup on, and even relax. She'd probably been here for an hour, sitting around, her location close enough to the finish line to indiscreetly assess the other contestants as they finished, noting their level of conditioning. It's what he would have done, and at that moment, he processed that Amity was clever, cunning, and dangerous. She'd come up with that solution with her hair that allowed them to snake by the fire challenge, and here she was, analyzing the cardiovascular fitness level of each competitor. He'd pegged her wrong. That was very unusual for him, given the number of people he met each week.

A blurred movement by his side caught his attention.

Forcing his eyes away from Amity, he discovered the crouching cameraman with a goatee stalking him. He screamed Hollywood like he regularly went to grooming shops. He looked a little like Miles but visibly more West Coast with the sleek way he wore gel in his hair. Cooper also noted the blue-blonde-haired woman intently filming Amity.

"How hard was it carrying that equipment up here?" he asked the gel-haired goatee man. "Or did the choppers fly you in?"

The cameraman shook his head, indicating that he couldn't answer, and Cooper smiled in amusement. It seemed that they were supposed to be silent while recording the drama. He wasn't used to that as he talked to everyone on his tours, and the camera crew, whether they liked it or not, were impossible to ignore, so out of place in the serene wilderness.

"I guess that means you're my designated stalker now?" Facetiously, Cooper continued, "The directors sicced a man on me. Is that so you can follow me even when I have to run off and take a leak?"

Goatee Man grinned silently but nodded, indicating that Cooper wasn't far off the mark. Well, at least the streaky-blue-haired woman would make it easy for Cooper to locate Amity, and immediately after the thought, he creased his brow. It wasn't like him to puppy dog after a woman. Yet, here he was, walking over to sit by Amity rather than going to get the water he desperately needed.

"So, you're a runner then?" Cooper asked, cupping his hands in the stream and splashing cool water across his steamy forehead and neck.

She squinted her eyes at him.

He dried his face on his dark green shirt, his neck hairs standing on end as he waited intently for her to speak.

"Thought you hated me?" she finally asked. "I'm certainly not your biggest fan."

Cooper exhaled. "Listen, I owe you an apology. I'm not proud of my behavior during the fire challenge or even afterward. I don't know you well, and I made some harsh, unfair judgments and said some really stupid things." He swallowed thickly. "I'm sorry."

Amity glared at him cautiously. "Okay, we'll see. Time will tell." Her chin shot up. "Why attempt to make amends? A racing strategy?"

He relaxed his muscles. She was giving him a chance. One he didn't deserve, but he'd gladly take it. Shrugging, he pasted on a warm smile, attempting to put her at ease, and said, "Nah. I mean, I don't want anything to do with you during the race. We're like oil and water." He gently nudged her knee. "And you're a high-maintenance princess, but other than that, you're okay."

"How kind." Her pursed lips softened when she caught on to his teasing, and a gentle laugh drifted out of her, which baffled him. "But agreed," she continued. "I don't want anything to do with you during the race either. You're a total caveman jerk." Her lingering grin let him know that she enjoyed the banter.

"So," he drawled out, "halfway friends then? When we're not competing, at least?" He grinned in return. "And when I call you Princess from now on, I promise I don't mean anything by it. It'll remind me how wrong I really was about you. It'll be my new way of letting you know how fierce of a competitor you are." He shrugged. "And feel free to call me Caveman all you want as a reminder to keep my act together. I deserve it."

Amity stared at the swells in the stream, chewing on her glistening lower lip. After a long pause, she looked back at him with curious eyes and said, "Okay, why not?" with a tiny shrug of her shoulders. "We can try friends, though I'm not sure I understand your motives."

"I don't have any," he said instead of, 'My eyes and mind are addicted to you,' thank god. He was in no mood to embarrass himself. He cleared his throat, plucking a long blade of grass and twisting it around his fingers. "So, you like to run?"

Amity watched him fiddle, contemplating him with her eyes, then sighed. "I suppose there's no point in hiding it. Yes, running is my thing. If I could do that run back there every week, I would."

"Not every day?"

She gently shook her head. "No, I'd miss the desert."

"Ah." Cooper nodded. She ran in the sun—that explained the tan. "Well, that's an advantage, isn't it? Acclimatization to the heat."

"Yes, it is." She glanced at him pointedly. "But so is acclimatization to elevation."

"I suppose so." Cooper cracked a grin, knowing that she assumed he had experience in the mountains. "Didn't seem to bother you much, though."

A cute little furrow appeared between her brows. "I think the ease of running in the cooler weather offset the elevation gain for me. Will we get even higher in elevation, you think?"

Her poke at his knowledge had his stomach jumping in confusingly pleasureful knots. He glanced at the PCT, following the trail with his eyes through the meadow to where it disappeared into another patch of trees. He couldn't help but let her in on what he knew, realizing that he wanted more than for her just to like him—he wanted her to trust him.

"I don't think so," he told her honestly. "Bandon said we'd stay on the PCT, and if that's the case, then we'll have moderate inclines and declines, but we won't be rock climbing any mountains."

Amity pulled her feet out of the water, placing them on the grass between them. "Do you wish we were?"

Red welts and bug bites covered the smooth surface of her

skin on the tops of her feet. He felt that protective surge inside him as she shifted more comfortably toward him. Her eyes locked onto his, and a full-on burst of adrenaline blasted through him. Funny, he rarely got adrenaline rushes anymore after being on so many steep cliffs, but this woman—she did things to him.

Cooper shook his head in response to her question. "Not as a challenge on this race. I don't want to pull an inexperienced woman up a cliff face. But to come back here and do it with my guys, absolutely."

"Girls can't do it?" Amity shot at him brusquely.

"Of course they can. I go climbing with women all the time. My sister can give me a run for my money. It's just that the guys I hang out with would be more likely to travel with me."

Amity's lips curved into a smile, a true, genuine smile, and it melted him. He needed to get away from her. It was too much.

"Ah, so you're kinda sweet then?" she asked. Although it sounded like she meant it in jest, he guessed that she was genuinely curious. "A protective big brother? You'd be nice enough to take me and a group of women climbing?"

Cooper tugged on his shirt collar—he'd be getting his knife out to slice the neck wider *tonight*. "No, definitely not. We'd never get along." He stood up quickly. "I need some water." His body felt leaden as he turned and stomped off.

"I was wrong," she said to his back as he walked away. "Trying to be friends is a bad idea."

No, she was exactly right. He could not handle the push and pull he felt for her. Just when he'd made progress at an amiable friendship that he couldn't help himself from wanting, he'd gone and pissed her off on purpose. He sucked at getting close to women. Usually, he didn't care if a woman was kind or even flirty with him because he knew that he wouldn't pursue her beyond sex. But with Amity, he was drawn to her like a compass, always pointing to her exact location.

The minute she'd gotten flirty, he'd panicked because he didn't want to care. Caring led to falling in love and falling in love meant commitment. It meant being trapped. It meant having to change yourself for a woman. Or worse, it meant watching someone you love more than yourself wither away from a disease while you watched hopelessly from the sidelines. He glanced at the trees forcing the desperate image of his best friend's wife from his mind. Amity was probably confused as hell by him.

A few hours later, after a pointless interview where he dodged questions about his feelings for Amity and his helpless position of not being able to choose a partner for the next leg of the race, he lined up behind Bria for some grub.

"So," Bria said, swatting at a mosquito that buzzed around her bleach-blonde hair with her hand, "looks like we're stuck with one another again. Unless some woman plucks ya up for your mountain skills. Is Hollywood choosing you? Saw your little convo by the stream."

Cooper chuckled in defeat. "Nah, she hates me again. Probably for the best." He tapped Bria's shoulder with his fist. "I should be decent at the next leg. A skills challenge, thank god."

Bria let out a little humph sound before saying, "Well, hopefully, that means we'll kick butt. Can't see anyone else choosing either of us. Who would be stupid enough to take on the biggest time penalty?"

"No one," Cooper agreed. "I owe you for accidentally doing that last time."

Bria nodded. "Yeah, you do."

After they each got a full serving of beef stew, Bria's eyes scanned the contestants at both campfires. "Hollywood's campfire or not?"

"Not," he said decisively. "Always keep me away from her."

Bria barked out a laugh. "'Cause you do such a good job of that yourself?"

Cooper sat in silence at the campfire listening to the other contestants try to lock in solid partners. Becky and Liam were popular and had about two suck-ups fawning over each of them. He didn't feel like it was the right time for him to build alliances since he was in no position to be chosen by anyone. After the next challenge, he thought, when he'd proven himself. He should be good at whatever they threw his way tomorrow.

Earlier in the afternoon, Cooper and all the other contestants noticed a large pile of logs that must have been brought in by helicopter. Perhaps a woodchopping challenge? If so, he had that made. He heated his cabin with a wood stove in the winter and spent countless hours outside chopping wood with his golden retriever by his side. It was a great stress release. Anytime his family or friends got on his nerves or an especially ornery group of tourists, he let out steam with the swing of his ax.

After a few minutes of listening to his competitors grill at one another's talents, he couldn't help but lose interest in their conversation and allow himself the relief of looking over at Amity. People seemed to be warming up to her. She'd fallen into conversation with Isaac. Cooper had overheard Isaac talking briefly in the tent last night. He'd had a decent collegiate basketball career, and now he coached high school kids in competitive leagues—again athletic—everyone here was.

Of course he was jealous. The intent, easy smile Amity held for Isaac as they talked was one that he'd never received and one he didn't deserve. If only they hadn't started out at odds with one another in the first place. But she'd had a difficult time with the fire challenge, and at the time, he didn't think she belonged. He'd learned his lesson now that *he* was the one in last place. He laughed, and Bria shot him a look like he was crazy.

"Sorry," he explained. "Just thinking."

"Yeah, about Hollywood. We know. The cameras love ya."

Cooper scanned the contestants around their fire—Becky, Liam, Kim, Justin, Jade, Sean, and of course, Bria—staring at him. Shit, he was doing a piss-poor job of making connections. If anything, he was networking himself out of ever being chosen by a decent partner. Liam tipped his cowboy hat in a direct gesture of what—recognition? That he had a crush? Unless Cooper let this be his wake-up call, he was screwed. He would ignore Amity—pretend she was dead—whatever it took to get to the end and win that money.

He couldn't even say anything to redeem himself. Denying his feelings would peg him as a liar and bring even more attention to the issue. His only way of changing their perception was to show them all that he had no interest in Amity. Cooper would have to walk the opposite way anytime he felt a pull toward her.

An unwarranted dislike of her sprang through his mind. She was no more than a means to an end, like everyone here. He should be focused on grilling people, too, although he wasn't too concerned about that, as he was learning everything that he needed to know just by listening to them. But still, he should be planning his moves.

Maybe he'd actually benefit from his temporary fixation on Amity by appearing the lovesick underdog—they'd rule him out as neither an ally nor a threat, and then he could take them out one by one with his mad outdoor skills. He took a deep, recalibrating breath. In the morning, he meant to do just that.

Nine

Amity woke up stiff after another miserable night in a sleeping bag, this time on a thin, uncomfortable back-packing air pad. The canvas cots from the previous tent must have been a one-night luxury. With a huge yawn, she lifted her frozen feet out of the stuffy bag, kneading her toes through her thin wool socks. Given that this was a conveniently set-up group camp, she dreaded the nights to come. Why couldn't they stay in cabins? They had those in the woods, right?

She let out a sigh, pulling on her purple coat to offset the cool morning air, and searched the main compartment of her red pack for her trail shoes. Her mouth spread into a grim line when she considered the effort required to carry the massive bag up a trail. She knew it wouldn't take long before she wanted to toss the whole load down the side of a cliff. And what a mistake that would be—she'd need every single thing in there—well, she thought with a smile, aside from perhaps her heels and fancy dress. Maybe she should ditch the useless items in the trash to lighten her load? But then it was survival; who knew when the satin fabric or spiky heels might come in handy.

So far, they hadn't been required to use much of their gear

other than the hiking clothes, trail shoes, flint, and knife, but she'd seen her own personal tent, sleeping bag, cooking supplies, and freeze-dried food packed tightly in the bottom of her pack. That could only mean one thing—she'd only touched the surface of this adventure—much more rigorous camping lay ahead.

If that realization hadn't done it, the confidence she'd built yesterday was shot anyway. This morning, they were heading into a skills challenge. Hopefully being able to select her partner would get her through it because she was out of her depth on this one. Amity had seen the tall, neatly-piled stacks of logs, and even she knew that they had to be related to the show. There were no roads around here for trucks to bring in large pieces of wood.

If they were going to play lumberjack, Miles was not the man for the job. She'd still like to scoop up Liam. A cowboy had to deal with things like that on a ranch, but she suspected Becky, having come in first twice with him, would choose him and vice versa.

Not wanting to incur too big a time penalty from a lower-finishing team, she planned to choose Isaac. She'd spent a good portion of the evening getting to know him, and even though he wasn't outdoorsy, his arms were ripped with muscles. A basketball coach who lifted weights in his free time should be able to do heavy lifting—dumbbells or logs—really, what was the difference? She'd be glad to watch him lift what-ever flexed his rockin' hot biceps, and she expected it to be him, not her, that had to do so—thank goodness.

All the contestants thought it was the men's turn since the women were required to start the fires. Yesterday after dinner, they'd inspected the skills-challenge stations, noting that each had a pine bench nearby. They'd put two-and-two together and decided it was the women's turn to park it. Amity was fine with that. Though she didn't want to give up control of her fate, anything to do with wooden logs was a nonstarter.

Alex Bandon had them line up, men and women, across from their prior teammate. Her designated camerawoman had her streaky-blonde hair up in a bun with the wispy blue strands fraying out. She smiled at Amity and zoomed in for a closeup, reminding her of the suffocating way the crew moved in when they'd filmed her interactions with Easton.

Amity thinned her eyes at the camerawoman, shooting her a curt look. She tried to forget about the pleasant way Easton had treated her yesterday, before his weird mood swing anyway, and the camera lens painfully reminded her. Their conversations always became heated, whether under pressure or not, and that made dramatic prime-time television.

Amity returned her focus to Alex as he explained what he lamely called the woodchuck challenge. She noticed that each man in line currently had some sort of tool, an ax, she guessed, lying by their feet. The camera crew focused on some of the men as they picked up their axes to examine them. She rolled her eyes skyward at the show's attempt to dramatize every scene. Noting the camerawoman catch her exasperated expression, Amity snubbed her nose at the lens. How many sour looks had the camera caught? Oh well, she thought while flicking a disgusting bug off her forearm. She had the prissy princess label, so why not go with it and continue to prove them all wrong?

Alex continued his explanation of the woodchuck challenge, saying that the men were to compete while the women sat on the benches—thankfully, they'd been right. She'd be her guy's own personal cheerleader. Anything was better than chopping wood and tearing her hands to shreds again like she'd done during the fire challenge. It'd be a few weeks before the deep cuts in her palms healed as it was.

Alex carried on, "The man from the first-place team will

choose first this time, followed by the female from the first-place team—" and Amity let out a disappointed huff even though she'd expected it because, unfortunately, that meant she'd choose after Miles, and he didn't deserve to go before her.

She looked across the divide at Miles, and he purposely locked eyes with her. His mouth lifted in one corner, a mischievous grin forming. He wasn't planning to choose her, was he? The blood rushed from her head, her skin prickling with icy beads of sweat. She hadn't anticipated that he actually would, but she'd been stupid—he'd do anything for ratings, and a guy that never went to the countryside would *not* know how to chop wood. She took in slow breaths, relaxing her shoulder blades to try and calm her racing pulse.

"Do not choose me," she mouthed at Miles. "I suck at skills challenges. You'll get eliminated."

Miles laughed in satisfied amusement, smiling like the trained professional he was as a camera narrowed in on his face.

For some reason, in Amity's moment of hopelessness, her eyes sought out Easton. For comfort? He'd never do that. What was she thinking? He'd react with an equally sly, calculated grin knowing that Miles as a partner would be her downfall, wouldn't he?

But to her surprise, Easton seemed to be doing everything he could not to look at her. In some ways, it was a relief not to have it tossed in her face, but in others, it was simply perplexing. He'd gotten under her skin yesterday when he'd sought her out and grilled her to learn all he could about her skills, just like the other contestants. But then she'd decided, as she lay in her tent last night, there was something else there besides pure strategy. He'd been too attentively aware of her for the past thirty-six hours.

And now, he avoided her gaze like she could kill him with

her eyes? It didn't make sense.

While Amity would admit that she'd all but hated him after the fire challenge, she'd be lying if she said she felt that way now. She didn't like the distance he'd deliberately put between them. His sudden use of the cold shoulder after being temporarily friendly by the stream was a mystery; then, Easton had continued his childish behavior of pretending she didn't exist after dinner last night. He'd passed by her on the way to the men's tent and visibly looked in the opposite direction. He certainly wasn't smooth at turning a woman down, if that was even his goal.

More than likely, he didn't want her to choose him for the skills challenge. That stung, especially given her time advantage and the fact that she'd be sitting this one out anyway. After her performance on the trail run, it was silly he didn't want to build an alliance with her. She'd argue that they were equally strong competitors, with him being the skills challenge master and her being the trail run queen.

Easton needed a woman on his side to balance him out, and Amity didn't think Bria was that woman. Even though he'd likely had to slow his pace for Bria, he'd been plenty winded after that run. He needed someone with an opposite skill set—someone with different ideas than him. But it was probably dumb of her to imagine that they'd be good racing partners, both because of how they'd gone at it during the fire challenge and because, right now, he wouldn't even look at her.

So odd. This was the second time Easton Cooper had allowed her to survey him shamelessly, and for some incomprehensible reason, looking at him calmed her, so she kept at it. She was sure he felt her gaze—she'd certainly felt every one of his, and it was hard to ignore someone who seemed so focused on you.

Amity decided he was kind of cute. His dark brown hair

was a couple of inches long and went this way and that, like Joshua Tree branches looking for different ways to point toward the sun—it didn't appear that he cared to comb it. Amity grinned at his disheveled appearance and watched him shift slightly. Oh, he noticed her gaze all right, and now that she'd allowed herself free rights to have him in her thoughts, she was enjoying every minute of it.

Easton scratched the surface of his chin and tipped the brim of his blue cap over his eyes, still shuffling like he couldn't quite handle her attention. She smiled in satisfaction, feeling pulses of warmth course through her, emboldened by her ability to affect him. She raked her eyes across every inch of his lengthy body, enjoying the way his hiking clothes molded to him like the mannequins at an outdoor adventure store.

And his eyes, my gosh, remembering their green-hazel depths from their conversation by the stream, spiked her pulse. She swallowed through quickened breaths as she thought of how his gaze coiled her stomach and sent tantalizing tingles across the surface of her skin. He'd trained them on her like he was trying to solve a puzzle; whether he was trying to put the pieces together regarding her or him, she didn't know. Did she want to find out? Unfortunately, the answer seemed to increasingly point toward yes.

Easton peered up at the sky, fidgeting his fingers and rocking around on his heels. Making him squirm was kind of fun. Though it seemed pointless to provoke him, honestly, it was her turn to do so. He'd had his fair share of inciting comments.

Alex repeated the process. "So this time, the man in the first-place team will choose first, followed by the woman in the first-place team. We'll start with the winning team and go down to the last-place team. Once you're chosen, you're chosen. You are required to race with that person, and I will disclose that the time penalty of the lowest-finishing member of your team will again apply, so choose wisely. Let's begin."

Selections happened quickly, as they always did. It was like people thought that if they didn't shoot a name off fast enough, their turn might be skipped. Liam, of course, chose Becky. Then, Miles was up, followed by her. It was a strange feeling to be so close to the top and potentially able to choose her own partner—as long as Miles didn't mess it up for her.

"Miles," Amity power-whispered across the divide, ignoring the three cameras catching her newest drama. "Do not choose me. Do *not*. I am not going down with you."

"Like I told Amity in the last leg," Miles announced to the cameras, "two hours a day in the gym, babe." With an arrogant grin, he turned from looking at the lens to meet Amity's eyes. "Don't worry, *Miss* Amity. I'm not going down without a fight." He then glanced at the host, basking in the attention. "I choose Amity."

"No," Amity huffed out and stomped her foot. "You really are such a dick."

Alex cleared his throat. "We'll have to check if we can air that one on television. All the same, we'll at least hear the bleep." He laughed before continuing, "So, Amity?"

Amity had her hands in her hair, grasping the strands to prevent a further outburst, likely ripping it out of the neat ponytail she'd styled this morning. "Yes, Alex," she finally managed.

"I take it Miles wasn't your first choice."

"More like my last choice to the nth degree—besides Easton, of course," she added in irritation. Now Easton's silent treatment, or rather silent gazing, was getting to her, and he wasn't the only one who had a right to lash out. She *wanted* the comfort of his constant gazes.

Miles grinned in complete satisfaction, enjoying the spotlight, she was sure, while she'd probably somehow look like the villain again for rejecting a selection from a second-place teammate—but he would never have come in second!

Alex continued to capitalize on the drama by asking, "Amity, may I ask who you would have chosen?"

"Isaac," she answered without hesitation.

"Isaac," Alex inquired, "your thoughts on that?"

"Be fine with me." Isaac flashed her a killer smile. "Amity would be a solid partner. She proved that on the last leg, sprinting past us at the end. Knocked my socks off. She almost took first. Probably would have if she hadn't had to drag Miles along."

"Yeah, keep telling yourself that, Isaac," Miles threw in.

Ignoring Miles, Amity felt the warmth of a blush and returned Isaac's smile. She noticed Easton shifting around, but he held his face so that his gaze was glued to Bria. Interesting. He wouldn't even look at Isaac or Miles while they spoke, let alone her.

"Thanks, Isaac," Amity said sweetly. "And yes, I would have taken first, but I'll save that for the next trail challenge."

She couldn't help but shoot Becky a competitive glare. The woman hadn't been nice to her in the tent last night. Amity's performance in the previous leg probably threatened her flawless co-partnership with the sexy cowboy. Too bad. Amity had her eyes on Liam and the bicep-bearing perfection of Isaac. Both of them were incredibly kind, and she'd like to get to know them.

Maybe Easton would actually look at her again if she became more respected and popular among the other men. After all, this was supposed to be a race for riches or *romance*— and surprisingly, a guy appeared more obtainable, as the money seemed like an obscured pot at the end of an insurmountable rainbow. For now, she'd play for the guy, but if that didn't work out—well—she'd focus on having a fun adventure and perhaps even take the win.

Ten

Cooper's skin flamed so piping hot he felt like he'd been dipped in molten lava. He ached to jump into the frigid stream, clenching every muscle in his body to keep his feet planted on the ground. He'd done everything he could to convince himself that feigning indifference would be for the best. That way, he could concentrate on winning the cash and prove to the other contestants that he'd somehow freed himself from his uncontrollable crush on Amity. But the flirtatious, encouraging comments from Isaac and Amity's quick acceptance of his support were all but torture.

Before she'd sweet-smiled Isaac, he'd felt her eyes on him. How could he miss it? She'd stared him down unashamed for several seconds, and he'd barely been able to breathe. He'd pathetically hoped it meant something, but what were the chances? He was a loose cannon, inconsistent with his behavior. And Isaac? What a smooth talker that guy was. He needed to take lessons.

Now Amity was forcibly paired with Miles, and he couldn't wait to let out his frustration with the swing of his ax. At least Amity's response today had been unfavorable toward Miles. Cooper had been confused when she'd temporarily teamed up with him yesterday—until he realized it was nothing more than her racing strategy—but her new interest in Isaac and even Liam ate at him. He barely knew her, for god's sake. This was insane, and evidently, he'd tuned Bandon out because he heard his name being called a few times with volume.

"What was that, Alex?" Cooper's head popped up. "Sorry, was lost in thought."

Alex laughed. "I can see that. You're automatically partnered with Bria since you're the only two left. How do you feel about that?"

"Great. I owe Bria one, and I've got this challenge in the bag."

"Do you?" Alex asked.

"Yep, I live in the woods." Cooper chuckled at the eeriness of his statement. It sounded like a horror movie opening. He could play that up. "All *alone* in my wood-stove-heated cabin. I'm pretty decent with an ax."

Cooper swung his splitting maul up, let it rotate in a circle a few times, and caught it in his hand to show off a little. He often did that when he answered his cell phone outside. He got bored just sitting around talking on the phone in his yard, waiting to split wood again, so he played around. Mostly, he threw a tennis ball for Jax, but even that ran its course during a phone call, so he had to find other outlets. He'd tried to split once with his phone wedged between his chin and shoulder, but his mom had freaked out, thinking he'd get hurt. She'd made him swear he'd never do it again.

"Neat little trick," Miles shot at him. "Just like those creeps in the movies. Do you know how to pull off a good ax murder with that thing, too?"

Cooper grinned but didn't look directly at Miles because he knew his eyes would involuntarily seek out Amity. "Only on the city slickers," Cooper fired back.

Miles snickered, trailing off with a polished glance at the camera.

Cooper ground his teeth and continued looking at Bria in front of him, trying not to let Miles get to him. He knew the guy was here solely for the attention of the cameras and whatever career he wanted to build—his new strategy seemed to be to stay near Amity and attack the other men who threatened his airtime. That was his real reason for trapping Amity and trying to make him seem like a backcountry creep.

Two days ago, Cooper never would have expected to be one of the men drawing the camera crew's attention, but anyone near Amity instantly seemed to do so—which had him wondering—was she here for the cameras too? His brow knitted. Did it really matter if she was? It wasn't like he'd see her after all of this.

"—the male contestant from each team will be required to chop a quarter cord of wood—" Bandon announced as Cooper let the pertinent information filter into his brain, but he'd already guessed this.

Earlier this morning, helicopters brought in eight giant metal bins dangling from chains. They'd set the bins in the meadow near the piles of wood. After breakfast, Cooper and Bria carefully inspected the challenge stations. Substantial round logs that had been chainsawed in sections from a tree, each about a foot wide by a foot-and-a-half long, lay in stacks between the metal bins. A scale lay underneath the bins for measuring the weight of something—obviously chopped wood. A quarter cord of wood would take an experienced person no more than half an hour to chop, but for someone inexperienced, like he expected Miles would be, it could take at least an hour.

Bandon went on to explain how contestants were required to chop each log into quarters, first by bringing their splitting maul down on the flat section of the round log to chop it in half, and then again to cut each of the halves in two, creating fireplace ready cuts of wood. When the scale tipped with the proper weight, each team's flag would raise. Bandon and several assistants would watch to ensure no team cheated by throwing improperly chopped pieces of wood into their bin. Piece of cake—for him anyway.

The first-place team drew for location, followed by Miles and Amity. Miles pulled out a green stick, placing him and Amity right at a center bin location with four teams on one of their flanks and three on their other. Cooper drew yellow, which of course, was right next to Miles and Amity, front and center. The drawings had to be rigged. Though the drama might play out naturally, the crew would do everything in their power to throw certain contestants at odds.

Cooper walked over to the yellow station and analyzed the cleared-out flat section near his bin to set his logs on for chopping. Closing his eyes in his own form of meditation, he put his mind back to his cabin. He imagined his woodpile, his chopping area by the woodshed, the rocks and trees that surrounded his open field, and his dog jumping up excitedly, hoping to play fetch before he grabbed his splitting maul. Chopping wood was home for him and his favorite form of exercise aside from backpacking and climbing—he was ready *right* now—but unfortunately, he'd have to suck it up and wait.

Bandon counted down to start the challenge for the first-place team. Cooper sat down against a grand fir and placed his hands behind his head, loosely listening to Liam start chopping. He could hear by the sound of the split that the Montana country cowboy knew what he was doing, and, of course, he wasn't surprised—Liam and Becky would take first again. Even if Cooper was faster than Liam, the time penalty was too extreme for him to catch up to a decent woodchopper. This challenge would move faster than yesterday's trail run, and it would be more difficult for him to overtake the other teams with his advanced skills than it had been for Amity yesterday with hers.

Speaking of which, after Miles' and Amity's five-minute penalty, the buzzer went off, and Miles was allowed to start courtesy of Amity's incredible trail run. Cooper watched Miles swing from the corner of his eye, and instead of feeling euphoric to see the man's oncoming downfall, he tilted his head down and dug his fingers into the back of his neck. The jagged noises that bounced off Miles' awkward hits jarred in his ears. Miles was having a hell of a time, as Cooper knew he would, and Amity could be eliminated because of it.

After what felt like countless minutes, all the teams had started, aside from him and Bria. Most of the men were flying through their cuts, making Cooper edgy. It was time for him to get in on the action so he could catch up. There were only a few contestants that he could easily overtake, one of which, not surprisingly, was Miles.

The judge for Miles' station had just signaled to Alex Bandon that another rule had been violated. Miles had missed, cursed, and missed again while managing to only split a small sliver off the side of one of the logs; Miles was trying to claim the tiny scrap as an acceptable piece. Bandon moved over to Miles, making announcements, while the cameras trailed to record the scene properly. Without the crew members helping, there were simply too many teams for Bandon to hover over them all.

"Miles," Alex lectured calmly, "per the rules, you must cut all four pieces in mostly equal sections and throw them in the bin together. You can't get credit for a small piece that you split off the side."

"This is crap." Miles tossed the splinter into the trees, but to his credit, he plucked another round log off the pile and tried again. He would have some nasty blisters tonight. Hands like Miles' probably hadn't seen anything other than free weights and computer keys.

After an excruciatingly long thirty-five-minute penalty, their buzzer went off. Bandon pointed at Cooper and said, "Go, team eight."

Cooper grabbed log after log, lining them up production style. He couldn't believe none of the other men considered a production line time saver. After lining up ten logs, he then went down the row chopping each one in half. He set up all the halves, doing the same action to slice them into quarters, and within minutes, he had forty pieces of wood to throw into his bin. Bria gave 'yeah, cut that up' and 'you nailed it, man' type chants throughout each perfect swing.

Cooper used other shortcuts to speed his progress, like searching for cracks in the logs. The trick was to select logs, if any were visible, with cracks in the middle and then, with a precise swing of the ax, slice more easily right through. He'd never do that at home because he'd have to chop every piece anyway, but today was about accuracy and speed. Fortunately, accuracy in chopping took lots of practice, so shortcuts wouldn't help most of the men here.

"Miles, focus." He listened to Amity's anxious tone, and his thoughts drifted to her. "Watch Easton swing for a minute so you can understand how to do the motion." A deep jolt shot through him at hearing Amity say his name. Powered by a pulsing rush of his blood, he chopped with more force, his ears now craving more of her voice. "Also," she continued, "Easton seems to be lining them up. He's doing more cuts at once and choosing certain logs. I don't know why, but there's a reason."

With a quick check over his shoulder, he noticed Miles had withered away his entire lead, and, with shaky, tired arms, he was only able to execute his hits by luck.

"Amity," Miles yelled, "I can only hit the log with the

damn ax half of the time. I don't think lining up more logs will make an 'effing bit of difference."

"Just trying to help."

"Yeah, well, don't."

Cooper winced at the tone Miles used with Amity, and a pain twisted in his gut that he'd been even worse to her during the fire challenge. He knew it would take something monumental to earn any admiration for him in her eyes and found that with each hard swing of his ax, he hoped Amity was as impressed with his chopping skills as he'd been with her run. Her caveman nickname for him had him chuckling while he 'neanderthaled' the wood. He might be a bit lanky for a caveman, but it sort of fit.

Cooper peered at Miles again as he went to grab another set of logs. Miles was yanking fiercely on the handle of his splitting maul. The sharp blade was stuck in a log, and his bin was only a quarter of the way full. His cuts on the ground were pathetic; literally, he'd mauled them, but it appeared that the judge let it go if there were technically four solid pieces from the same log.

Amity's next words rang through Cooper's core, her whiny tone now prickling the hairs on the back of his neck and rushing adrenaline through him. And to think, her high-pitched voice used to grate across his eardrums like fingers on a chalkboard.

"*Please*, Miles, aim. It takes up so much of your energy when you miss the center of the log. You're slowing down."

Her desperate words continued over the next few minutes, her voice cutting through him like each piece of wood he sliced. His breathing accelerated while a clammy sweat moistened his palms, loosening his masterful grip on his ax. Cooper set down his ax and rubbed his hands down the sides of his cargo pants. Trying to push her voice out of his mind, he took a longwinded breath to recalibrate himself.

He resumed his work and cut through multiple groups of logs, methodically taking the resulting chopped forty pieces from each group and throwing them into the bin. After only fifteen minutes of chopping, he realized about eight more pieces would tip the scale.

And he couldn't do it.

"You have enough wood, Cooper," Bria yelled. "Stop chopping and throw the rest in. We're golden. *Now, man!* We'll get third."

Damn—third, Cooper registered. That was pretty incredible with how short the task was combined with their huge time penalty.

Cooper lifted his head to check on Miles' progress. Even with the time advantage on almost every team, his bin was still only half full, if that, and Miles sucked so badly at chopping that he wouldn't have time. He glanced at Amity, recognizing the same propelling urge he felt while climbing, followed by a deep, stinging pain in his chest. He could not lose her.

"Yo, Cooper," Bria continued in an agitated tone, "let's do it! Throw the wood in. Come on, man."

Cooper spaced her out and went to grab another set of ten logs. He chopped them all into fourths, filled his lungs with air, and, with a crazy rush of 'what the hell am I doing' while his arms worked, threw the pieces into Miles' bin.

He heard an audible gasp from Amity, followed by a scream of "What the fuck" from Bria. "Have you lost your—"

But again, Cooper tuned her out, the mad adrenaline rush driving him forward. He moved quickly, tossing the cuts into Miles' bin until all forty pieces were thrown in. He then went back to grab another ten logs, noticing Miles' dumbfounded stare.

Cooper shouted as he grabbed another log, "Man, get off your ass and chop. *Now.*"

Miles glanced at Amity. "Your boyfriend's gone mad."

"Chop," Cooper yelled at him. "I can only risk this for a few minutes."

"Okay, man," Miles said, shaking his head. "You've lost it, but I'll take it." With a light snicker, he added, "Must be the cabin life," and swung his ax.

Cooper heard Miles' sloppy hits continue through Bria's string of constant cuss words in the background. He could only imagine how pleased the directors were with his psychotic behavior and the dramatic scene unfolding.

"Alex," Bria called out angrily to the host, "this has to be against the rules."

Bandon, who'd been speechless, shook his head with an equally flabbergasted stare. "There's nothing in the rules that says he can't fill another team's bin. The cuts are within the required regulations. We never specified which male contestant had to fill each team's bin. Just that the ladies had to stay on their bench and couldn't participate or touch anything." The host scratched his chin in thought. "And that no one could remove completed logs from a bin."

Bria swore and started yelling at Cooper again. He tried to only register her comments when they were relevant. "Dammit, Cooper, we're in fourth now. Justin just finished." If he listened to her beyond that, then the guilt he'd feel for putting her in this situation would have him changing his mind.

A few minutes later, Cooper checked on the other teams. Several of them were glancing at him in wonder. A few asked if, while he was at it, he'd fill their bins too, to which he just ignored them and kept working. He was probably sinking his chance at being selected by anyone ever again. That's when Dominic sprung into his mind. He *needed* that money. What was he doing? But he couldn't help himself because right now, he could have both—keep Amity here and have a chance at the money. Later in the race—well, he'd worry about that then.

Cooper tried not to look at the shocked faces of the contestants while he analyzed their progress and chopped wood simultaneously. He'd already made this crazy choice—now he needed to see it through *and* still get a decent finish. As Bria said, Justin and Kim had finished, but none of the other teams were close enough to cost them any more places, especially since his behavior distracted them from their task. Several of the men seemed to have panicked that he was helping another team, their frantic movements hurting their accuracy and slowing them down.

Cooper flew through multiple cuts of wood. He caught Miles up to where he was, tossed almost all the remaining cuts Miles would need on the ground in front of him, and then turned and threw the remaining eight pieces of chopped wood into his own bin, which did indeed tip the scale. Even with all of that, he'd managed fourth place.

Letting his breath out in a rush, Cooper allowed himself the pleasure of locking eyes with Amity. His lips curved into a satisfied smile, warmth radiating through his body and loosening his tense frame. After not looking at her all day, it was a huge relief to give into her pull; but from her bewildered stare, it was clear that he had more to do to win her over. Confusion, shock, distrust, curiosity, and frustration were all wrapped into one look. Not just from Amity as he glanced around but from every contestant, director, producer, and camera crew member there.

"You want to explain yourself, jackass?" Bria finally said.

Cooper shrugged. "Not really."

All he knew was that Amity wasn't going anywhere because he couldn't stomach the thought.

Eleven

What just happened? Was it part of his strategy? Why did he smile at her when he'd finished? Did she owe him something? And then it occurred to her—the next leg of the race was a trail challenge. If it was anything like the last one, she could win, and Easton was here to win. He did see the advantage of racing with her to offset his skills.

Still, it surprised her that he wanted to be partners with her, even if it did get him ahead for one leg. Heck, he flat-out told her that he didn't want to race with her. Why not get rid of her now and choose the next fastest runner? Maybe it was because most of the stronger teams had finished ahead of him, and if he kept her in the race, then he, too, would have a fast runner for the next leg.

Whatever his reason, good golly, that boy could chop. It was one of the sexiest things she'd ever seen. Amity was no expert but watching him bring down his ax and seeing the firm, layered patterns of muscles flex across his arms was beyond hot. For such a slender guy, she couldn't believe his strength. He had her attention now, but did she have his?

Amity huffed out a soft sigh, so confused and wound up that her limbs were shaking. What a morning! She still hadn't gotten over the stress of almost being eliminated, followed by Easton's miraculous rescue, but thanks to Easton, Miles finished only a few minutes after him. Easton had chopped enough wood so that Miles only had to split one more log to tip the scale, putting them at an undeserved fifth-place finish. The rest of the teams trickled in with their finishes shortly thereafter.

Alex Bandon jumped up on the camera platform by Easton's station, cupping his hands around his mouth to project out his voice. "Please head to the main part of camp to grab a sack lunch. Another challenge will occur today—a trail challenge, so be ready with comfortable, flexible clothing and trail shoes at one o'clock. The current group camp will again be your sleeping arrangements for tonight, so only the detachable daypacks are required for today's trail challenge. You can leave your larger packs in the tents."

Miles groaned, clearly spent from the effort of bringing down his ax in skill-less, energy-exhausting ways.

Amity bubbled with laughter. "Too bad for you." With one gauzed-covered hand on her hip, she pointed a bandaged-clad finger at Miles with her other. "Just so we're clear—you're on your own this time. I'm not dragging you down a trail again." A sudden thought occurred to her, and she perked up, quickly adding, "I don't think you get to decide before me. We both finished in fifth." She flashed him a smug smile. "And I do believe it's *ladies'* turn to choose first."

"You owe me," he said, "for choosing you—twice."

"Nice try, Miles. You chose me for your own selfish agenda —both times, and you know it. I owe Easton. You got enough airtime on that last challenge, so you can give it up now."

"No, your boyfriend got airtime, not me." A concerned frown crossed Miles' face, distorting the perfect crescents etched below his hollow cheeks. Amity couldn't believe she had ever found him attractive. "Quality airtime while I looked like a fool. Maybe you should question *his* agenda."

She shook her head. "He's not here for the cameras."

"Sure." Miles laughed cynically. "Keep telling yourself that or buck up and realize there's nothing else to gain. You, of all people, know that a million dollars only goes so far, especially after tax."

Yeah, right! Amity wished she knew. Miles had no idea how far a million dollars could go if you weren't an over-spending, conceited moron. She could probably live the rest of her life on that, even after tax, but she'd never tell him that. If Miles knew her financial situation, he'd use the information to his advantage and tell Easton. How likely was Easton to race with her if he knew how badly she needed money? Still, she reminded herself, she wasn't here for a million dollars. An adventure—that was the goal. There was no reason to get her hopes up beyond that.

When she didn't respond, Miles droned on with a crabby sneer, "Cooper's no different than me. He wants screen time. You're better off racing with me and taking him out. He's a threat. I give you my word right now—I'll go to the end with you."

She drew back with a scoff. Did he really think she was that dense?

"You'll figure it out eventually," Miles said, stalking off toward medical, probably to get bandages for his hands.

His cuts and scrapes looked almost as bad as hers from the fire challenge—almost. How embarrassing to have been injured even worse than Miles. She couldn't believe Easton would want her as a partner, even if she could run.

Amity searched for Easton and located him walking toward camp. She casually followed at a distance, stopping when he stepped in line for food. Bria strolled up behind him with her arms crossed and a nasty scowl on her face. Amity didn't blame her. If Easton had been her partner, and he'd pulled that stunt, she'd be pissed too.

But he hadn't been her partner, so—what now?

She ambled over to them, catching the last few words.

"I don't get what you're up to, but I can't understand how giving up placement to save Hollywood really benefits ya. Sure, she can run, but we don't even know if…"

Bria turned and glanced at her like she was an inconvenient new recruit.

"Sorry to interrupt," Amity said, "but Easton, can I please have a minute?"

Amity didn't know why she still wasn't calling him Cooper. She didn't hate him anymore. In all honesty, she never really did, so she should get over her promise to herself that 'she would never call him Cooper,' but she couldn't. His last name didn't sound right in her ears. She didn't think of him as a 'Cooper.' And on top of all that, calling him Cooper would reveal that she cared to please him, which she definitely didn't want him to know.

"How about you step into line behind Bria?" As Easton spoke, Bria grunted like Amity stepping behind her was a curse. "We'll need to get as much food and water in our system as possible before this next trail challenge. Then, we can chat as we eat—if you'd like?"

Amity nodded. "Good plan."

She waited behind Bria, biting her lip and looking up the trail. She tried to imagine what the day would bring, wanting to ask Easton a dozen questions. Where did the trail go? How much elevation gain? What type of terrain? But she knew there were too many ears listening nearby, and he might not tell her anyway. She had no idea if he planned to partner up with her or if he would answer her questions until he was sure he could.

Really, there were no guarantees when it came to who

would choose either of them. There were teams above them who could choose one of them first, either to select a strong partner or to make sure she and Easton were not partners— especially since Easton's erratic choice to sacrifice his own finish for her could inspire the other teams to keep them apart. A shocking lightning-like pain shot through her—she didn't want to be separated from him.

She reached for a veggie and provolone pre-made lunch bag, her hand brushing against Easton's arm as he selected roast beef and Swiss. With a quick intake of breath, she tried to process the tingles that raced through her fingers and up her forearm. She quickly snatched up the bag and jerked her arm away, noting that Easton did the same, while Bria, still standing between them, thinned her lips and snagged a turkey and cheddar bag.

To Amity's relief, Bria walked the other way, mumbling something under her breath that sounded like 'damn teenagers,' while Easton led her to a patch of grass by the little stream.

Amity plopped down, anchored her gaze to his, and said, "*Thank you*," in a fervent tone, "but I don't understand… why?"

Easton's mouth quirked up, his grin unreadable. "Straight to the point. Usually, I like that."

"Usually?"

His smile faltered. "Yeah."

After a few minutes of silence, Amity asked, "You're not going to explain it to me?"

Easton shrugged. "Your speed." He dipped his hands in the stream, cleansing the dirt off from the woodchuck challenge. "I'm hoping to choose you for the trail challenge today. It'd be nice if you helped me come in first as a return favor."

She inhaled a relieved breath and tried to hide the smile that tugged at her lips. "That kind of makes sense. A little crazy, though, if you ask me. It cost you a third-place finish and put you at odds with a lot of the other contestants."

"Ah, yeah." He chuckled, grabbing the back of his neck and roughly rubbing the muscles as he spoke. "I had a 'what-the-hell-am-I-doing moment,' but the rules for this race are all over the place." Shrugging again, he continued, "It's hard to say if it was a bad move or not. Strong contestants will have a target on their backs now regardless. Only seven teams left, and both of us are less of a threat than Becky and Liam—even if we're not partners."

Amity hadn't spoken to the team that had just been eliminated in the woodchuck challenge. It was the brown-haired team with the teal and yellow shirts who'd tried to block her and Miles on the trail run. They'd been furious, staring her down with evil glares before their exit interviews. As if it was her fault! She hadn't done anything offensive. Easton was the one who'd made the unpredictable move.

Speaking of unpredictable, he stared at her again, spiking her pulse and lighting her nerve endings on fire. Easton Cooper had no idea she wanted his long, secretly sculpted arms wrapped around every part of her—but she needed to be careful. What other secrets did he have?

She cleared her throat. "We may be less of a threat than the top two teams but with higher visibility. We make a scene every time." In jest, she tacked on his line. "Even if we're not partners."

His mouth twisted into a smile. "That's your fault."

Amity let out a carefree laugh. "I don't think you can claim that after that last move you made. That scene was all you."

She gazed into the depths of his eyes, trying to read him. The green-and-brown hazel pattern of his irises blended in with the forest. Everything about him fit in out here—his eyes, his physique, his attitude, his clothes—whereas everything about her did not. Her skin flushed when she realized how long she'd returned his intent gaze. It was at times like this that the cameras felt like an intrusion.

"I still don't fully understand why you did it," Amity said softly. If Easton could read her, he'd pick up on her growing desire for him, but thankfully he seemed clueless. "I'm not sure there will be many more trail runs in this race. Seems like we'll move on to backpacking here soon."

Easton shrugged. He did that a lot, she noticed, almost as if it was his way of keeping things light. "You're in shape," he said. "You've proven that. It's a big asset on a race like this—for backpacking too."

It didn't entirely add up. All of the women in this race were in shape. Amity decided to let it go for now and dumped the contents of her lunch bag out on the grass. She'd wanted something lighter today than the heavy chilis and stews she'd been eating. The first bite of the fresh veggies on rye was just what her system needed.

"Be sure to drink water, too," Easton instructed.

Amity lifted a brow. "Okay, Caveman. I may not have any outdoor skills, but I do know how to stay hydrated. I'm a runner, remember?"

His smile returned, a cute little dimple forming on his left cheek. "Yeah, I guess that hasn't fully sunk in yet. I didn't get to see you much on that run. Second place! Damn, I still don't know how you managed that."

"I run anywhere from three to twelve miles a day back home."

He coughed, choking on a bite of his sandwich. "Speaking of why...*why*?"

A soft giggle escaped from her throat, his whimsical side tying her stomach in knots. "Just like one might wonder why you start a fire using a *flint* or live in a cabin that requires splitting wood with an *ax* for heat." She brushed the grass with her fingertips, the silver charms of her bracelet ringing and dangling with the movement. "Or why you want to willingly sleep in the cold on an uncomfortable air pad all night."

A concerned look crossed his face as his eyes followed her hand across the ground. Was he worried about her cuts? She'd had medical reapply the bandages this morning. Heat climbed up her neck. How long would it take the wounds to heal so she could save face?

He hesitated before saying, "Amity, you do realize that this race is going to get more difficult—you know—more rugged? Our packs are full of hardcore backpacking gear. I'd guess that tonight will be our last group camp or soon anyway."

And there it was—he already regretted his choice to save her. He didn't think she could do it. "Yeah, I could work that much out for myself, thanks." She dampened her lips with her tongue, craving her gloss, and looked up the trail. "I'm going to have to learn how to survive in the wilderness."

Easton's eyes searched her face. "Is this race worth it for you?" He knitted his eyebrows. "Since you don't seem to need the money? A woman like you doesn't have to do this."

She shot him an icy glare. "Why work so hard to keep me in this race if you think I'm going to bail out like a wimp?"

Cooper's eyes widened. "I didn't mean...I do want...I just meant that..." He braced his hands on his knees and took a deep breath before speaking again. "Why are you doing this? Do you want visibility for your career or something?"

"Nice." Amity stood up and brushed the dirt off her bottom. "You make no sense, *Easton*," she said, drawing out his name, watching him flinch, and immediately feeling her chest tighten. This man was getting his hooks into her, and she didn't need the pain of rejection from a guy who was only after the money. "If we're partners for this leg, then I'll help you get a first-place finish because I *owe* you for keeping me in this race, but if you're going to be an ass, then leave me be."

Amity turned and marched away, noticing that, again,

they'd drawn the interest of all the cameras and contestants within hearing distance. She blew out a puff of air, already regretting her quick temper. Easton only reacted to his first name now if she said it in a rough jest, but he'd deserved it this time. She twisted around to peek at him, still sprawled out by the stream, and quickly looked away from his injured expression. Ugh, she shouldn't have said any of that!

Her back-and-forth emotions had her acting like a middle schooler. Dealing with Easton was like swinging on a pendulum. His actions never really made sense with his words. Why did he save her if he didn't truly believe she could help him win?

Twelve

Every time! Cooper shook his head. Every time he got into a conversation with Amity, he screwed it up; but he'd seen her look of unease as she'd glanced up the trail, and he'd wanted to make it all better for her. He still didn't understand her motives. Why was she here?

When she'd stepped into the clearing on the first day, everything about her screamed money. It still did even now—veggie sandwiches, polished fingernails, sparkly silver bracelets, and running like she'd been trained by a personal coach. He'd misjudged her racing skills; perhaps he was misjudging her motives as well?

Whatever her reason for being here, Cooper didn't want her to go home. Anyone with a wit of sense could see that—except her. He played it off like he'd saved her for his own personal benefit, but strategically, he never would have kept her in the competition. Both because he was sweet on her, as his sister would say, and because, just like she'd guessed, a partner who could run wasn't enough to risk his position in the race. But how could he tell her why he'd done it when he didn't even understand it himself?

Having lost his appetite, he stared at his roast beef sandwich for a few seconds and then swiped it up with his hand, knowing he'd have to force himself to eat the rest of it. Calories were essential for the next leg, and he'd burned plenty, chopping almost double his share of wood.

Cooper turned his head as a shadow blocked his sunlight. "Show's over, Miles. No more airtime here."

"You did it for the cameras, didn't you?" Miles asked. "Some of the guys said you run a tour business for this outdoor shit. So you need the tourists to see how good you are?"

Cooper overheard Miles trying to convince Amity that everyone was here for the cameras. How wrong this guy was, while Amity seemed to have smartly picked up on the truth. But he'd rather Miles not know how desperately he needed the money, so it was better if he played along in a scumbag sort of way—and that meant disagreeing without giving anything away. He'd met Miles' type on his tours, and if you agreed with them, they became skeptical, always expecting everyone's hidden agenda to be similar to their own.

"Man," Cooper said, grinding his fingers from his sandwich-free hand into the back of his tense neck, "your time was up this morning. I won't be saving your city ass again, so let's just give each other space until you're on your way."

"What do you think your girlfriend will think when she finds out?"

Cooper froze, holding his sandwich to his lips mid-bite. "If boasting my skills was my motive," he said before finishing his bite and beginning to chew, "which it's not, I doubt Amity would care. She's not my biggest fan."

"She's here for the cameras too, you know?" Miles raised his brows. "A rich girl like her."

That's what Cooper feared—that the woman he suddenly couldn't avoid would never want anything to do with him. Why would she? He was a regular, everyday guy. He didn't know anything about the road to fame. Gulping roast beef down his parched, swollen throat, he pressed his fingers into a spasm he'd unleashed in his neck. Did he really want to deal with a woman right now anyway?

That was the weird thing about this strange crush. He wanted to help her every time she was in trouble, so she wasn't hurt or upset—but also so he could keep her around him. What the hell? He lived alone and liked it. That's what he wanted, wasn't it? No expectations. If not, then he wasn't on the right track because when he did actually get to speak to her, he turned around and put his foot in his mouth.

"You know I don't plan on making that stunt up to you, right?" Miles continued, trying to bait him. "If anything, it makes me want to take you out. Can't have some dude making me look like a wimp and going after my partner."

When the full meaning of Miles' statement sunk in, Cooper started laughing. Take him out? How? The guy couldn't do anything other than work out in some multi-story gym. He'd heard rumors from the other contestants that he'd begged Amity to slow her pace so he could keep up. He *should* leave it alone, but he just couldn't.

"Yeah, and how do you plan to off me? With that ax your delicate hands can't handle? Or by having Amity drag your butt down another trail?"

Miles uttered a few expletives at him before his shadow disappeared.

"Good luck," Cooper yelled over his shoulder, chuckling until the loudspeaker interrupted.

"Only thirty minutes until all contestants are required to reappear on the mats for official filming," McKenzie called out. "Please dispose of your lunches and meet the camera crew for a sound and film equipment fitting."

Cooper sighed and tanked down some water from his bottle. It felt like official filming all the damn time to him. His goatee camera guy never left his side unless he slipped into the tent or went to take a leak—and it was time for him to do both. He shoved his sandwich wrapper, followed by the untouched red apple that he should've eaten, into his lunch sack, fisted his water bottle, and headed toward the tent to pack his gear—or double-check it, really—he'd packed at first light.

"If I make a run for it, do you have to follow?" Cooper asked the cameraman as he walked along, tossing his lunch sack into the trash.

Goatee Man laughed quietly so the camera wouldn't pick it up.

Cooper shook his head. "Whatever." He grinned mischievously and pointed at him. "But there will be a time that I make a break for it. Just warning you. It's damned annoying to be followed around."

A few minutes later, Cooper emerged from the tent with his small, gray daypack slung across his shoulder, his eyes involuntarily searching for Amity. He felt sick to his stomach when he located her talking to Isaac and laughing. Really? It gutted him after all he'd done for her. Or had he done it for her? Technically, he'd done it for himself, though he wasn't getting much out of his dumb decision. Damn, her way of flirting. Isaac was a lucky man.

Amity glanced at him, guilt ghosting her features before she masked the expression and turned back to Isaac. A peal of her laughter echoed across the clearing. That did him in. He wanted her to like him—to trust him—and flash *him* that killer smile. The next time he spoke to her, he vowed to do better.

Cooper met the camera crew to attach his voice and camera equipment for the trail run. He refilled his water bottle from the cooler, knowing in his gut that the luxury of pre-pumped water before trail legs would soon be in the past, turned his back on Amity's antics, and flopped down in a camping chair.

It was time to think things through. If the pattern remained, it was the ladies' turn to choose first.

Becky would choose Liam—even now, the pair stood alone by the water cooler, plotting their moves. He'd learned that Becky was from a remote town in Alaska and knew as much or more about the outdoors than he did. Together, she and Liam were virtually unbeatable.

Second place on the woodchopping challenge had been Isaac. It took Isaac only a few minutes to get the hang of chopping wood, figuring out an effective motion for his swings quickly—perhaps from the experience of learning routines through his coaching experience? And with his lead time from the previous challenge, Isaac hadn't fallen behind any of the more experienced choppers that were trying to catch up.

Cassie had been Isaac's partner. Cooper looked at Cassie, who had now joined Becky and Liam by the water cooler. That was an interesting alliance—and a dangerous one that needed to be broken up. Cassie's natural blonde hair was in two of those braided pigtail things again. He didn't understand why grown women bothered to take the time to do that—having those things flop around would be annoying.

He narrowed his eyes as he continued to analyze the group. How would this play out for him? After Becky chose Liam, then what? Cassie would likely choose Isaac again—though he wasn't positive because Isaac didn't have much outdoor experience. Still, unlike Miles, Isaac was a fierce competitor. He worked through his weaknesses and came out on top.

Third place was Justin, who'd been partnered with Kim. Justin, he knew nothing about. The man kept to himself and seemed reclusive, even hiding behind a large bushy red beard and mustache combo. He held his own in the challenges, so he must have some kind of experience.

Kim seemed to work well with Justin, as they were both

relatively quiet about their personal lives while vocal and to the point during the challenges. Cooper did hear Kim tell Amity, of all people, that she worked a corporate job at North Face, which explained why she'd been decked out in their gear on the first day. Amity seemed very interested in Kim's job, and the two had continued to chat about athletic clothes.

Cooper thought North Face headquarters had recently been relocated to Denver, so Kim's home base was only about two hundred miles from his location in Aspen. He could use that information to open her up to him if they were partners. Which had him wondering, would Kim choose him? It was possible after his performance in the last challenge, but since he'd labeled himself unpredictable, maybe not. He wouldn't choose someone who'd sacrificed their own team for another, so he couldn't expect someone else to do so either.

Then, of course, there was Bria. If ladies went first, Bria could choose him—but he doubted she would after what he'd done.

Did he *want* Kim or Bria to choose him? In his head, the answer was yes, but his gut churned uncomfortably at the thought because he couldn't deny that he wanted to run the leg with Amity—badly. Amity had promised him that she would help him win the leg, but if someone else chose him first, there would be nothing that she could do. Which gave him the undeniable realization—if he didn't already have a partner when it was his turn, then he planned to choose Amity. Who would have thought?

AMITY COULDN'T HELP but notice Easton staring at Becky and Cassie. Becky, with her stunning glossy black hair and flawless honey-brown skin radiating in the sunlight, wearing her tight, light blue shirt. And then Cassie, looking like a blonde supermodel, even with the childish braids in her hair, wearing her hot pink sleeveless exercise top.

All of the women had talked non-stop about which color shirts they'd been given in their packs by the props crew. Amity still preferred her vibrant purple, but the constant clothing chatter brought front and center how amazing the other women looked compared to her.

She still had bandages around her hands, and her hair was up in a ponytail that looked a bit ragged on the ends, like a feather duster used for catching dust. Bug bites peppered her skin worse than any of the other contestants—obviously, she had no clue how to prevent their vampiristic interest in her blood. And puffy circles had developed under her eyes from her inability to sleep well on an air mattress all night in the freezing cold.

She laughed in defeat, feeling like Cinderella standing before her two evil stepsisters, and then furious with herself for caring, turned hastily toward the mats. They were nice women, and she was acting petty.

Bria suddenly appeared out of nowhere and startled her. She nodded toward the two women, still standing by the water cooler. "They're a threat."

Today, Bria had chosen a long-sleeved, light green shirt from her pack. Her assigned lime green color matched well with the camo pants that she'd worn since day one, looking badass with her spiky, bleach-blonde hair and strong figure. Amity knew that long-sleeved, UV-sun-protective clothing could keep you cooler, contrary to what most people believed, but she'd never been able to bring herself to do it during her runs. She'd continue to use the long-sleeved purple shirt they'd given her during the cooler evenings.

Amity cocked her head to the side and met Bria's water-blue eyes. This was the first time Bria had initiated a conversation with her. "Are we friends now?"

"No," Bria returned, but she grinned. "I don't make friends with prestigious California types. It would ruin my image."

Amity scrunched up her nose. Bria was joking, right?

"Stop stressing, Hollywood. About *everything*. He's not into the girls over there, just taking surveillance."

Amity shook her head, indicating that she didn't understand.

Bria sighed. "He's analyzing the competition. That boy is still into *you*. Why? I don't know, but he is."

"I wasn't worried about—"

"Yeah, you were. I'm good at reading people—watched all different kinds in the barracks. There wasn't another reason for Cooper to save ya this morning. That's why I'm pissed at him. It wasn't strategic, and it cost us both."

"He said it was strat—"

Bria let out a throaty laugh. "Yeah, I'm sure he did. That boy doesn't know what to say. Nor should he. He's lost his mind." She eyed her curiously. "Hope you're worth it."

Amity watched her walk away to stand on the mat right across from Easton, who was already in position. She'd felt his glare as she talked to Bria, but now he seemed to be focused on Bria's scowl. Amity was glad that Bria didn't seem to be taking her frustrations with Easton out on her.

She sauntered over to the fifth-place mat, smiled at Bria beside her, and received a curt nod. She'd take it. Bria seemed to have opened a door for her, and she'd like to have a girl-friend during this race. Talking to men all day wound her up, especially these men.

Amity glanced across at Miles, shooting him an indifferent glare. She hoped he'd get bored with her and look somewhere else for ratings. If she got stuck with him again, it might be the end of her. He raised his eyebrows at her with a provoking grin while she balled her fist as an outlet. The cameras captured his nonsense, and naturally, Miles loved it.

Looking away from Miles, she met Easton's eyes for comfort, and her stomach did a giddy little flip-flop. They shared a smile before McKenzie counted down for Alex Bandon to start his official spiel. "Welcome to the trail run compass challenge. Again, we will schoolyard pick partners, so I urge you to choose wisely so you can make it into the final six pairs."

Compass challenge? What did that mean? Would they be running around aimlessly in the trees in all different directions? Amity scratched the bug-bitten welts up and down her arms and scanned the row of men. At least she could choose her partner.

"—and although the lady of each team will select first today, followed by the gentleman," Alex continued, "you must choose a contestant you have *not* worked with on a previous leg."

Oh no, Amity thought, her head spinning. The hot sun suddenly felt like bright interrogation lights as beads of sweat formed along her hairline.

All kinds of noises erupted from various contestants. She heard a few cuss words, several gasps, and even a few joyful shouts, but all Amity felt was mild alarm. She hadn't worked this scenario through. No one had. So much for helping Easton win as a return favor—they'd been partners before, so he couldn't choose her now. Would she get stuck with another guy who couldn't compete?

Selections rapidly began. Amity had to snap to and focus. Alex immediately jumped into having Becky choose. Unable to select her usual partner, Liam, Becky's eyes darted between Isaac and Easton. After hesitating twice, she chose Easton, and Amity wanted to scream. A fiery pain burned in her chest, and suddenly, she didn't just dislike Becky—she loathed her. Amity actually felt her nostrils flare.

"Becky, why the hesitation?" Alex asked.

"His thing with Amity and the time disadvantage," Becky replied. "But he knows the outdoors better than Isaac."

"Cooper, your thoughts?" Alex asked.

"I'm thrilled," he said with a pleased smile. "Becky and I will tear this leg up."

Easton rocked back and forth on his heels with his hands shoved snuggly into the pockets of his zipper-compartment pants. Why did he look so friggin' relaxed? Well, duh—because he thought he could win with Becky as a partner, but she still wanted to smack him. Bria had been totally off base with her thoughts. Easton clearly didn't give a rat's ass about her.

"Amity?" Alex asked, causing her to jump. "How do you feel about Becky and Cooper as partners?"

Her throat was clogged with emotion, and she made a few scratchy sounds to clear it. "How do I *feel*? Like they're both threats in this race that need to be taken out."

The host pasted on a grin. "Very well."

Amity's arms shook as she pulled them tightly to her chest. How did she *really* feel? Confused, frustrated, jealous—but mostly intensely angry with Easton Cooper. He saved her, and she was grateful, but now she had to deal with an onslaught of feelings that she didn't understand.

The jealousy thing was new to her. She'd been on her own, trying to make it from paycheck to paycheck, and never once had she felt envious of the tourists that spent whatever they wanted while dining and smooching at the outdoor tables lining the streets; and now to have this feeling—over a man— it sucked.

Alex went down the line in order of finishing rank and gender, accordingly, moving on to those who had still not been chosen. Liam chose Cassie. Isaac chose Kim—that hurt, but Amity understood. Kim finished higher in the last leg of the race and didn't come with all the drama that Amity had surrounding her.

Justin was next, and he chose *her*. Amity released her breath and beamed a smile at him. Justin was a mystery to everyone. He hadn't revealed much about himself, hiding behind a mass of facial hair, but he typically had decent finishes.

"Justin," Alex prompted, "why Amity?"

"She's fast," Justin responded quickly as if he didn't want to speak at all. "This is a trail leg."

Bria chose Sean, the blond surfer-looking guy, followed by Miles, who chose Jade, the woman with the dark curly hair. By default, the final team became Lucy, a gymnast who talked so fast no one could get a word in, and Carlos, a Spanish bicyclist who kept to himself.

"The finish for the trail challenge will be right back here," Alex said, pointing to a mat on the trail. "This is the final test of your physical, mental, and social skills before the backpacking part of the race begins. We want to be sure only the strongest contestants are left for the upcoming multi-point portion of the race."

Amity kept turning the word *social* over in her mind. There was more to this race than outdoor skills. They'd have to build connections—alliances.

"On this leg, you'll be provided with a detailed map of the area and a compass. Your current location is marked on the map with a red X. We're on the PCT by Mesa Creek. As a team, you must find six flags at six different locations, each marked with a blue X on the map.

"One member of each team must grab a flag of their own color. You cannot touch another team's flag at any time throughout the challenge, or you'll incur a twenty-minute penalty. The ladies will draw sticks for your team's color. I'll hand the ladies the compass while the gentlemen will get the map. After the items are distributed, you can decide as a team how to approach the challenge."

Alex went down the line, extending different colored sticks to draw from a round container. Amity smiled when she pulled out a dark purple stick that matched her shirt; that had to be good luck. She waved the purple stick so Justin would see their color.

Justin nodded in response.

Alex then handed her a compass. Amity scrunched up her forehead in thought. Why a compass? Couldn't they just follow the map?

Thirteen

"I want to work together," Cooper said to Justin, running up to him a few seconds after Alex finished speaking.

The contestants had all dispersed, dividing into huddles with their partners and desired alliances.

"What?" Becky bared her teeth. "No, I chose *you*. You don't get to decide that."

"Sorry," Cooper said to her, "but you should have known better." He turned to Amity. "If Justin's okay with it, you're going to run with me." Cooper glanced at Justin for confirmation. "We'll split the flags up—three and three. Justin and Becky can find three, we'll find the other three, and then we can reconvene at the finish. Agreed?"

Justin eyed Cooper for a brief moment, then nodded. "Agreed."

"You're really okay with this?" Amity asked Justin.

Justin scratched the side of his pirate-like beard with the backside of his fingertips. "Cooper's right. We need to work with another team, and they're the logical choice since we'll leave only five minutes after them. It seems I can trust him when you're involved. He let me have third on the last one because of it."

Justin frowned at Becky before meeting Cooper's eyes to continue. "The other teams will try something similar, but some might turn on one another. You can't trust her." He motioned his thumb at Becky. "She'll want to work with Liam, and he's a serious threat."

"Are you really going to keep talking about me like I'm not here?" Becky asked through gritted teeth.

Cooper nodded, ignoring Becky. "I'll keep that in mind at the finish line, but you're the one who will be finding the flags with her. I'm not sure she can do much along the way without jeopardizing her finish in the race."

"I'm counting on that," Justin said. "Let's watch which way Liam goes when he starts, and then Becky and I can head in the opposite direction."

Cooper was surprised by the flood of words coming out of Justin's mouth. He'd rarely spoken at camp. Although his secretive approach wasn't Cooper's style, he liked the guy; and they seemed to have formed an alliance that might come in handy. At the same time, Liam and Isaac were chatting as they spoke and seemed to be solidifying one of their own.

Becky looked over her shoulder at Liam and Isaac and mouthed to them, "I won't follow Justin."

"Yes, you will," Justin said, surprising them all as Becky wasn't even his actual partner. "Unless you want to lose this race, then going the same direction as Cooper won't be fast enough. Only the teams that split up will have a solid chance, and this afternoon, whether you like it or not, your fate is tied to Cooper's."

"I know. I was just calling your bluff—or trying to anyway." Becky glared at Amity and randomly added, "You shouldn't be here."

Cooper gave Becky a sharp look. What was the point of that? An outlet for her frustration? He couldn't understand why Becky even cared.

Amity mumbled something about her evil stepsister prediction not being too far off, which Cooper also didn't understand.

"Do you know how to use a compass to take a bearing?" Cooper asked Justin.

"I do," Becky cut in, ignoring Justin's nod. "Like you said —I *have* to finish this challenge with you, so you can stop pretending like I'm not here. I should have chosen Isaac. What was I thinking?"

"You were thinking that Isaac would struggle," Cooper responded. "Which he might if Cassie doesn't know how to use a compass."

Cooper had no doubt that Liam would swap partners with Isaac so they could divide up the flags too. That meant Cassie would be running to find the flags with Isaac and Kim with Liam, even though the pairs weren't officially partners for the challenge. It was a lot to keep track of, and Cooper thought it was best to just run like hell and find their own flags, not spending too much time thinking about the other teams' strategies.

Cooper and Justin studied the blue Xs on the map, which marked the locations of their flags. The map made it even more apparent that the challenge was set up for the teams to split up. Three of the flags were south of their location around an area called Sisters Mirror Lakes, which contained multiple small lakes in one region. The other three flags were north around a large meadow area called Separation Creek. He suspected the directors wanted to mix the contestants around and had purposely selected a challenge that would do so.

Cooper looked at Justin. "Your thoughts?"

Quietly, Justin said, "I'd rather go toward the lake area."

Justin's eyes followed Becky as she walked a few steps away to whisper something to Liam. Cooper realized Justin was simply making sure Becky couldn't overhear and didn't even care what she whispered. Justin must have come to the same conclusion about only focusing on their own plan.

"Between you and me," Justin continued, "I'm a nautical guy. I'll be able to find these flags around the water areas easier than the ones in the middle of that field."

"We'll see." A frown creased Cooper's brow. "I'd rather you went the opposite direction from Liam, so Becky doesn't team up with him." Cooper pointed at the locations on the map in sync with his words as he continued, "Taking a bearing for the Xs on land won't be any different than the Xs around the lakes. I think that theory is in your head."

"Completely," Justin said with a crooked grin, "but I still hate dryland."

Cooper smiled in return. He hadn't met someone quite like Justin before. Occasionally, he'd meet a sailor on one of his tours—usually a retired guy or gal, but rarely people who didn't care for land.

"You're Navy," Cooper guessed suddenly.

Justin nodded, continuing on in his quiet tone, "Fifteen years of service. Started when I was eighteen, but it's time for a change. I'm thinking of getting into something like you're doing now, except *boat* tours. That's why I'm competing for the money. Maybe you could give me some tips on the tour business after all this."

"Anytime," Cooper said as the timer beeped for the non-existent first-place team to leave. No one could leave in the first-place time slot since Becky and Liam had been forced to choose contestants that finished in a lower-ranking place.

Technically, that meant Liam and Cassie left with a five-minute penalty due to Cassie's second-place finish with Isaac, but it wasn't even relevant since they'd be the first team to leave anyway. It was all more complicated than necessary, but the producers and directors wanted to create drama, and he supposed that meant mixing teams up.

Five minutes later, the timer beeped for Liam and Cassie to head out, but instead of running down the trail, the pair sat on a log near the start, waiting for Isaac and Kim. Another five minutes later, Isaac and Kim's timer beeped, and the two leading teams swapped partners.

To Justin's benefit, Liam and Kim headed north toward the trail that would take them to the Separation Creek meadow area. That meant Cooper and Amity would go toward the meadow as well, keeping to their plan that they'd force Becky away from her strong partnership with Liam.

Cooper hadn't had time to absorb the relief he felt in having Amity paired with him to find the flags, but he knew it was the reason he could focus. Without her by his side, he'd have spent the whole leg worrying about her, and he needed his head clear so he could win the money.

He leaned casually against a tree as the timer counted down for his start with Becky. There was no hurry, as he and Becky would have to wait five minutes for Amity and Justin's timer to go off anyway. He closed his eyes, using the time to relax and mentally prepare.

5...4...3...2...1, and Becky ripped the map out of his hand.

"Shit," Cooper said, his eyes popping open.

She took off like a bullet, sprinting north toward the meadow.

He launched off the tree and scrambled after her, pushing his long legs into a full-on sprint. Twenty seconds later, he raced up beside her, sprung for the map, and got a solid grip on the folded corner while yanking her shoulder back and pulling it out of her hand.

"No," Becky screamed, sliding to a halt, her hands flying up in frustration. "That's breaking the rules."

"How so?" Cooper countered. "You're not hurt."

Becky kicked up some dirt on the trail and paced. Perhaps trying to think of a rule that she could exploit? Coming up short, she snarled, "Fine, rip it in half. I'll take my half, and you take yours."

"You want to run on your own? Go for it." Cooper ripped the map in half, keeping the half with the lakes and throwing her the meadow portion. He wasn't too worried about her finding their flags. "Your strategy is boneheaded. We have to finish together anyway. You might as well work with Justin."

Becky smirked at him like she'd gotten away with something and took off north, obviously planning to meet up with Liam.

McKenzie, the head director, stood on the side of the trail grinning from ear to ear while his designated cameraman trailed suffocatingly beside him.

"You want to give me five paces of space, Goatee Man?" Cooper tugged on his shirt collar. He'd sliced the back of the neckline with a knife this morning, but it still felt tight. "I think you captured the moment."

Goatee Man jerked back in surprise, then chuckled quietly. Cooper realized his astonishment was related to being called Goatee Man, not being asked to step back.

Cooper tapped him on the shoulder with his fist. "Maybe you can buy me a beer after all of this? Or better yet, I'll agree not to consistently bolt for the trees if you come hang out on one of my tours and record it for me, so I can advertise."

The cameraman gave him a thumbs-up.

Just like the last trail run, Cooper would get some space here soon anyway when the bulky equipment the camera crew carried couldn't keep pace along the trail, and their body cameras took over to catch the drama. Regardless of how suffocating it felt, he still liked making friends with new people. Genuine friendships mattered, even with Hollywood cameramen that likely had nothing in common with him.

Returning to the start line, he walked over to chat with Justin for the remaining minutes of their time penalty.

"Sorry, man," Cooper said. "Looks like you're running the meadow solo now instead of going to the lakes at all. Don't let the idea of land versus water get into your head. Just find the landmarks and go."

Justin glared north up the trail, surveying his new route. "I'm glad Becky betrayed us upfront, so I don't have to worry about when she would have. I knew it would happen. Damn, that girl's smart."

"Why is that? I thought it was a dumb move on her part."

Justin rubbed his hand across the back of his neck. "Thought a wilderness guy like you would have thought of this. Becky has the other compass."

"Oh that." Cooper grinned. "I did think of it. That's why I let her have the other half of the map—in case Liam burns her. I have an extra compass in my pocket." He shrugged, patting his zipper pants' pocket. "Always do when I'm on a tour. The 'keep the clothes on your back' thing was beneficial."

Justin belted out a hearty laugh. "You really are a back-country bum."

"I'm not the one who looks like he's lived without a razor for five years."

"Touché," Justin said, running his fingers down the red mane on his chin.

Cooper noticed Amity's thoughtful grin, but he continued talking to Justin. The alternative meant speaking to the woman that made his brain turn to mush. "Becky will assume you don't have a compass, which will give us an advantage. Stupid move on her part. You could have easily decided to take the other compass, thinking that I would be able to figure out the waypoints without one and that I'd help Amity for you. Becky would have slowed me down instead, her *own* partner."

More guessing than asking, Justin said, "If we did have only one compass, you would have given it to me?"

Cooper masked his expression. Yes, he would have—so

that Justin could have found his flags—and so that Cooper could have made sure Amity was able to stay in the race with him. Because he could still beat some of these teams without a compass if he had to, although it would have put a lot of stress on him and taken him longer.

But Cooper didn't want to divulge any more of his insane thinking, so instead, he said, "I wouldn't have let Becky have the other half of the map in the first place, so she never would have run off on her own. She doesn't trust Liam *that* much. But as you said, it's better that she betrays us upfront while falsely thinking she has an advantage over us."

Justin glared at him with a knowing grin, probably guessing the direct answer to the question that Cooper wouldn't give, which had Cooper adding, "I think we'll be in touch even after this race."

Justin nodded. "Yeah, I expect so."

Cooper glanced at Amity, who was still looking back and forth between the two of them curiously, and asked her, "Can you please hand Justin your compass?" He didn't want to give up his own familiar compass, so he plastered on a sugarcoated smile. He wanted to be on her good side, knowing from experience with his mom and sister that women didn't like to be bossed around.

"Wait," Amity said. "I have a better plan."

Cooper groaned. Any plan that didn't involve him being with her was a *hell* no.

Amity continued, "I'll catch up to Becky and follow her. I'd have no problem keeping pace with her, especially in a meadow where I can see ahead and—"

"No," he and Justin both said together.

"Why?" Amity protested. "I'm really fast. That way, Justin can head for the lakes with you. I almost caught Becky on the last trail run, and that was with a *much* larger time penalty. She won't be able to shake me."

"Amity," Cooper began, hearing the pathetic plea in his voice—this caring stuff was a pain. "I have no doubt you can more than keep pace with anyone in this race—however, Becky and her group will throw you off over the course of finding *three* waypoints. A single missed flag would mean you'd be on your own. Justin can use a compass to take a bearing, so he doesn't need to rely on anyone for this challenge. Regardless, it's a moot point. I wouldn't be able to focus if you went the other way."

Cooper snagged the compass out of Amity's hand and passed it to Justin. In chorus with the beep of their timer, he said to Justin, "Go, before we overthink this."

Justin smirked—translation—go before Amity tries to run off on her own, and Cooper loses his mind.

Fourteen

"Not going to talk to me?" Easton asked.

Amity exhaled a long breath, enjoying the sight of his lengthy, lean form as she ran behind him. After seeing the defined muscles in his arms, her eyes kept drifting up and down his body, looking on in wonder. The forest green shirt the crew had chosen for him did little to hide his definition. She imagined being locked in a kiss while running her hands along his firm shoulder muscles, down his narrow back, into his flimsy shorts, and then gripping his butt and pulling him hard against her. After all, she'd been staring at his full broadside for a mile now and had plenty of time to let her mind wander.

Her daily growing interest surprised her, given her gangly and rude first impression of him, but now, his wayward ways amused her. He had a hang-loose way about him, and his hair —oh gosh—was so cute. He had it mashed under his blue-faded baseball cap that said Rocky Mountain Inspiration in dirt-stained white letters across the front.

"I don't like being the tagalong follower," Amity finally answered. "I'm feeling bitter about it."

"Sorry about that," Easton said. "It's my fault. You're fully capable of staying in this race yourself."

"You know you kept me in it. Please don't placate me."

"Amity." He looked briefly over his shoulder at her before refocusing on his steps. "You could argue that you kept me in this race when you found a way to light that fire. This show is just a mixed-up set of events staged for drama. It's about being athletically skilled and *lucky* enough to survive what they throw at us. Miles chose you and then couldn't handle the challenge. That's not on you. He wasn't creative enough to pull off a win with the wood the way you did with the fire. Don't for a second think that I don't believe you can win this yourself. You've got just as good a chance of that as I do."

A smile broke across Amity's lips, her heart pitter-pattering against her ribcage. This guy who'd been her archenemy just days ago was actually a total sweetheart. "Why didn't you just let me run off after Becky if you have that much faith in me?"

"You could have." He shrugged. "But that would have lowered your chances of staying in this race."

She nodded to herself. "Because I don't know how to use a compass to take a bearing? Ugh, so frustrating."

"Yes, and alliances, of course. Together we're more likely to succeed because we can take chances to help each other out. At least," he let out his breath and added, "you're more likely to succeed."

"What?" Amity wasn't quite that confident in herself. "That doesn't make any sense. Why me and not both of us?"

Easton remained quiet for a few paces before he spoke. "I think it's pretty obvious that I'd like us to be in an alliance. I don't know if the feeling is mutual. You still might want me gone."

Her skin flushed, and she swallowed down her nervous butterflies. "I did after the fire challenge, but now..." She trapped her lower lip between her teeth and watched the small plants fly by along the trail. How should she answer him?

"But now?" he prompted.

"I..." Amity paused, thinking. How much did she want to give away? "I don't want you gone."

Easton laughed. "That's a start."

"What you did at the woodchuck challenge—that was pretty out there. I mean, I get alliances, but after nearly being eliminated when you were partners with me...I just...I still don't fully understand why you did it." She let out a confused little huff. "And then you said something about not being able to focus if I went the other way. Why?"

Amity listened to their thumping footsteps. She *wanted* to understand. Was it his racing strategy? Was he playing the romance angle just in case he needed a relationship to win the money? That would kill her. She wanted his *genuine* interest.

"I don't know what to tell you, Amity," Easton finally said. "I was kind of hoping you wouldn't ask me that." He chuckled anxiously. "I...oh, shit...might as well just say it—I can't stand the thought of you being eliminated." He took a deep breath. "I *really* like you."

It was the first time in months Amity found it hard to breathe while running. Her throat screamed for moisture, constricting with emotion. His voice was so sincere that guilt pulsed through her for even thinking he would fake a relationship for the show. He just wasn't the type. Miles was, but Easton—no way.

For a few steps, her brain couldn't form words to respond, and when her neurons finally did fire, she blurted out, "I meant what I said by the stream."

"What?" Easton asked, a tense edge to his voice. "Which part, exactly?"

"I'll help you win this leg and any others that I can." She swallowed through her jitters, wetting her dry throat, and went for it. "I don't want you eliminated either. I enjoy racing with you."

"I'm glad to hear that." He shot a grin over his shoulder. "So, hopefully, that means you like me too? As a friend, at least, I mean."

Tingles continued to dance inside her. What was she getting herself into? "Yes." She smiled as the warmth of her feelings spread. "I can't believe I'm saying this after everything, but I *really* like you too."

Easton exhaled. "Well, that's good news...um..." He tugged his shirt collar, causing a little ripping sound, and she put together that the slash in the back of the fabric was probably his own doing. She giggled quietly at his adorableness before he finished rambling, "this pace okay?"

Amity would never have guessed Easton would be interested in her or that *she* would be interested in him, but maybe opposites did attract? Perhaps she just hadn't met a guy who brought out the passion in her by completely clashing with her before? She wrinkled her nose. Did she need an adventure in her relationship, too, not just in life?

She'd always thought her biggest obstacle with her past relationships had been her lack of funds, but it had to be about more than that. Perhaps she needed a guy that would push through life's most challenging obstacles with her? Like fires and flints, woodpiles and axes, trails and compasses—no matter what—Easton Cooper never gave up.

She scraped her dry tongue over her teeth, pulling a worried lip into her mouth. Even if that was the case, Easton wanted money too—just like all the guys she'd ever dated before. Her previous boyfriends didn't want to work *hard* to settle down, have kids, and go on adventures with her like her parents had done. They wanted it the easy way—handed to them. Would Easton even date her if he found out she had virtually nothing?

Almost forgetting to respond, Amity snorted a laugh to hide her tension. "Oh please! Don't insult me, Caveman. You can speed up if you want."

Easton chuckled and picked up the pace. Was he distracting himself with a harder workout? If so, it helped her blow off some of her nervous energy too, and, after a few additional paces, his quiet confidence added to her calm. She found it beyond sexy that he knew where to go. She could see that they were following the PCT and headed south, but how he knew it wasn't time to stop was beyond her.

If he was her boyfriend, she'd definitely boast about him. Her friends back home would probably roll their eyes, just like she always did when they went on excessively about the 'my man's the best' details. But perhaps she was beginning to understand—you fall for everything about them, just the way they are—like a sappy Hallmark movie. It certainly felt like they were living in a fictitious dream.

Across the valley, a stunning mountain came into view, like a scene from a coffee table book. Finally, she couldn't contain her curiosity, even though it would likely give him an ego boost. "What's that mountain over there?"

Easton's head swiveled to the left. "That's the South Sister, and, depending on where we are on the trail, you can catch glimpses of the Middle Sister and North Sister behind it. Together they're known as the Three Sisters."

Easton didn't come off as smart-alecky at all. In fact, he seemed to enjoy sharing it with her. Another flood of warmth went through her that had nothing to do with the run. Amity realized that she felt comfortable asking him questions.

"How do you know where you're going?" she fired off.

"Besides studying the map that they just gave us?"

"Yes, besides that, smartass."

He laughed softly. "Some of it I learned from talking to people from Oregon. I fall into conversation about trails very easily." He took in some air and continued, "But the precise details of this trail, I figured out from studying maps of the Cascades on my phone apps and handheld GPS on the bus ride over. As soon as I saw what direction we were headed, I analyzed the trails. This stuff is sort of second nature for me."

"How's that?"

"I'm a backpacking and climbing tour guide in the Aspen area. My best friend and I started our own business together ten years ago."

The image of him as a helpful tour guide suddenly fit perfectly into her brain—him bringing willing participants up challenging trails for endless days.

"Oh." Not wanting to contain her thoughts, she added, "That must be awful. The backpacking and climbing part, I mean, not the business."

His full-hearted laugh that followed was incredibly sexy. "Why's that, Princess?"

Amity didn't even react to him calling her Princess this time. He could call her whatever he wanted when he acted like this—especially if he meant what he said about her being a fierce competitor.

"Oh, I don't know," she began. "I think we started to cover this in our conversation by the stream, but—cold tents, bug bites that itch, uncomfortable sleeping pads, unbreathable sleeping bags, no shower, no mirror for makeup—"

"I get it." Chuckling, Easton repeated, "I get it." He shook his head like she was insane. "So what do you do then? Something in the more civilized world I'd venture."

Amity didn't know why she couldn't say it. If he didn't want a relationship because of her financial status, then it would be best for her to know that upfront anyway. Perhaps it was because she was ashamed to admit that she wasn't the spoiled princess he seemed to imagine.

She was more like Cinderella, who needed a prince to

rescue her and take her to the ball—but not in the caveman, 'I'll provide for you' type of way. What she really wanted was a fairytale-type love. A guy that wanted *her* so badly that he'd search the country for her, just like the prince had done to match the glass slipper on Cinderella's foot. A guy that would whisk her off her feet in a romantic way and be willing to put her first—*always*—because that's how much she wanted to love someone in return. But maybe that was asking for too much.

Amity grinned, realizing that she had stereotyped Easton as well—as a bossy caveman, but she knew he really wasn't. He seemed like the type of guy that enjoyed life. Would someone like him be her prince? Would he prioritize her and whisk her away on adventures? Maybe—but maybe not, given that, unless she went running, she basically couldn't afford to leave her house.

Amity cleared her throat. Her mom would automatically know she was about to lie. "I'm in fashion." Maybe not a lie, but definitely not the whole truth.

"That figures. And your parents?"

"My mom works in the resort business," Amity explained, another half-truth. She could have added—in housekeeping—as she was very proud of how hard her mom had worked for them, but she didn't want him to know that just yet. "We live in Palm Springs, where there are lots of high-end resorts. My dad, unfortunately, passed away when I was young."

"I'm sorry," Easton said, his voice heartfelt.

The back of her throat burned as she choked up. She swallowed and took in a few calming breaths.

"Siblings?" he asked.

Amity noted that he was a decent conversationalist, probably from talking to all the tourists. It surprised her since their earlier conversations had been rough, but she'd revisit that thought some other time.

"No, just me," she said. "You?"

"Yep, a firecracker of a sister."

"Oh, yeah. You mentioned her when we talked by the stream after the trail run. She can climb?"

"Yep, and ski. Hannah's a full-time ski patroller at Aspen Mountain. In the summer, she has extra time, so she helps me on climbing tours. Especially this summer…"

Amity wondered why he trailed off. "Especially this summer?"

Easton skidded to a halt. He grimaced through the cloud of dust surrounding them.

"Too fast?" Amity asked.

She was pretty sure that it wasn't too fast for him. He was breathing hard from the solid pace they'd maintained while chatting, but she'd let him determine the pace, and they hadn't gone that far yet.

"No." He wouldn't meet her eyes. "I need to check the map."

Amity wondered what he'd been about to say, but she let it go. Whatever it was, he didn't want to talk about it. It wasn't like she had revealed her innermost secrets either.

"We've gone about four miles," Amity said.

"Almost exactly." Easton finally looked into her eyes. "How did you know that?"

"I can feel about how far I've gone. I wear a Garmin watch when I run." She raised her eyebrows. "Why does that surprise you? Seems like you'd be good at sensing mileage too."

Her Garmin watch had been a birthday present from her mother about two years ago. It was her favorite splurge item aside from her cell phone, both of which were now tucked safely away in her fancy pink case. The crew would have taken them away anyway, even if they had been 'on her person.' The directors were adamant about no electronics—not that it mattered—it wasn't like there was anywhere out here to charge devices.

"Yes, but our pace threw me off until I saw the trail connection here." He nodded toward another trail that branched off. "I'm used to a hiking pace. To tell you the truth, running isn't my favorite thing to do. It seems like unnecessary torture."

"You and I have different ideas of what constitutes torture. Although I will say, it's gorgeous out here." She held out her hands and spun in a circle. "As long as I'm not in a skills challenge or sleeping in a tent, I love it. Runs out here are amazing."

Easton crouched down and held his compass to the map. His head turned in various directions, locating what she assumed were landmarks while he somehow oriented the compass to point in the direction of one of the blue Xs.

"Can you show me how to do that?" Amity asked eagerly, squatting down next to him. It looked like something she should understand for the backpacking portion of the race.

"How about back at camp? We've only got a few teams behind us. We need to make sure we beat them back to the finish."

"Okay." Amity put her hand on her hip, pasting on a pouty frown. "Although I think we'll come back first with you doing that," she said, pointing at the map, "and our fast pace."

"Let's kick some butt then." As Easton eyed her, his features tightened with concern. "Don't worry, Princess. I *will* show you when we have time. I want you in this race."

Amity's mouth slowly lifted into a pleased smile, her insides tangling as he flashed her one in return.

Clearing his throat, he continued, "You're not even breathing hard or sweating yet. I'll try to go a little faster."

After tucking the map and compass in his small pack, he unexpectedly reached for her hand. An electric shock went through her system as their fingers touched.

"Wow," she said, sucking in a quick breath.

Easton froze, eyes wide like she'd spooked him, and fixed his gaze on her mouth. Was he going to kiss her?

She leaned in.

He yanked his hand away, hissing a rapid intake of breath through his teeth like she'd seared him.

"Are you okay? Did a bee sting you?"

Backing away, Easton flexed his hands. "I...um..." He pulled off his hat and ran his fingers through his hair before looking around like he'd lost his bearings. "Sorry, was trying to guide you this way."

He pointed and then took off down a trail. She followed, sprinting to catch up. His erratic mood swings were confusing and insanely irritating. So what did that mean? He liked her but didn't want to touch her? If that wasn't a confidence killer, she didn't know what was.

"Problem, *Easton*?" she asked sharply after a few minutes.

"No, Princess, just trying to focus on the race. I've got a million dollars to win."

"Don't call me Princess when you're being an ass," she shot back. The stupid money! And now that he'd dropped the playful undertone, it reminded her of her first impression of him.

"I'll stop calling you Princess when you stop calling me..."

"*Easton*," she finished for him a few seconds later when she realized that he didn't intend to say it. "Are you going to tell me why you don't like your first name?"

He ignored her, and they ran on in silence for several minutes. She pumped her fists harder with each step and ran uncomfortably close to his heels.

Easton's breathing accelerated, as did his pace, but when he finally spoke again, it was annoyingly about the race. "We're going for our flags that are farthest away first. They're

137

on land and off the trail, from what I can tell. There's no water near the X."

Easton took in a few deep breaths, filling his lungs with air. Amity hoped to have him full-on gasping soon. She clipped his heels with her toes.

"Once we find those flags," he continued, his voice laced with irritation, "we'll work our way back, going for the X that appears to be in the smaller lake, followed by the one that's in the larger lake, which will likely be in the water. I want to wait until we've found the first two flags before we get wet."

Get wet? Amity wanted to ask him, but she didn't want to give him the satisfaction. She'd been running behind him like a dog on a leash. 'Thanks for asking me my opinion,' she wanted to say as she continued to provoke him with her childish heel-clipping.

After tensely trudging through a thick foliage of scratchy bushes and fir branches to find their first flags, they were on their way to their second ones. Her arms stung from the scratches, and, at one point, Easton had let go of an evergreen branch that had whacked her in the face. He'd apologized profusely, and she'd believed him when he'd said he didn't mean to—he really did seem to hate it when she got hurt—but she'd still opted not to look at him. Too little, too late, in her mind.

Their first flags had been strung along a pole in a batch of trees behind a small clearing. Easton had explained that they'd be very difficult for most teams to find. Amity had rolled her eyes when he'd said it, not wanting to give him the satisfaction of being 'the man' when she was already angry with him.

Now, they were back following the trails again. The lakes they passed were crystal clear and endless—one after another. Pine trees, fallen logs, and rocks lined the lake edges. She watched water bugs and dragonflies dance on the surface as they passed. What a shame to run by so quickly without even stopping to dangle her feet in the cool water.

As they came upon yet another grassy clearing, she could see Isaac and Cassie in the distance. Easton told her that he thought Isaac and Cassie would struggle to find their flags in the off-trail trees—that it required precise use of the compass and map by taking a bearing off some butte in the distance. Amity, still upset by his businesslike treatment of her, wasn't really paying attention to the details.

"Perfect," Easton added, bringing her out of her thoughts. "We're way ahead of Isaac and Cassie. They're not even wet, which means they've probably only found the easiest flags to get—there"—he pointed toward a batch of trees with glistening water visible through the cracks—"is the small lake."

Cassie shot Amity a dirty look as they ran past while Isaac smiled kindly at her.

"Hi, Isaac," Amity said brightly.

Isaac gestured with a nod instead of saying anything, probably for Cassie's benefit.

Easton clenched his fists in front of her. Good! She hoped it irritated him. He remained quiet, both fists curled, until they reached the lake's edge, split in two by a narrow passage. Stopping to survey the scene, they looked for the flags. Easton's features were taut, his lips tight, and his eyes crinkled. Perhaps the tension between them affected him as badly as it did her? He just handled it differently.

She threw out an olive branch. "What do you mean small lake? Looks big enough to me."

A brief smile tugged at his lips, loosening his features. "It's smaller than the other lake we'll go to, and according to the map, the flags are in a shallow section of the lake."

Not able to see the flags from their current location, they took off again, sprinting along the lakeside. After a few minutes, he pointed behind a narrow patch of trees. "There they are. The flags are on that island."

A tiny rock island sat in the middle of a shallow part of the lake with a long pole of flags. She could see the five remaining flags dangling down, blowing slightly in the breeze. Unlike the first pole they'd found with all the flags intact, two of the seven were missing on this one, as they had already been retrieved by Isaac and Cassie.

"We'll have to take our shoes and socks off," Easton said as they reached the lake edge close to the island.

Amity slid off her trail shoes, followed by her wool socks, scrunching her face up at the divide between her and the island. She liked dipping her feet in, but this water was deep enough to reach above her knees.

Easton motioned in front of him, smirking at her hesitation. "It's better if you just go for it, kind of like ripping off a Band-Aid."

Amity nodded, sucking in her breath as her foot touched what felt like ice. She walked carefully on the smooth, slippery stones until her legs became numb. "This water is freezing," she screeched, picking up the pace by pulling her feet in and out of the water with fast-paced pitter-patters.

Easton chuckled, trudging through the water behind her like he was immune to its temperature. "Yep, it may be sunny, warm, and free of snow at this elevation in the summer, but you're still in the mountain range."

Amity reached the smooth surface of the stone island and felt the sun-soaked heat radiating into her heels and toes.

She moaned in relief. "Oh my gosh, so much better."

The rock island was about the temperature of hot sand but without the luxury of stepping into warm ocean water. She snagged her and Justin's purple flag and rotated in a circle to enjoy the surroundings. A steep rocky shore lined most of the lake, as well as scraggly pines that looked weathered from the harsh conditions of winter.

"Time to go," Easton said the instant he grabbed his and Becky's yellow flag.

"Just enjoying the moment."

"The next lake will be more impressive. If the tree line is low enough, we should be able to see the South Sister in the background. This group of lakes is called Sisters Mirror Lakes for a reason. The mountains can be seen as a reflection in the water at some of the lakes."

"Really?" Amity exclaimed.

"Yes, really."

"How cool. I always thought pictures of scenes like that were computer-generated."

Easton turned and grinned at her with a look of surprise, filling her with warm butterflies as she reveled in the return of his carefree side. "There are reflection lakes in several states," he said. "Some in Colorado too. I'm surprised you haven't seen one before. I think you need to get out more."

Amity waded behind him in the calm, cold water toward their socks and shoes, their conversation keeping her mind off her frozen feet. "That's the point."

"What do you mean?"

"Of me being out here," she explained with renewed ease. He was so nice when he was like this. "To get out more."

"To get out more? Can't you just pay for a vacation to do that?"

"Like those incredible tours of yours, you mean?"

"Yeah, like that," he said, his voice amused. "Or a tropical beach for you instead?"

"Now you're talking. But then," she added sweetly, "how would I see my first reflection lake?"

Easton cleared his throat. "Let's hope I'm right about that."

"If not, can you take me to one someday?"

The words were out of her mouth before she'd thought them through, and the result was painful—dead silence.

Her heart lost its rhythm. Did he like her or not? Because she'd had enough wishing for things to happen in her life. If he wasn't interested, then she didn't want to get her hopes up.

Fifteen

Cooper felt like such an ass. He wanted to tell her—yes, anytime, he'd take her on any tour she wanted—but he tried not to make promises he didn't intend to keep. Amity needed a man that could cater to her—that could take her on fancy vacations to the upscale resorts and shops she seemed to enjoy—and that wasn't him. He came home to a backwoods cabin with floor heaters and a wood stove, cooked most of his meals at home or went to his parents' or sister's places, and then spent the other eighty percent of his time in the wilderness.

He liked her a lot, but he wasn't her guy. At least not long-term. Perhaps you could argue he was her short-term guy because he wanted—what did he want? To keep her safe, to be the one to make her smile, to take care of her? He didn't even know. But he did know from the touch of her skin that he wanted her. If she leaned in again, he'd kiss her without question and regret it. Amity wasn't a one-and-done type of woman.

He could tell her type instantly. They listened and showed emotion. They asked lots of meaningful questions, and just as she'd done moments ago, they suggested doing things together in the future. When her type came along, he'd learned to run. He would *not* change for another woman.

Ironically, his one big downfall in relationships was that he put those he cared about before himself. He had yet to have a fifty-fifty romantic relationship, his girlfriends always wanting him to change for them. He'd tried changing four times now, and it made him unhappy every time.

So lately, he'd resorted to short flings with the tourists rolling through town. Not the women who went on his tours, of course, but instead, women he met in bars or on the slopes. Easy in, easy out. Never women like Amity. She'd expect a commitment, and he'd bet his million dollars that the lucky man she chose could pamper her.

One day, maybe he'd find a low-maintenance gal that understood give and take. Perhaps, they'd even be fortunate enough to get married and have kids and somehow figure out how to work through his weeklong absences. That would take an extremely patient and understanding woman, which his best friend assured him was out there. After all, Dominic found his wife, and Cooper and Dominic were gone on their tours for exactly the same amount of time.

Cooper cringed, thinking of how Dominic had looked the last time he'd seen him, his pale skin and frail figure, and the tears in Chelsea's eyes. He needed to win the million dollars at any cost—no one was more important than the people he'd loved for his entire life. He took a deep breath and focused on the dirt beneath his feet, pumping his arms with more force.

After a few minutes, they crested a ridge, and the large lake containing their final flags came into view. Cooper heard voices. Whoever it was, the endless trees concealed them.

Amity turned to speak, and he held his finger to his lips. "I don't want them to find us," he whispered. "They might try to follow us or ask questions about the other flag locations."

She nodded, and they ran on until he realized that the

group was coming toward them. Pivoting in the opposite direction, he motioned for Amity to follow, frowning at the vivid purple glow that bounced off her torso. Of course, her shirt color stood out, while the green color they'd chosen for him was perfect for camouflage. Why was everything about her always so eye-catching?

He leapt behind a group of leafy, green bushes and swiveled into a crouch, propping himself against a thick fir tree trunk and pointing to his lap with his index finger.

She shook her head, her eyes fixed on his lap.

"We don't have time to argue," he whispered. "They'll see your shirt. This is the only spot we can hide."

Amity glanced up, measuring the angle of the bushes with her eyes, and sighed. Holding out her hand, she said, "You're right. Help me up."

Cooper hauled her into his lap and tucked her soft hair beneath his chin, instantly realizing he'd made a mistake—damn, he knew better than to touch her. His pulse hammered while an unwelcome erection grew in his running shorts. The thin fabric did little to conceal his junk, one of the many reasons he preferred more substantial khaki hiking shorts.

Amity, clearly feeling his excitement, tried to shift away from his groin, her bottom rubbing on him like an intimate lap dance, and instead of relieving him, his cock went from rigid to rock-hard.

"My god, Amity," Cooper croaked out in a gravelly whisper. "*Please* hold still. Believe me, that doesn't help. It's turning me on."

A quick intake of breath whistled through her teeth, and she froze, confirming that her goal was just the opposite.

He closed his eyes and tried to imagine the least sexy thing he could think of. A walrus at the zoo. A compound fracture bleeding out. A bird crapping on his car window.

His eyes popped open as the voices echoed off the nearby

trees, and through a crack in the bushes, he could see Bria and Miles come flying around the corner, clothes dripping wet. What a stupid decision to leave them on. They'd likely chafe.

The pair stumbled around and swatted at a swarm of mosquitoes drawn in by the moisture and heat radiating off their fragrant skin. He chuckled to himself. Poor Bria—having to run the leg with Miles, who proved yet again that he knew nothing about the great outdoors.

"Miles, let's go," Bria said impatiently. "Lucy or Carlos, whichever comes this way, will follow if we don't get moving."

"Yeah, in a minute," Miles fired back. "Damn mosquitoes."

Bria and Miles had swapped partners too, which meant that Jade and Sean went to find their flags in the Separation Creek area. That left the final pair, Lucy and Carlos, split up and on their own with no team to help them. He and Amity probably had loads of time to find their final flags, but he still had no intention of slowing his pace.

"What the hell?" Bria shouted. "What are ya doing now?"

Miles peeled off his shorts, going down to his black boxer briefs, which the idiot should have done before he'd gone in the water. As he turned and grabbed the small pack off his back to stuff his shorts in, his eyes temporarily lined up with their location. Cooper adjusted his body to shield Amity's purple shirt, her frame wrapping around him like a pretzel. He squeezed his eyes shut, trying not to think about how perfectly they'd fit together in bed.

"Good idea," Bria said.

Cooper let out a yoga-like breath while Amity shimmied around on his groin. She felt so...damn...good. "Stop wiggling, please," he whispered into her ear. "You're killing me."

"I can't help it," Amity whispered back. "I'm slipping. Stop adjusting your legs."

146

Cooper clenched his teeth. Yeah, because every guy could hold a multi-second squat with a woman on his lap without moving a muscle. She tightened her grip, painfully digging her purple fingernails into his arms. The pain helped a little, but not enough. He shut his eyes again, squeezing tighter, reimagining things that would calm his excitement. Blood-soaked gauze. A nail in his tire. Spoiled lunch meat. Miles and Bria.

He peeked through the bushes. Bria was now stripping off her wet layers, too. He smiled at her girl version of camo boy boxers—lucky for her, she wore underwear that looked like shorts.

Amity shifted and slipped backward, somehow grabbing on like a trapeze artist and training a set of icy brown eyes on him.

His smile fell. What was her problem? *He* was the one suffering. He slammed his lids shut. A worm in a bird's mouth. The guts of a fish. The smell of a wet dog.

Amity shuffled back into his lap, her sexy little bottom rubbing enticingly against his eager cock, and visions of her potential undergarments popped into his mind instead. Pink lace. Blue silk. Black satin. A low, deep groan ripped out of him while a soft, wispy intake of breath slid through Amity's teeth.

He was going to die.

"Hold still," he growled as beads of sweat broke out across his skin, and his legs shook like a miniature earthquake.

"I am," she whispered through raspy little breaths that turned him on even more.

A long, painful minute later, Bria and Miles finally ran on, somehow without noticing them. Their voices faded, and Cooper eased Amity to the ground in front of him, letting go once he was sure her legs were stable. He yanked on a tree branch to pull himself up, his wobbly legs protesting and his groin in serious, serious pain.

"For fuck's sake." Cooper groaned, planting his hands on his knees, barely able to stand. "Ouch." Thank god, he'd likely never date her—the woman was fully capable of giving him blue balls, not that he'd ever let her in on that knowledge. Harsher than he intended, he added, "Let's get moving."

Amity glared at him, lifted her chin, and said, "Agreed," before running up the trail like a track star.

Cooper cracked a smile. Her anger turned her into a sexy little firework, and unfortunately, it was better for both of them if she stayed mad. He took off after her with a much-needed intake of breath, staggering for a few steps before his legs woke up.

A couple of minutes later, he caught up to her, standing on a clear, rocky shore; and just as he'd anticipated, there was an incredible view of the South Sister reflecting off the lake. Catching a movement in the distance, he noticed a cameraman unsuccessfully hiding in the trees on the opposite bank. To capture shots of the teams as they jumped into the water, he assumed? Cooper smirked. It gave away the location of the flags because just across from the cameraman, a large group of rocks jutted out into the lake.

"We need to go out there," he said, pointing. "Looks like we've got to cross those fallen tree logs first to get to the other shoreline. Then we can go out on the rocks." When she didn't respond, he glanced at her. "Amity?"

"I've never seen anything like this," she whispered in awe. "The mountain reflecting off the water is like…like something out of a postcard. My dad would be so happy I'm out here."

Cooper wanted to keep moving, but he could sense that this was somehow a pivotal moment for Amity, and he was insanely curious to know more about her. "Did your dad like backpacking?"

Amity's eyes flashed to him. She hesitated, then seemed to come to a decision. "He liked to travel—not backpacking necessarily—just anywhere. My dad's dream was to experience the best adventures of his life with me. My parents had a difficult time conceiving, so I was their miracle. He had all these plans to take me places like this before…"

"Before?"

"Before cancer." Amity swallowed hard and blinked back tears. "Anyway, no reason to dwell on that. He's up there somewhere." She pointed at the sky and spun in one of those circles again. "And he knows I'm here." She fanned her hands out in front of her. "Seeing this incredible place."

"I'm glad that you're here seeing it too."

She took another long look at the scene, sighed, and said, "We should go. I know how much you want to win this."

"You don't?"

"Of course I do. Who doesn't want to win a million dollars?" She laughed softly, bent down, and grabbed a flat rock, unsuccessfully skipping it across the water's glassy surface. "But I didn't sign up for the show expecting to win money. Honestly, I didn't even think they'd select me at all. There were so many people standing in that line," she trailed off in a whisper, shaking her head. "No, the chances of winning the money are still so farfetched. I don't want to get my hopes up."

She tossed a few more stones that plunked sideways into the water but never came back up and cast him a sheepish glance. "I've always wanted to skip a rock three or four times in a row, like in the movies."

Cooper picked up a flat, gray stone and sidearm tossed it with trained ease, watching it skip seven consecutive times across the surface.

Her mouth fell open. "Showoff."

Shit! He hadn't been thinking. Way to woo the girl—by one-upping her. "Sorry, I…" He braced his hands on his head, running them down his cap. "I didn't mean to do that. I really wasn't—"

"Is there anything you're not good at?"

Yes! Everything that wasn't in the mountains.

She laughed, surprising him. "That sort of sounded like a loaded question."

He startled, looking at her in wonder. If she meant sex, he'd happily boast about his skills—sex he could do, but he'd never measure up to her other 'boyfriend' expectations. "So, you were explaining—why you're out here?"

"Oh." Amity paused, then shrugged. "Yeah, I guess I was." She placed her hand on his bicep, standing his arm hairs on end. "This might sound crazy, but I swear it's the truth—I'm out here for an adventure."

Cooper narrowed his eyes. Really? She thought he'd buy that.

Her mouth dipped into a frown. "No, really, Easton, I'm serious."

Had she read his thoughts?

Amity continued on in a persuasive tone, "I know it sounds like I'm covering some hidden agenda, but I'm not. I want a decent finish, too—so I can stay." She tried to skip another rock and pursed her lips as it splashed straight down with a loud *thunk* into the lake. "That and I'm a super competitive racer. Ingrained from my track years in high school, I suppose. I can't *stand* to lose."

As Cooper suspected, Amity didn't need the money, but he couldn't understand why she didn't just stay in a mountain resort town and go on day trips. Why put herself through this? He'd already asked her that, and she'd smoothly evaded the question. Was he supposed to believe that she wanted to compete in the wilderness for fun? When she hated almost everything about it? Yeah, right. How dumb did she think he was?

It left only one disappointing, sensible possibility—the one he'd suspected all along—that she wanted exposure for her high-profile career. He'd better keep his head on straight. Everyday guys like him didn't make headlines with Hollywood stars. She'd burn him in the end.

He swallowed with a click. "We'd better get moving. The other teams will come through here, just like Bria and Miles. Let's get our flags and haul tail so the other teams can't see us and mark our location."

Amity nodded, and they headed out to cross the logs, cutting off the need to hike around a small inlet of the lake. Amity flew across the logs with amazing grace while Cooper struggled to balance, his shoes slipping on the wet, slimy wood as his reedy legs wobbled.

Amity turned around to watch him, giggling. "Come on, Caveman. Speed up. The water won't bite if you fall in."

"Yeah, but my man parts won't take well to wet shorts," Cooper yelled and cursed himself afterward. If another team heard him because he was joking around, he deserved it.

Amity's laughter rolled out. She was so cute he couldn't even bring himself to tell her to be quiet.

Cooper jumped off the log and grabbed her hand to lead her along the rocky shoreline. "Come on." A burst of energy shot through him at their touch, and he quickly dropped his hand.

They reached the opening of the rock peninsula and ran to the tip. He frowned at the murky water in front of them. Bria must have purposely stirred up mud from the lake bottom to conceal the flags. Smart woman, he thought, assuming Miles would never have been clever enough to think of it.

Cooper removed his bodycams and soundbox as instructed by the camera crew, setting them on the rock. His backpack, hat, shoes, and socks came next before he peeled off his shirt. He couldn't help but say, "Enjoying the show?" as Amity gawked at him. He laughed and slid his thumbs into the sides of his shorts, ready to strip them down.

Amity's eyes widened. "*What* are you doing?"

"I'm not chafing from wet clothes—especially not on my nads. Don't worry, Princess. I'll wear my boxers into the water, take them off before I put my shorts back on, and then go commando on the run back. You'll never see me naked." He grinned at her. "Unless you take a peek after we get wet"—he waggled his eyebrows—"while I strip my boxers off."

Amity cast her eyes toward the water while he took off his shorts, a cute pink blush on her cheeks. "So, I'm supposed to strip down to my undies? In front of the cameras?"

"Oh, relax. It's just like a swimsuit for you ladies, and they'll put one of those blur bars over you. If they even air this," he added. "I don't see why they would. The race is what people will care about."

"Is that what you think?" Amity choked out, shooting him an amused look. "Easton, this show is a hundred percent going for social drama. Yes, people will follow the challenges, but mostly they want to see heightened tension between contestants."

"I'm well aware," Cooper responded dryly, glancing at the cameraman on the opposite shore. "I just don't see why they'd air us stripping down."

Amity bit her lip, holding back laughter. "Do you want to see me almost naked? Answer honestly. I'm just making a point."

"Yes," he said quickly. "Any straight guy would be lying if they didn't."

"Exactly. They'll air it. Because lots of people will enjoy seeing us naked." Amity shrugged. "And to see our reactions —whether we check each other out." Continuing to smile, she added, "Which I intend to do."

Shit, if that didn't turn him on. He didn't expect her to be so bold.

Amity's eyes scanned unabashed up and down his lengthy form. "Not bad. Strong upper body." She tilted her head. "You still have your boxers on, though. What a shame." Then with a sigh, she turned a brighter shade of pink and said, "Fudge. I should have worn a different set."

"Set of what?" he said.

"Bra and panty set. Here we go, America." Amity took off her shoes, socks, camera gear, and pack. She paused, glancing at the camera across the lake, before quickly stripping off her purple tank top and black shorts.

And Cooper lost all mobility—frozen erect and speechless. To put it simply, Amity was gorgeous. Her tan body carried toned, athletically curved hips. A barely-there, hot pink lace thong provided a side view of her perfect bottom with skin he could only dream of running his hands across. Her matching intricate lace bra fit snuggly over a full-sized set of breasts.

His jaw must be hitting the rocks because he'd never seen a more beautiful woman. Unlike those glossy supermodels, Amity had a healthy, satin glow, and to him, the bug bites and scrapes peppered across her skin turned him on even more— they made her seem real. Her jagged hair stuck out of her tiny ponytail reminding him of how she didn't even hesitate to hack it off—so they could stay in this competition.

The despicable boner in his boxers returned full force. He could only hope that because she'd checked him out, she'd be fine with him doing so in return. "Why are you wearing *that* for a trail run?"

Amity crossed her arms to cover her chest. "The sports bra and underwear the show provided in my pack got all sweaty on the first trail run, so I washed them in the creek. I didn't know how long the fabric would take to dry in this climate. In Palm Springs, things dry quickly." Her lips lifted into a flirty

153

smirk. "This is what I had on during the fire challenge. Under that orange dress, I wore. When you called me Princess for the first—"

"Yeah," he interrupted hoarsely, drawing in shallow breaths. "Believe me, I remember."

Amity locked eyes with him, not comprehending that she'd rendered him motionless. The only movement he wanted to make was to pull her up against him and feel every inch of her.

"Can we jump in now, please? I don't want additional airtime"—she motioned her hands up and down her body—"of this."

With both reluctance and relief, Cooper returned his focus to the churned-up water. He didn't even look up to see if Amity continued to check him out, not having an ounce of willpower left to resist her.

"I'll dive under and find the flag bar," he said, listening to the husky tone in his voice. "After I retrieve my flag, I'll signal you in."

"Works for me. I'll let you freeze your nuts off."

Cooper grabbed a long stick and poked around in the murky water, checking for rocks under the rippling surface, not wanting either of them to break their necks or backbones. Determining it safe, he slid into the murkiest part of the lake, assuming that was where Bria had attempted to conceal the flags. It took him a few minutes of bobbing up and down to find the bar and unlink his yellow flag from the clasp.

He popped up and rubbed the muddy water out of his eyes with his flag-free hand, calling out to her, "Okay, the flags are right under me."

Amity took a deep breath, jumped in, bobbed to the surface, and screamed, "Fuck, that's cold."

"Quiet down, please." He splashed water on her. "Every team within a mile will hear you."

Amity swam toward him, her teeth already chattering. "Water in Palm Springs is warm or better yet, *hot*."

"Yeah, well, welcome to the mountains, Princess. Dive under, feel around for the flag bar, and open your eyes. You'll get a time penalty if you grab the wrong one."

Amity scowled at him, probably due to his lack of sympathy for her. He, however, was extremely grateful for the icy water. Anything to calm the raging hard-on he'd developed after seeing Amity's incredibly sexy body firsthand. She looked like a—well, 'beautifully sculpted runner' if he had to choose a phrase. Another reason among many that she would never want a guy like him—he wasn't even in her league.

Quite impressively, it only took her two tries to find and unhook her purple flag. "Wow, a runner and a swimmer?" Cooper asked, still processing that she actually had the flag in her hand.

Amity glided toward the rock. "There are a lot of pools in Palm Springs. *Warm* pools. When I was young, I used to dive down for rings and batons at the resort pools with my friends. Got quite good at it." Moving like a graceful otter, she added, "I want out of this lake!"

Cooper swam toward the giant rock, making larger strokes with his long arms, wedged his foot in a crevice, and easily climbed a few feet, launching himself out of the lake. He turned and watched her from the rock's surface.

Amity reached the bottom of the rock, struggled with her grip, and slipped on the wet edge, splashing back into the water. After three more tries, she let out a frustrated huff and yelled, "*How* did you do that?" She waded around, crinkling her features. "Oh duh, you're a rock climber. Well then, Mr. Spider, can you get me the hell out of here, please?"

Cooper crouched down. He couldn't begin to understand why he wasn't hurrying. Probably because he knew they were lightyears ahead of the other teams, and he didn't need to.

There was always team placement to worry about, but right now, his mind was on Amity.

"I'll get you out." He grinned mischievously at her. "If you promise, you'll choose me as your partner for the rest of the race, regardless of what happens."

"What?" she exclaimed. "No! You're all over the place. One minute you're nice, and the next, you're an ass."

Cooper bit back a grin. "You look awfully cold, Amity. Your lips are turning blue. It's a simple promise and one that will ease my worries."

Amity looked behind her at the opposite shoreline.

"That's a difficult way to go," he drawled out. "Slime-covered logs are very slippery, and those rocks over there look just as jagged as these ones."

"You want to win this race badly, don't you? Leaving me in here is of *no* benefit to you."

He propped his chin under his hand. "Hmm...I think you'll get cold before I get antsy. What do you think?"

"That you're unpredictable," she squeaked out.

"Exactly, so you should really just take the deal. Honestly, how often do either of us actually get to choose anyway? Someone else usually scoops us up first."

"Get...me...out," she stammered.

"So, you'll select me then? As your partner? Every time?"

"Do you promise not to be so crazy erratic?" she asked, goosebumps breaking out across her skin. "I can't s-st-*stand* your mood swings."

Cooper sat on the warm rock, letting the hot sun dry his cool skin. "Nah, no promises."

"I d-don't understand," she chattered. "You want to win this r-race for that s-st-stupid money, and now you're r-risking it."

"Not really. We're pretty far ahead of the other teams." Cooper watched her doggy paddle to keep afloat but also, he suspected, to keep her blood flowing. "I imagine you won't last long in there with your heat-acclimated skin. What's the downside, Princess? You told me you like racing with me."

"I told you—I h-hate it when you call me Pr-Princess when you're being an a-ass. And that promise is cr-cr-crazy! This r-race could be going on for f-five more weeks. Remember? We s-signed away s-six weeks of our life."

"An awful lot of talking for someone so cold." Calmly, he added, "Uses lots of energy."

"I'm terrible at sk-skills challenges *and* c-camping. You might c-cl-claim that you like me for the t-ten minutes it takes you to realize that you really d-don't. And partners will get sh-shifted around anyway. Show d-dr-drama, remember?"

Cooper's smile faded. He couldn't imagine watching her race with another guy. It would churn him up inside, which was ridiculous because when they went home, he'd never see her again. "I'll take that risk," he said, but he didn't feel elated anymore—because Amity was right.

"Okay, Easton, your f-fu-funeral. Get me *out* of h-here!"

"So, that's a promise, then?"

"Dammit. I p-pr-promise."

Cooper crouched, reached for her hand, and with the strength of a full-time climber, easily pulled her out of the water and into his arms. He enveloped her in his warmth; her silky body pressed against the heat of him. Feeling somewhat guilty about the ice-cold temperature of her skin, he rubbed her back with the friction of his large hands, her hard nipples poking through the thin lace of her bra into his chest.

"Amity," he groaned into her wet hair. "My god, Amity. *Please.*"

She reached up and tilted his chin down, so he met her eyes. Running her soft fingertips along his jaw, she nodded—that was all he needed—confirmation that she wanted him too.

Gripping the back of her neck, Cooper molded his mouth

to her frozen lips, his own warming them instantly as he ground every part of himself against her.

Amity kissed him back with throaty little moans that nearly made him come in his boxers, her hands eagerly exploring the muscles in his shoulders before she trailed them down the spine of his lower back.

Instinctively, he grabbed the bare skin of her ass, pulling her hard against his groin, the feel of her wet skin more intoxicating than his mind could handle. He slid his tongue into her mouth as she moaned and bucked against him. Roping his thumbs through the strings of her thong, he slid the tiny strands down her bare hips—and froze.

A blurred movement in the distance caught his eye. He couldn't take her in broad daylight with a damn camera filming, just like the playboy he'd sworn he'd never be. Not to mention, Amity would never settle for just sex. He'd given her the wrong idea.

With extreme effort, Cooper pulled away. He looked into her hungry, sparkling brown eyes, noticing brilliant flecks of gold in their depths, and said, "I'm only able to have a fling."

The resulting slap across his cheek was well deserved.

Sixteen

Amity's body shook. She ran behind Easton near tears, and—oh gosh—she could *not* let him see her cry. He didn't deserve the satisfaction. Only another eight or so minutes—that's all she *had* to make it before they returned to the finish line. Screw Easton and her promise to him that she'd choose him as a partner. When hell froze over.

He'd made her feel and, now that she thought about the cameraman on the opposite shore who'd filmed them, look like a total slut. The only smart thing he'd done since their sultry kiss was to not say another word because if he had, she'd have slapped him ten more times.

A fling? Really? The voice recorders lying in their heap of clothes on the rock caught that, as they'd been instructed not to turn them off. So everyone in America would hear those disgusting words when the show aired. Maybe that was a good thing, though. Surely, Easton would come across as a jerk when her reaction made it clear she wasn't that type of girl. People still rooted for guys to make a commitment, right? Or did they just accept any kind of sexual drama?

Anyway, it didn't matter because that was the last time Easton Cooper would get a taste of her lips. She was *not* a one-night stand. If America wanted a race for riches or *romance*, then she and Easton were not it. Guys who wanted flings never changed. It was like—once a cheater, always a cheater— once a flinger, always a flinger. You could not change men.

"You made a promise to me, Amity," Easton said as the finish line came into view. "Just remember that tomorrow when we choose partners."

She clamped her teeth together. "Like hell."

Easton stopped, and she slammed into his back, stumbling. He twisted around, grabbing onto her shoulders to steady her. "You made me a promise." He looked pleadingly into her eyes. "We agreed that regardless of whether or not I was an ass, you'd choose *me* as your partner. I was an ass, and I'm sorry. I panicked. You're too good for me." He released her shoulders and backed away. "But that doesn't change the fact that we're in this race together."

"You're so confusing," she said, beginning to sniffle. "What does that mean?"

"It means that a guy like me could never make you happy." Easton took off his hat and rubbed a hand through his floppy, damp hair. "But I'm attracted to you, and I can't help it. I just don't do relationships. All I meant is that if you get involved with me, I can't offer you anything after this race."

"Then *don't* get involved with me, *Easton*," Amity whispered harshly, "because I *only* do relationships."

Easton flinched, and Amity ran around him, her pulse hammering as she headed for the finish line. He'd deserved that! She rubbed her misty eyes with the hem of her dusty shirt and pulled out her three matching purple flags as Justin came into view.

The flags in the Separation Creek meadow area must have been easier or closer to find because she and Easton had gone extremely fast. Becky, standing with Justin by the finish line, scowled at her as they neared while Liam and Kim waited off to the side. It appeared that Isaac and Cassie still hadn't returned from the lakes. She wasn't surprised, given her and Easton's speed, and she had to admit Easton was impressive with a compass.

Just steps away from the line, Easton motioned at Justin. "Go ahead, man. You and Amity take the win."

"Are you kidding?" Becky yelled. "You are so blind. She's playing you. Do you really want to give Amity a million dollars? Because I promise she cares *nothing* about you. She's after the money."

"You go," Amity muttered to Easton. "You're here for the money. Don't let me get in the way of that."

"So is Justin," Easton whispered in response.

"I'm fine, man," Justin said. "I think Amity's right. You left before us. Finish it out. It likely won't change things for me, but for you"—Justin stroked his beard—"if you finish first, then hopefully, you can choose Amity on the next leg. I think I'd rather be free of that drama. What if she decides to choose someone else? You're a little crazy when it comes to her."

Easton nodded. "I think you're right."

Amity jerked her head back. "You're on his side," she whined to Justin.

Justin shrugged, quirking a brow. "You're the one who suggested he take the win. Am I missing something?"

Easton motioned Becky across the finish line.

Becky turned and said, "You'll lose because of her."

Amity rolled her eyes. How many contestants had said those words to Easton? *You'll lose because of her.* She kept hearing it over and over. She'd prove them all wrong.

She shot Becky a competitive glare, watching her step over the line in front of her, then finished in second place with Justin. She would *not* let Becky beat her on the next leg. In a month or so, the show would air, and these contestants would watch it all play out step by step on their television, wondering how they'd been stupid enough to let her walk away with a million dollars.

~

THE WORDS KEPT RINGING through Cooper's mind. *You'll lose because of her.* He looked at Amity sitting by the campfire, confused by his motivations. If he didn't pursue her, what had been the point of keeping her here? Why torture himself?

He'd been truthful with her. He did believe she could remain in the race just as easily as him. There was so much luck involved. It was about dealing with curveball rules. It was about making connections with strong partners. And it was about getting chosen by the right person at the right time.

Miles would have lost the woodchopping challenge no matter who he'd been partnered with, and since he'd chosen Amity, she would've been eliminated because of it. Another reason Cooper hated these shows—they weren't fair. Of course, you could argue that Amity kept herself in the race by building an alliance with him since he was mental enough to save her, but the chances of that had been almost zero. Who would have guessed he'd be into her? Himself included.

Cooper's eyes betrayed him as they focused comfortably on Amity. She'd pulled her short, chopped-up hair out of its ponytail, allowing the lake-soaked strands to fan out and dry in the sunlight while she chatted with Bria. His stomach re-knotted in confusing tangles while his groin hardened with the memory of his hands cupping her bare ass. He felt like a damn teenager. He *should* grab his food and beeline for the second campfire, but it pained him to think about distancing himself from her.

"Hi," Cooper said lamely as he snagged a nearby camping chair and sat down beside her. He twisted a forkful of spaghetti covered in meat sauce and shoved it into his mouth, realizing five seconds later that he hadn't eaten a meal in front of a woman he wanted to impress in months. Did he come across as a backcountry slob?

"Really?" Amity asked. "Hi? Now we're friends again?"

Cooper shrugged, enjoying the carbs and dense meat, the ground beef heartily filling his empty stomach. "I don't know if we could ever use the word friends to describe our *relationship*," he emphasized for fun, flashing her an ornery smile.

"So," Bria cut in, clearing her throat, "you two are an official thing now?"

Bria looked back and forth between them, taking a swig of beer. Beer? At least he was pretty sure that's what it was. He could smell the barley and hops coming off of her breath. Where had she gotten that? He swung his head around, looking at the dinner line, and then swiveled back, deciding that intoxication was a bad idea—around Amity anyway—he couldn't think straight sober.

"No," Amity responded when he didn't, glancing at Bria with her face scrunched up. "We're friends at best. Easton made it clear he only wants a fling, and I'm not into that."

Bria choked, pulling the bottle down from her lips. She covered her chuckle while wiping foamy beer droplets off her chin with the back of her hand.

Amity turned to Cooper and held out her hand. "Friends, Easton? I think it's best if we try to get along, given that we're in the same alliance."

How did he want to handle this? Here he was, thinking that he couldn't win both the money and the girl—after all, the damn show was titled *The Race for Riches or Romance*—but how could anyone possibly enforce that? The money or the girl? Is that what it came down to in the end? And how impossibly classic of him—to go right down the path the stupid producers dreamed up on a crap reality TV show he hated. No wonder the cameras loved him.

Screw it, he thought. How could he *lose* the money if he went after her? He'd bet the directors didn't even know how they planned to end it. As he'd thought many times before, this race was a damn shitshow. He had about the same chance of winning it whether he got mixed up with Amity or not. And if he had to choose the money or the girl at the end? Well, he'd take the money, and then they could get together afterward. All he had to do was tell Amity his plan. How could they stop him?

And his messed-up past relationships? Well, women that tried to change him left eventually, and it hurt, but he got over it. Why not take a chance on Amity? She could walk away if he wasn't good enough for her, and he wouldn't have to continue to live with the blustering-aching need he had for her. He could enjoy himself. Relief instantly flowed through him at the thought. He could concentrate on winning the cash—because having Amity apart from him did *not* work.

"Nah," he said, ignoring her hand and leaning toward her lips. "You said you *only* do relationships, right? I think I'd like to give that a try. If you want to anyway?"

Amity scoffed, looking mad enough to kill, moved away from his lips, and flipped the bird in his face. "Not funny." She turned and asked Bria, "Why do guys play games like this?" She dropped her hand and shook her head. It took a few seconds before Amity saw his determined gaze and parted her lips in confusion. "Oh my gosh, you're actually serious?"

Cooper nodded, purposely holding his steadfast gaze. "Dead serious."

Amity swallowed hard, playing with the hem of her shirt. "Sorry, I didn't mean…" She sighed. "I'm so confused."

Cooper wrapped her hand in his and caressed her palm, avoiding her injuries—thankfully, there were only a few bandages over the deep cuts now. "I bet you a week-long, private-guided tour in the Colorado mountains that I can stay in this relationship longer than you. With no tricks or games involved. A genuine relationship that we're both putting our *full* effort into. I will outlast you."

Amity glared at him in disbelief. "You're crazy." After a few minutes of deep thought, she scrunched up her brows. "Half of the time, you don't even like me."

"Not true. Half of the time, I'm trying not to get involved with you, but the unsensible half of me always seems to win, so I vote we give it a try."

Amity stared at him with her mouth agape, probably waiting for the punchline. When he didn't waver, she cleared her throat and nodded. "Okay." Cracking a grin, she leaned toward him. "So, what do you get if *I* break it off first?"

To Cooper's surprise, Amity seemed to be enjoying herself. So were the cameras, he suddenly noticed, as well as every other contestant in the race. Granted, some of the racers were just analyzing it, not enjoying it, but their interest was intently focused on them.

He pushed them all out of his mind. If he had to win this dumb show with a girlfriend just to keep himself sane, then he'd do it. He'd put a massive target on his back, but he was pretty sure he already had one anyway. The new goal here was to win both the money and the girl—or at least win the girl until she dumped him but any amount of time with Amity would be worth it.

Cooper rubbed his hand across the stubble on his chin. For some reason, this decision seemed important. When it came to him, he snapped his fingers. "I know what I want if I win the bet." But would she think he was a selfish guy who didn't care about her? Or would she realize it was part of his plan to be with her long-term?

Amity braced her elbow on her knee and put her chin on top of her hand, leaning in with interest.

"If you break it off first," Cooper said, "I want your every effort to make sure that I come out of this race with the money."

Amity's eyebrows shot up. She shrugged a shoulder, confirming his suspicions that the money meant less to her than it did to him. "Okay, Easton, why not. You'll last ten minutes, but I'll humor you." She brushed some short, escaped wisps of dry hair behind her ear. "That trip you're taking me on. I want it to be all-expenses-paid. The plane tickets, the tour —everything. And I want a glamping tour. None of that hard-core, backbreaking rock-climbing stuff. I want to be pampered."

Cooper chuckled, not fully understanding her. Did Amity just want to stick it to him if he lost? Not that he couldn't afford plane tickets, but she could probably go to Italy on a whim if she desired. Oh well, figuring out this strange connection was worth the risk. He didn't care about a couple thousand dollars.

"It's a deal." Cooper nodded and grinned, feeling the pleasure of their commitment roll through him. "But, Princess, being pampered and the woods don't exactly go hand in hand."

He was just bantering with her. The details of their ficti-tious Colorado tour didn't really matter. He wasn't going to lose the bet.

"When you break up with me," Amity tacked on sweetly, "I guess you'll have to figure it out. You've got lots of skills," she added, biting her lip after her words.

Bria, Justin, and Sean laughed while Miles' face dropped into a perturbed frown. Counting Amity and himself, there were six of them around their fire, while a few feet away, Becky, Liam, Cassie, Isaac, Kim, and Jade sat around the other fire, watching them with predatory glares. They didn't like the tight alliance. He'd been right about having a major target on his back, but those six would be better off focusing on the

166

threats at their own fire. Aside from himself and Justin, he considered the other group the bigger threat. He meant to take their entire group out of the race. A line had been drawn.

Too bad Carlos and Lucy had come in last place on the compass challenge. They weren't as big a threat in his eyes, whereas Liam, Becky, Isaac, and Cassie were. Although, he wouldn't miss Carlos or Lucy either. He didn't know them well, so no trust or bond had been formed, and in some ways, he'd even prefer Miles to two unknowns, which was saying a lot.

Cooper thought about talking alliances and teams with Amity, Justin, Bria, and Sean, but since the show had a way of mixing contestants around, it seemed like wasted breath. Amity had finished eating, and he wanted some time alone with her, though he itched to tell her that she should eat more carbs. She'd eaten more salad than spaghetti, and soon they'd be reduced to backpacking food.

"Amity, would you like to go for a walk?" Cooper asked.

Amity ignored the grins of the contestants around the campfire. "Of course."

The others probably thought they were sneaking off to get it on, but Cooper wasn't even in that mindset. He still vowed not to be a playboy. If they got more intimate, he'd find a private way to go about it. He meant to lose the cameras sometime anyway—it would be fun.

Cooper led her into a patch of trees along Mesa Creek and found a grassy bank near a cascading waterfall to sit. "The water noise should drown out our conversation some," he said while plucking a few blades of grass, "so there's less chance we're overheard."

Amity hugged her legs to her chest and sat like a roly-poly beetle with her chin resting on her knees. "Did you mean what you said by the fire? Are we...*dating*?"

"I meant what I said. If that's what you want?"

"Yes, I do. I have a major crush on you, Caveman."

His lips curved up, probably into a geeky grin. "I have a major crush on you too."

"I like your eyes," she added suddenly. "They blend in with the trees. It's like you belong here." She looked over at her blue-blonde camerawoman and sighed. "I'd love a little privacy, but this will have to do." She uncurled from her ball and crawled over to him, bringing her lips slowly and seductively across his.

Everything about her undid him—her words, boldness, toned body, and soft, satiny skin. His hands roamed everywhere as he lowered her to the grass, climbing above her and deepening the kiss. His fingers traveled down to the edge of her running shorts, ready to slide into the fabric.

Amity moaned, breathing out, "*Easton*."

His heart stopped beating. With a masterful amount of control, he pulled away and rolled off her, catching his breath.

"I'm *so* sorry," she said, burying her face in her hands.

"It's okay, Amity." Cooper reached out and ran a hand up and down her arm. "I got a little carried away. I stopped because I wanted to shield your sexy body from America's eyes—that's all. Some other time, we'll sneak away."

Amity looked perplexed. "You're not upset?"

He shook his head, still mentally calming his body's hungry reaction. "Believe me, you can come on to me anytime you want. I'm a guy. I reacted a little too intensely. It's my fault." He furrowed his brows. Did she have an abusive ex or something? If so, he'd maim the guy. "*Why* would I be upset?"

"Um…" She sucked her bottom lip into her mouth. "Well, you pulled back when I called you Easton, so I thought I'd upset you."

"Oh," Cooper said, drawing back in surprise. After a moment of thought, he whispered, "Truthfully, I think it turned me on. There's something about *you* calling me that, I guess—at least when you're not mad at me anyway."

Amity sat up and studied him, running her hands across the grass, a pink glow still present on her cheeks. "What happened? Why don't you like your name?"

He stared at the waterfall that cascaded like a veil onto one of the rocks and kneaded the muscles in his forearm. "Yeah, okay. I guess we're dating now, so I can't exactly avoid this stuff."

Amity laughed softly. "Is that what it takes for you to open up? A first date?"

"Do you want me to tell you or not?"

Amity motioned a zipper movement across her lips, taming her smile. Her face grew serious when she could sense his genuine discomfort.

"This isn't exactly a story I like to tell, so please bear with me as I get through it." He cringed, feeling like a hundred people suddenly started to yell out his name. "Let's just say it's not a subject I'd bring up."

Amity reached for his hand and gave him a reassuring squeeze, running her fingers across his wrist.

"Here goes. Hopefully, I'll earn some sympathy points." He twisted the grass in his free hand as a distraction while he took a deep breath and tried to drown out the voices. "I wasn't exactly a popular kid in elementary school. I was the geeky-looking, tall-and-gangly kid. I wasn't into team sports, didn't get picked first for anything, you name it. I wasn't super smart either. I had all the dork labels without the good grades. In short, I was a total loser in most kids' eyes."

Amity's warm expression settled inside him, earning his trust.

"So," Cooper continued, clearing his throat, "I avoided other kids. That's when I began to use a compass so I could disappear. You see, in Colorado, the woods are the perfect way to escape the neighborhood." Amity massaged his arm with her fingernails, and his eyes fastened to hers, urging him on. "And at recess, I went for the safety of the fence lines behind the trees. I played with my compass because I had no one to play with."

She continued running her fingertips across his sculpted forearm, the warmth in her eyes branding him. "A group of the popular kids caught on. At first, they tried insults like 'Easton should go East,' which just sounded lame. It wasn't very creative, and it didn't catch. So eventually, they started this chant. East...on, Freaks...ton, Go east, Freaks...ton. Also, dumb and unoriginal. It didn't stick either, but," he said with a sigh, "the nickname did. They started calling me Freaks*ton*, with this uptick in emphasis at the end.

"For days upon days, they just didn't let up on chanting Freaks*ton* as loudly as they could until the sound of it was seared into my nightmares. Believe it or not, it stuck through middle school until the jerks that started it moved on to other targets."

He sighed again, hating the memories. "So when I went into high school, I started filling out on those get-to-know-you forms that I wanted the teachers to call me Cooper. The nickname dropped off. After that, I couldn't stand the sound of my first name. It became a trigger after four years of solid teasing. When I hear Eas*ton*..." He flinched. "I hear a hundred voices saying Freaks*ton* instead."

Amity looked at him sympathetically. "Kids can be so mean."

"Yeah." Cooper chuckled dryly. "And the worst part was, I *really* liked playing with other kids. I'm a total people person, always have been." He squeezed her fingers, throwing the blades of grass from his hand into the stream. "Anyway, my high school years were way better, and my job now—I love it. I don't ever want to do anything else."

"I'm sorry." She hugged his hand to her chest and took a deep breath before forcing out, "*Cooper*."

Amity's soft voice saying his last name echoed in his ears, and to his surprise, he felt like he'd been punched in the gut.

"Sorry, feels weird saying Cooper," she continued, "but I won't call you by your first name anymore. I shouldn't have, but I didn't know the whole story, of course, and well, you *really* pissed me off during that fire challenge." She wrung her hands around his wrist. "Did I say something wrong?"

He cupped her cheek, rubbing his fingers tenderly across her satin skin, loving that he was finally allowed to do so. How should he explain? He always seemed to screw up their conversations. "This might sound weird, but please don't call me Cooper."

He felt her body jolt, and she shied away from his hand.

With a loud exhale, Cooper said, "Sorry, I never seem to say the right things around you. Just know that I want to." He smiled uncomfortably. Ugh, feelings, but this was what came with commitment. He *could* do this. He looked into her beautiful brown eyes and went for it. "I actually like it when you call me…" He paused and closed his eyes, choking out, "*Easton*. It's sort of intimate or something like it's reserved just for you. When you called me Cooper just now, well, for some reason, it just felt wrong."

Her face lit up, beaming like he'd just asked her to marry him or something.

Whew, he must have explained it all right then.

"Okay, then I'll call you Easton." Her smile broadened. "I wish I could kiss you, but we seem to lose control. That's probably a good thing, though. Means we won't struggle in that department."

"No." He laughed and eyed her meaningfully. "We won't."

Amity leaned toward him, her features turning sultry. "We should definitely lose the cameras sometime—outrun them."

She flashed a challenging look at the blue-blonde woman, who smirked in return. Amity's eyes drifted down to his lap. "I can't wait to see *all* of you."

Cooper grinned, loving her forward nature. It gave him the confidence he desperately needed. "You won't be disappointed." He wasn't half as perfect as the creature sitting before him, but as long as she wanted him, that's all that mattered. "Believe me, I feel the same as you times ten."

Amity bounced up on her knees, like the ball of energy she seemed to be, and leaned even closer to him. "I know this is off-topic, but you are being *so* open and honest right now; I feel like I need to ask everything I can while the iron's hot." She continued rambling, "And since I can't kiss you…it's a good time to talk…so can I ask you one other thing? And maybe try not to get mad…because it would make me mad if you asked me this."

Cooper tried to process all of her words and shrugged. "Sure, go ahead. What do you want to know?" He paused and scrunched his features before adding, "My relationship history or something?"

She tilted her head. "That's not what I was thinking, but if you want to go there."

"No," he said quickly. "No, no. I'm sorry I brought it up. Stupid new relationship thing to do. I just assumed you'd go there." He smirked at her. "By the way, I probably shouldn't let you in on this secret, but not much makes me mad. As long as the people I love are safe, I'm pretty easygoing."

"Oh, well, good then." Amity moved into a crisscross-applesauce position and avoided his eyes.

"*What?*" he groaned after a few seconds. "Come on, Amity. You have me in suspense here."

The words flew out of her mouth so quickly that he had to listen carefully to hear them over the steady rumble of the waterfall. "I was wondering if your business was going under."

Cooper looked at her sharply.

"I mean…" Amity stammered, brushing her hands across her thighs. "Why do you need the money?" She closed her eyes. "Oh, I'm stupid. Why can't I keep my mouth shut? I shouldn't ask you that. Not when I just got you to date me."

He shouldn't be surprised—he wanted to know her motivations as well, but she'd cleverly avoided his questions so far. Did he trust her enough to reveal his true motivation? What if they broke up, and she used it against him? The other contestants would know just how desperate he was to win the money.

He reached out and held her hand, squeezing it reassuringly. "I think I've revealed enough today."

"You don't trust me?" she guessed.

"Can you say that you fully trust me?"

"I don't really have anything to hide, but I'll admit that I trust you to keep me physically safe more than emotionally."

Cooper let out a soft chuckle. "Ah yep, emotional safety. We're definitely in a relationship." He kissed her temple, stood up, and lifted her up with one arm. "Come on. We'd better get back to camp." With a wink, he added, "People will get ideas about what we're up to out here."

Seventeen

"Hey, Hollywood." She felt a pair of hands shake her shoulders. "Your boyfriend's worried about you."

Amity twisted around like a worm, stretching her sore muscles, and sucked in an unwelcome breath of moist tent air. She missed real beds or, at a minimum, the semi-comfortable cot from the first night. And she missed heating and cooling systems, the sweaty dampness inside the stuffy bag enveloping her like a confined sauna. In the middle of the night, she froze, and in the morning, she baked. Camping really sucked.

Squinting her eyes against the bright sunlight seeping in through the mesh fabric, she made out Bria's face illuminated by the rays, a nasty burn framing her nose and upper cheeks.

"Why's he worried?" Amity grumbled. She heard the scraping of titanium breakfast plates, and her nostrils registered the faint smell of bacon mixed with campfire smoke.

"'Cause you're gonna miss breakfast if you don't get your butt moving."

"Can you tell him to stuff some food into his pockets for me or something?" She rolled onto her chest, yawning widely, and flopped an arm over her eyes to block out the light. It had taken her forever to fall asleep while she'd pondered the events of the past three days and, in all truth, the intense feelings she had for Easton.

"No," Bria said, poking at her shoulder, "you're in my alliance too, and I can't have you wimping out on granola. Let's get some eggs and bacon in you. I'll warn ya—you've only got so much time this morning. The directors are even more hyper than usual about us getting equipped with all the mini cameras and sound boxes. They'll pounce on ya before you're even allowed to eat—or pee, for that matter. Damned annoying."

Amity sat up and unzipped the bag, scowling at the onslaught of cold air. She wrapped herself in her heavy purple coat, pulled her scrappy hair into a miniature ponytail, and grabbed her small makeup case, taking out a slender, foldout mirror.

Raising an eyebrow, Bria folded her arms across her chest. "Really, Hollywood?"

"What?" Amity asked with a grin, touching up a few mosquito bites with a light layer of foundation. "I have a boyfriend now, and there's no reason not to look good." She narrowed her eyes at her reflection. "Well, as good as possible without a shower and real mirror anyway."

Responding with a humph, Bria shook her head and turned to leave.

"Bria," Amity said before she could zip open the tent door to escape. "Here." She threw her a tiny bottle of sunscreen.

"That's okay, Hollywood. I don't want any favors. Hate owing people."

"Oh, for heaven's sake, use it." Amity rolled her eyes. "We're in an alliance. You don't owe me anything. Anyway, I'm not the type that keeps score."

"Just the type with money?"

Amity froze, her pink lip gloss clenched between her

fingers. "I guess I deserve that. I gave quite a first impression, didn't I?" She met Bria's eyes. "It's true. I really didn't come here for the money." Letting out a wistful sigh, she added, "But it would be nice."

"Why *are* you here?" Bria wiped a dollop of sunscreen across her cheekbones and wrinkled her nose. "This shit smells like coconuts."

Laughing, Amity brought her hand to her mouth. "Oh no, you can't smell nice."

"I feel like I'm waking up at a damn girly sleepover."

"Oooooo." Amity clapped her hands together. "Can I do your makeup?"

"Hell no!" Bria shouted and threw up her hands. "Look, Hollywood, just be careful. Your boyfriend *is* here for the money. Don't get too attached. I just don't want to watch you give up the win for some stupid crush. Not that I want you to win either," she added meaningfully, "because I plan to, but still, I'd rather race against you at the end than Becky or Cassie."

"I'm not giving up. I'm here for an adventure, and I intend to have one—as long as possible." She shot Bria a pointed look. "Besides, if I help Easton win, why can't I win too?"

"Girl, this show is likely going to force you to choose. If you aren't partners with Cooper at the end, would you let him win the money with someone else? Because I've been watching ya, and I don't believe you've got millions."

"How would you know?"

Bria threw the sunscreen back to her and started ticking off points on her fingers while she spoke. "You value relation-ships, you're resourceful, you stand up for people, you work hard, you're unselfish, you don't like owing people for favors…" She pointed at Amity. "That one is a dead giveaway. People who don't have much to give don't like to owe people. I know because I'm one of them."

Amity hadn't expected what basically turned out to be a string of compliments. "Okay, let's say you're right?" She jutted out her chin. "What's your point?"

Bria unzipped the tent door and reached for her trail shoes, talking over her shoulder. "My point is—don't give Cooper more than you receive. I like him too, but I'd hate to see ya get hurt in the end. This bit about the race being about romance is garbage. It's about creating television-worthy drama, and they're giving away two million dollars to do it."

"Bria," Amity said before she could step out. "Can we trade digits at the end of this? Stay in touch? You're different than most people I know."

Bria grunted. "Yeah, sure, why not? But I'm waiting until you're done crying over Cooper before I text back."

"Wait."

Bria sighed. "What, Hollywood?"

"You really think Easton will dump me?"

A tight frown formed on Bria's lips. "No, I think you'll dump him, but not because you want to." She stepped out and zipped the tent door closed. "Hurry up, Hollywood," she yelled through the mesh. "There's not much time left to eat before we're due on the mats."

Not because she wanted to. What did Bria mean by that? Then, it occurred to her—this was a race for riches *or* romance. Had Easton just proposed a relationship to her because he thought he needed one to win the money? The thought had occurred to her before, but she'd glossed over it. Perhaps he expected some sick twist at the end where he only had a chance at the cash if he feigned love? Amity wrapped her arms around her middle, feeling sick to her stomach. Was she about to get burned?

∼

THERE WAS DEFINITELY SOMETHING WRONG. Here he was, trying to make sure Amity got a full, healthy breakfast in her before they were reduced to backpacking food, and instead, he'd already screwed up somehow. Did she think he was being bossy, or controlling, or what? Dating was such a headache. It was less than a day into their 'relationship,' and she already didn't want to talk to him.

"You going to tell me what's up?" Cooper asked, watching her dab at the scrambled eggs on her plate.

With an animated cough, Amity fanned her hand through the smoke that curled in the wind. "I hate smelling like camp-fire all the time."

"Yeah, I believe it, but that's not what your problem is." Cooper opened his mouth to continue but quickly snapped it shut as he noticed Becky listening intently. Cursing, he scooted his camping chair closer and dropped his voice to a whisper. "Amity, we've got to be on the mats in five minutes. If you've got something to say to me, then say it."

"It's nothing." Amity stood up and headed toward the trash can. He wondered if she realized this was the last time luxuries like cleanup crews would be present. "Just nervous about the next leg," she said over her shoulder.

Cooper didn't buy it. There was something else bothering her. Why didn't she just spit it out? How was he supposed to succeed if he didn't even know what he'd done wrong? He braced his hands behind his head and fumed out a breath. Forget it! He wasn't going to beg. She could take him or leave him just the way he was.

He flung his body out of the chair, grabbed his full pack as instructed by the crew, and headed for the mats. It was back-packing time—what a relief—as long as he could be with Amity. As much as Cooper vowed that he wouldn't change for her, he couldn't focus without her by his side.

He stood across from a glowering Becky and sent her

provoking grins in return. If the directors played by the previous rules, it was the men's turn to choose first, and given his and Becky's first-place finish in the last leg, that *should* mean he could select Amity. Yet, an uneasy feeling stirred in his gut. It felt too simple.

"Good morning, contestants," Alex boomed out. "It's another clear blue sky today in the Cascades. As you've probably guessed, we're moving into the backpacking segment of our race. Each day will be unique. You may have to switch partners or complete challenges on a whim.

"For day one, you'll start at the red X on your maps and end at the blue X. A list of required tasks for the day will be handed out. The first team to finish gets an advantage for the next leg. Advantages will be critical in order to remain in the race. There will be no more crew support for eating or sleeping. Supplies in your packs will be refreshed as deemed necessary by the directors, and campfires are now prohibited until otherwise noted.

"It's the male team member's turn to go first, and *yes*," Alex emphasized as he smiled and nodded at the contestants, "we will honor that."

Cooper let out his breath, gripping the back of his neck and rolling his shoulders. Finally, a lucky break.

"Happy, Cooper?"

"Very happy, Alex."

The host chuckled. "We shall see."

Oh shit, Cooper thought, what now? He tightened his jaw, waiting for the twist.

"Becky," Alex quipped, shifting his eyes to her, "who would you choose first?"

Through stiff lips, Becky said, "Well, Alex, I don't think anyone would believe me if I didn't admit that I'm planning to choose Liam. I feel like that's a loaded question."

Alex nodded, fastening on a smile. "Yes, unfortunately for

both you and Cooper, you don't get to choose first. Today, we're starting with the lowest finishing team and working up."

"That's bull," Bria shouted.

"What?" Justin yelled. "That *is* bull."

Miles grinned greedily like he'd just been given a Christmas present.

Jade smiled and glanced at Isaac.

"That's crap, Alex," Becky threw in. "*Completely* unfair."

"Stupid," Liam said, throwing his hands over his cowboy hat. "Why bother to win a leg if there's no benefit?"

Sean shrugged, looking at Cassie.

Kim shifted slightly but contained her reaction.

Amity's hand flew over her mouth. Her eyes sought his, wide as a squirrel caught by headlights.

"It'll be okay," Cooper mouthed to her, hiding the gut-wrenching twist inside his stomach that made him feel like he wanted to puke. How could he win over Amity if he wasn't even with her? This show was the most unfair, dumb thing he'd ever done in his life. He'd be lucky to leave with either the money or the girl.

Amity nibbled on the corner of her mouth, her wispy pony-tail swishing around as she tried to assess the row of men and guess how things would shake out. Good luck with that. There was no telling what went through people's heads. Whatever happened, he'd find a way to get both of them through to the next leg.

"I see we have some mixed feelings here," Alex finally said after the cameras caught their various reactions. "Even though we're throwing this curveball at you today, I can promise that coming in first will matter greatly for the remainder of the race. Advantages *will* go to first place."

Yeah, right, Cooper thought—they threw a curveball every

minute. The key was just not to come in last and get eliminated.

"Miles and Jade," Alex continued, "since you came in just before the eliminated team, you'll select first. Miles, you're up, followed by Jade."

A cold sweat broke over Cooper's brow. He removed his cap to wipe his forehead. If that guy chose Amity again, he'd lose it. He tightened his fist but imagined his feet staying in place.

Miles grinned mischievously, running a hand through his trimmed black hair. He'd developed a sunburn on his pale skin over the past few days, and Cooper hoped it hurt like hell. Miles looked back and forth between Amity and Becky. Cooper squinted his eyes menacingly, ready to tell the guy he'd pull him down the trail by the tip of his goatee if he threatened Amity's position in the race, but to his surprise, Miles said, "Becky," with an arrogant grin.

Cooper released his breath and watched Becky's eyes shoot open, her hardened face losing its tinted glow. Too bad for her, but he loved it. Becky was a tough competitor, and Cooper respected her, but he wanted her eliminated.

"Becky?" Alex asked. "Your thoughts?"

"Miles better not slow me down," Becky forced out, her voice laced with venom. She glanced at Liam, who nodded reassuringly.

Were they a couple too? Cooper hadn't put much thought into relationships versus alliances. Relationships were stronger and much more dangerous. Of course, that would make him and Amity the biggest threat, but it seemed they now had company. Clearly, other contestants were more than friends.

With a shy smile, Jade selected Isaac. Cooper sensed a crush there on Jade's part, at least, which was fine by him. Amity liked Isaac too, and he didn't want competition to win her over.

Sean was up next, and surprisingly, he selected Cassie. Cooper was shocked as he thought Sean had been slowly gravitating toward their side.

"Sean?" Alex prompted. "Why Cassie?"

"Cassie's a fierce competitor," Sean responded, "and she's dope."

"Cassie?" Alex motioned his hand toward her. "Your thoughts on Sean?"

Cassie cocked her head to the side. "I don't know yet, Alex. We'll see if a surfer can keep up on land."

Sean grinned at her. "Don't worry. I'll keep up."

Bria was up next, and she selected Justin, thank god. Finally, someone who had the sense to keep the alliance together. Bria was extremely smart, and it probably helped that she didn't seem to be pining after anyone.

Due to the order in which people had been selected, Liam was up next, and Cooper's pulse quickened. Liam had two choices—Amity or Kim.

With a smug look flashed directly at him, Liam said, "I'll take Cooper's girlfriend."

Cooper felt like the wind had gotten knocked out of him. He took deep breaths, trying to recover, and straightened into a rigid stance. Before long, he curled his fists and stared Liam down like a jungle cat, completely unintimidated by Liam's hard glare in return. He would pay for this.

"Just for clarification, Liam," Alex said with a touch of amusement in his voice, "you mean Amity, correct?"

Liam tore his eyes away from Cooper and looked at the host. "Yes, Alex."

"Amity?" Alex asked. "How do you feel about Liam as a partner?"

Amity rocked back and forth, fidgeting with the hem of her purple tank top. "Obviously, Alex, there are alliances now, and we're not in one. I think Liam's a nice guy, but I can't trust him."

She thinks Liam's a nice guy? Amity might as well walk up and knock him directly in the gut. Liam was even worse than Miles because he was outright competition for the race—and for his girl.

Alex continued questioning her. "Can you trust Cooper?"

"A hundred percent," Amity said without hesitation. Well, that was better, at least, and a very interesting comment, given their discussion by the stream last night. "Liam made a big mistake," she continued, "because I'm not here for the money." His mouth fell open. What was she doing? The less information she revealed, the better. "And I fully intend to make sure that Easton wins it. I'm a terrible person to select as a partner." She shrugged. "Because I really don't care if I get eliminated."

Cooper finally caught on. Amity was trying to make herself an unappealing choice in the future, but she was trying too hard.

Alex grinned like Amity's spiel was a wonderful load of screen-worthy crap, which, of course, it was. That made him nervous. *Was* she here for the cameras? How long before he didn't provide any benefit to her screen time, and she tossed him aside?

"Liam, your thoughts?" the host asked, snapping Cooper back to attention.

A hint of a smile touched Liam's lips. "Amity's full of it. I don't care how much money she has. She's here for attention, at the very least, which will keep her fighting to stay in it. I call bull on her sacrificing her race for Cooper."

The host turned his head. "Amity?"

Amity flashed a brilliant smile and glared Liam down. "You're not so sure, are you, cowboy? I've got you sweating under that designer hat."

"Darlin'," Liam drawled out, "you're going to be the one

sweating when I take your boyfriend out, and no one is there to bail you out of all the challenges."

Amity pinched her lips together, her hands in tight fists. "I take it back, Alex," she spat, her head swiveling around to meet the host's eyes. "Liam's not a nice guy." She twisted back toward Liam. "Maybe don't piss off the woman running the next leg with you. I will *not* forget that comment."

Liam laughed, shaking his head, while Miles' face hardened. Miles probably regretted selecting Becky, as again, the drama surrounded Amity. The camera crew continued to eat up the scene with the zoom lenses.

So caught up in the drama himself, Cooper almost forgot that his own partner was yet to be announced. He'd be partnered with Kim automatically since they were the only two left.

"Cooper, how do you feel about Kim as a partner?" Alex asked.

"Great," Cooper said. "I think leaving her to be partners with me was a huge mistake by the other men."

Amity folded her arms across her chest and looked away, probably as jealous as he was by her initial praise of Liam, but she had nothing to worry about. He couldn't focus on another woman if he tried.

Alex moved along the line of women, handing them a combined map and task list before shuffling over to the men and having them draw for colors. Cooper selected blue and noted that Liam pulled out orange and Justin green. Cooper meant to keep track of his alliance and enemies.

Alex returned to the center mat, clapping his hands together. "Okay, contestants, as you've probably noticed, a map for each team and a checklist of required tasks along the way have been handed to the women. You must complete every task on the list and cross the finish line as a team *together*. The cameras will catch any cheating. Uncompleted tasks will result in a two-hour time penalty.

"We're starting this leg of the race even, meaning you'll all leave at the same time, and advantages from here on out will only go to the first-place team. Also, keep in mind that the last-place team will receive a disadvantage. This leg is not an instant elimination."

Alex looked at McKenzie for the go-ahead to start. "...3...2...1," he counted down and pointed at the contestants to begin.

Cooper sprinted toward Amity, sideswiping as Liam jumped in front of him. He attempted to bypass Liam's block, but Liam reached out, firmly grabbing his arm.

"Hey," Cooper shouted while body-slamming into Liam's shoulder, "you're going to lose time if you don't let me talk to her."

Cooper plucked the cowboy hat off Liam's head with his free hand and tossed it in the dirt, distracting Liam enough to wrench his arm free. But just as he dived for freedom, Liam reached his foot out and swiped Cooper's feet out from under him.

Face in the dirt, Cooper scowled. He could not lose a pissing contest and appear weak, especially in front of Amity. He pressed up on his forearms, swiveling around on the ground and swiping Liam's feet out in return. Liam crashed down on his back with a loud grunt.

They both rolled over, facing one another, fuming, before standing up and charging like rams. With a solid collision, they fell and began tussling on the ground. Cooper's baseball cap flew off as he maneuvered to keep his arms free.

"Steer wrestler, dumbass," Liam said into Cooper's ear. "I'll have you pinned in minutes."

Cooper locked his arms on Liam's shoulder and yanked him off, then punched him hard in the arm and rolled away.

"High school wrestling team and rock climber. You'll never pin me, tumbleweed."

Slowly, they both stood up, covered in dirt. Deep breaths puffed in and out of their lungs while they glared, sizing each other up. Cooper realized they were an even match and watched a grin spread across Liam's face when he came to the same conclusion.

Liam brushed the dirt off his clothes, picked up his hat, and walked toward Amity, who studied the map and task list in her hands with scrunched-up brows. Cooper also snatched his hat off the ground, raking a hand through his rumpled hair and watching the dust fly out. He rubbed a sore spot on his elbow before replacing his beat-up cap.

It would be nice if Amity were even remotely worried about him. Stupid, he thought suddenly—she was exactly right to take in the information in case Liam took the map and tasks from her. Amity couldn't wrestle Liam—outrun him for sure—but not wrestle, which gave him an idea.

Cooper glanced at the other contestants, who were still looking at their maps. If Amity took off toward the first task, Liam would have to follow, giving them a lead.

"Amity," Cooper said urgently. "Do you know where the first task is?"

"Generally. There's actually only one task today." Amity sighed, eyeing his scrapes with what appeared to be annoyance. "Are you okay? I don't know why you guys are dumb enough to—"

"Don't worry about me, Princess." He motioned with his hand for her to take off and shouted, "Go."

"*What?*" she exclaimed.

"Go." He shooed her with another hand gesture. "As fast as you can."

Amity caught on and lifted her huge backpack off the ground, stumbling around. Cooper was afraid it might tip her over and started toward her but caught himself and stepped back. He didn't want to hurt her ego by running over to help in front of the other contestants. She could do it.

After rocking around while snapping the waist and shoulder straps in place, she blew him a kiss and sprinted north up the trail like a bullet, even with the weight on her back. She wouldn't be able to maintain that pace, but she'd get herself and Liam so far ahead it wouldn't matter.

"Giving us first place?" Liam asked, slugging Cooper in the shoulder as a return jab before he snapped on his pack and took off after Amity.

"I hope so," Cooper whispered to himself, rolling his newly injured arm in circles and walking over to Kim, who studied their map.

Bria and Justin came over to meet them.

"Idiot," Bria said to him.

Cooper nodded. "I know."

"We've got to get moving," Justin said. "These teams are an even mix. I don't think there's a weak link now. The directors know what they're doing."

Yeah, they sure did—producing a show that was going to make him lose his mind. Cooper could pretend that watching Amity run off with his strongest competitor wasn't a big deal, but he still felt as unsettled as he did face down in the dirt.

Eighteen

Amity's legs burned. The thirty-plus pounds on her back were not conducive to distance running.

"Dammit, Amity, let me see the map," Liam shouted. "Where did you put it?"

He'd been reaching for her pockets and grabbing at her pack for two miles. Honestly, she couldn't blame him. He had no idea where they were going or if she knew what she was doing.

But she did know. The map was straightforward, and the task was near the finish line for the day. The directors appeared to be going for a max-drama finish.

"Relax," she gasped between breaths, "we still have several miles before the task, and talking will wear us out."

They slowed a speed walk, weighed down by their supplies, and finally, after four miles in, Liam said, "That's it. I don't know why I didn't think of this before." He fisted his fingers through a loop on her backpack and pulled, adding testily into her ear, "Probably because you're a woman, and it's not polite."

Amity involuntarily jerked back, her feet skidding to an uneven stop on the dusty trail. Since she'd buckled her pack across her chest and around her waist, she couldn't go anywhere. "What the hell, Liam?" she yelled over her shoulder, flailing around, trying to free herself. "Easton's going to knock your face in when he hears about this."

"I doubt that," Liam said. "He should have known there'd be payback to his girl when he tackled me. I'm not letting you go until you give me the map, and I might just shake you around a bit while I'm at it."

Amity kicked the backside of her foot up and nailed Liam's groin with the solid heel of her shoe. "How about payback for Easton instead?" she shouted as he let go of her pack. She ran a few paces away and turned.

Liam buckled over with his hand on his balls, gasping for air. The weight of his pack sent him falling face-first into the dirt, his ivory cowboy hat askew.

After rolling around in pain, he crouched and pointed at her, yelling through clenched teeth, "That's got to be a violation of the rules. A man's nuts are off-limits."

"Oh, please." Amity put her hands on her hips, rolling her eyes. "You're not harmed enough that it's *impossible* for you to adequately finish the race. You should have been nicer to me earlier. Telling me, I need someone to bail me out of the challenges. What a stupid thing to say."

"Is that what you're raw about? *Honey*," he said roughly, "this is a competition, and your backcountry boy is way too willing to carry you along."

"Tell me something, Liam, because I really want to know." Amity dug her nails into her hips, relaxing her fingers when the pain irritated her cuts that were on the mend. "I'm here slowing down my hike so your country legs can keep up. We," she said while pointing back and forth between the two of them, "have to complete today's challenge together. Easton isn't here, and I'm just fine. What will it take for you and the rest of the contestants to believe that I can handle myself?"

"Nothing you do will change my opinion." Taking advantage of their pause, Liam took off his gaudy hat, looking much less impressive covered in soot, and wiped the sweat off his forehead with the hem of his preassigned maroon shirt. "You'll buckle. Somewhere along the way—you'll buckle."

Amity pushed her palm out, hissing through her teeth, "Fine, no more talking. It's pointless." She kicked a rock on the trail and watched it fly into a patch of wildflowers before turning back to the hike. "Gosh, I want to knock you out of this race, and to think that I thought you were nice in the beginning."

She sped up, hoping to get under Liam's skin as much as he'd gotten under hers. If she could make him pant for air like a tired puppy, then maybe she'd feel better; but after another mile, even Liam's labored breaths didn't appease her because she knew that he still believed her weak.

Hot blood pulsed through her veins, and when the sun rose further overhead, beads of sweat inevitably trickled into her eyes. Her running headbands were tucked in the side of her borrowed pink case, grouped securely with the only other items she actually owned—practical, affordable items that she used every day. She didn't need expensive sun hats or designer sunglasses. In truth, she didn't *need* a million dollars.

Amity needed to experience life. She needed—well, she didn't *need* Easton Cooper, but she sure as heck wanted him. Drowning out her hike, she closed her eyes and brought him to the forefront of her mind. The beautiful green color of his eyes blending in with the dark, rich colors of the forest. The passionate heat of his wet body against her ice-cold skin. The lopsided grin he'd given her this morning when she'd loaded up her plate with eggs and bacon. Gosh, she missed him. It was an odd feeling for a woman who had been on her own her entire adult life.

Her assumption this morning that he'd offered her a relationship purely for personal gain didn't make sense. He'd saved her in the woodchuck challenge and lost his time advantage. He'd made sure to run the compass challenge alongside her and offered her first place. He'd told her to run ahead today and leave him behind. And he'd made himself a huge target because their alliance appeared unbreakable.

Why had she questioned his motives? His actions said it all —Easton Cooper was a complete and total loyal sweetheart and the first guy she'd ever met that checked off every single box on her list. Who would have thought that a few days ago?

But now that she knew him better, there was no *way* she'd break up with him. That man was crazy if he thought he'd win their ridiculous bet. Amity wanted him, and she planned to fight for him. She had time to weasel her way into his heart, didn't she? Besides, if he got cold feet and broke it off first, she had a week in Colorado to change his mind.

For the next few miles, Amity felt as light as the hawks floating in the sky as she glided along the trail. She wasn't sure if it was because of her new goal to permanently win her man or because she was completely dehydrated. Lifting her head, she noticed a small stream—at least, that's what she thought it was, but her vision blurred a little.

"Amity," Liam choked out between breaths, "we need some water."

Oh, shoot! Now she *really* missed Easton. She didn't know how to pump water and admitting that to Liam would embarrass her beyond recovery. But she had to have water, even if that meant she'd make a fool of herself. She'd pass out otherwise.

"I agree," Amity huffed out, watching an orange batch of butterflies flutter up from the grass surrounding the stream. Smart little buggers—if she were a butterfly, that's just where she'd hang out. They even had a mountain view, though she supposed insects didn't care about that.

Amity unbuckled her pack, checking to make sure the camera equipment and soundbox were capturing the scene properly as instructed by the crew. Cool air rushed up her sweaty back as she dropped to her knees in front of the rippling water. She filled her palms, splashing the glacial-cold liquid across her flaming face and down her heat-stroked neck, repeatedly soaking her skin and shirt until she felt some relief.

Liam rummaged through his pack without a glance at her. He appeared so thirsty there was little chance he'd notice if she knew how to use a purifier or not. Copying his actions, she pulled out her own water bottle and pump. The contraption had a small, squishy handle like a turkey baster and a long, clear hose. All Liam did was drop the hose into the stream and hold the baster-like handle over his bottle, squeezing repeatedly; the purified water flowed directly into the bottle. With a relieved smile, Amity copied the simple process. No one would ever have to know she didn't have a clue.

With the bottles halfway full, both of them eagerly drained the contents before filling them again for the remaining miles. Her hand ached from the repetitive squeezing motion, but she'd take that ten times over hauling the heavy weight of water from the start line. Heck, she should take one of these purifier things in her running pack all the time.

"Is this enough water for the rest of the hike?" Liam asked, the irritation in his voice piqued. "Or do we need to fill the second bottle they gave us?"

Amity put away her purifier and water bottle, heaving on her heavy pack. "I guess I can fill you in. If you wanted to run back to your alliance, you already would have."

"I won't." He shook his head. "It's not to my advantage, so let's work together, okay? Short-term truce. Two heads are better than one."

Nodding, Amity pulled out the map.

"You put it in your cleavage?" Liam exclaimed, followed by a grumbled, "Well, that explains why I couldn't find it."

She pointed to where they were going. "Right here. We're supposed to hike to this blue X on the obsidian hills and complete a task on the PCT, so not even a side trail. It's a very straightforward eight miles. We've gone about five, so we only have three left."

Liam furrowed his brows. "You know this for sure?"

She nodded. "I'm good at estimating distance. I track my runs."

With a thoughtful look, Liam glanced north up the trail. "So then, how far ahead of them do you reckon we are?"

"Probably a mile or so." She shrugged, regretting the gesture as the pack's weight dug into her unseasoned shoulders. "We're moving out, but all of them are too. Since they're likely traveling in alliance groups, there will be some comfort in numbers, but they know a challenge is at the end, so they'll be high-tailing it anyway."

Appearing satisfied by her explanation, Liam stuffed his purifier and water bottle into his pack. "We'd better get going then. I don't want them to catch up."

Amity raised her eyebrows. "So, you're okay with ditching Becky? I didn't think you would be. It's why I hid the map."

"You didn't need to. I won't risk my race for her." He eyed Amity with a probing look. "When push comes to shove, your boyfriend won't either. You honestly think he'll risk a million dollars for you? I don't care what BS he's feeding you. A guy doesn't fall for a girl that fast."

Amity shrugged again, wincing at the pain. Easton's signature gesture was rubbing off on her, but the pain was not. "I guess I'll deal with that when and if it happens."

Accusingly, Liam said, "I thought you didn't care about the money." He raised his chin like he'd caught her in a lie.

"I don't really, but I do care if Easton puts me first."

Liam snickered. "I don't believe you. A million dollars is a lot of money."

To a certain degree, Liam was right. Who could honestly admit they didn't care about money? A million dollars could put her in a full-sized apartment and help her mom have a chance at retirement—and shoot, she could actually pay her bills. It would *really, really* help her out.

"Just as I'd hoped," Amity said, "no one, including you, has a clue what I want. What does it matter anyway? You won't trust what I say regardless."

"Good point. I actually find you incredibly hard to read."

Amity jerked back in surprise. Was she difficult for Easton to read too? She hoped so. That sounded like a girlfriend advantage.

"You'd better watch out," Liam continued. "Even though I think it'll come down to your boyfriend versus me at the end and whatever women we're partnered with, I still think you're a major threat. You're smarter than I thought this morning."

"What a compliment," Amity forced out. "You've got quite an ego."

Liam let loose a carefree chuckle, the pleasure of his tone grating at her ears. "Too bad Cooper claimed you first. You sure you wouldn't rather have a strapping cowboy? I can be really nice to a girl when she's mine."

Amity scoffed, glancing over her shoulder. "*Very* sure."

He tipped his hat. "Okay, darlin', but you're missing out. There's a lot more man to me than that twiggy mountain guide you're with."

She eyed him in challenge. "He's going to beat you, you know? In the end. If it's you versus him, you'll lose."

The side of Liam's mouth quirked up. "You think he can best me, do you?" He nodded once. "We'll see. Tell him I'm looking forward to it."

"Oh, and by the way," Amity continued, scrunching her

nose at a determined black bug buzzing around her hair, "you've got way bigger problems than Easton. Becky won't sacrifice anything for you. Pay attention to the way she looks into your eyes. She doesn't *care*. You did choose the wrong girl."

Again, Liam chuckled, but Amity sensed that this time, he tried to mask his unease. She'd gotten to him.

A few seconds later, Liam drawled out, "Problem there, Amity? I can lend a hand. Squash the sucker for you—in return for a pucker up?"

"Nope, I'm good. I can handle a few mosquitoes."

The way she flung her head around probably looked like a horse swishing its tail on Liam's ranch, but she didn't care. She swished her frizzy mess of hair with a huge smile on her face. Amity could not wait to help Easton burn Liam. The pleasant idea even made dealing with the forest bugs tolerable.

With renewed energy from her motivating thoughts, and probably more accurately, the hydration break, they took off and covered the remaining three miles quickly, power walking until Amity could see sparkling, black obsidian rocks come into view. The fifth-grade boy in the apartment across the hall from hers was obsessed with rockhounding, and though most of his collection was sandstone from the cliffs in Utah, he'd shown her a piece of obsidian. She knew it was volcanic glass with a shiny luster.

But seeing the hills covered naturally in the shimmering volcanic glass was a whole different experience than a single rock in a collection. Her eyes glossed in awe as she looked across a valley of sparkling black, like a fantasy world on a distant moon. Swallowing through a lump, she pretended her dad stood next to her, and to her surprise, Easton appeared in her illusion next to them.

"Amity," Liam said, cutting her pleasant moment short, "there's Alex. Looks like the task."

Nervous butterflies danced in her belly, reminding her of the ones she'd just seen flutter around at the stream. Hopefully, this challenge was something she could handle. She'd like to think she was getting more rugged, but experience didn't happen overnight.

As they approached, Alex pointed to a large gray mat in front of him. Multiple cameras surrounded the central mat, while six different colored stations with additional cameras appeared to be set up around the perimeter for the various teams. There were huge wooden blocks all over the ground in each team's color, with a central table to build something in the middle of their task area.

"Amity, Liam," Alex boomed out jovially as they stepped onto the mat, "you are the first team to arrive. You can begin the task immediately. One team member will complete the puzzle. The other must remain on the side mat in your chosen color's area and can assist verbally. If the team member sitting out *moves* off their mat, then your team incurs a thirty-minute time penalty. If the team member sitting out *touches* a block, then your team incurs the entire two-hour time penalty required for not completing a task. Keep in mind that the partner who completes today's task must rotate and sit out tomorrow."

Bouncing up on her toes, Amity glanced at Liam. "This is a perfect task for me. I'm *really* good at puzzles."

"Don't care." Liam shook his head and pointed at the stations. "This is a physical challenge."

"But you don't understand how many puzzles I've done with my mom. We—"

"Those blocks are probably forty to fifty pounds apiece. I lift hay bales daily, darlin'. I doubt you can even pick some of those up. Besides, you'd chip those fancy polished fingernails of yours."

Amity puffed some air out through her nose. Her fingernails were already chipped to bits anyway. The cuts on her hands were more concerning, not that she'd mention those to him. "I'm sure I can manage it," she said, "just not as fast as you, but that's not what concerns me—the puzzle does. You're *not* thinking this through. What happened to two heads being better than one?"

Liam smirked, shaking his head. "I said that to get a look at the map, and it worked. I'm not about to let a woman boss me around. The puzzle won't be hard, and for the record, that whiny voice you use on your boyfriend doesn't work on me."

"It doesn't work on him either," Amity grumbled, "but it matters less when it doesn't work on him because he's smarter than you."

Liam flashed her a look. "Alex, I'll do the task, and Amity will watch."

"Very well," Alex said, "but keep in mind, the team member who touches the first block of your chosen team's color must complete the task."

"Liam," Amity said fiercely as they walked toward the orange station, "what about the task tomorrow? What if it's something like the fire challenge and I bomb—"

"Enough," Liam said roughly. "The directors aren't likely to have two heavy-lifting tasks in a row. Just sit down and relax."

Amity huffed in astonishment. "Even though it looks physical, this is a brain challenge. Tomorrow is likely some other impossible outdoor thing—probably right up your alley. Why take a risk when *this* I know I can do?"

What was the point in continuing to argue? Amity could run past him and touch a block, but that just seemed so first-grade. Instead, she plopped down on the ugly orange viewing mat that reminded her of the color of her stuffy sleeping bag. A few jagged rocks stuck into her backside from underneath the hot plastic. She scowled, watching Liam throw his backpack and annoying cowboy hat down next to her. Should she steal a critical item from his pack, like the flint or water purifier?

No, she wasn't that evil—yet. Plus, he'd retaliate, which sucked because right now, all she wanted to do was get back at him.

Liam picked up a giant, rectangular orange block like it was as easy as lifting an oversized feather pillow and threw it onto their matching orange platform. One after another, he carried and tossed the heavy, multi-shaped blocks. She had to admit the Montana country cowboy looked mouthwateringly hot, carrying blocks that looked like hay bales around, but not as sexy as Easton when his rippling muscles chopped through a solid chunk of wood.

Five minutes in, Liam took off his maroon shirt, using it to wipe the sweat off his hands and forehead, and damn! He was ripped with an eight-pack so smokin' hot she had to fan herself a little with her hand, but still, nothing about Liam would ever measure up to her man. She perked up, thinking of Easton. He would be here soon, and she could stare at his lean muscles instead while imagining what his calloused-back-country hands could do to her body. Maybe he'd take his shirt off too?

Amity sighed longingly and returned her focus to the challenge, squinting her eyes to study the pieces. The blocks were in various L-shapes, zigzags, and rectangles that appeared to slide together.

"Liam," Amity shouted, "I think it forms a square."

"I can see that," he said, gesturing a hand toward the pieces, "but which ones go on the bottom."

"That is the point of a *puzzle*. You have to figure it out." She received a killer glare but had no sympathy for him. "Just start sliding the pieces together to form a square on the bottom, and the rest should fall into place."

Liam stood there, staring at the blocks with a blank look on his face.

Amity glanced at the trail and yelled, "Do something. The others will be here soon."

Liam tossed his shirt aside and began to powerhouse the orange blocks around, quickly losing his temper and flinging a few of them so hard they fell off the platform. Like that would help! Amity dug her teeth into her lip and swayed back and forth on her bottom like a rocking horse, looking around at the glittering hills.

She should have been the one to do this task. She and her mom had spent countless hours building puzzles over the years. Every Friday night, they'd go to Goodwill and purchase used games, puzzles, toys, DVDs, and CDs for weekend entertainment. It always amazed her the wide variety of cultural items that were donated and the knowledge she'd gained from building, using, and watching materials from all over the world. This challenge would be a cinch for her, but from down here, where she couldn't really see, there was nothing she could do.

"Not so much like hay bales now, are they?" she threw out facetiously.

"What do you want me to say?" Liam sat on a zigzag block and took a swig from a pre-provided water bottle. It appeared that the directors wouldn't allow the contestants to actually pass out from dehydration. "You were right. I should have listened to you."

Amity stood up. "Yes, that is exactly what I want you to say because we'll probably be stuck with each other tomorrow, and you need to park your ego. We're running out of time." She pointed at the flat-rock valley beside her. "Why don't you bring the blocks down here so I can help you?"

"Amity, I'm not carrying all these damn blocks off the platform and then back up again."

"I have to be able to see. I'll instruct you on how to build the puzzle from down here on the obsidian, and then you can carry each block back up to the platform and build it in reverse. There is nothing that says which blocks have to be on the bottom. We'll just flip it as you dismantle it."

Liam stared at the blocks, scratching his head. "Shit. We'll have to go with that. I'll never figure this out myself."

Just as Liam began to throw their blocks back down on the rocks, Amity could see the other contestants approaching, racing toward the central mat in a huge, stampeding herd.

Locating Easton's tall form, relief flooded through her, and she hopped up on the balls of her feet, waiting for him like a giddy teenager. Her stomach fluttered with nerves. If he knew how much she wanted him, he'd probably run the other way. Play it cool, she thought, but then as Easton approached, he flashed her a wicked smile, and her emotions broke free. She was ready to bear-hug him unconscious.

Nineteen

"You have to come to the mat," Amity yelled. "I can't step off of it."

Cooper raced to the mat like the lovesick fool he was and tucked her into his arms. Standing on tiptoes, she wrapped her tiny limbs so fiercely around his neck that it felt like she hadn't seen him in months. A protective instinct flooded through him, but it was beyond that now. He was a goner. Whatever was bothering her this morning seemed to have faded, thank god. He'd spent eight miles worrying she'd connect with Liam and leave him brokenhearted.

"I hate being away from you," Cooper whispered into her ear. He found her lips, covering them in fresh salty sweat, but she didn't seem to mind. In fact, she gripped him tighter like she couldn't get enough of him. Dominic first, he thought, and slowly pulled away. "I've got to start the task."

Amity peeked around him, sucked her bottom lip into her mouth, and nibbled on the flesh, completely oblivious to the fact that he was turned on. He imagined tangling his tongue with hers and dipped his head.

"You're having Kim sit out?"

"Huh?" Cooper froze before reaching her lips, shifting his

gaze to her eyes. "Oh yeah, that's the plan." He shook his head, furious with himself. "Shoot, I need to go."

Amity frowned at him.

"Sorry," he said abruptly, gripping the back of his neck, "it's just that I've got to win this race. I *can't* get eliminated."

"So you've said. And I want to help you—wait, Easton." She reached for him as he backed away.

"Amity, really, I've got to—"

"Please just listen," she said, her voice stern. "This is important for the task. You'll need to be good at puzzles. Are you?"

Hesitating, he assessed the size and shape of the large, blue blocks that were spread out across the jagged obsidian rocks. There were *a lot* of pieces. "Not particularly."

"If Kim is, have her do the task. The puzzle is *hard*. Liam wouldn't let me because the blocks are heavy, but I don't think he can, so we're going to build it down here where I can see and reverse it."

Kim agreed that he should do the task, as the pieces looked very heavy, but maybe they were wrong. He sucked at puzzles, algorithms, and all the other brainteaser stuff. He'd been average at best in math and would never be an analytical genius. Dominic did all the finance and marketing for their business while he planned the routes and packed the gear.

"Let me guess," he said, "you're good at puzzles?"

She grinned, a sheepish glow on her cheeks. "Yes, they're a strength of mine."

"Somehow, that doesn't surprise me," he grumbled. "Prep school or something, right?"

"Um…"

"Never mind explaining now. I've got to get moving." He looked for Kim, who walked up to them tentatively. "Are you good at puzzles?"

With a thoughtful nod, Kim said, "I'm decent at them."

"Alex," Cooper yelled, "Kim and I would like to switch places. You said that was allowed, right?"

"Until one of you touches a block," Alex shouted back, "it's allowed."

Cooper walked quickly to the blue mat, which fortunately wasn't far from Amity's orange one. He made sure Kim started the task before glancing back at Amity, who beamed at him like it was Christmas morning.

"What?" he asked curiously. "You look pleased."

"It's just that you listened to me."

"Brownie points for trusting my girl?" Cooper chuckled, his nerve endings on edge.

He shielded his strained expression from her, scanning the rocky black hills, and found that when his eyes returned, Amity continued to smile adoringly at him like he was her own personal miracle. Damn, if that didn't make his heart swell. It reminded him of—he lost his breath. Amity was looking at him like Chelsea looked at Dominic—like she *loved* him. An icy burst of adrenaline rushed through him, and he took a few desperate breaths.

"Are…you…okay?" Amity mouthed to him.

He pasted on a smile, nodding in return. It was too early for her to actually be in love with him, but he recognized that look, nonetheless. He'd dreamed about having a woman look at him like that, and the idea of living up to her expectations sent him into a panic. Would she be able to accept his lifestyle? Would he survive if she couldn't?

Cooper tugged on his shirt collar, ripping the fabric a little more as Kim struggled with their bulky, blue blocks. He yelled words of encouragement to her while she powered through, lifting each awkward piece onto their platform.

Amity's confident voice funneled into his ears as she stood on her mat, pointing and instructing Liam on how to slide their blocks into place. Amity wasn't kidding—she was good at puzzles. Their giant orange square was over halfway formed already, and unlike everyone else, the pieces appeared to fit together correctly; however, their puzzle was down on the ground, and Liam would have to reassemble it up on the platform. That would take a good chunk of time.

The minutes ticked by, and Kim started constructing their puzzle, making quick progress, but she kept having to pull pieces out that didn't fit and try again. Amity had finished instructing Liam on how to build their puzzle, and he knew Liam would make quick work of reassembling their blocks up on the platform. Most of the other teams weren't far behind.

The task remained intense, yet he felt confident since Kim was almost halfway done and appeared to have correctly formed the bottom of their square. Sean and Cassie struggled the most with Sean on the puzzle, but this wasn't an elimination, so Sean would be around longer regardless. Still, the directors had to be playing some kind of angle for the viewing audience. Coming in last would likely cost them.

Several minutes later, Amity and Liam finished in first, followed shortly thereafter by Kim and himself in second. As he understood it, only first and last place mattered now, and his girl had gotten first. If only her advantage could be to choose him as her next partner, but he didn't think they'd get that lucky.

Standing on a gray hosting platform with the title of the race painted across it in bright-multicolored letters, Alex turned toward the largest camera. "Amity and Liam came in first, so they will have an advantage during one of the tasks tomorrow—"

Cooper released a ragged breath, took off his cap, and wiped the sweat off his brow with his shirtsleeve, trying to relax his muscles. What was his problem? He should be at ease now that Amity had an advantage—it would kill him if she were eliminated—yet he tried to battle the underlying feeling that maybe he shouldn't have helped her come in first. He shouldn't even be thinking it. She'd warned him about the difficulty of the puzzle and saved him from coming in last.

Yet, Cooper still felt like he should have sacrificed everything to make sure *he* came in first. He should have taken off down the trail *with* Amity, not let her run off to take the first-place win for herself. What was he thinking? Dominic could *die*. From now on, he had to take every advantage for himself that he could.

The race wouldn't affect whether Amity remained in a relationship with him anyway. She already admitted that she didn't need the money and seemed to understand how desperately he did. Heck, she'd even gone as far as to say she'd help him take the win.

He glanced at her with pride. Amity was a keeper—smart, selfless, and sexy as hell. Whatever happened, he'd call her the minute his cell phone was back in his hand and make sure she was on the first flight to Colorado for that weeklong camping trip.

"As a reminder," Alex bellowed, flashing a cheeky grin, "team members who completed the puzzle today must sit out of tomorrow's individual task—"

At least he and Amity would be doing the task tomorrow at the same time. He still meant to help her out when he could, but never again when he'd lose his edge. There weren't enough people left to provide a buffer for making irrational decisions.

"Sean and Cassie," Alex continued, "will be required to complete a sudden death challenge against the team that comes in last tomorrow. Unless Sean and Cassie finish in last place again, in which case, they will automatically be eliminated."

Relieved looks crossed the faces of the contestants. Cooper fist-bumped Justin. Finally, a fair and understandable way to eliminate teams—one that was less based on luck—and both he and Amity had strong partners this time. Perhaps it wouldn't matter that he'd just given up a chance for an advantage.

Alex went on to reiterate that they would no longer receive staff support for meals or sleeping but that staff tents were nearby for emergencies, and no changes would be made to filming hours—cameras would be rolling twenty-four hours a day. After the host finally finished his announcements, Cooper grabbed his pack off the rocks, watching Amity wobble around as she lifted hers. Before she could snap it on, he snagged the strap and slung it across his shoulder to the side of his own.

Amity raised her eyebrows, the corner of her mouth lifting.

"We don't have to go far." Cooper pointed to the top of a rocky hill. "No reason for you to deal with strapping it on." He peeled back the edge of her purple tank top with his fingertips and frowned. "Your shoulders look pretty raw."

"Running with a heavy backpack does that—to normal people anyway," she trailed off in a mumble. "You must have seasoned your shoulders into steel rods."

Cooper chuckled, taking Amity's hand to lead her up the hill, their current alliance trailing alongside—Bria, Justin, and Kim. With a smirk, he watched Amity adorably flail around on the loose rocks while he held a firm hand to steady her.

Amity slipped, gripping his hand so tight he lost the blood flow to his fingers. "Gosh, I miss sidewalks. I mean, I love it out here—don't get me wrong." She smiled up at him. "But I don't have much experience on loose terrain. The funny thing is—I'm really good at balancing on beams and floats and things like that." With a thoughtful look, she shrugged. "Guess it's a different skill set."

"I suppose so. Seems we complement each other well."

"Awe, what a sweet thing to say."

Caught off guard, Cooper grinned. "Sure, sweet. If I can

inadvertently make you happy, then I've got this relationship thing made."

He noticed Goatee Man with a camera balanced on his shoulder, focusing a lens on them from a cliff edge. Though the pining smile on his face probably made him look like an infatuated nitwit, Amity's adoring smiles in return made him so hopeful she'd be in it for the long haul that he pushed the cameras out of his mind. Maybe he'd finally found the one. Daring to hope, he planned to go into full boyfriend mode tonight. Any break from the race was a chance to solidify his relationship and walk away with more than just the money.

"So, I know for sure you're good at balancing, except on rocks," Cooper said. "And you've told me a little about your running and swimming background, but we got sidetracked before you could explain why you're a puzzle whiz. Private school or something? I don't even know where someone learns that sort of thing?"

Amity tightened her grip on his hand. "Um, no, not private school. Actually, by spending time with my mom."

"Really? That's neat."

"Yeah, my mom and I do puzzles and games, watch movies, listen to music—things like that when we both have an evening off from work. We go shopping for them at…um… on Fridays, so we have a new set of things to look forward to each weekend."

"Wow, shopping every Friday—that sounds fun," Cooper attempted to add with fake enthusiasm while hiding his panic-stricken face. Rolling his shoulders back, he opened his mouth to draw in more air. How could he afford to please her? Hopefully, she made a decent salary on her own.

Bria narrowed her eyes, glaring at Amity.

"Yes, the shopping part can be fun," Amity said, "but the best part is the quality time with my mom. I wouldn't trade it for the world."

Cooper relaxed his shoulders. Amity cared about people with every action she took and every word she said. She wasn't after money—he could sense it—but what would happen when she found out he wasn't into the expensive lifestyle?

"So," he said casually, "do you have any big shows coming up after the race?"

Amity wrinkled her forehead. "What?"

"You know, for your fashion line?"

"Oh." She looked at the rocks, clearing her throat. "I said I was in fashion, not that I had a fashion line, but yes, I'll be right back to work when I get home. Look," she added suddenly, "we can see the mountains from the tent sites. What is that? The South Sister?"

"Yes." Cooper nodded while noting her quick change of subject. Bria wasn't the only one who could read people. Perhaps Amity was afraid that her lifestyle would scare him off? Which he'd admit was true. They'd work it out somehow, but only if she could take him as he was. For now, he'd let it go. He pointed his index finger toward the horizon. "And you can see the edge of the North Sister behind it. The Middle Sister is hidden between them from this angle. Boy, would I like to climb them someday. All of them."

"I'm not sure I like that idea," Amity said.

"Why?"

She stared at the mountains, nibbling on her lip.

"Oh," Cooper said, nodding in understanding. "You think I'll be in danger?"

Having her worried about him, he could deal with. Not being allowed to climb, he could not. His pulse sped at the thought of her concern for him, and he dropped their packs, lifting her into his arms. His heart rate accelerated as she tangled her legs around him.

She wiggled against him to get a better grip, and he sucked

in a sharp breath. "Damn, Amity," he whispered hoarsely, "I don't need to teach you how to climb me."

She laughed.

Bria made a gagging sound, and she, Justin, and Kim walked away.

Naturally, Amity was still on their previous debate while his mind was on devouring her lips. "It's just that I don't want you to get hurt." Her mouth tightened. "I'm not a fan of heights to begin with…cliff edges are dangerous…they have to be…so I just don't get it."

Cooper squeezed her bottom with his palms, rubbing playfully against her and listening to her gasp. "Don't worry, Princess," he whispered, planting a few reassuring kisses by her ear. "I'm a *very* good climber. I promise to come home alive and in one piece."

He molded his lips to hers before she could protest further. Sexy little moans came out of her throat, and she rocked against him, roughly gripping the back of his neck. A burst of heat shot through his core. Yearning to slip inside her, he fantasized about gliding in and out of her soft flesh with each rocking motion of her hips until he had to pull away, gasping for air.

"Wow," she said in a throaty whisper. She ran the tip of her tongue along her glistening pink lips, and his eyes followed. Her mouth lifted into a seductive grin.

"You're torturing me," he said roughly.

"I know," she whispered. Her eyes darted to his mouth. "I want more."

Cooper groaned and moved in to kiss her, sucking her soft lower lip into his mouth. Amity whimpered, digging her nails into his shoulder blades. My god, their chemistry. He'd never had a woman turn him on like this.

A loud rumbling sound blasted off to his side, and he quickly broke their kiss, turning his body instinctively to shield Amity. Looking for danger, he prepared his legs to bolt for safety, bending his knees, but he quickly realized that the rockslide occurred below Goatee Man. The cameraman was fine, but he'd ruined the moment.

Cooper frowned. "I want privacy."

With a soft intake of breath and a nod, Amity said, "Same."

He reluctantly lowered her onto the rocks. Would they ever be alone? Releasing his breath, he looked at the position of the sun. The directors said they'd be taking them aside one at a time for interviews, so there were only a few hours of useable daylight left. "We'd better get our tents set."

He gripped Amity's hand and led her the rest of the way up the hill, taking deep breaths to relax his over-excited body. They arrived at a simple set of rectangular dirt-covered areas surrounded by rocks meant for backpacking tents. He dumped their packs on the ground next to a log, feeling at home. Finally, he thought, *real* camping.

"This is it?" Amity scrunched up her nose. "Dirt and more rocks?"

"And, as you pointed out, a killer view of the mountains." Cooper looked out across the valley. A shallow stream about twelve feet across ran through a wide, grassy canyon with a view of the snow-capped mountains in the distance. It didn't get much better than this. Cooper clapped his hands together, a little annoyed that he'd used the same motion as Alex Bandon. "Let's get some water pumped."

"Seriously, Cooper," Bria grumbled. "Tone it down. We finally have a break from our host."

Cooper grinned. "Yeah, sorry. Hope Bandon's clapping habit doesn't rub off on me." He placed his hand on Amity's back. "Do you and Bria want to purify some water while I set up camp?"

"Sure." Amity bounced up on her toes and gave him a

quick peck on the cheek, flashing him a confident smile. "I learned how to pump water today, so I like that plan."

"Did you?" Cooper nodded, hiding his frown. Though he wanted her safe and independent in the woods, he hated the image of Liam teaching her anything. "Good to hear."

"Should we get some wood for the fire too?"

Cooper shook his head. "We can't have a fire out here, sweetheart." He reached for her hands, surveying her cuts gently with his hands, guilt lining his features. "Are these healing?"

～

Amity's insides melted at his use of a term of endearment for her—his first. Easton's concern for her hands was sweet too, and the tentative hitch in his voice had her smiling. "Yes, they're fine. Got the bandages changed this morning." She rubbed his palms, which also had cuts and scrapes, probably from the woodchuck challenge. "I remember Alex saying something about campfires. Why can't we have one?"

Easton cleared his throat. "Alex said campfires won't be allowed until advised by the crew. They likely have to enforce that because of the potential for forest fires. With equipment and a full safety crew, they can monitor fires at a group camp in the backcountry for a TV show, but with us mostly on our own out here right now—no way."

"Then how will we cook our food?" Amity asked, her voice rising in pitch. Before he could answer, she shook her head. "Never mind. I'm sure you'll show me. Talking about it will stress me out. Bria," she added, "ready to pump some water?"

"More than." Bria uncrossed her arms and headed to her pack for supplies. "Let's get a move on, Hollywood. Justin, Kim, Cooper—we need your water bottles."

Amity trotted down the rocky hill with multiple water

bottles in her hands and a purifier hose strung around her neck, trying not to slip on the loose rocks. She somehow reached the picturesque stream without falling and sat on the grass.

"So," Bria said, dropping her purifier's hose into the crystal-clear water, "you gonna tell me the real story behind your mastery of puzzles? Whatcha trying to hide from Cooper?"

"Oh." Amity looked behind her, locating the boys in a group of weathered pines up on the hill, well out of hearing distance. "Yeah." She cleared her throat. "I mean...what do you mean?"

"Save the lies for your boyfriend, Hollywood. You want a friend? Then spill it."

With a long-winded sigh, Amity dropped her purifier's hose into the stream just down from Bria's and met her eyes. "Okay, fine." She took a deep breath and blurted out, "I'm dirt poor," already feeling better about admitting it to someone. "I'm here to travel and get out of the rut my life has become."

Before Amity lost her nerve, she quickly continued, "Sometimes my mom and I shop on Fridays at Goodwill. That's where we pick up puzzles, games, DVDs, clothes, and such, and they are *never* brand new. My fashion job," she rushed out, making quote marks with her fingers, "is in retail where I make mediocre, at best, commissions." Pausing, she put up a finger. "Oh, and while I'm at it, I live in a *tiny*, one-room apartment with a bathroom that's as tight as an airplane lavatory, and I *drive*"—she made quote marks with her fingers again—"a beat-up car that I can't afford."

Amity had only signed up for the show because she barely had enough money to pay for a tank of gas, let alone a plane ticket. Her fifteen-year-old Volkswagen Jetta couldn't sputter more than a few blocks—it needed oil, license plate stickers, and new brake rotors, whatever those were.

She'd almost given up her travel dream entirely when a

cop fined her for illegal parking at a resort complex. He hadn't been sympathetic that her mother worked in the building. Flirting with the cop hadn't worked either—not that she was any good at schmoozing. Still, she had to try since the parking ticket would set her back another week. With the cost of bills, repairs, and stupid tickets like that, she'd had to focus on just doing what it took to get by.

Then, she'd seen a flyer in the window of a Palm Springs shop to try out in L.A. for an action-adventure reality show. After hitching a ride with her boss who was on her way to a shoddy fashion show, running twenty blocks, and standing in line for the interview, here she was—finally—on an all-expense-paid trip to an undisclosed location to have an adventure, just like she'd promised her dad. Never in a million years did she think that adventure would include a too-good-to-be-true, sweet and thoughtful guy—and she could lose him. What would he say when he found out?

Bria started laughing. "So what?"

"*So what?*"

"Yeah, so what. There's no shame in any of that. Quite frankly, it makes me like ya even more, and I really don't want to because I have to beat you at the end of all this." After a moment of silence, Bria added quietly, "The viewing audience will like you too."

"Really?" Amity jolted up on her knees while she continued to squeeze the pump. "You think? I've been assuming I'd be a villain on TV."

"No, you telling me this on camera for America to hear will make you a fan favorite. Hopefully, I'll be one too." Bria winked. "Anyway, I'm glad you told me because it helps me understand you better. Trying to figure you out has been giving me a headache. You're far too capable to fit the 'wealthy, spoiled girl who has had everything handed to her' stereotype. I've had to work my tail end off in life too. I recognize the signs." After filling one bottle with filtered water, Bria twisted the lid on, set it aside, and grabbed another. "So, why are ya lying to Cooper? You think he'll care?"

"No…yes…it's just that at the start of the race, I didn't want to throw a pity party, and now that the assumption I have money is out there, I just can't admit that I don't." Amity sighed. "I've had some boyfriends leave me in the past because I didn't have enough money to go out and do the things they wanted to do, and it's different telling a guy I like that I'm not very successful versus telling a friend."

Bria's face dipped into a frown. "Success is relative, Amity. You don't strike me as the type that thinks a fortune will make you happy. Besides, you're selling Cooper short."

Amity shook her head. "But *he's* here for the money."

"You don't know why, though, just like you don't know why I'm here. Careful about making assumptions." Bria screwed the lid on another bottle. "Think about the assumptions Cooper is making. He thinks that you've come from money based on your clothes, makeup, lackluster outdoor skills, and whatever else is going on in that boy's head, but he's way off."

"You're right, Bria," Amity whispered, nodding. "And a good person—you're real."

Bria made a humph noise. "I suppose—real with the people that I like anyway. So now that I know you're a hard-working gal, how about getting your lazy hands pumping harder again so we can fill this water? I want some food. I'm starving."

"Yeah, if I'm even able to walk back up that hill. Everything hurts. I went so fast today with that pack on that I have ruts in my shoulders." Amity closed her eyes in dread and groaned before continuing, "And we have to sleep on those air pads… in those stuffy sleeping bags…in the cold…again tonight…and again tomorrow night…and again the night after that."

"Okay, stop, right there. You're ruining your tough girl image for me. I even slipped up and called you Amity a moment ago." Bria snorted. "Try basic training, Hollywood."

Amity shook her head. "Hell no. Not *ever*!"

And they laughed, still laughing as they approached the camp with handfuls of water bottles while Bria told Amity entertaining stories from her time in the barracks. Easton looked at them curiously. He probably hadn't expected a hard-core Army girl and a so-called prissy princess to hit it off.

Justin and Kim were lighting what looked like miniature Bunsen burners with tiny stove grates on top—the back-packing stoves, she assumed.

Easton walked over to her and gestured behind him with his thumb. "I pitched both of our tents. Hope you don't mind."

Amity blinked before looking at the tent setup with wide eyes.

He put out his hand as if to comfort her. "I wasn't trying to imply that you couldn't do it," he rushed out. "I just like doing this stuff, and I didn't think you would. Please don't be mad."

"She's not," Bria threw in. "You don't have to grovel."

Easton shot Bria a look.

"No, Bria's right," Amity said. "I love that you put the tent up for me, actually. It's just that—there's no cover. I'm going to freeze." She didn't really want to admit to everyone, especially Easton, that she'd be scared out of her wits if she was exposed to the dark night by herself, with only an open mesh cover over her. She hadn't forgotten Easton's comment about the bears, and these tents were nothing like the large base camp tents full of people. It would be just her and the elements. After a long pause, she asked, "Can't I sleep with you?"

"Uh." Easton chuckled. "Amity, they packed us one-man tents. Hence there's only space for *one* man or *wo*man." He pulled off his tattered baseball cap and scratched his head while analyzing the scene. "Tell you what. I'll move our tents together, so the zipper doors join on one side. That way, you can at least kind of snuggle up to me. How does that sound?"

Amity pecked a quick kiss on his cheek. "Much better."

"Good." Easton nodded. "I think I'm learning how to put a smile on your face."

Twenty

The sun set, revealing a mostly full moon and the light twinkle of thousands of stars in the night sky. Cooper had spent the daylight hours showing Amity how to use a backpacking stove to fix freeze-dried food, so she'd be fully prepared if they got separated during a future challenge. That meant revisiting the use of her flint to light the stove, which fortunately was full of laughs and lighthearted comments this time around.

After washing their dishes with biodegradable soap, they completed their daily interviews, put on warm clothes, and, looking for privacy, sat on a log away from the tent sites—not that they had solitude anyway with the cameras bearing down on them, but at least it was quiet.

"I want you." Amity pressed slow and sensual pecks across his lips. Becoming more urgent, she fully molded her mouth to his, running her hands up the back of his neck, before gripping his untidy hair in her fists and continuing to kiss him.

Jolts like fire woke every nerve ending in his body. "By that," he said, hearing the raspy sound of his voice, "you mean make out or more than that?"

"I mean, I want you in the tent tonight. *All* of you. If I'm going to be uncomfortable, I might as well enjoy my man."

"Damn, Amity," he whispered, "you have *no* idea what I'd be willing to do to make love to you, but I don't have any protection. I don't think the show packed condoms in the side pockets of our packs. I'm pretty sure you would have found them during the fire challenge. You went through the contents enough times."

She smacked him on the shoulder. "Hey."

He flashed her a grin, loving that they could joke about it now.

"We don't need condoms anyway. I've got an IUD, so I won't get pregnant, and I haven't been with anyone for a long time, so you don't have to worry about other things."

Cooper was losing his willpower, but he cared too much about her to get caught on film. "I'm clean too, but Amity, what about the other contestants and the cameras? Princess, tent walls are *not* soundproof."

"Then quietly," she said seductively into his ear. "You're a mountain god. Can't you make serene love to me? Come on, you let the girl do all the seducing?"

"Yes. In today's world," he said, laughing quietly, "for sure yes, and rightfully so. I have your official permission, correct?"

Amity held up her hand like she was in a courtroom. "Yes, kind sir, you do. I give you my full permission."

She swung her leg around, straddling him like a flexible yoga guru, and began to rock her hips against his groin in the same way that made him come undone on the rocky hill. She kissed him with a passionate hunger so urgent that he couldn't think. He moved in harmony with her until he was ready to come in his pants.

"Amity, I have…to…stop…"

Breathless, they broke apart and touched noses, making intimate contact with their eyes. A sassy smile spread across her strawberry-flavored lips, the lingering taste still tormenting his tongue. What was that stuff anyway? Lip gloss? How the hell had she gotten that out here? And when did she put it on?

Amity had him mesmerized and hooked. She made him feel like he could climb Everest without oxygen. Deep down, he knew she was the one, and if she went home to California, it would destroy him. But she was so incredibly gorgeous and smart—and completely out of his league. How would he convince her to stay? Why would she pick him over the hundreds of other guys out there?

"Are you okay?" she asked.

Cooper blinked his eyes, not realizing he'd vise-gripped her arms. "Sorry," he said quickly, loosening his grip.

Amity smiled warmly at him. "It's okay." She reached up and ran her fingertips along his jaw before swirling them on his lips. "You can hold me as tight as you want."

Cooper closed his eyes and drew her index finger into his mouth, sucking on the tip. Her sweet, little gasp drove him mad and tugged on his heart. He had a one-week tour in Colorado to convince her that she couldn't live without him, right? He could figure out how to glamp the hell out of her experience. He'd continue to pitch tents, carry her bag, or whatever it took to please her.

"Can we promise each other we'll do the week-long Colorado camping trip regardless of our bet? No matter who breaks up with who?"

"What?" she asked, tensing up. "Why are you talking about breaking up?"

"Oh, no, I'm not," he said quickly. Nice, Cooper, you moron. Could he be any denser with his wording? "Quite the opposite, in fact. I just want reassurance that I'll have more time with you after the race."

Amity's body relaxed, and she began to explore his

shoulder muscles with her hands. "Oh, that's a cute thing to be thinking."

"There I go, being cute again."

"Easton," she said, beaming at him like he was some sort of miracle and she'd won the lottery. His name on her lips with that vehement smile permanently etched its way into his heart, while each touch of her fingertips made him fall even deeper under her spell. "You don't need to worry about that," she continued. "The Colorado trip was the bet if you break up with me, so we can have our trip whenever you want because I'm *never* breaking up with you."

Sucking in a shocked breath, he said, "That's a promise you just made to me, Amity. Don't forget you said it." He couldn't believe the intensity in his voice, the hope and possession laced in his words. Was he in love with her? Shit! If so, he'd never recover if he lost her, especially if he moved inside of her.

His panic bubbled up. What would happen when he couldn't afford her lifestyle? What would happen when he left on his tours, and she was without her man for five nights in a row? Would he be worth waiting for?

"Maybe we should—"

"Easton," she whispered again, sending another jolt through him, "are you thinking with your head or your heart?"

"My head," he stated simply.

"Then don't think."

Cooper tightened his hold on her. He could not resist living in the moment, even if he fell in love with her and left this damn show with a broken heart. "Fine, but just remember..." He took her mouth and was met with a satisfying moan. "I warned you."

Her soft lips quirked into a grin. "It's not a warning when I want the same thing."

Amity truly did seem to want him, and he was a fool if he didn't do everything in his power to strengthen his hold on her heart. "Hang on just a minute," he said. "I'll be right back." He picked her up, placed her gently on the log, and ran to grab the sleeping bag out of his tent. Returning, he whispered in her ear, "Now we run."

"What?" she asked, looking around in confusion.

"Do you want to have sex in front of America?"

"Um, no."

"Then hold my hand and run."

Together, they took off like track athletes on an obstacle course, holding hands while somehow maintaining their balance. He guided her down the rocks, across the valley, and into the forest. Goatee Man and the blue-blonde-haired camerawoman raced after them, but with the weight of the heavy cameras on their shoulders, they quickly fell behind.

After fifteen minutes of skilled aversion through the forest using the moonlight to see their way, Cooper led them to a secluded location in the trees. "They shouldn't be able to find us. If they had more time, maybe, but those camera folk can't match my off-trail skills."

Amity laughed softly. "Oh, so that's the benefit of having an outdoorsy guy. I was beginning to wonder."

"There are a lot of benefits." He placed her hand on his bicep and listened to the adorable sound of her continued laughter.

Locating an area covered with a soft bed of pine needles, Cooper unzipped his dark blue, down sleeping bag, wishing he could own a dozen himself, and threw it folded open like a blanket onto the ground. The props crew had bought the finest camping gear on the market for the show, probably to advertise it ten times over.

"Mine's orange," Amity said with a pouty frown. "But not

a pretty blood orange like the dress I wore. This ugly rust-colored—"

Cooper silenced her with a kiss, not at all interested in talking about the color of their gear, and hesitated before taking things further. "You really want this, right? Because, Amity, if I touch you, I may never recover if you leave."

She looked at him curiously. "I'm in this for keeps." Nodding firmly, she said, "Yes, I really want this. I want you, permanently. So please?"

Cooper took in a quick breath, feeling his heart skip a beat. "Do you have any idea what *permanently* means?" he said fiercely. "What happens when I show up on your doorstep in California and ask you to come home with me?"

The bewildered look on her face almost made him backtrack. He hated being weak, but he wanted her more than he'd ever wanted anything.

Amity slid her arm through his and began to nibble on his ear. "Easton," she whispered, seeming to fully understand the hold his first name coming from her lips had over him. She tugged his arm gently toward the sleeping bag, and he followed, falling onto the fabric and pulling her into his arms. "I make commitments," she continued, running her fingers down the firm muscles in his arm, "and I keep them. I *am* falling for you. I want this, and I want *you*."

Her words warmed him, and he relaxed his rigid pose. Amity was being very transparent with him on purpose, clearly catching the drift of his uneasy thoughts. She intended to stay, and he believed her, but they still had to make it work in the real world. It hardly mattered, he decided, if she left him after this, he probably wouldn't recover whether they made love or not.

"Just don't forget your promise to me, Princess."

With an incredulous look, she said, "I didn't actually promise anything because I don't need to. However, when you take me backpacking or camping or whatever, because we *will* be together, and I'll have to compromise and do the things you like too—I want a *two*-man tent."

A pleased grin spread across his face, and Cooper allowed himself to believe her words. He braced an arm on the ground and traced her collarbone with his fingertip. "I've got absolutely no problem with that. I'll sleep with you whenever and wherever you want, and I'll carry a truckload of girly shit into the woods if it makes you happy."

"Good." Amity smiled, nodding. "Now that we have that settled." Placing a hand on his chest, she flipped over, so she was on top and took off her coat, shirt, and sports bra. She sucked in a quick breath as the ice-cold evening air rushed up her torso. "You'll warm me up, right?" she asked while he stared speechless at the most beautiful woman he'd ever seen.

In awe, he reached up and ran his fingers over her peaked nipples as she gasped and arched her back in the moonlight. Grinding against him, she leaned her chest toward his lips, letting him suck one of the perfect pink peaks into his mouth.

Cooper loved her boldness. Her taking charge allowed him the confidence to lose himself completely to her. He devoured her nipple with his mouth, sucking and swiping his tongue across the tip while tantalizing the other with his fingers. Her sultry moans had him throbbing in his pants, and with each hungry pulse of his cock, she rubbed enticingly against him.

A few desperate groans escaped his throat, and with a satisfied smile, she shimmied her body down his legs before stripping off his hiking pants and boxers and moving seductively toward his groin.

"Amity," he cautioned, "I'm probably a little salty from all the sweat."

"Don't care." While holding his eyes, she added, "What's the problem with a little salt? At least I know my man gets out and exercises."

Without a second thought, she slid her breasts against his bare skin and took his full, raging hard-on into her mouth. He groaned and did everything in his power not to come on the spot as her soft lips slid up and down his tender skin. She placed her hands on his backside, encouraging him to move his hips in rhythm with her mouth.

Overcome, his breath came out in desperate, shallow pants. "Amity," he tried to force out, "I'm going to…"

Amity held his eyes with a provocative glance, continuing to slide her lips up and down the length of him. He allowed himself to drown in the flood of sensations while she climbed into his soul with every glance. He'd never felt connected to a woman like this.

"Amity, please," he said in a gravelly voice, trying to guide her body back up with his hands.

She slid up to him, and together they removed her leggings. Cooper smirked as he tossed aside her lacy pink underwear, having a flashback to their first day where she'd flailed around in that orange satin dress, never guessing that he'd be removing the sexy thong she wore beneath it only days later.

Cooper brought his mouth to hers, roaming his hands down the sleek skin of her back to her soft, round bottom, grabbing both cheeks in his palms and pressing against her. He was being reckless, letting his heart loose, but he wanted to take things all the way.

"*Easton*," Amity begged, her tone raw and vulnerable. She held his eyes with a look of pure trust and adoration, and he knew he was in love with her. There was no going back.

But he couldn't tell her yet. She'd panic if she knew he'd fallen in love with her in such a short time—no matter what enamored looks she sent his way.

"Please," she continued, tugging eagerly at his arms, "I want you inside me."

Cooper maneuvered Amity beneath him on the sleeping bag and slid inside her, proceeding to make love until they came together with her shouting his name and tightening her already permanent hold on his heart.

Within seconds, the cold air rushed against his sweaty skin. Amity would freeze if he didn't do something fast. Pulling her against him, he grabbed the down fabric with his free hand, enveloped both sides of the sleeping bag around them, and zipped it closed. It was a little tight, but she fit against him so nicely that it seemed to work.

"That was incredible," she breathed. "I'm addicted to you."

Cooper chuckled. "I mean to keep you that way."

He'd keep her addicted and hope that one day she'd fall in love with him too. Claiming her swollen lips, he prolonged the return to reality until he had to abruptly break free of their kiss.

"What is it?" Amity asked, a worried furrow between her brows while she looked around at the trees.

Cooper smirked. "Not a bear, Princess. I was teasing you about that. Bears are very uncommon here."

He hated that he'd had to ruin the moment but saw when it dawned on her that there were voices in the distance. She turned to scan the woods while he reached for their clothes. He piled them up next to the sleeping bag and listened to hear the direction of the voices over the soft rustling of evergreen tree branches in the light breeze.

"Bummer." Amity relaxed against him, seeming to conclude that wildlife wasn't going to eat her but that their time was up. She began to run her hand through his unruly hair. "I like your style now, by the way. During the first challenge, everything about you drove me nuts. It still does—just in a totally different way. Turns out, you're exactly my type."

"I'm glad." He grinned, taking one last mental picture of her after-sex glow, memorizing the incredible, soft set of lips that just claimed him in the most intimate way. "If you're nuts about me, then I'm doing something right."

"You are. I'm absolutely crazy about you. Earlier today, I was thinking about what a gem I have for a boyfriend."

"Yeah, okay." He chuckled. "Keep telling yourself that, and maybe I've got a chance. When you're with a woman that looks like a goddess, the compliments help." He unzipped the bag, stood up, and took her hand to lift her from the sleeping bag. "They're coming. We'd better get dressed."

She started shivering, having lost both her cover and his body heat.

"I'll warm you up in the tent," he said in response while quickly getting dressed. "It'll be a little chilly until then."

"O-Okay," Amity said, her teeth chattering while she, too, slid on her clothes. She looked flushed, happy, and cold. "I don't mind fr-freezing if I get to do things like that with you. Tonight was p-perfect."

"I think I'll look forward to anything with you for the rest of my life. You just ruined other women for me."

Shoot, did he just say the rest of his life?

But thankfully, Amity laughed. "I'm not going to complain about that."

Well, she *had* said she wanted him permanently earlier, but he didn't know how much she considered the weight of her words. He meant them and hoped to hell she did too. He tucked the sleeping bag under his arm and took her hand, leading her back toward camp. After weaving through a few sets of trees, Goatee Man smirked and nodded to him as they walked past.

With a grin in return, Cooper said, "Told you I'd find a way to ditch you."

The cameraman chuckled silently while Amity asked, "You talk to your stalker?"

"Yeah, he's all right," Cooper said, shrugging. "He's just doing his job."

She shook her head. "You're such a people person. It's cute."

"Okay," he said, feeling increasingly content. "I've learned cute is a good thing. Glad to hear it."

Amity was the true gem between them. If he could keep this up, he might come out of this hellish experience a very lucky man. He gripped her hand tighter and continued to lead the way.

Twenty-One

Amity cringed while rappelling, or rather falling, down the side of a huge rock face, bursts of adrenaline pumping through her veins. Having sat out of the puzzle challenge the previous day, both she and Easton had to compete. The task required them to rappel the cliff twice, with Amity and Liam's advantage from their prior win being that she only had to scale the daunting face once.

Easton held her hand the whole way down, saying all the right things to put her at ease. Amity realized she'd just experienced what he did for a living, only with the added benefit of boyfriend treatment; however, watching Easton's masterful talent was the only positive thing about hanging suspended in midair. Though the scene surely made good television, she hated everything about it, which probably meant that rock climbing was out for her too. A runner through and through, she wanted her feet on the ground.

"We should wait for the other teams," Liam said as she reached for her gear. "I'd rather stay with the pack today. If it comes to it, we can beat them in a foot race."

Easton nodded in agreement and then scrambled back up to complete his second round. Waiting for the other teams meant that her and Liam's advantage didn't really matter, but she chose not to argue with either of them, as being alone with Liam and away from Easton sounded miserable. Still, it made her wonder. What was Liam's motive? To help out Becky? Or did he mean to sabotage someone? And Easton's motive? Did he want her to help him with the tasks? Hopefully, it was the right decision.

Cupping her hand over her eyes, she located Easton's firm backside. Watching him scale the cliff for a second time was nothing short of amazing. He flew down the rocks, looking like a spindly mountaineer version of a spider. She covered her mouth with her hand in both awe and fear. How did he do that so fast without killing himself?

Her stomach filled with butterflies as a flood of delicious memories from their scandalous disappearance in the forest ran through her mind. Gosh, she loved him. Without question, she was head over heels. Locking eyes with him in every intimate way had brought her feelings to an unbreakable level. She'd do anything for him, and it scared her. What if he was just after the money? She didn't think so based on his actions, but still, what if?

She puffed out a breath, furious with the direction her thoughts had taken, and readied herself for the ten-mile hike that was required to arrive at the finish line for the day.

Alex jumped up on his hosting platform. "You all are making it easy on me. I was going to make this announcement team by team as you left," he boomed out in his chipper voice, "but all of you leaving together should make for an exciting finish. And less bouncing around on the trail for me." He motioned his hand out toward the chopper he rode from point to point.

Shaking her head, Amity rolled her eyes, but she liked their host, so she laughed at his obnoxious comment anyway, peeking at Easton to share the moment. He'd been distant since the leg began, wearing an intent look on his face. Aside from his sweet treatment during the rappelling task, he was focused on winning. She shrugged when he didn't make eye contact and decided that if it was that important to him, she'd help him come in first.

"As a reminder," the host continued, "a team will be eliminated at the end of the day either by a sudden-death challenge or by Sean and Cassie coming in last place again. I recommend you give it your all because, in a couple of days, teams will get a short break at a designated camping area before the final challenges begin."

Amity sighed in relief at the thought of a much-needed break. The physical demand of the challenges and miles traveled were starting to make her feel like she'd entered an Ironman competition, although fortunately, they hadn't been required to swim or bike yet. She groaned at the thought. Would that be next? Her muscles ached, she still had cuts on her hands and feet, and she felt like a dirty, half-lifeless zombie. When she got to an ice-cold lake, she'd cleanse every inch of her skin without a complaint after miles of sweat and dirt in the summer mountain sun.

They set off in a herd, speed-walking through patches of trees and occasionally stopping for a task, all of them so far, a simple true-or-false question about the race. The rules stated they couldn't discuss their answers with the other teams, which was enforced by a crew member accepting and checking each team's answer on a whiteboard. If they answered correctly, their team raced on, while incorrect answers resulted in a five-minute penalty. So far, all the teams had gotten the correct answers, and they'd hiked on as a group.

About five miles in, they crossed a rocky stream bed where Amity heard a loud scream followed by a splash. Looking behind her, she saw Cassie clutching her ankle.

"I think we should keep moving," Easton said, glancing at both her and Kim while marching on.

"Becky," Liam shouted behind him. "Don't wait for her. She can't keep up with an injury."

"You're kidding," Sean yelled in return. "Bunch of douches."

Amity shrugged. Whatever, she thought, Cassie wasn't in any life danger. If Easton and Liam wanted to secure a win, fine by her. She'd never been a fan of Cassie anyway, but moments later, a shot of guilt hit her conscience—it wasn't fair to Sean—but someone had to go home.

Nine miles in, they came to the final task on the list, which turned out to be an opened-ended question differing from the true-false questions they'd received thus far.

"How many sandwich options were offered for lunch after the third challenge of the race?" the card read.

"Who the fuck cares?" Easton ground out. "That isn't even a relevant question about the race. Ask us how many packs of freeze-dried food were provided in our backpack, and I can tell you. Fifteen! That matters in case we get stranded in the middle of nowhere, but this is dumb as shit." He spiraled around suddenly, looking at Kim with a hopeful expression. "Do you know?"

Kim's face dropped into a disheartened frown, and she shook her head.

A male crew member standing to the side said, "Contestants, I must remind you to step onto your team's mat to discuss the task, or you'll automatically incur the penalty. This isn't an open debate."

"It doesn't matter anyway, Easton." Amity rubbed her hand soothingly across his arm. "We'll all get through this leg. Cassie and Sean won't be able to catch up."

"Yeah." He dug his fingers into his jaw. "But *first* gets an advantage, and this is trivial nonsense. At least keep the race a 'race.' This *task*," he said into the microphone attached to his shirt, "is for TV ratings. You just want to screw somebody over, don't you?" before adding in a grumble, "Wait to give an impossible question until the end of the leg to create senseless drama."

"You're the one creating it, jerkoff," Miles threw in. "Drawing attention to yourself? For your tour business?"

Easton flipped him the bird.

"Stupid," Bria agreed with a nod, glancing at Justin. "Do you know?"

"Contestants, I already reminded you—" the crew member began.

"Oh, shove it," Becky shouted at him. "We won't share the answer. Leave us be."

Amity smiled. It was the first time Becky had ever said anything she respected.

Justin ran his fingers down his shaggy red beard before shaking his head and locking eyes with Bria. "No. There was a big row of lunch bags. I grabbed one and moved on. Didn't give it a second thought."

Bria shrugged. "We'll all get it wrong, Cooper, and have a fair race to the finish. No one can do more than guess."

But Amity knew. She'd thought it odd at the time that so many sandwich options were offered for a simple lunch in the woods. Even through the tingles that danced in her stomach at brushing arms with Easton, she'd read all the labels on the bags, wondering if the show was concerned about dietary restrictions or if Hollywood expectations were just that posh. Turns out, it was a setup for drama—just like everything else.

Her emotions tangled. What should she do? Easton wanted to win the leg for an advantage, but they were a team. *Together*, they could win the race. Separate, they didn't have a chance. Alliances mattered. It was better to win the leg with Liam than let some other team take the win from them both.

Amity grabbed Liam's arm and dragged him over to their mat. She wrote 'nine' on their whiteboard.

Liam jerked his head back. "Are you sure?" he whispered.

"Very."

He laughed in amusement like he'd been handed a surprise birthday present. "I did say you were dangerous and smarter than I thought."

Ten minutes later, she and Liam crossed the finish line in first. Amity glanced around, taking in the crystal-clear lake at the edge of a rocky lava field. She didn't even know such a place could exist. Spinning in a circle while enjoying the fresh air, she waited for Easton to cross the line.

The minutes passed quickly, and Easton jogged across in third place with a huge scowl on his face.

Amity ran up to him and jumped into his arms. "Remember, we're a team," she whispered. "If you'd been in jeopardy, I'd never have run off without you. The advantage matters for us both."

He cracked a slight smile. "I'm not asking you to give up your race for me, Princess. I'm just pissed at their show tactics. Their ploys and rules are garbage. I *hate* that I even had to come on this dumb show."

Amity's face fell. "But we wouldn't have met."

Easton shook his head fiercely. "I didn't mean it like that. Believe me, I didn't." He kissed her forehead. "Just give me a minute to cool off."

"Can we do that together? I actually *want* to jump in the frigid water today."

"Not what I meant." He laughed, his smile slowly reaching his eyes. "But yeah, that should help me clear my head."

They set up camp, and she and Easton quickly snuck off in their knickers for a much-needed dip. The water felt like a fresh mineral spring poured right out of an Evian bottle, surrounding her battered skin like a liquid miracle. The cameras were rolling, so she and Easton had to keep every-thing PG-13, but even while standing on slimy lava rocks in the chilly water, their steamy French kisses sent surging rushes of blood through her, warming her goosebump-covered skin.

"What's this?" Easton asked as they waded around. She held her arm out while he ran his fingers across the glistening charms on her silver bracelet. "You never take it off. I've been meaning to ask you about it."

"Oh yeah..." With a bittersweet smile, she looked at her bracelet. "My dad got it for me. Every time he found a charm representing a place he wanted to take me, he'd add it to my bracelet. He never waited for a holiday to give them to me; he'd just clasp them on. Before he died, he asked me to visit as many of the places as I could to see things—to live life." She swallowed through a lump in her throat. "I haven't actually been to any of them yet."

Easton rubbed his fingers across her quivering lip. "Don't be sad. Your dad wants the best for you. He wants you to live life even though he can't be here with you. That's a good thing. Maybe we can visit some of these places together?"

"Really?" Amity perked up. "That would be amazing."

Easton hesitated. "I'll have to save up."

"I'll save up with you."

"Okay." He nodded, a confused look on his face. Amity knew he was processing her supposed fortune—the one she should admit that she didn't have, but before she got the guts to tell him the truth, he shrugged it off. "Let's see," he contin-ued. "Where do you still need to go? Hmm...this is the Eiffel Tower, right? So Paris. And Big Ben? So London. Gosh, there's about thirty of these things."

"Yeah, it'll take a while to get to them all."

"What's this?" he asked curiously, pinching the only charm etched with a brilliant shade of golden yellow among the silver dangles.

"Good eye. That one's super special." Balancing on a flat, slippery rock with her teeth chattering, she drew him closer for body heat and clasped her fingers through his. "I worry about losing the charms, especially that one, when I wear my bracelet places like this, but my dad believed in using things— wearing them—not putting them away in pretty boxes. We only have so much time." She squeezed his hand and pulled him closer. "Live life, right?"

Easton nodded. "Yeah, for sure. *That* I understand. So what place does it represent?"

"Not a place for this one. He gave it to me the day he died. It's like he knew it was his time. A yellow rose for Amity Rose —his baby girl—friendship, love, and harmony forever." Her eyes welled up. "He meant for it to be happy, of course," she added with a sniffle, splashing lake water over her face to hide her tears. "For me to always know how much he loved me."

"Amity Rose? That has a nice ring to it."

"Yes. Amity means friendship and harmony, and Rose is my last name."

Easton smiled warmly. "Your name suits you. I wish I could meet him. I'd like to think that we'd have gotten along. I just hope I'm that great of a dad someday."

"You want kids?"

He paused, then nodded. "Yeah, I guess I do."

"Me too," Amity said, her insides tangling in giddy knots.

She wrapped her arms and legs around him, molding her mouth to his. Pressed up against him, she yearned to slide her panties aside and allow him inside her, but the rocking motions would be caught on camera. Surrounded by an open field of endless lava rock, there was nowhere to even try and run away from the intrusive lenses.

Amity let out a loud sigh. "Too bad there are no trees around here." With a mischievous grin, she continued, "Would be nice to sneak away with those heels I've been carrying around."

Easton's brows shot up. "You're kidding? You still have those? A sensible person would have chucked them. They add unnecessary weight to your pack."

"No!" Amity huffed out a shocked breath. "Chuck them? I couldn't do that. They're expensive, and besides, they're sort of sentimental now. Thought you might like to see me naked" —she flashed him a sultry glance—"in nothing but those."

"Anytime, Princess," he whispered. "Anytime and anywhere."

The hungry look she received from him stayed with her all night.

~

"CONTESTANTS," Alex Bandon announced, motioning behind him at the vast landscape, "today's trail challenge is a flat-out grind across a barren lava field with an instant elimination. As I said yesterday, give it your all because, after this leg, you'll have a three-day break. Partners will remain the same until the next leg of the race."

"Amity," Easton said, his tone eager, "you'll need to fill up your two-liter pouch and water bottles. This section of the PCT is twelve miles of lava rock with no vegetation or water sources. It'll be like walking on the hot surface of a meteorite— slowly cooking your skin, parching your throat, and tearing your shoes apart."

To which she wondered, why would anyone willingly do this? And then laughed because she did have a choice in the matter. She could walk away at any time.

Amity filtered water out of the lake, filling her containers, and turned to give Easton a kiss before heading over to the start line. Having won the previous leg again, she and Liam were given the advantage of a five-minute head start. It wasn't much, but she'd take it.

Easton ended their kiss quickly, motioning toward the start line. "Run ahead today. Don't worry about me. This leg is about speed."

"But—"

"Amity, you need to go. Your timer only has a few seconds left."

"Okay, but what about you? The numbers are dwindling down. There isn't a buffer."

"I can handle myself."

Amity hesitated, oscillating on her feet. There really wasn't anything she could do to help him. Truthfully, she worried about being a weak link herself on this leg. Her body felt like it had been through a meat grinder.

"Let's go," Liam said impatiently. "Your twiggy boyfriend's gonna have to win a leg himself. Hmm...wonder why he hasn't yet? Probably because his girlfriend's *smarter* than him."

Amity winced while Easton narrowed his eyes menacingly at Liam.

"There aren't even any tasks on this leg, Amity," Liam continued, coaxing her while smirking at Easton. "There's nothing you *can* do to help him." Then he mumbled, "Directors are going for a trail leg from hell," while staring out across the lava field.

"Go, Amity," Easton said, clamping his teeth together. "Before I knock your partner on his ass."

Liam chuckled while Amity pursed her lips. She didn't care for Easton's delivery, but she'd let it slide. Liam was being an ass. "I'll see if I can take first," she said with a decisive nod. "Bet our next advantage has to do with partner selections."

The timer beeped, and she and Liam set out on the trail across the lava. After only minutes, the burden of her pack was enough to nearly kill her. The added weight of outright carrying all the water made running impossible, so they power-hiked across the treacherous, space-like surface, scuffing their shoes and sometimes even the bare skin of their legs on the jagged rocks.

Her muscles ached, her joints were raw, her brain was tired, her lips were chapped, and her cuts hurt—ugh, she thought, desperate to push all the aches and pains out of her mind. She glanced around for a distraction, taking in the scenery and their lead on the other teams, who marched along as a group of tiny specks in the distance. Though the terrain was difficult, it was a huge advantage to be able to see across the miles of rocky landscape.

"What's that mountain over there?" Amity asked, pointing at a peak shaped like a needlepoint.

"Don't know," Liam said. "Don't care."

"I was just trying to distract myself from the scorching heat. Geez."

"You're dragging today. Just focus on your feet."

Amity scoffed, glancing over her shoulder. The other teams were gaining on them, but she wasn't too worried as she *could* kick it into gear if need be. Squinting her eyes, she made out Easton's tall, scraggly figure in the distance, with his untidy hair poking out from around the sides of his blue-faded baseball cap. She giggled at his adorableness. Gosh, that man did things to her.

"Focus on the trail," Liam said. "You'll trip and sprain an ankle like Cassie."

"You're no better," she returned.

He'd glanced at Becky multiple times, too, perhaps not as much as Amity had looked at Easton, but there was definitely something there.

Over the grueling twelve miles, the teams gained on them, and Amity struggled to put one foot in front of the other like never before. With the weight bearing down on her shoulders and her tired, shaky legs, she had to dig into her last ounce of energy to cross the line with Liam in first.

Literally seconds later, Easton and Kim powered across the finish in second place, followed by Justin and Bria and Miles and Becky.

Becky tossed her pack on the ground. "You almost got me eliminated," she shouted at Miles as Isaac and Jade strayed across the line in last place.

With the remainder of her energy, Amity dragged her feet over to Easton and threw her arms around him.

"Nice job," he said with a tight smile.

Amity ran the tip of her tongue across her dry lips, swallowing to wet her parched throat. "You're not mad, are you? I didn't know you were the team right behind us. Should I have let you pass?"

"No," Easton said quickly, "of course not."

But Amity wasn't so sure. She knew he wanted the money —badly—and now, she really, *really* wanted to know why. Was a million dollars more important to him than her? She narrowed her eyes, watching his retreating figure as he slid past the cameras. They'd catch him eventually for an interview. No one could avoid it, although all of them, aside from Miles, had tried.

Jade and Isaac made a surprisingly friendly exit, congratulating the other teams while holding hands. Maybe they'd date after the show? But Amity didn't speculate long. Barely able to move, she limped over and dropped her backpack next to Easton's at a designated campground on the side of a giant, oval lake; the location Alex announced they would stay at for a three-day physical and mental break.

With the cameras rolling, Amity hardly felt the mental break part of the host's comment was accurate, but they did have primitive toilets and running water at this campsite which was a major bonus. She eagerly gulped down two bottles of water, ran her small brush through her hair, and even applied some makeup again, having all but given up on her appearance over the rigor of the past few days.

"Wow," Easton said as she approached him dangling his feet in the water off the side of the dock. "You look incredible."

"Thanks." Amity smiled, her cheeks tingling with a blush as she reveled in the novelty of his attention. "What's that mountain?" she asked, pointing behind the trees toward the direction of their strenuous hike. "I wondered all the way across the lava field." She sat down next to him, took off her shoes and socks, and dipped her sore feet in the water, letting the soothing water surround them.

"Mt. Washington," he said. "Looks kind of like a sewing thimble at the top, don't you think?"

"I guess. I was thinking more like a spinning wheel needle." *Ask him about the money*, she thought, but instead, she said, "Can you climb it?" like a coward and immediately regretted the question.

"Yep, but it would be technical. I'd need a rope, harness, and climbing partner. Maybe I'll bring Dominic..." He trailed off with an anguished look on his face.

"Easton, I really don't like the idea of you climbing that rocky mountain or any mountain for that matter. Repelling that cliff yesterday was awful. If you fell, then—"

"Princess, you're just going to have to trust that I know what I'm doing, okay? I love to climb. I'm *not* giving it up."

Amity released her breath. She'd hit a nerve, and it wasn't even the one she wanted to hit. "Okay, I guess I'll get used to it."

Easton reached for her hand. "Sorry," he said, slumping his shoulders forward. "I'm not trying to be unreasonable. It's just that I can't change what I like to do. I've tried that before in relationships, and it made me unhappy."

Pinching her lips together, she forced out, "Then you'd better not fall."

"I won't," he promised, grinning like the idea was unheard of, but then the smile slowly drifted off his face. "Do we have that settled? You'll stay even if I go climbing, right?"

"Stay?"

"Yeah." He tightened his hold on her fingers. "Like not leave because you can't deal with me being out on climbs and stuff?"

"Leave? Easton, I just said that I'd get used to it. I also said that I want you permanently, remember? I don't know how much clearer I can be."

After a few tense seconds, he relaxed and moved in to kiss her, but she couldn't really get into it.

"Something wrong?" he asked, pulling away, a nervous edge to his voice.

Not wanting to upset him again but unable to stop herself, she tentatively asked, "Are you planning to tell me who Dominic is and why you have that pained look on your face when you mention him?"

"Oh." Easton grabbed his shoulder, digging his fingers into his muscles. "Not at all what I thought you were going to say. Thought you were going ask questions about the future or why I want the money so badly or something like that." He sighed. "But, yeah, I wondered when you were going to ask about Dominic too."

"I *do* want to know why you want the money so badly," she blurted out. "I *really* want to know. I mean, we all want money, but…"

"Yeah, I would want to know too." Taking off his cap, he splashed some cool lake water on his forehead. "I suppose I'd better explain. I can't continue to keep secrets from you. Besides, it'll help you understand why I've been a bit of a jerk."

241

"I didn't say—"

"No, no." He held his palm out. "I have, Princess. I can see it on your face when I get intense about the race. I'm sorry about that. There is a reason."

"Okay, I'm listening."

Easton nodded, glancing out across the lake. "Dominic is my business partner." He took a deep breath before meeting her eyes. "We met in high school and have been best friends ever since. After school, we created Rocky Mountain Inspiration together."

"That explains your baseball cap," she said, smiling softly.

"What?"

Amity pointed at the battered blue cap in his hands.

"Oh, yeah." Chuckling, he twisted his cap to look at the dirt-stained white letters and mashed it back over his dark brown mass of hair. "The caps were our first for-sale items for the tourists to pick up after they'd gone on a tour—when we were a small-nothing business right out of high school. Now, we've built Rocky Mountain Inspiration up to be one of the top tour companies in Aspen."

A pang of pride went through Amity, but also a few nervous jitters. She wasn't nearly that successful. "That's amazing," she said, rubbing her fingers across the muscles in his quad.

He nodded and plucked a wet leaf off his leg, tossing it into the water. "Yeah, we're a success story. We created the life we always wanted. Everything was going great."

His features scrunched up. In frustration? In pain? He paused so long she couldn't handle it.

"Until?" Amity prompted and reached for his hand.

Letting out another breath, Easton began to play absent-mindedly with the charms on her bracelet. "Dominic came down with a rare heart problem a few years ago," he said, his Adam's apple bobbing as he swallowed. "His health quickly went downhill, and with all the testing and research, his medical bills went through the roof. He almost stopped fighting to live, arguing that we all needed to get on with our lives.

"But Chelsea and I—Chelsea's Dominic's wife—wouldn't let him give up. Dominic and Chelsea found a doctor that thinks a specialty medical procedure might save him, but he can't afford to pay outright, so he won't be prioritized for the surgery." A muscle beat in his jaw, and he looked down, gluing his eyes on their interlinked hands. "Probably not in time anyway. We make a decent living, but it's *a lot* of money. If I win, then…"

"You can afford to pay for the procedure in time," Amity finished.

He nodded and went back to tinkering with her bracelet. "That's the hope."

"I'm sorry." She squeezed his hand. "That's a lot to go through."

"Yeah, it sucks. He's too young. We've always joked about going through our mid-life crisis together, but we're not even thirty yet."

Amity understood all too well. Dominic was probably about the same age as her dad when he'd become really sick. Life wasn't always fair. She'd already planned to help Easton win the money, but now she would make *sure* that he did. A man's life was on the line and one that meant the world to Easton. She'd have done anything to have had the chance to save her dad.

"I'll help you win," she whispered.

"Amity." He shook his head. "I'm not asking you to do that. That's not fair to you. I was simply giving you an upfront answer. Honesty is vital for a successful relationship."

Amity sucked her bottom lip into her mouth, looking out

across the lake, afraid to meet his eyes. She hadn't really lied to him, but she hadn't been honest with him either.

"Um, Easton, about that—"

"Hey, man," Easton said suddenly.

Amity jerked in surprise as Justin approached. For a brief moment, she'd actually forgotten about the other contestants and somehow even the cameras.

"Hey," Justin returned, "I was just thinking I might jump in the water for a swim, and you two love birds are in my way."

"I'll join you," Easton said, rolling his shoulders back. "I could use a few laps across the lake to loosen my muscles— though I probably can't keep up with a sea captain."

Justin smirked. "You never know. You've got limbs like an octopus."

Easton burst out laughing. "My best feature."

Amity smiled at them. "Have fun. I'm going to find Bria and see if she's hungry. I'm starving, enough to even crave backpacking food." She placed her hand dramatically on her forehead. "Oh my, what's happening to me."

With a little relief and cowardice, she bowed out of their conversation without admitting a thing about her financial status. Then it occurred to her that if she did, Easton might feel guilty about taking the win. Perhaps, she thought, it was better that he didn't know she was broke until after the show.

Twenty-Two

Cooper could not sit still. Three days of rest! How would he stay sane? While Amity couldn't stop talking about how wonderful the time off was and how her sore muscles were in heaven, he was stressed beyond belief. With both his best friend to save and the most incredible woman on the planet to impress, he'd do anything to be on the airplane home with the money and the girl. She'd changed his life, and if he could save Dominic, then he'd truly have it all.

After his second leisurely lap across the lake with Justin, he realized he'd starve if he didn't make some food and located Amity sitting at a picnic table in the campground.

"I love benches," she said, smiling up at him like she'd just discovered heaven, "and tables."

He laughed, pleased that such simple pleasures could now make her day, while he grabbed the backpacking towel from his pack. Hopefully, that meant she'd be fine without a mansion and extra-large walk-in closet full of designer clothes.

"I made you some dinner," she added. "All by myself. Even lit the stove with the flint."

"That's my girl. I'll have to thank you properly later."

That evening, Cooper led Amity on an off-trail sprint

through the woods with her strappy black high heels in hand. He needed a distraction—he needed *her*.

He wasn't too worried about the physical exertion of racing through the trees, as they'd have another night for their muscles to recover before the competition resumed—not that it would have stopped them from running away like horny teenagers anyway.

She stripped off her leggings, changing into her heels, while he tossed their trail shoes aside. They fell onto his open sleeping bag, shedding the rest of their clothing, him in near desperation.

Amity pulled him on top of her, flashing him the sexiest smile he'd ever seen—wearing nothing but her heels. "Let's hurry," she said. "I don't want to miss the chance. Those vultures aren't going to let us escape again."

Cooper smiled at her. She didn't have to ask him twice, but he also didn't want to hurry on someone else's account—the show shouldn't dictate their private time together. "I think I'll warm you up first."

"What?" she asked, followed by a little gasp. "Oh."

Cooper pulled her nipple into his mouth, nibbling and savoring the strawberry peak. In this case, the cool breeze worked in his favor as he warmed her body and enjoyed each heightened pebble. Amity rocked and moaned with every slide of his tongue.

He returned to her lips for a kiss before positioning himself on top of her. "You ready?"

"More than," she whispered. "I've been waking up all hot and bothered since the first time. My body knows it wants you."

He thrust into her, and Amity cried out, stifling the sound with her lips pressed into his shoulder. She rocked her hips with him and pulled his hand to her chest.

"Hard and fast," she begged. "Please, *Easton*. I need you."

When she said his name, it wrapped around his heart, healing the years of endless taunts and replacing them with her love. She felt like silk—and home.

"Easton, please," she continued. "Move faster."

Cooper moved in and out of her, shots of heat searing through him with each motion until he spilled every ounce of his soul into her. He called out her name, despite the potential of being overheard, and collapsed on top of her, shuddering from the pleasure.

Chilly air rushed up his back, making even him cold, so he shifted Amity into his arms, cracking a smile at her provocative heels and chipped-up, bright-purple toes while he zipped the sleeping bag around them. The day they met flashed through his mind, and his stomach dropped as he thought about how incredible she was. She deserved to be warm in a luxury hotel on soft bed linens, not freezing her buns off in the forest on a rumpled sleeping bag.

He wanted to tell her how much he loved her, but he just couldn't—not yet. Admitting that to her and then having something go wrong would rip his heart out. He'd tell her when they left the competition together—in just a few short days.

THE BREAK WENT by quicker than Cooper expected. Spending time with Amity had helped him force the race out of his mind, but now he had to dig in and finish it. The sun rose over the horizon, and he did everything he could to prepare—ate a solid breakfast, stretched every muscle in his body, and even jogged a lap around the campground—anything to calm his nerves.

Alex stood on his hosting platform, announcing expectations regarding their camera equipment, interviews, and supplies, so far, most of it garbage in Cooper's mind. Until Bandon resumed his discussion about the actual race, he didn't process a word.

"New partners will be chosen today," the host continued, and Cooper's head popped up. "Please listen carefully because several of you have asked the directors about the romance stipulation in the title of the race during your interviews." Having adamantly been one of them, Cooper now strained his ears to hear every word. "Since we are getting so close to the end, I would like to reveal that romance has no bearing on winning the riches we promised you at the end of this race—"

Cooper slowly let the air out of his lungs. Thank god. He wouldn't have to make some dumb decision that would potentially tick off Amity. Finally, a curveball rule that was on his side.

"—a motivating refresher, two million dollars will be handed to the winning team, a one-million-dollar check to each contestant in the final pair. The reason the show is titled *The Race for Riches or Romance* will be fully explained during the reunion episode—"

Cooper closed his eyes, sucking in a few replenishing breaths. He could do this—he *could* have it all. He just needed to focus and make the right choices along the way.

"—teams are resetting, Amity's and Liam's advantage for winning the previous leg is that they get to choose first—"

Amity pushed up on her toes and swiveled her head around to lock eyes with Cooper, her frayed ponytail swishing with the movement. She flashed a smile at him like they'd just been handed a winning lottery ticket.

And his heart dropped. He did everything he could to send her a pleased grin in return, but the game had just changed. Even before the host announced there was no romance requirement to win, Cooper wasn't so sure they should be partners— but he hadn't said a word to Amity because he was afraid that she'd take it the wrong way. Maybe he should have said something?

Yes, he *wanted* to race with her, but as he'd made abundantly clear, he had to win, and he wasn't sure what the challenge was. If it was a trail run or puzzle, then Amity for sure. But if it required outdoor experience, he'd be better off racing with someone else.

But then he had made her *promise* him when she'd been stuck in that lake that she'd choose him as her next partner—whenever possible—no matter what. Practically begged, in fact. At the time, it had seemed like a good idea, but now, he didn't know.

"It's ladies' turn to choose first," Alex continued. "Therefore, selection will begin with the woman in the first-place team, followed by the man in the first-place team. We'll start with the winning team down to the last-place team—"

"Finally together," she mouthed to him.

Okay, obviously not planning to choose someone else. Cooper held his expression in what he hoped was one of agreement. There was no reason to stir things up with her when he didn't even know what the challenge was, was there?

He hesitated, hoping to hear if the challenge was a footrace, a puzzle, or some other strength she had, but Bandon went straight into partner selections.

"Amity, your selection?"

"Easton," she announced, clapping her hands together.

Alex pasted on his screen-worthy smile. "Cooper, your thoughts?"

If only Bandon could feel the turmoil that he felt inside, then the peppy host would probably explode.

"Never felt better, Alex," Cooper lied, forcing the first full-on fake smile he'd given in the competition. Pathetically, it wasn't even for the benefit of the cameras; it was for the benefit of his girlfriend.

Amity's eyes moved from him to the host, and Cooper's mouth slid into a frown. He kneaded the back of his neck with his long fingers, hiding his face behind his arm as Liam selected Becky and Kim scooped up Justin. Unfortunately for Bria, that meant being automatically paired with Miles, and the scowl on her face made it apparent that he was her last choice.

"Teams will have simultaneous skills challenges, with one partner participating in a swim race through the lake," Alex explained, motioning behind him at the water, "and the other partner a bike race around it." The host swirled his finger in the air to indicate a circular pattern. "Both challenges begin in five minutes. Teams can select which member participates in each respective challenge.

"As always, give it your all. The last-place finisher from each challenge will put your team into a sudden-death competition—unless the same team has both members come in last, in which case, that team will automatically be eliminated."

"If you're ready, get set," Alex called out. "…3…2…1."

Cooper sprinted to Amity.

"I'd prefer the swim challenge," she said. "I haven't ridden a bike since I was twelve, but I swim in the resort pools all the time."

"Fine, yes." Cooper patted his legs. "My quad muscles should be good on a bike from all the climbing."

"That works out then." Amity wrapped her arms around him. "We make the perfect team. We balance each other out," she added, standing on her tiptoes for a kiss.

Cooper gave her a quick peck on the lips. "We should get to it. They limited our time to discuss this on purpose."

She nodded. "I'll head over to the lake. I promise I'll do well."

"Okay, thanks," Cooper said. "Good luck."

'And I love you,' he thought. Damn, he should have said it, but he *had* to focus.

Cooper ran over to the start line for the bike race and pulled a blue-framed mountain bike off the rack. He propped the frame against a tree, pushing on the tight knots in his shoulder blades. It would take him months to recover from the stress of all this, and the frustrating part was, without the cameras, crap rules, and pressure to win a million dollars, he'd love every minute of it.

A crew member handed him a map—ten miles through the trees. It would go fast, and he'd have to pedal at record speed. Increasingly antsy, he filled his bottle from the cooler, took a few swigs, and dumped the excess into his hands, mopping up the loose ends of his hair and pressing them into his bike helmet.

Liam pulled a green bike off the rack, propping its frame against an adjacent tree. "Time to see who's the better man?"

"I don't care about a bike race, moron. I care about winning."

"Me too." Liam shot a strained look toward Becky, who stood by Amity waiting for the swim challenge. The women were in their black sports bras and underwear, staring at their maps. With a light chuckle, Liam added, "By winning, do you mean the money or the girl?" He tipped his cowboy hat. "Must admit, I've been trying to figure that out myself regarding Becky."

Cooper couldn't contain his shocked expression. "Most honest thing I've ever heard you say."

"Yeah, well, shit. I didn't expect to like her."

Cooper grinned. "It sort of creeps up on you, doesn't it?"

"From Alaska, of all places," Liam grumbled, chucking his once-white but now dirt-stained hat to the side before putting on his bike helmet. "What the hell am I going to do about that?" He sighed. "I don't care if romance has no bearing on the win. It's still going to be a disaster somehow."

With a smirk, Cooper said, "Hopefully only because I'll be fighting to kick your country ass."

They remained cordial until the timer beeped, but six miles into their ride, the truce was over. Far ahead of Bria and Kim, they jockeyed for position. Near the finish line, Liam crashed into Cooper, and they ended up in a footrace, pushing their battered bike frames alongside. Just before the finish, Liam stuck his foot out and tripped him to secure the win.

Liam would probably get first dibs to choose his next partner, and that was huge—it could even determine the race.

"I'll make sure you pay for this," Cooper said to Liam, clenching his muscles to keep from tackling him.

Liam just shook his head and laughed. "You're too *nice*, Cooper. Didn't want to be partners with Amity today, did you?" He put his hat back on, tipped it, and added, "She's why you'll lose," as he walked off.

Cooper tossed what remained of his bike on the ground in a crumpled heap and ran over to see the end of the swim race, his body so tense he thought he might pop some veins. He let out a sigh of relief as he took in the scene. About fifty yards from the finish, Amity glided through the water with Becky to her side. Justin, being a natural in the water, had already finished. And then there was Miles. The dope was yards behind both women, flailing and clutching at his leg.

Cooper sat on the dock and splashed some cold water down the back of his neck, watching Becky swim across the finish line, followed by Amity. Miles paddled across a few minutes later. Thank god for Miles.

"My leg cramped up the whole damn time," Miles complained. He continued to whine to McKenzie, trying to manipulate her into a redo before giving up and limping off the dock. "Should be a redo. Totally unfair."

"Unfair like when Cassie sprained her ankle?" Justin called after him. "Or are you just special, Miles?"

"Dickhead," Miles threw at Justin over his shoulder, glancing at Bria. "Who lost the bike challenge?"

"Kim," Bria grumbled. "We still have a chance in the sudden-death challenge, or I'd be cussing ya out. Leg cramps, really? You're dehydrated. Drink some water."

A few minutes later, a sudden-death archery challenge took place. Bria and Miles beat Kim and Justin with Bria's tactical skills giving them the edge. Shock, sadness, and guilt flitted across Kim's face while Justin assured Kim it wasn't her fault. Cooper felt bad, but what could he do? The good people had to go home for him to win.

"Man, I'm sorry," Cooper said to Justin. "You don't deserve to go home."

"Yeah, I don't, but this is a shit competition. We both know that." Justin shrugged. "Maybe I'll get a loan." He punched Cooper softly on the shoulder, adding, "If I do, come help me set up my tour business, okay?"

Cooper nodded and said, "Will do," watching Justin walk away for his exit interview. At least he didn't have to compete with someone he respected as much as Justin at the end.

"Contestants," Alex announced, "we're approaching the last two days of the competition. You are the final three teams, or should I say the final six contestants. Be prepared for a mix-up tomorrow. Get some rest and congratulations."

After the host's announcement, Cooper turned toward Amity, his nerves on edge. She had her arms wrapped tightly around her torso, her teeth chattering, and her lips blue, with goosebumps covering every inch of her skin. They'd been required to watch the archery challenge—not that any of them would have missed it anyway—and she must not have had time to change. In all the commotion, he'd been distracted.

"Princess, I can help warm you—"

Amity pressed her icy lips to his, apparently not shaken up about a thing. "Sorry, Easton, but I am *fr-freezing* my butt off." She ran toward the bathroom in her undergarments, covered only by her tiny backpacking towel, trailing behind Becky with her clothes in hand. "I wish there were *actual* showers," she yelled.

Cooper laughed as he watched her gorgeous, bug-bitten, rock-scraped, tan form disappear. Clearly, she planned to shed her wet clothes before getting dressed, which was smart—but Amity was smart and perceptive—which meant that she understood what he needed to do to win. It was time for him to buckle down and make it happen.

Twenty-Three

Morning came, and though Amity felt physically ready to race, her insides were tangled up in knots. Standing on her mat with her arms crossed over her chest, she tried to calm herself with deep, yoga-like breaths. Her guaranteed time with Easton was coming to an end, and they hadn't talked about the future. The list of potential obstacles repeated in her mind like a singer looping the main riff of a song.

What if money was more important to him than her? What if he changed his mind when they went home to different states? What if he dumped her when he found out she was dirt poor? What if he'd never fallen in love with her to begin with? What if, what if, what if... Okay, maybe ten songs. She needed some aspirin.

Massaging her temples, Amity held on to the one certainty she had—if he broke up with her, she'd hold him to that week-long camping trip in Colorado, that was for sure. They had a bet.

"Contestants," Alex barked out, startling her, "congratulations on making the final six. It's time to select three teams for today's rowing skills challenge. The first team to finish will receive an invaluable advantage for the final leg. The last two teams to finish will go straight into a head-to-head, sudden-death challenge where one team will go home.

"Men choose first today based, as always, on finishing rank. Liam, you won the bike challenge and Justin the swim challenge. However, as Justin has already been eliminated, we won't need a tiebreaker for yesterday's unique instance of two men coming in first on simultaneous challenges. Therefore, it will go from Liam choosing first directly to the second-place finishers—Cooper from the bike challenge followed by Becky from the swim challenge."

Amity clasped her hands out in front of her and smiled at Easton, pushing her apprehensive thoughts aside. She loved him, and it truly seemed like he loved her, too—that was all that mattered. They were a team, and she had no reason to believe they wouldn't go through life as one.

"Liam," Alex called out, "your selection?"

Liam tipped his hat toward his girlfriend, stating, "Becky," without a hint of doubt.

Becky grinned at Liam like they had the challenge made. They were kind of cute together, and Liam's new caring attitude toward Becky won back a few points for him in her mind.

"Cooper?" Alex asked. "Your selection?"

Butterflies of excitement danced in Amity's belly, never actually having been selected by her boyfriend before. With a giddy smile, she tried to lock eyes with him, but he stared straight ahead at Alex, never glancing her way.

"Bria," Easton announced, clear as day.

Amity's breath caught, a sharp knife-like pain twisting and replacing the butterflies in her stomach. She must have heard him wrong—but no, he still avoided her eyes. Gasping, she tried to draw in air. Her lungs wouldn't fill, and the world started to spin, everyone's voices fading.

In slow motion, Becky's blurry figure ran toward her, her hands outstretched. Becky grabbed Amity's arm before she collapsed and braced her against the solid support of her side. At that moment, Becky officially became her new favorite person because she'd just saved her from being touched by Easton—the only other person she'd been able to concentrate on. He'd rushed to her as well, and she just couldn't.

Through a silky mass of black hair, Amity whispered, "Thank you," into Becky's ear.

Becky turned and nodded, her features taut with concern, while Amity faltered, trying to stand on her own.

"Woah, there," Becky said. "You're white as a sheet. Give yourself a minute."

At Becky's statement, blood rushed to Amity's cheeks, replenishing her clammy skin with plenty of color. She stared at the lakeside dirt, avoiding everyone's eyes. Who nearly faints because their man doesn't choose them in a silly school-pick lineup?

But it was more than that. Easton betrayed her. If he'd planned this, he should have told her. Blindsiding your closest ally was cold, especially when it was your girlfriend.

Easton reached for her, a look of acute anxiety etched across his pain-struck face, but Amity wasn't about to offer him her sympathy. She swatted his arms away with one hand while clinging like a koala bear onto Becky with the other. Still flushed from her head rush, she closed her eyes. The splotches in her vision began to disappear, allowing her mind to reel. Did he really have so little faith in her?

Amity knew it was because the rowing challenge would require arm strength, and Bria was hands down stronger physically, but still, they were a team, more likely to succeed together than apart—or so she'd thought. She'd proven herself in this race again and again—*never* had she come in last place, and *never* would she.

"Amity, are you alright?" Easton asked, his voice rising in

panic while his words rushed out. "Please tell me you're okay. I didn't know you'd react like this. I'm sorry. It's not personal."

It was *entirely* personal! What a clueless idiot. To him, she was a *liability*. Not a partner, but a weak link. Had Easton been carrying her along, leading her on, until she was no longer a benefit to his racing strategy? Now that there was no romance stipulation to win the money, he didn't need her? No, she didn't believe that, did she? But the timing was hard to ignore.

Or maybe he'd just held his thoughts back, not wanting to tell her he might choose someone else in fear of her reaction. If that was the case, what else was he hiding?

Amity needed answers, but for now, she was strong enough to handle this—strong enough to put on a show, at least.

"I'm okay now," she said to Becky. "Thanks again. You have no idea how much I appreciate what you just did."

"Yeah, I'd want the same"—Becky shrugged—"if it were me. For what it's worth, I think he's wrong."

Amity cracked a faint smile. "We'll see." She recentered her feet on her mat, feeling numb.

Alex, who'd abandoned his hosting platform, touched her shoulder. "Amity, can you continue?"

"Oh, yes." She nodded. "I can *definitely* continue. Sorry about that."

"No need to apologize," the host assured her. "What happened there?"

"Just a little surprised, Alex, that's all."

Her skin flushed as she met Easton's eyes. He rocked around on his mat with a look of pure misery on his face, running his hands through his messy, dark brown locks, trying to mouth something to her, but she looked away, too mad to consider his words just yet. How could they be a couple in real life if he didn't join forces with her when it mattered?

Alex cleared his throat. "All right then, we'll continue. Cooper, any response to Amity's words?"

"Just that." Easton paused, grabbing the back of his neck. "I thought she'd understand. She means *a lot* to me—she knows that."

The host looked at her. "Amity, any response?"

A lot to me, really? She wasn't expecting a declaration of love, but he was digging his own grave. "No, Alex, can we please move on?"

"Okay," Alex mused. "Since you and Miles are the final two left, you're automatically partners."

"Fantastic," she spat, frowning as the blue-blonde camerawoman zoomed in on her face.

Amity tore her eyes away from the camera, glancing at the men while trying not to imagine what that whole dramatic scene would look like on television. To her surprise, Liam looked smug, almost pleased, while Miles, on the other hand, shot daggers at her with his eyes. Miles was probably too close to a million dollars to be solely interested in ratings now and likely didn't want a fainting headcase for a partner. For once, she agreed with him about something. She wasn't at her finest.

Alex continued, "The rowing challenge will be a kayak race on the lake—"

But Amity tuned out most of his words, still too flustered to concentrate.

"—you have five minutes until the start timer beeps."

Alex did his countdown, and Miles grabbed her arm, pulling her aside. "I need you to listen to my instructions. I'll sit in the back to propel us and get better leverage. The most important thing is for you to rotate your paddle in sync with mine on the straightaways. On the turns, I want you to pull your paddle out of the water. There isn't time for you to gain enough experience for the turns."

Amity placed her hands on her hips. "Oh really? What are you? An expert rower?"

"Yes, actually. I did collegiate rowing for Cornell in New York."

Her mouth dropped open. "You're kidding."

"Not in the slightest." Miles grinned like the haughtiest version of the Grinch. "We're about to bury your boyfriend. Or should I say ex-boyfriend?" He quirked a brow. "Hope you can handle that."

She nodded, still processing his words. Miles, the sly, calculated underdog, kept his rowing skills a secret, playing up his workouts in the indoor gym—never once telling anyone about the countless hours he'd spent on the miles of open water surrounding Manhattan. She might be saved by the one outdoor skill Miles actually possessed.

As she walked toward the dock, Easton ran up to her. "Amity, I'm so sorry. It's just I have to win. You know that."

Her skin lit on fire to the degree that she felt like she'd spent countless hours in a hot spring. "If you want to win so bad, go *win*."

A tormented look crossed his face, and guilt tore through her. Ugh, now he was the wounded puppy? This sucked! She wanted to kiss him until they were both breathless and call the whole thing a stupid misunderstanding, but she wasn't so sure it was.

"Okay." He touched her arm gently, sending tingles down her spine. "I...um...I'll see you after."

Amity walked up to Miles, who stood beside their red kayak. She took off her long-sleeved shirt and bent down to splash cool water on her face and across the bare skin of her shoulders, letting the droplets run down the front of her purple tank top. Determining her head to be as clear as it would get, she reached down to grab a life vest.

"No," Miles yelled, "don't touch *anything*. Didn't you listen to the rules?"

"Not really." Amity shrugged and bit the corner of her mouth. "I couldn't focus."

Miles whispered something that combined eloquently with the F-bomb before adding, "We can't touch the life vests, paddles, or kayak until the timer beeps, or we get a time penalty." His jaw tightened. "Look, I get that your dumbass boyfriend didn't choose you, but get over it. *You* can still win."

That woke her up. If Amity won, she could give Easton the money to help him save Dominic. Two fighting for the win was better than one. And maybe—no, she shouldn't be selfish —but it was impossible not to think about keeping a chunk of the change to help her mom retire or even pay her bills and fix her car.

"Okay, Miles." Amity nodded. "Let's do this. What do I need to know?"

"That's more like it." An eager expression lit up Miles' angular features as he proceeded to explain everything she'd tuned out. She heard most of his words, becoming only slightly distracted by the ingrown hairs peppered throughout his once-perfect goatee. The elements were taking it to them all.

Moments later, the timer beeped, and she jumped in the front seat with her life vest in hand, bending her legs slightly and setting the long one-piece paddle across her lap as Miles had instructed. Miles pushed their kayak off the dock, sliding into the back and rotating his paddle through the water, gliding them weightlessly across the surface like they were floating on a cloud.

Amity glanced over her shoulder, noting that the other teams also chose to have the ladies sit in the front, probably for weight distribution. Not surprisingly, Easton and Liam struggled more than Miles getting their kayaks launched, but they weren't far behind.

The course was set around the outer edge of the lake as a large loop. Buoy-like cones marked a wide waterway with the shoreline off to their left.

Miles took a quick lead. He rowed at an impressive speed, his arm muscles bulging with each rotating stroke as they drifted through the water like the Olympic kayakers she'd seen on TV. Amity dutifully followed Miles' instructions as he shouted them out with each stroke, rowing in sync on the straightaways and lifting her paddle on the turns. She'd learned twofold during this competition that everyone had different strengths, and given that rowing wasn't one of hers, she needed to listen.

About three-quarters of the way through, the lake shallowed out, and their designated path led them into a solid section of stringy pond plants.

Miles slowed their pace. "We're going to have to choose the left or right side of these plants. The middle section is too dense."

"You choose," she said quickly.

Amity had no clue which way to go. The swimming challenge had been on the other side of the lake by the campground, where there were no plants. Clearly, the directors had planned for the teams to encounter this obstacle near the end of the challenge to heighten the drama. She'd already had enough drama to last a lifetime. Closing her eyes, she thought, two more days. She could do this.

Miles went right, away from the shore, which appeared deeper. Amity turned to see the other two kayaks about twenty yards behind them. Bria and Becky were better rowers than her making the other teams almost as strong. Miles' impressive talent was bogged down by her. Maybe Easton was right? Maybe she was a liability? But she shook off the thought, not wanting to give him an excuse. He should have told her his plan.

Liam and Becky followed behind them on the right, while Easton and Bria turned left. Amity heard Bria say something to Easton about the left side being less dense with plants even though it was closer to the shoreline. Perhaps Bria had hiked around the lake to check out the surrounding area during the break? Amity should have done that, too, instead of spending all her time falling hard for a man that didn't believe in her.

Several yards into the unforgiving plants, their kayak snagged on the viny tendrils. Miles shouted at Amity to pick up her paddle while he frantically thrashed at the vines with his. Liam and Becky paddled their way through, gaining on them until they bumped hard into the back of their kayak, pitching Amity forward.

Miles turned around and pushed his paddle off the front of Liam and Becky's kayak, rotating their boat and pulling them side to side with their own. He then braced his feet on the underside of their kayak's rim and placed his hands on the bottom edge of Liam and Becky's boat.

"Alex never said we couldn't do this," Miles called out, putting all his arm strength into flipping them over.

Amity stared in shock as Liam and Becky's kayak capsized, Liam cussing and Becky screaming as they splashed into the water.

"We have to get them out," Amity shouted, trying to stand but slipping on the wet surface beneath her feet. "They'll drown tangled up in those plants."

"No, they won't." Miles laughed comically. "It's shallow enough to stand." He tugged on her arm, and she fell back into her seat.

Amity glared at Miles as he continued to chuckle in delight, but his expression quickly sobered as he looked to his left, locking eyes with Easton. Rowing in unison, Easton and Bria glided seamlessly through the plant-filled water closer to shore.

"Miles, this feels like cheating," Amity said, ignoring his concerns over Easton and Bria's progress. "We can't win the leg this way."

"The hell we can't." Miles twisted around, grabbed his paddle, and rowed, maneuvering around the plants with renewed energy.

Amity held her paddle defiantly across her lap and whipped her head around to search for Becky and Liam. As Miles had correctly predicted, they were able to stand, shuffling frantically through the water to get their kayak flipped over.

She turned back around with a huff, no longer interested in helping Miles win. Miles put everything he had into his strokes, but after choosing the wrong side coupled with their dramatic delay in the plants, he couldn't catch Easton and Bria. A few yards behind, they rolled into second place.

"That was pointless," Amity yelled after they docked. "We have to go into a sudden death with Liam and Becky anyway as one of the last two teams to finish."

"Yeah, but I almost beat your *ex-boyfriend*, and then we wouldn't have had to." With a pointed glare, he added, "And I would have won for sure if I didn't have *you* for a partner. Bria would have cinched it for me."

Amity drew back like she'd been slapped while Easton came toward her with his hand held out, a sympathetic look on his face.

"I don't need your pity," she spat at him, hating how desperately she wanted to take his hand. "It seems you agree with him."

Easton scrunched his features. "Amity—"

"No." With her palm held out, she added, "I don't want to hear it."

Easton dropped his arm, looking at her like she'd thrown him into a pit and left him for dead, his eyes rimmed with stress, his hair disheveled in a fray, and sweat breaking out across his scratched-up forehead.

"Does anyone else want to tell me I'm dead weight?" she yelled toward Bria.

With a tight-lipped frown, Bria shook her head. "Don't take it out on me, Hollywood. I think they're underestimating you."

"Yeah, sure you do." Pulling roughly on the ends of her frayed ponytail, Amity turned back to Miles. "You're such a dick. What an unmotivating thing to say"—she stalked off toward the mats—"right before another challenge together."

Amity tried to calm her emotions while she listened to Alex explain the sudden-death challenge, but his words just flowed soundlessly into her ears. Should she just throw the challenge and go home? As mad as she was at Easton, she still didn't want to get in the way of his win, and if being here wasn't going to help, then why stay?

With a sigh, she glanced out at the lake. Crew members were setting up four pyramid-shaped, buoy-like platforms from the side of a large motorboat, throwing anchors down to hold them in place. It wasn't hard for her to guess the challenge on her own—balance and endurance. It appeared each contestant would get their own platform, which was confirmed as she heard the last of Alex's words.

"—and the team that still has at least one contestant standing on their pyramid will win, continuing on to the final leg with Bria and Easton to compete for their chance to be one of two that will go home a million dollars richer."

Amity almost didn't want to win the sudden-death challenge out of spite—to end Miles' chance at a million dollars—but she'd be good at this, and she wasn't a quitter. Plus, she thirsted to prove herself after literally *everyone* doubted her.

Alex offered her a container, and she drew a yellow stick for her and Miles, leaving Becky and Liam with the remaining color of blue.

Miles walked up to her. "Can you do this?"

Amity smirked at his arrogance. "Can you?" she challenged.

"After racing boats and balancing on the rims my whole life—yes, I can."

"Then what does it matter? Only one of us has to stay on the platform longer than Becky and Liam."

Miles hid his expression. "It would be nice to have a safety net," he grumbled.

Amity noticed a movement out of the corner of her eye and swung her head around. Easton stood, rocking back and forth on his feet, wringing his fists around the sentimental baseball cap in his hands—no wonder his cap was such a wreck. It sent a small pang of guilt through her conscience after the intimate discussion they'd shared about his friend.

"Just noticing your backstabbing *ex-boyfriend*?" Miles asked. "How about getting lost, man? Amity needs to concentrate."

Easton didn't acknowledge Miles, but his jaw strained at his words—words she selfishly believed Easton deserved to hear. Although, Amity wished she hadn't looked into his beautiful green eyes because a deep sadness now shone from their depths. Did he regret his decision?

Easton swallowed deeply and croaked out, "Is there anything I can do to help, Amity?"

"Like what?" Amity chuckled without humor. "Go back in time?" She shook her head. "I'm fine. I can handle myself," she added, repeating the words he'd said to her earlier in the race. It hadn't bothered her then, but now that she understood what he'd meant, his words hurt. They were individuals, not a team. How had she not picked up on that?

Amity stripped off her purple tank top and tossed it onto the dock, letting the sun warm her torso. She wore her show-provided black sports bra and running shorts, prepared to get wet yet again. The crew boated the contestants out to the platforms, dropping Amity and Miles off at the yellow pyramids before taking Becky and Liam to their respective blue ones. Easton and Bria stood on the gray viewing platform with Alex, which had also been anchored securely to the base of the lake.

Her confidence in winning this challenge was high, as she used to play on the floats in the resort pools while her mom cleaned the rooms. To increase her seniority, her mom had worked loyally in one Palm Springs chain, and the staff became practically like family to them, taking turns watching out for her as a child.

With the beep of the timer, the challenge began, and the afternoon winds picked up, gusting in stronger blasts than they'd experienced in the race thus far. Waves moved across the crystal-clear water, causing the platforms to shift in unison with each ripple. Amity stood loosely with her arms out to her sides, palms down, concentrating on her balance, her tiny feet wedged painfully on the flat bar of her tall, narrow pyramid. The small foothold made it even more difficult to balance, probably on purpose, so the challenge wouldn't last forever.

Closing her eyes, Amity went into a yoga-like trance, letting her body flow in sync with the back-and-forth motion of the waves and allowing her mind to drift through the events of the past several days. An icy, tingling burst went through her core when she put together the obvious—she was more invested in their relationship than Easton was.

Amity had never put much stock into the expression 'blinded by love,' but how blind could she be? She'd been the one to believe in him as a partner, while he'd put his faith in someone else. She'd been the one to bet for more time with him, while he'd asked for her to help him win the money.

She'd been the one to say she wanted him permanently, while he'd said nothing about *forever*.

And his comments throughout the race? How had she missed their meaning? *I can handle myself. I hate that I even had to come on this dumb show. I'm only able to have a fling. I don't do relationships. If you get involved with me, I can't offer you anything after this race.* Blind...blind...blind...blind...blind! Or should she say stupid?

Sure, he cared about her—but not enough. Once he pocketed the money, she'd probably never see him again unless she came to Colorado. Isn't that what he'd said? That she'd come home with *him*, not the other way around? It *wasn't* an equal relationship.

After what felt like twenty minutes, she heard a collection of voices shouting her name and came out of her stupor. "*Amity*," Alex repeated in chorus with the other voices. "You can come down. You won."

She opened her eyes and saw Miles swimming toward the group platform while Liam and Becky sat on the edge, Liam with his shirt on and Becky covered in towels. Involuntarily, her eyes located Easton behind them. He looked alleviated, probably glad that he didn't have to feel personally responsible for her elimination.

Well, he was about to be relieved of all burden concerning her. Amity hated what she had to do, but she could *not* be invested in an uneven relationship. Her dad would have taken a bullet for her mom, and she wanted nothing less for herself.

Amity jumped into the frigid water, her legs so shot she could barely swim. She dog-paddled across the divide, and Liam reached for her hand, pulling her onto the group platform. With a smirk, he said, "You're pretty badass."

She wrapped her shaky legs in her arms and began to knead her exhausted feet with her fingertips, shivering from the cold as someone wrapped a towel around her shoulders. "That's a nice thing to say."

Liam shrugged. "I fell after about five minutes, so I've had a while to get over it. Becky hung in there a long time, though. She almost beat Miles." He turned and pecked a sweet kiss on Becky's cheek, staring adoringly into her eyes.

Amity tried to force a smile. Liam had just lost his chance at a million dollars, but his face glowed with such love for Becky it was like it didn't even matter to him. Gosh, she wanted that.

With a frustrated sigh, she hobbled across the platform and stumbled onto the motorboat, plopping onto a plush, padded seat in the back.

"You have to stand," one of the female crew members said. "Like you did on the way over."

"You gonna make me?" Amity asked, shocked as the words flew out of her mouth. Did she just say that out loud? It sounded like something Bria would say.

McKenzie shook her head at the crew member, making a gesture with her hand.

"Guess not," the woman finally said, hiding a smile.

Amity laid her head back on a soft cushion. It was the first time in days she'd been comfortable. She trickled out a laugh thinking she should just stay put for the night. Could they really make her move? Didn't they desperately need her for their stupid drama? More than she needed them, she thought wryly. She was a major part of the reality show's plot now.

Bria, Becky, Liam, and even Miles eyed her like they thought she was losing it. Maybe she was. Stick a fork in her, she was done. Oh wait, they only had a spork in their back-packing supplies. The ridiculous thought made her laugh even harder. Easton looked at her with a concerned frown.

Within minutes, they arrived at the dock, where she was immediately pulled aside for her daily interview. After evading countless probing questions from the directors about her relationship with Easton, she rushed off toward her tent to change.

"Amity," Easton yelled, jogging up to her. "Wait, please."

The cameras surrounded them, suffocating Amity in her current emotional state. She tried to draw in consistent breaths of air, not wanting to hyperventilate and almost faint like she did before. This had to end quickly for her sanity—like removing a Band-Aid—rip it off and cry out in pain all at once. If Amity didn't dump him now, she'd fall even deeper in love with him, and it would hurt worse when she finally admitted to herself that she could no longer give more than he took.

"*Cooper*," she began, holding her face even.

He flinched. "Cooper? What the hell?"

"Yes, Cooper. It's what you like to be called."

"Not by you."

"You don't need to worry about me anymore," she continued, listening to her voice shake. "I'm breaking up with you."

Easton's face crumpled, the pain of it stabbing at her heart.

"You win the bet," she whispered as chilling shivers wracked through her body. "You have my every assurance that I'll help you win the money—just like we agreed."

Easton drew in some air, looking at her with a dejected frown. "Amity, I don't think you're being fair. *One* decision that you should understand why I had to make, and you dump me."

She shook her head. "It's not just about that."

"It's not? Because before that, we were fine. The race is entirely separate from how I feel about you." With a determined glare, he continued, "And I'll prove it to you. Tomorrow when we leave here, let's leave together. Not just for one week on a silly camping trip from a bet. I want you to come *live* with me in Colorado. I'm crazy about you, and you know it. If you don't know, then you haven't been listening to me."

Listening to what? Empty promises with not even so much as an 'I love you.' She wrapped her towel tightly around her shoulders and backed away. His words confirmed her fears—he wanted *her* to make all the sacrifices. Move to Colorado with no guarantee for a future? He hadn't even considered her life in California. What was she supposed to do? Just up and leave her mom? And he hadn't considered how lack of communication during the race would affect their relationship. He'd chosen to put his trust in someone else when it mattered the most. Why should she trust *him*?

Amity met his pleading eyes. He looked confused, hurt, angry, and clueless—like *she* was the unreasonable one. Women had tried to change him, he'd said. Well, she wouldn't be one of them. Here she'd thought she'd hold him to that weeklong camping trip in Colorado to convince him that he couldn't live without her. But to gain what? She had dreams too, and she wasn't willing to give them up to be somebody's second priority.

Amity thrashed her head from side to side, focusing on the mud covering her still-wet bare feet. Unable to look at the emotion blazing from his captivating green eyes for a second time, she whispered, "I'm sorry, Cooper. I just can't anymore," and sprinted away before he could see the tears run down her cheeks.

She sat on a log in the backwoods and cried herself out, hugging the first full-sized towel the show had provided around her frozen, goosebump-covered skin. This was the worst pain she'd felt since her dad had died. Amity would survive and mostly move on—she always did—but first, she had a bet to uphold. She would do everything in her power to help Easton Cooper win the race. Not just because she'd promised him, but because she loved him.

Twenty-Four

ooper wished he could go back in time, just like Amity had jokingly suggested. He was in *agony*. The worst part was he didn't even have to do it. Amity was like some sort of acrobatic goddess or something because she'd never have fallen off that platform; his eyes hadn't left her for those fifteen-plus minutes. She'd stood on her pyramid in her sports bra and running shorts, her short, highlighted-brown hair up in a wispy ponytail with her eyes closed, so relaxed and beautiful, while he'd been tense enough to drive nails into the viewing platform boards.

There had not been a moment since he'd said 'Bria' that he hadn't regretted it, but all he could think of when it was his turn to choose a partner was what if he lost and Dominic died. He would *never* forgive himself. The logical choice for a strength challenge was Bria, who lifted weights and trained on strenuous equipment.

And he hadn't been wrong. Bria brought him an instant win.

But he hadn't been right either. Amity would never have lost that balance challenge; even if he'd fallen in the water, their team would still be in it.

Cooper understood her hurt and disappointment—that he didn't believe she could get him to the next leg—but he'd told her why he needed the money. Did she expect him to chance his best friend's life? Her continued reaction didn't seem fair. He'd thought she would get over it. That *he* was more important to her than winning the race.

But the real head-scratcher was being dumped when she didn't even get eliminated—they *were* both still in the race. Regardless of who he'd selected for a partner, the result was the same. The only difference was that he had an advantage on the next leg she wouldn't have. There had been several legs where she'd had the advantage when he didn't, and he'd understood. Why couldn't she?

Now his head was a jumbled mess because he'd gone and done exactly what he'd said he wouldn't do—fallen in love on a damn television show for other people's entertainment where the relationships didn't last. Because they weren't *real*. Nothing but a few weeks of heightened drama with intensified experiences that failed when the couple realized they had no solid foundation. He was such a fool.

How many times had Cooper told his sister, Hannah, that television relationships weren't real? And he was still too stupid to listen to his own advice. But it *felt* so real. He felt in love. He felt raw, hurt, and miserable. He felt—*ugh*—he hated the sappy way it sounded—but he felt like his future had been ripped away from him.

Cooper kicked some loose rock beneath the picnic table and poked at his soggy, freeze-dried eggs with his spork. Dammit, who was he kidding? He still loved her, and nothing about it was fake.

He'd tried to win her back after the challenges yesterday, but Amity hadn't given him the time of day. After disappearing and nearly giving him a heart attack, she'd tiptoed out of the woods, still in damp clothes covered only by a towel, her face red and splotchy from crying. She'd changed without a word to anyone, made her own backpacking food, and re-pitched her tent next to Bria. That killed him. He'd gotten used to falling asleep holding her hand between the open mesh doors of their side-by-side tents every night.

He didn't think things could get worse—but they did. As the sun set, increasingly high winds brought with them a sharp drop in temperature. Amity, having been wet for hours, never recovered from her nearly hypothermic state. He'd tried to give her every layer he owned, even throwing his sweat-shirt, heavy coat, hat, and gloves into her tent, but she'd tossed them all out.

At the beginning of the race, when he'd hoped the elements would take her out, he had no idea that a few weeks later, he'd be listening to the woman he loved attempt to conceal the sounds of her anguished moans for ten hours straight, not letting him do anything to help her. He didn't get a wink of sleep and felt even more like crap this morning—if that was even possible.

If Amity didn't want him, he'd have to move on, but man, the pain only intensified the longer they were apart. It just didn't make sense. She'd broken up with him out of nowhere. He'd played it over and over in his head, and he still couldn't piece together her permanent rejection.

Perhaps she'd planned to do it? She'd had some fun for a few weeks at his expense and then pulled away just in time to go home to her California mansion. Did she also plan to blind-side him and go for the cash? Or was she just creating drama to gain exposure and draw attention to her fashion line? Cooper shoveled a load of eggs into his mouth, forcing them down his throat and into his unsettled stomach. Man, he wanted answers.

He narrowed his eyes as Amity emerged from her tent with her flint, backpacking stove, water bottle, and a bag of freeze-dried breakfast food. Her eyes were red-rimmed, her ponytail was an unbrushed mess, and her hands shook violently as she tried to light the small stove. She wasn't fooling him. Amity was hurting, too, from much more than just the elements. Even if she was here for the money or cameras, she cared about him.

"Having a tough time?" he asked.

Amity looked up at him, narrowing her exhausted eyes in return.

"You know the easy way to solve that, right? Tell me what I did pissed you off, and then forgive me. Why make us both miserable?"

Bria and Miles exchanged looks, Bria a pinched frown and Miles a pleased smirk.

Amity huffed out a breath and continued heating the water for her food. After pouring the scalding liquid into her freeze-dried food pouch, she began to walk toward the dock to eat alone.

Avoidance—interesting. If she thought he would give up without answers, she had another thing coming. "You know, Amity," he said to her retreating figure, "I seem to remember the first challenge of this race starting off about like this. You hated my guts—the only problem for you now is that you really don't."

She paused, hesitated, then turned. "But we won't be partners today, will we? Because you don't *think* I have the skills to win."

"When are you going to get over that? I do think you can win. The difference is I *have* to win. I'm not just here for shits and giggles."

Amity's face dropped into a shocked frown, the deep hurt that crossed her features stabbing at him. Why in the hell did he just say that? Damn, she made him crazy.

"You will win, *Cooper*." She took a deep breath and nodded. "I'll make sure that you do."

His last name coming off her lips shot a twisting pain through his stomach. "This isn't over yet," he said as she walked away. He wasn't going down without a fight—for the money or the girl.

~

WITH RELIEF, Amity finished her final backpacking meal of the race, but the reprieve didn't last long. Shortly after, she was called to *another* interview where the suited-up panel of directors hammered her with questions. Normally, she liked the head director, but her eager devotion to splash her breakup across TV for entertainment disgusted her.

"Amity," McKenzie probed, "can you tell the viewing audience why you broke up with Easton?"

"*Cooper*," she corrected tersely. "And no. It's no one's damn business."

"Do you love him?"

Amity threw up her arms. "You know what? Why not? Everyone can tell anyway. Yes, *I love him*, but it doesn't matter, does it?"

"Can you explain to America," McKenzie said, smiling like they were filming solid gold, "why you can't tell Cooper that you love him?"

"No," Amity snapped, giving them exactly the kind of ratings-worthy TV they craved, which made her grit her teeth even harder. "Did Alex lie to everyone a few days ago? Is there some sort of sick twist at the end of all this so you can have your Race for Riches or *Romance*? Do we need to tell another contestant that we *love* them to win the money? What a joke," she added, rolling her eyes. "Can I leave now and get my mics and cameras on for the *actual* race."

Amity sounded like the spoiled brat she'd been painted as in the beginning, but she was in no mood to regurgitate her pain. Walking onto her mat, she took a deep breath and snapped on her smaller pack, which contained two pre-filled bottles of water. Now that they were almost finished, the show had taken away their heavy packs. It seemed the days of pumping water by hand and pitching tents were finally over.

Easton stepped onto his mat and locked eyes with her, determination strewn across his rugged features.

Amity tore her eyes away, wanting nothing more than to run into his arms, but she couldn't let herself do it. She'd wind up giving up on her dreams and focusing all her energy on his. It took everything in her not to look at him. She scanned the forest treetops, frustrated that the picturesque scenery no longer offered her comfort. Without Easton by her side, her passion for adventure in the great outdoors was over. Mountains, pine trees, and glacial lakes would forever remind her of the man she loved, and she needed to be away from those reminders.

Amity would have moved to Colorado for him. She'd given it some thought and decided her mom would probably be willing to move too, as Amity's happiness had always been her focus in life. There were plenty of resorts in Aspen, likely in the same chain as her mom worked in now. They'd miss the heat and their friends, but they'd acclimate. Easton was more important to her than where she lived. He had his established business, whole family, and best friend in Colorado. She understood his reasons. It's just that—if he really loved her, he'd be willing to do anything to be with her—and he wasn't.

Alex Bandon stepped onto the hosting platform with the lake silhouetted behind him, flashing a broad smile at them. "Good morning, contestants. Congratulations on making it to the final leg of the race. Today, we'll be handing out two million dollars, one million for each partner on the winning team—"

Amity squeezed her eyes shut and imagined stacks of one-hundred-dollar bills in her hands. My gosh, all the things she could do with that money.

"—Bria and Cooper's advantage from winning the previous leg is that they each get a five-minute head start, regardless of partner selections—"

Amity's heart sank. She'd been secretly hoping that Easton would choose her in the end, but Alex's announcement solidified partners. Bria and Easton would be stupid not to choose one another and leave with a five-minute head start. She'd just lost him for sure—and the money. Amity shook her head, frustrated by her selfish thoughts. It didn't matter. Money was never the goal—an adventure was, and she'd certainly had one.

"It's ladies' turn to choose first," Alex said. "Therefore, selection will begin with the woman in the first-place team— Bria. Since we're down to only four of you, Bria's decision will decide both teams. A major advantage, but only fair as the men chose first last time."

"So, Bria," Alex continued, fanning his hand out toward her, "your choice is?"

"Cooper," Bria stated firmly with a head nod.

"No surprise there," the host said. "Cooper, your thoughts on that?"

He nodded. "I probably would have chosen Bria as well."

Amity curled her fist, trying to hold an indifferent mask on her face.

Easton's eyes shot nervously over to look at her before drifting back to the host. "It's the logical choice for a win," he continued. "Especially given the five-minute head start we share."

"Amity," Alex chirped out, acting way too chipper for her mood, "are you feeling all right this time?"

"Yeah, fine." Amity held up her hand to ward off the attention of the cameras. "I told you I wouldn't react like that again. I'm over it."

Easton's jaw twitched, and he shifted around on his mat. She really shouldn't have added a zinger, but his easy agreement with Bria hurt. He'd proven that she wasn't his rock. You had to be each other's rock in life, and real life was even tougher than this—at least for her.

But it didn't change the fact that she still loved him. Easton needed the money, and he would get it. Because no one could *make* her cross the finish line.

"Contestants," Alex began, "there will be a mile-long footrace—"

Easton's hands flew up to cover his face. One part of her wanted to tell him, 'Don't worry, you'll get your money,' and the other part wanted to watch him sweat. Were the directors feeding into *her* strengths? Perhaps? They'd want their standard max-drama finish.

"—with hurdles along a paved road. The run will end at a parking lot at the base of Hoodoo Ski Resort, where your team will be expected to complete a puzzle—"

A string of profanity flew out of Easton's mouth, and Amity smiled, somewhat pleased to watch him squirm.

"—skills challenge before finishing the race. It's been a long journey, and I wish you all the best of luck for the win." Alex clapped his hands together. "Okay, let's get started. Men will draw for colors today."

Easton stomped toward the host, thrusting his hand into the container so hard he almost knocked it out of Alex's hands before pulling out a green stick. Amity couldn't hold back her amused grin—green to match the rich color of his eyes and the vast expanse of trees in which he belonged—how fitting.

Miles drew the remaining stick—purple—and she sucked in a shocked breath. The same color as her shirt, just like Easton had drawn the color of his. Was it some sort of sign their team placement was as it should be? Amity shook off the thought that the universe was telling her something and decided she might as well do her best to enjoy the end of her heartbreaking adventure.

Miles walked toward her with a resigned frown on his face. "You'd better not lose this for me."

Rolling her eyes, she returned, "I thought you only cared about screen time."

"We have a fifty-percent chance at a million dollars. Now I care about money."

She laughed. Too bad for him that he wasn't going to get any.

"What's your deal?" Miles asked, squinting at her. "You're not planning to let your shithead ex-boyfriend win the money, are you?" He leaned closer toward her. "Because he doesn't care *anything* about you. He's proven that."

A shot of pain so intense Amity had to hold back tears went through her. "I'm not stupid," she said, crossing her arms. "Give up a million dollars? Of course not. Who would?"

Easton, who now stood on the start-line mat, glared at them over his shoulder, his features taut. What? Was he mad she wasn't spouting about upholding the terms of their bet? She wasn't going to tell him what he wanted to hear.

Sending a sweet fake smile his way, Amity asked, "Problem, Cooper?"

He pointed at her. "This isn't over yet."

She scrunched up her nose. What wasn't? The race? Or their relationship? She couldn't help but ask, "*What* isn't?"

"*Us*," he said, sending a confusing jolt through her.

Easton and Bria's timer beeped, and they ran off, jumping over the first set of hurdles and slowly disappearing into the distance. Scanning the scenery, Amity did her best to ignore Miles; and five slow minutes later, their timer finally beeped.

She bolted forward.

"Wait, Amity," Miles shouted behind her. "Slow down. My calves are 'effed up from all the cramps."

Speeding up, she let loose an immature chuckle.

"We need to stick together," Miles said, continuing on with even more aggressive protests until, thankfully, she could no longer hear him.

The hurdles were spaced fairly far apart, and she hopped over each bar with ease, using her experience from all the garden fences and bushes back home. The run was a nice release of her pent-up emotions, and given that her placement no longer mattered, she enjoyed her surroundings. A small ski mountain with a few lifts towered in front of her, all the snow currently melted off by the summer sun. Camera cars followed alongside now that they were on flat, open pavement, and a golf cart sped past with Alex Bandon riding toward the endpoint.

"Hi, Alex," she called out with a wave.

Alex waved back and shouted, "You forgot your partner."

Amity shrugged, and the host laughed, lightening her mood.

Seven short minutes later, the endpoint flags were in sight, and Amity sucked in her breath at the scene. Bria was lying on the ground next to the final hurdle, holding her ankle with Easton by her side. How had Bria managed that? Amity had expected them to already be working on the puzzle.

Easton helped Bria up and supported her weight while they hobbled toward the checkpoint mat.

Amity raced past them and jumped in front of Alex—alone. Fortunately, Miles was nowhere in sight.

"Amity," Alex announced, "you cannot begin the final challenge without your partner."

Shrugging again, Amity said, "He'll be along," as Easton and Bria arrived at the mat.

The host cracked an amused grin. "I see." He then turned

to look at her competitors. "Bria and Cooper, you may begin the challenge. The team that completes the puzzle first wins the race. Announce your completion, and we'll check your work. Please note, you are not allowed to touch a member of the other team or their puzzle—doing so will result in a thirty-minute time penalty." He motioned his hand out. "When you're ready, go ahead."

Easton hurled himself onto the green platform while Bria slowly made her way up on one foot. He frantically began to slide pieces around on what appeared to be a flat, tile slide puzzle. Amity would excel at this. Hopefully, she wouldn't be tempted to take the win at the last minute. After all, it was a million dollars. She sighed, trying to push the counterproductive thoughts out of her mind, but over and over, her brain repeated, 'Think of all the things you could do with that money.' Ugh! The longer Miles took to arrive, the better.

Twiddling her thumbs, Amity tried not to stare at her sexy ex-boyfriend's backside while he thrashed the pieces around. Gosh, she wished he was still hers. She would miss him—terribly.

Easton and Bria exchanged heated words, and Amity began to feel guilty they had to go through being distraught for no reason. She opened her mouth to admit her plan, but just then, Miles arrived.

"Dammit, Amity," he spat at her, wiping his face with his sweat-lined fluorescent orange shirt.

She smirked at him.

"Amity and Miles, you may begin the challenge," Alex announced before monotonously repeating the instructions for Miles' benefit. The host finished with his same statement of, "Go ahead."

Miles jumped onto their purple platform and reached down to pull Amity up; one-armed, he lifted her. Miles was strong—she'd give him that. In a bossy and condescending tone, he said, "Okay, solve it."

Amity could have some fun with this. With feigned effort, she slid the brightly painted tiles around. She glanced at her camerawoman, absentmindedly working the puzzle. Today the woman had her hair up in two separate pigtail-like, blue-blonde mounds on top of her head. They exchanged a smile before Amity returned her eyes to the puzzle.

"Shoot," she said to herself, wrinkling her brow and pulling her hand back. She'd slid the starting words into place. 'Riches *and* Romance…'

"Problem there, Amity?" Alex called out.

Bria peeked over and saw the start of the phrase. Oh perfect, Amity thought. It didn't occur to her to help them out in that way.

"Um, no, Alex," Amity mumbled, deciding then and there to get the puzzle as close as possible without actually solving it.

Easton, who still manically slid pieces around, shot a frantic look their way. The beads of sweat dripping off his skin pricked her conscience. She hadn't meant for him to squirm that badly.

"Keep your eyes on your own damn puzzle," Miles yelled, blocking theirs from view with his hand.

Amity grinned. Too late, dummy. Bria had already seen it.

"Amity's about to win your precious money," Miles continued. "I never understood why a creepy mountain recluse like you needs money anyway. Don't you live in your cabin in the woods all by yourself with your murderous ax and no electricity?" Miles chuckled menacingly, sending a chill up her spine.

Easton ignored Miles, putting all his focus on the puzzle. "Bria, you try," he finally said.

Amity shuffled the remaining pieces into place—except one. The cameras circled her from every angle, ready to record the win. Leaving the last tile out of place, she stared at the phrase, 'Riches *and* Romance. Can you really win it all?'

And the answer was: A big fat no! You could *not* win it all. The directors planned a ratings-worthy blockbuster—at her expense.

"That's it," Miles shouted. "Amity, that's the last part of the phrase. Slide it down!"

Easton shot another frantic look their way, and just when Miles locked eyes with him, Amity reversed her thought process. One at a time, she began to slide the tiles out of place, counting to herself, 'One, two, three, four, five, six, seven—'

"What the hell? What are you… No," Miles shouted, darting for the puzzle.

In what felt like slow motion, Amity turned and placed her small frame in between Miles and the puzzle.

Miles chuckled and said, "You couldn't stop a mouse." He grabbed her around the waist and locked her against his side with her feet sticking out.

Miles' embrace filled her with a yucky combination of embarrassment and nausea, spurring her into action. She wildly began to shake her feet around.

Unfazed, Miles kept his grip around her waist and, with his free hand, began sliding the few remaining tiles back into place. "Didn't think your plan through too well, did you? The smart girl isn't so *smart* after all."

No! Amity couldn't let Miles win. In a panic, 'Easton… Dominic…Easton,' went through her mind. She wrenched her arm back and elbowed Miles between the ribs.

"Ouch, fuck," Miles shouted, dropping her and grabbing his side. He staggered backward, regained his balance, and before she could react, reached for her ponytail, gripping the frizzy ends and pulling her head back. "Nice try, *Princess*," he mocked. "But even your ax-murdering ex-boyfriend can't beat me in a fight."

"Ow," she screamed as he gripped her hair even tighter, tears of pain pooling in her eyes. "*Let go.*"

Easton locked eyes with her, a torn look of agony on his face. He stood in limbo like he was ready to run over and defend her, but she could take care of herself. She didn't need him to *defend* her; she needed him to *love* her—as much as she loved him.

"Amity," Easton yelled from across the platform divide, "I can't stay out of this much longer—"

Her man's voice sent adrenaline pumping through her. If Easton got involved, he'd take on a time penalty. Regardless of what her needs were, right now, his were more important. And he needed her to win this fight.

Amity turned her head and hissed into Miles' ear, "No one calls me *Princess* except Easton," as she smashed her heel down on the tips of his toes.

Miles grunted and loosened his grip, allowing her to twist her body around. Cocking her leg back, she kneed him as hard as she could in the balls, and with a loud yelp of pain, he fell over and began rolling around on the platform boards.

"Serves you right, you creepy *troll.*" Ignoring the pain in her scalp, Amity sprinted back to the puzzle and thrashed the pieces around, moving ten more out of place, knowing she only had seconds before Miles recovered. She continued counting in her head, 'Eleven, twelve, thirteen—' until he slammed into her.

Shoving her out of the way, Miles turned to stare at the puzzle and tossed his hands over his head. "We only had *one* tile left—one friggin' tile—and then a million dollars. A million dollars!"

Amity bit her lip, a wide smile bursting through. "Yeah, it's a real shame—one tile—and then we had the phrase 'Riches *and* Romance. Can you really win it—'"

"*Shut up,*" Miles yelled, a vein popping out on his forehead.

"Shut the hell up." Still holding onto his sore groin with one hand, Miles pounded his other fist against the puzzle table. In whiny desperation, he continued, "Why would you let them win? *Why?*"

Bria chuckled from across the divide. "Thanks for the info, Hollywood."

Swearing profusely, Miles returned to the puzzle and shuffled the tiles around like a maniac, but even knowing what the phrase said, he couldn't slide a single piece into place.

Amity laughed, and Easton turned to glare at her with an incredulous look. She put her fist into her mouth, averting her eyes.

"Do something," Miles yelled at her. "I can't solve this."

"Not so different from being dumped in a lake," Amity said, continuing to muffle her laughter. "Is it, Miles?"

"You're going to give them a million dollars each. A million dollars," he shouted. "You're crazy!"

"Yeah." Amity shrugged, grinning. "Turns out I am."

"Alex," Miles called out frantically, eyeing the host. "She's throwing the race. She's throwing the fucking race. It's got to be a violation of the rules."

Alex shook his head, holding back his own grin. "There's nothing in the rules that states a member from one's own team can't touch the puzzle or their other team member within contract guidelines." The host placed his finger to his lips as if thinking through the conditions. "Neither of you injured one another such that you can't adequately continue the race. So, no"—the host shrugged—"there's no violation of the rules."

Giving up on Alex, Miles turned back toward Amity. "You'll never see him again," he said, pointing at Easton. "He'll take the money and run. I told you, that guy doesn't care *anything* about you. Selfless people don't get ahead in this world, Amity."

"I think they do," she returned sweetly.

"Got it," Bria called out, stepping back from the puzzle with her arms out wide.

Alex moved in, along with a dozen cameras. "That's it. 'Riches *and* Romance. Can you really win it all?' We have our winners! Congratulations, Bria and Cooper."

"Yeah!" Bria jerked her arm back and pumped her fist out in celebration, balancing on her healthy leg. She wasn't one of those women who ran into people's arms for hugs, though she did shout out several whoops of joy.

Easton let out his breath as if a huge weight had been lifted off his shoulders, which of course, it had, but when he met Amity's eyes, intense guilt lined his features.

Tears welled up in her eyes, and she looked away. This was it—the last time she'd ever see him.

Alex jumped up on his platform. "Congratulations to the winners of the *riches* for *The Race for Riches or Romance*"—the host motioned his hand out, flashing a jovial smile—"Bria and Cooper. In a few minutes, we'll present each of you with a check for one million dollars."

Amity cheered while Miles scowled like the sore loser he was. He walked over to McKenzie, making one last desperate plea to claim he was wronged while she laughed again, enjoying his downfall.

"The reason we added *romance*," Alex continued, facing a large camera, "to the title of the race will be revealed to you at our reunion episode. Be sure to join us and *all* of this season's contestants live on stage. Find out what's happening with our couples two months from now," the host added dramatically. "Will Isaac take Jade on that date he promised her? Will Liam move to Alaska for Becky? Will Amity forgive Cooper and give him a second chance?"

Amity squeezed her eyes shut. Thanks, Alex, she thought, for pouring more salt into the wound.

"And find out the contestants' perspectives on key

moments from this season's race," Alex continued. "Did Amity really throw the race for Cooper? If so, why did she dump him and leave him brokenhearted? What do Cooper and Bria plan to do with their million—"

Amity covered her ears and tried to control her breathing. Would she make it through the reunion episode?

Appearing to have finally finished, Alex jumped off the platform, and Amity removed her hands from her ears. "Contestants, don't go far. After the ceremony, we'll be recording exit interviews for all four of you."

Amity groaned. Did she really need to tell the world that she loved Easton again? The man would be confused enough when he watched the show back and listened to her confess her love for him. It was a question everyone would want to know—if you love him so much, then why did you break up with him?

"AMITY, WAIT," Cooper yelled, running over to her while Goatee Man moved in to capture the scene. Cooper turned his head and whispered, "Can you cut us a break? Please, man. I need a minute."

Frowning, Goatee Man shook his head.

"Yeah, yeah, I get it. It's your job even though the race is over. Do you plan to come move in with me too?"

Goatee Man chuckled and then backed up slightly, focusing in on them from a distance.

Cooper released a nervous sigh before turning to meet Amity's guarded expression. He finally had a million-dollar check in his pocket, and he wasn't even happy. "Thank you," he said to her and swallowed through his clogged throat. "I wish I could say more, but there aren't strong enough words for what you just did. I'll never be able to repay you."

"No problem," she said with a shrug. "We had a bet, and we both know that I don't need the money. I'm only here for shits and giggles, right?"

Flinching back, Cooper shook his head. "Amity, I—"

"I didn't mean to say that so harshly." Forcing a smile, she clasped her hands out in front of her. "I didn't mean to say that at all, actually. Sorry, no hard feelings. I hope Dominic makes a full recovery. I sincerely mean that. A person's life is more important than anything."

Cooper nodded. "Thanks, but I don't want this"—he motioned his finger between the two of them—"to be over yet. I'm not giving up on us. Why are you? Because of the money? I'm not keeping a dime of it for myself. I want *you*, not money. I meant what I said—I want you to move in with me."

Amity searched his eyes, hope blossoming across her features.

Silently, Cooper cheered. He was making progress.

She tilted her head to the side. "Will you come to Palm Springs instead to live with me?"

He froze, fear ripping through him. *What?* Come live her plush lifestyle and give up everything he'd worked so hard for? Leave his family and friends? He couldn't do that. Even if he tried, he'd never live up to her expectations in a setting like that. He'd have to change everything about himself.

"I can't move," he said.

Her face dropped, all signs of hope vanishing.

In a panic, he added, "But I can give you more time. We could date until you're ready. Maybe fly back and forth for weekends?"

Amity let out a frustrated huff, gnawing on her lower lip. "I'm so sorry, Cooper. I can't..." She fanned her palm out and, with a shaky whisper, added, "I just can't," before jogging away.

Cooper stood motionless, watching her leave, a permanent

hole ripping open inside him. He'd been here before—with women not wanting him enough to stay. The difference was that he'd never really been in love with any of them before. Not like this. He felt like he'd just lost one person to save another.

Spacing out, he mumbled incoherent answers through his final interview and boarded a bus with the remaining contestants and crew members. The bus driver dropped them off at a hotel in Bend for the night to rest and clean up before shuttling them to the airport the next day.

Amity shot out of the bus's front seat like a cannon with her shiny, pink suitcase in hand, wearing a royal blue running shirt and splotchy-patterned black leggings. Everything about her screamed expensive again, like she'd stepped right out of a catalog. Cooper jumped off the bus and forced himself to walk in the opposite direction.

Favoring her good ankle, Bria limped up to him, decked out in clean camo gear with her spiky blonde hair freshly gelled. "How ya doing?"

"Miserable," he said, grabbing the back of his neck. "Freaking miserable."

"Yeah, I figured as much."

Cooper dug his fingers into his muscles. "I should be ecstatic. I'm hopefully about to save my best friend's life, but all I can think about is how I lost her. I keep going through it repeatedly in my head, wondering what would have happened if I hadn't chosen you for that kayak challenge."

"Well, that would've sucked because then I'd be a million dollars poorer."

He let out a defeated-sounding chuckle.

"To answer your question truthfully," Bria continued, "not that you want to hear it—if you'd chosen Hollywood for that kayak challenge, you still would have won the race. She never would have fallen off that pyramid in the sudden-death challenge." Bria paused and sighed. "And then that final puzzle—looked to me like it was hand-painted. I reckon the design must have been pre-planned days before the finale—Hollywood solved that thing within minutes. If you'd chosen her, *both* of you would have won a million dollars."

Guilt tore through him as he acknowledged what he didn't want to hear. He'd cost Amity her share of the money. He already knew it but hearing it from Bria punched him in the gut. Good thing Amity didn't need money, or he'd feel even worse.

Letting out his breath, Cooper rubbed his forehead. "But would we still be together if I'd chosen her instead of you? That's what's really killing me. I'll never know for sure—she might have left me anyway."

Bria shook her head, laughing in disbelief. "Is that what you think?" Her eyes searched his face. "You do know that she loves you, right? Like really loves you."

He glanced at Bria, hopeful but not convinced.

"Come on, man." Bria raised her eyebrows. "You can't be that clueless. *Every* move that girl made was for you. The money, yes, but more importantly, she left because she didn't want to force you to make sacrifices for her."

Cooper shook his head. Could that be true? His mind was so exhausted he couldn't think. "I told her I wouldn't ever change again for a relationship, but I seriously don't think I'll ever be the same without her. I know it sounds ridiculous, but I'm not sure I can *survive* without her. I don't want to go through life alone."

Bria slapped him on the shoulder. "Then go tell her that, stupid, and don't give up until she understands."

He attempted a grin. "You're a good friend, Bria."

"So I've been told." Bria grabbed her suitcase handle. "Now, I'm going to go spend my million on a condo at the beach and never look back. Tell Amity I'd like her to come visit

291

after ya win her over. You can come too if you don't hump her like a rabbit in the guest room."

Cooper chuckled, watching Bria hobble off toward the terminal. Was she right? Could he win Amity back? And if so, what would it cost him?

Twenty-Five

The next several days were a whirlwind for Cooper. At first, Dominic wouldn't accept the money. Chelsea and Hannah went batshit crazy, yelling at Dominic to get his head out of his backend. Cooper joined in, having to go as far as to tell his best friend that another contestant gave up the win to save his life.

That woke him up. Dominic then realized that if he didn't accept the money, he'd be slapping some stranger in the face who'd given up a million dollars for him. Cooper would never stop owing Amity. Without her sacrifice, he wasn't even sure Dominic would have taken the money.

Since the show had ended, Cooper had been staying in town at his parents' house to be closer to Dominic. His cabin was a thirty-minute drive from central Aspen, up in the hills, and required an off-road Jeep to tackle the road. His sister, who had a townhouse at the base of Aspen Mountain, had also moved in temporarily to help Chelsea. He was mostly grateful for it, as Chelsea was barely hanging on, but his sister would *not* leave him alone. He felt like Hannah, Chelsea, and even Dominic had double the energy since he'd returned.

Still, Cooper tried to hide his mood and help out as much

as possible. Most evenings, the four of them ate dinner on his parents' patio, which eased the hassle of groceries, cooking, and cleaning for Chelsea and Dominic. His parents helped out, too but gave them space, eating inside most of the time. He hoped to be equally incredible if he was ever a parent, which painstakingly brought on a stabbing pain in his chest as he again thought of Amity.

After staring fixedly at the mountains in the distance, Hannah suddenly dropped her fork on her plate and shot him a look. "Who gives up a million dollars to save someone's best friend?"

Great, Hannah, he thought. Just what he needed was Dominic trying to reject the money again—right after his best friend had finally gotten his name moved up to a priority surgery slot too. Cooper shot a nervous glance his way.

"Don't worry, Coop," Dominic said, running his fingers over his shaved head. He'd buzzed off his wavy light brown locks to make life easier. Wearing a Hang Loose T-shirt, he slouched back in his chair. "Chelsea already put the money into our account and scheduled the procedure. I think she'd *kill* me if I tried to give it back now." Dominic started laughing, his usual high-energy shining slightly through his exhaustion.

"Dominic, that is *not* funny," Chelsea chastised, but Cooper could see the relief on her pale face. Chelsea's cheeks were typically covered in a bold set of freckles, which had faded when she'd cut out her outdoor workout routine. The fact that she'd also chopped off her strawberry-blonde hair to simplify life had pained his best friend.

"See, not funny, Coop." Dominic winked. "Guess we have a million dollars for a few more days."

Unfortunately, his best friend's begrudging acceptance of the money screwed him over in another way. Hannah and Chelsea began to fire questions at him about the mysterious donor. With each evading answer, their looks grew in curiosity until he finally got up and walked away.

The following day, he tried to sit on the couch and enjoy mindless Nordic ski reruns when Hannah plopped down next to him.

"You seem kind of strung out," his sister said.

He grunted and turned up the volume on the TV.

"This woman—on the show," Hannah continued casually while twisting a lock of her honey-blonde hair around her fingers. "Why did you say she gave up the money again?"

Gritting his teeth, Cooper forced out, "I never said it was a woman."

"But," she continued, leaning toward him with interest, "it *was* a woman, wasn't it?"

"Hannah." He kneaded his forehead with the tips of his fingers. "*Please* mind your own business. I really need some space right now."

"Cool," she said, jumping up from the couch. "When do I get to meet her?" She pulled on his hand, her words coming out a mile a minute. "Let's go. Does she live in Colorado? Does she like to hike? Does she like to climb? You need a break from all this stress with Dominic."

Cooper yanked his hand away. "You don't get to meet her. We're just friends...*period*."

Hannah started laughing. "Bull-friggin-loney, you're just friends. You look like a burnt marshmallow that's been raked over the coals. What did she do to you?" After a moment of thought, his sister pointed an accusing finger at him. "What did *you* do to her? You screwed it up, didn't you? With that no-commitment crap you've been into."

"Hannah, please." He sighed, hearing the exhaustion in his own voice. "I need to focus on Dominic right now, not made-up, girly romance BS. You're totally off base, making everything into something it's not. I told you before, and I'll tell you again—it's a damn television show. No one actually falls in love. It's not real."

"No?" she challenged.

"No," Cooper said with finality and stood up to walk away. He headed for his childhood bedroom, which was now a guest room, so he could shut the door, though he heard her trailing behind him.

"So this woman gave up a million dollars for you, but it's not real?" Nonchalantly, she added, "Oh well, I guess I'll see for myself starting tomorrow when the show airs."

Cooper froze. Oh shit! The show was going to air. He was so distracted with being there for Dominic while aching for Amity that he'd lost track of everything. Sleep wasn't something he consciously did anymore. The whites of his eyes had red streaks through them, he'd lost his appetite, and he plain flat could not think. Why try to hide it anyway? Everyone would see their relationship unfold over the next two months —damn television show.

"She didn't give up a million dollars for me," Cooper said in defeat. "She did it to save someone's life."

Hannah choked out another laugh. "Yeah, okay, big bro. Keep telling yourself that it had nothing to do with you." Bouncing up on her toes, she clapped her hands together. "This is going to be so fun."

"*What* is?" Cooper ground out.

"The show, dummy."

He groaned, pinching the bridge of his nose.

"I can't believe you're going to be on TV," she said, grabbing his arms in uncontained excitement. "And that you met a woman! I'm *so* going to guess who she is during the first episode. Is she pretty? Does she like the outdoors? Why won't you tell me? What about pedicures? I can't wait to hang out with her. I haven't been to the spa in *forever*!"

Cooper threw his hands over his ears and walked into his

room, shutting the door with the back of his foot. He made a beeline for the bathroom to search for ibuprofen in the medicine cabinet. His damn headache was about to turn into a full-on migraine. Hannah's constant reminders that he was heartbreakingly, exhaustively miserable without Amity were driving him over the edge, and he couldn't do anything about it.

After he'd landed in Colorado, Bria sent him Amity's phone number and address. Cooper had tried to call her multiple times, every time getting her voicemail. Finally, he left a pathetic message—and that was ten days ago. It was pretty straightforward—Amity didn't want anything to do with him. He went to bed with those same thoughts spiraling through his mind, just like every crappy night of sleep since she'd broken up with him.

The first episode aired the following evening, and Cooper stayed in the dining room while his parents and Hannah watched from the couch. There was no way he could see the woman he loved on-screen without having her by his side, but at the same time, he couldn't make himself leave the house. He sat on a wooden chair at the dining room table, rubbing his golden retriever's ears and listening intently through the wall.

Over-the-top intro music played like they were about to climb Mt. Everest. He chuckled at the stupidity of it all until he heard the contestant previews begin. Amity's pre-show interview mainly focused on her obsessive running habits and her time spent splashing around in lavish resort pools with her friends. There was nothing about her home or family life. He found that odd, but maybe Amity's family wanted privacy, which he totally understood.

Cooper tuned out again until he heard the scene unfold where Amity became his partner. He wanted to laugh at the childish things they were saying to one another, but hearing her voice was killing him.

"Well, Amity seems a little high maintenance. Huh," he heard Hannah say before yelling at him through the wall. "It's not *her*, is it?"

"It's not who, dear?" his mom asked Hannah. At least his sister had enough sense to keep his parents in the dark.

"Never mind, Mom," Hannah said, getting hooked on the show again.

He listened to the fire challenge unfold, knowing that in the coming weeks, Amity would sacrifice much more than her hands and feet for him. It tied his stomach up in knots. He'd *never* be able to repay her, no matter what he did.

"Oh my gosh," Hannah yelled. "You're going to get *eliminated*. How are you not going to get eliminated?"

His parents were shouting intense comments at the screen, along with his sister. He finally let himself laugh at that. Wait till they see the next part, he thought. Wait till they see *all* the incredible things Amity will do.

"Oh my gosh, oh my gosh," Hannah screamed. "She cut off her hair. Her hair! She's burning it." There was a quiet pause, then, "Oh, of course. She's smart. Oh, oh, she's got a flame. Her hands are bleeding everywhere. Poor thing. Wow…"

Cooper tuned everything out after that because he couldn't live like this. He would do anything to win Amity back—*anything*.

He walked silently to his bedroom, threw a few extra clothes and toiletries in his already-equipped backpack, and jogged out the door without a word. Amity would have to convince him that she could never love him back because he would *not* leave her doorstep until she did.

~

COOPER DROVE his rental car down a side street full of shabby stucco buildings and parked in front of the house number on

Bria's text. This couldn't be right. With scrubby, unkept cactus beds and peeling, chipped-up paint, a three-story apartment complex stood before him. A bent-up chain-link fence surrounded a small courtyard, which contained an empty swimming pool. Thirsty-looking weeds grew through the cracks.

He started a text to Bria, his fingers freezing before tapping send. Bria's original text had an apartment number. Cooper rubbed his fingers across his scruffy chin and glanced back at the building. He was already here, so he might as well investigate. Perhaps Bria had an outdated address from when Amity went to college or something.

Hot, dry desert air blasted him in the face as he stepped out of the car. No wonder Amity had frozen in the mountains—she was acclimated to a damn baking-hot palm paradise. Though he was already acutely aware, it sure felt different experiencing her climate in person.

He jogged up the cement stairs to the third floor, rounded a corner, and paused in front of apartment 316. Pulling off his tattered baseball cap, he mussed his hair, trying to unflatten the scraggly, brown mass and knocked softly. When no one answered, he pounded a little harder.

A muffled shout came through the door. "Coming, Mom."

The door swung open, and his breath hitched.

Amity stood staring back at him with her mouth hanging open. "Cooper," she finally said, wringing her hands out in front of her. "What are you doing here?"

His heart rate accelerated several beats faster than when he climbed the highest peaks. She was so beautiful, her rosy cheeks flushing vibrantly across her tan, oval face, but her eyelids were bruised, and she looked painstakingly thin in her pink V-neck shirt.

Replacing his cap, he cleared his throat. "Easton," he corrected, trying to peer into the apartment. "Are you housesitting for someone?"

"No." After a short pause, she squared her shoulders. "I live here. This is my place."

"I'm sorry. *What?*"

Amity looked at the concrete by his feet and whispered, "It's all I can afford."

"But the clothes, the suitcase, the fashion line, your mom's job at the resort?"

She timidly met his eyes. "I let you believe what you wanted to believe. You and everyone else assumed I had money. I never said that I did."

Her words sunk in, and he braced his hand against the stucco wall beside her door. "I don't understand. Why did you dress up then?" He sucked in a quick breath. "Was it all an *act?*"

"Of course not," Amity spat at him before sarcastically adding, "Yeah, *Cooper*, I gave up a million dollars to play dress up for the cameras."

"Then perhaps you'd better explain it to me," he said. "Because I'm not understanding. I don't *pretend*."

Amity crossed her arms, giving him that same sassy look she had the first day they'd met. "No, you just *choose* yourself."

Cooper pushed off the wall, shaking his head in confusion. "Spin my choices how you want, but I don't understand why you lied to me."

After spiritedly holding his eyes for a few seconds, she sighed and glanced away. "Look," she began, returning her eyes to his, "I never expected all of you to assume I had money, okay? Once you thought I did, I just didn't..." She shook her head, gnawing on her bright pink lower lip.

"Please, Amity, just explain," Cooper said. "I'm really confused."

"I didn't want your *pity*, okay?" Amity forced out. "I still don't, but that's inevitable now. The truth is... Do I really need to explain?" Her lips trembled, covered in their sparkly glossy pink glow. She was just full of contradictions and pretty fancied up for someone claiming lack of funds, or maybe just girly—shit, he didn't know anymore.

"I'd really like to understand," he said. Was she hiding something? A run-in with the law? A spending addiction? A nasty divorce? He loved her so much he didn't care; he just wanted answers.

Flushing a splotchy shade of crimson from her cheeks down to her neck, Amity puffed out her breath and said, "Fine, Cooper," before throwing up her arms. "If you must know, the truth is that I work retail on commission—that's my fashion job. My boss helped me borrow all those clothes and accessories—they weren't mine."

Raising her chin, she continued, "And my mom is a house-keeper at a resort chain here in Palm Springs. She's worked harder than anyone I know, scraping by after all the years of medical bills for my dad. I'm extremely proud of her for even putting food on the table for us. So there you go, all right? The truth," she added in a prickly tone before chuckling uncom-fortably. "Pretty glamorous, isn't it?"

Cooper stood frozen, hardly able to breathe while he processed her words. She hadn't done anything wrong. In fact, her reason for going on the show almost exactly mirrored his. "Why didn't you tell me?" he asked, tugging on his shirt collar. "Amity, I'd have done everything differently if I'd known you went on the show for money. And for a good reason too."

She shook her head. "But I didn't. I wasn't there for the money."

"Yeah, right. The least you can do is be honest with me like I was with you," he said, walking into her apartment without an invitation, desperate to wet his dry throat.

He owed her at least half of the million and could probably afford a hundred thousand outright if he sold his investments.

Then perhaps he could slowly feed her the rest out of his monthly paychecks?

Opening her small cupboards, Cooper searched for a glass. It didn't take him long, as there weren't many of them. He filled a sunflower-patterned glass and drained it.

With her arms crossed, Amity sniffled and began tapping her foot on the vinyl floor. "Just make yourself at home."

"Sorry," Cooper said. "I'm just processing this. It's a lot to take in." He refilled the glass, walked past her, and sat on her beat-up, blue leather couch. Letting out his breath, he stared at a hole on the armrest where the stuffing seeped out before glancing around.

The place was basically a single room. He could see her bed from the freaking couch. Next to her nightstand was a huge shelf of DVDs, all of which looked like they'd come from a resale shop. Only slightly more than an arm's length out in front of him sat a tiny television with a crack in the right-hand corner and a dented Blu-ray player that looked like it might crap out after its next use.

Cooper shut his eyes, trying to control the tremors that pulsed through him. Amity hadn't put on an act. What would she have gained from doing so? She needed money—it was that simple—and she'd given it all up for him. He owed her a million dollars.

She deserved better—she shouldn't have to live like this, but he shook his head at the thought, realizing he'd lost focus on his goal. He'd come here to win Amity back, not to pay her back. She'd get half of what he had anyway if she ever forgave him. His cabin wasn't fancy, but it was big enough to share a life together. A real house on a gorgeous property.

Cooper twisted the vintage sunflower glass in his hands. It looked like a 1970s tumbler you'd pick up at Goodwill, simple and practical. In a way, her lifestyle was a huge relief. He didn't have to live up to the crazy set of expectations he'd developed in his mind. He set the patterned glass on a fold-out end table next to the couch and met her eyes, pressing his fingers together.

"Amity, I came here for you." He stood up and walked toward her. "Would you consider giving me another chance?"

A dozen emotions flitted through him, but mostly panic as she backed away. Did he lose his chance with her? His sister had phrased it the best, 'Who gives up a million dollars to save someone's best friend?' Amity—that's who! Because she loved him. It was painfully obvious, and he was too busy being selfish, belittling her sacrifices, and questioning her motives. That's why she dumped him—he wasn't good enough for her.

But that was about to change. He *would* be the man she deserved.

Reaching for her, he began his attempts to grovel. "I'm so freaking stupid and sorry—"

"Cooper," she returned in irritation, "you don't need to feel guilty, and honestly, I don't have time for this right now. I have to go to work. I have a blood orange dress to pay for and a bunch of repairs on my car."

He dropped his hands. "That's fine. I can wait. I'll hang out here until you get back."

"Please just go home." Amity flashed her palm at him. "You don't owe me anything. Money is *not* why I went on the show. Remember when I told you that I promised my dad I'd live a life full of adventure?"

He nodded.

"*That's* why I went on the show. I don't want your pity money." She grabbed her purse and walked toward the door, jingling her keys as she went, hinting that he was supposed to leave.

Cooper obliged and asked, "Can I meet up with you after work?" as he walked out.

"There's nothing left to say." Amity locked the door and bounded down the steps without a backward glance.

That's fine, Cooper thought, watching her retreating figure —he could wait. He sat numbly on the concrete, brainstorming the words he would say to win her back. As afternoon turned into evening, he pulled out his cell phone and checked in on Dominic but refrained from calling Amity. He wouldn't convince her of anything unless they spoke in person. Hindering boredom, he finally resorted to playing mindless app games until the battery died.

It was midnight before he realized that she wasn't coming home, and he began to full-on panic. He was the world's biggest idiot. Cooper replayed everything he'd said to her, and it was embarrassing. He'd dug an even deeper hole for himself —now, he'd be lucky to ever win her back. But he would *never* give up. No woman on earth could compete with Amity. She was a selfless angel, and he could now safely say that he loved her more than he did himself.

He ran to his rental car, grabbed his backpack, and began to set up camp. Had Amity forgotten what kind of man he was? He could live here indefinitely without a roof over his head. He always traveled with his gear, and these warmer temperatures would feel like sleeping in a house. Chuckling to himself, he thought of her Caveman nickname for him as he pitched his tent beside her door, ready to settle in for the season.

He wasn't surprised when she didn't return that night, or the next, or even the next, obviously evading him at her mom's or a friend's place. She was smart enough to try and outlast his willpower before returning home—but she still thought it was because he felt guilty. Of course, he did, but honestly, he'd never try this hard to pay someone back. Since Amity was likely counting on that, she was in for a life-altering surprise.

After four days of bouncing a ball that he'd found beside the non-existent pool against a plastered wall, making good friends with the apartment complex manager in order to use the bathroom, and eating countless backpacking meals, he woke up with a foot on his chest.

"Ow," he yelped.

Amity screamed.

"Amity, it's me." Cooper bolted up, hoping she could see his face from the reflection of the streetlights. Apparently, he'd fallen asleep leaning against her door, so bored out of his mind he couldn't stand being in the tent anymore. "This apartment complex should at least replace the damn light bulbs in the corridors for your safety. I should chat with the manager about that. Don't know why I haven't already."

"*Easton,*" Amity mouthed in relief through her palm. She drew back, quickly adding, "I mean Cooper."

Cooper smirked at her slip-up. His first name coming off her lips felt like a warm caress. Perhaps he did have a chance?

Amity twisted her key into the lock and opened the door.

"Wait," Cooper said, pressing his hand against the frame. "I'm not leaving until I get a *real* chance to talk to you. Do you want me to camp out here all year? Because I will."

"Relax, Cooper. I'm just opening the door, so I can turn on the light." Amity reached into her apartment and flipped the switch, sighing as she eyed the rumpled sight of him. Pulling her arms tight around her waist, she asked, "*Why* are you still here? I already told you—I *don't* want your mon—"

"I'm not here to repay you," he interrupted. It was time for her to understand. "You're the strongest woman I've ever met. I know you'll be fine without me and that I don't deserve you, but Amity, I am miserable without you. I will live *anywhere* you want to."

She blinked before her eyes lit up, a smile tugging at her lips.

At her reaction, relief flooded through him. He was definitely on the right track. "I will do *anything* for you. I'll even give up backpacking and climbing if it gets in the way of us. All that matters to me is that I'm *with* you."

Amity beamed at him, smiling like she had when she'd thought him a saint. "Do you mean that?"

"Every single word. It's why I came here in the first place—because I'm in love with you—that's it. Please give me another chance. I'll never choose another partner—"

Amity jumped into his arms, bear-hugging him so unexpectedly that he lost his balance and smacked against the stucco wall. "Why didn't you just say all that when you got here?" she yelled before crashing her lips against his.

Pressed up against her, his body came alive, and he kissed her urgently in return. If he hadn't been such a moron, he could have avoided ever losing her in the first place, and he *never* would again.

A few of the neighbors had come out of their apartments to investigate her loud scream. "Princess," he breathed huskily between kisses, "we've got company. Not that being watched is new for us, but I could do without an audience for once."

Amity jumped out of his arms, landing solidly on what appeared to be her trail shoes from the race. She'd kept them? He quirked a grin, remembering the crew's strict instructions that all gear must be returned.

"I'm okay, thanks," she shouted to the neighbors, grabbing his hand and pulling him inside. She wrapped her arms around his neck and planted kisses along his scruffy jaw.

"I like your shoes," he whispered against her cheek.

"What are they going to do? Fly out here and pry them off my feet?"

"Not on my watch," Cooper returned, feeling so lucky to be inside her apartment enjoying the softness of her eager lips rather than outside sleeping on a hard slab of concrete. "If we're living in Palm Springs, we need a bigger place. I don't think I can fit on that bed." Feeling Amity freeze in his arms, he quickly added, "But I can if that's what you want. We can figure out how to get a larger bed in this apartment."

"You really will move here for me, won't you? To Palm Springs?"

"Yes, Amity, without question. I can't survive without you."

A wide smile spread across her face. "That's nice to know, but I'm going to have to get some warmer clothes because, in the morning, we're headed to Aspen."

"*What?*"

"I'd like to give your place a try. We'll have to work out how I'm going to see my mom, but otherwise, I'm good."

"But," he said as she continued to plant kisses on him, "I thought you wanted to live here?"

"I don't care where we live, Easton. I just needed to *know* that you're willing to make sacrifices for me too."

"Amity, I'm completely serious about moving here. The most important thing to me in life now is that you're happy—"

She pulled him down on the bed. "I *really* don't want to talk. I'm exhausted. I just want you—and sleep—and maybe sex if we have the energy. But I'm *so* tired. I haven't been able to sleep in days. Not since I lost you."

"Lost me?" He raised his brows. "How about dumped me?"

Amity wrinkled her nose. "Yeah, well, you deserved it." She giggled softly. "But my life just got a thousand times better because I'm *very* much in love with you too."

He released his breath, allowing the words he'd dreamed of for countless nights to fill him with warmth. "Just remember how much you love me the next time I do something stupid because I've been *really* stupid. I'm so sorry, Princess," he whispered, running his fingers across her lips.

"Apology accepted."

"Good to hear." He nodded, finally feeling content, then

frowned when he realized his feet were hanging off the bed. "I'm with you—sex or sleep—but I really am too tall for this thing. Maybe we should camp on the floor?"

"Sounds perfect," Amity said, "except…"

He tensed. "Except what?"

Giving him a reassuring kiss, she said, "It's nothing bad. Well, maybe to you it is…you see…it's just that…" She playfully pursed her lips. "I don't actually own a sleeping bag."

He laughed, full and hard. "Of course not. You're a spoiled, pampered princess used to glamorous five-star conditions."

She smacked him. "Hey, my place is *way* better than a tent. There's heat in here, at least. And no bugs," she added with pride. "And a toilet, and running water, and—"

Cooper picked her up, listening to her shriek in surprise. He tucked her under his arm, grabbed the comforter off the bed, and tossed it on the floor. Settling them down on top, he used it as a base layer, just like they had with the sleeping bag on the forest floor and proceeded to enjoy the best night of his life. No cameras, no challenges, or nosy contestants—just the two of them making love at full volume.

He was in his own private heaven until he thought about the next day.

Feeling him tense, Amity asked, "What's wrong? Please tell me you didn't change your mind."

"Amity, I'm more concerned about the reverse scenario. I will camp out on your doorstep every time we argue. I won't lose you again. I…love….you, okay? Got that?"

She nodded.

"I'll tell you every single day, I promise. No need to ever question that again."

Amity relaxed. "Good to know. So," she asked, making a little popping sound with her lips. "What then?"

Cooper let out a moan. "My family will be all over you

when we get to Aspen. It might make you go crazy. Please just don't run away, okay?"

"Oh, fun," she exclaimed.

He laughed. "Yeah, okay, *fun*, I guess." Something told him that Amity and his sister would get along just fine.

Epilogue

Amity sat in Easton's arms on his family's large, L-shaped couch, with Jax curled up next to them, a two-carat princess-cut diamond ring sparkling on her finger. Three nights after they'd arrived in Colorado, Easton had coaxed her into a large tent in his backyard, where she'd found countless red, white, and pink roses surrounded by candles. Adorably nervous, he'd proposed, leaving them both so irrevocably happy they decided the bumpy route to love was a godsend.

Now, after almost two weeks in Aspen, the third episode was about to air. Easton's family, his friends, and her mom, currently in the middle of her move to Aspen, sat on the edge of their seats, ready for the newest installment of the drama.

Amity had hit it off with Easton's sister right away. Hannah quickly picked apart her interests deciding that they should start off at the spa and that she'd like to go on some runs with Amity. In return, Amity had agreed to try skiing in the winter, unable to believe that the words had left her mouth. Ice, snow, and cold—she would freeze!

For dinners on his parents' patio, she still had to sit bundled in a light jacket, even in the summer sun. After dinner, they typically returned to his cabin, which was in the middle of nowhere down a beast of a road. Without her catching on to his motive, Easton went through each of her concerns with living there and then, the next day, explained his plan.

Amity was concerned about the 4X4 road—he'd hired a company to level and pave it all the way to his cabin. She was concerned about the fireplace as a heat source—he'd hired a company to install a modern heating and cooling system. She didn't have a car to make it to town—he'd bought her a brand-new Jeep.

The new car sent her over the top, and they'd gotten into their first fight in front of his family and friends.

"It's too much," she'd argued. "I don't need a *new* Jeep."

Easton had then been boneheaded enough to say, "You should have a million dollars, so too damn bad! Deal with it." He knew he'd said something stupid, so she watched him try to calm down. "Look," he'd added a little more levelheaded, "I've learned my lesson about making changes to compromise for you. You're going to have to get used to it."

She'd clenched her teeth. "I want you to slow down some. *You* have to be happy too."

It wasn't until she'd noticed Easton's sister smiling on the sidelines and Hannah had said, "I know why you both make good TV. I can't wait to see tonight's episode," that Amity had tried to calm down too.

"Fine, but the car is *it*, Easton. You're not buying me anything else. I'll get a job next week." To which his goofy, satisfied smile annoyed her all over again. "I'm still mad at you," she added, walking past his perplexed family and friends toward his childhood bedroom.

"You might be mad at me, Princess, but you're still calling me Easton. As long as you're doing that, I know we're still fine."

"Ugh," she'd said and shut the door, but she loved him so much she was over it by dinner.

That was the same night an outdoor heater had showed up on his parents' patio, and she was so tired of fighting with him that she'd just shook her head at his timid grin and let it go. Seeming to think that meant she was okay with it, he'd gently added, "I got a couple for our patio too," and she'd dropped a French fry from her fingers, taking in a series of deep breaths.

Hannah, Chelsea, and Dominic had glanced at the two of them with amused grins, seemingly unworried by their newest conflict. Though all they'd seen of their relationship on the show thus far was the two of them hating one another during the fire challenge and the drama during the first trail run, Amity suspected that they knew Easton so well that whatever they saw in his behavior since she'd arrived in Aspen made them confident that she was the one.

Last week, her impressive trail run had aired, and Easton was on the edge of the couch the whole time, saying things like, 'Damn, Amity, you didn't stop for water,' and 'Oh, you almost had them,' as she approached Becky and Liam near the finish line. He'd even gotten so into it that Jax had started barking at the TV, sending Amity into a fit of giggles.

Now, here she sat on the large, L-shaped couch with their family and friends, who were eager to watch the third episode. Amity was a little apprehensive about watching their relationship unfold with all of them present, but what did it really matter? They'd see it regardless. That was the crux of being filmed on TV. At least it wasn't an episode where they had their tongues down each other's throats yet.

Easton slung his arm around her shoulders, linking his fingers through hers and rubbing his thumb over her engagement ring with a content look on his face while the ridiculous theme music played for episode three. Her intro was a shot of her busting through a tree patch on her first trail run into the sun, while Easton's was this sexy, and yes silly, photo of his defined arm muscles bulging while he thrust his ax down during the woodchuck challenge.

It made Amity laugh, but she turned and whispered into his ear, "Can you do that at our house with your shirt off?"

"Every damn day," he whispered back with a huge smile on his face. She suspected he loved hearing her say 'our' house, though truthfully, she was still getting used to the idea.

A portion of Amity's morning interview popped onto the screen—an interview that had taken place just after Miles had selected her for the woodchuck challenge. She buried her head into Easton's shoulder, both hating to watch herself on TV and knowing what she was about to say.

"I've got to say, though I can't *stand* Miles, I'm just glad it's *anyone* other than *Easton* Cooper," sounding just like the snotty villain she'd imagined. Hopefully, the coming episodes helped to improve her image.

Hannah giggled. "Wow, Amity, it's nice to know you'll keep my brother in line."

Amity glanced sheepishly at her fiancé.

Easton waggled his eyebrows at her and told Dominic, "Just wait till you watch the stupid-ass decision I'm about to make."

Amity slapped Easton's leg, loving that he didn't hold anything against her that she'd said during the race. "Actually," she said, moving her eyes to meet Dominic's, "you're about to see why Easton can stop going on about how I would have won a million dollars. Both of our idiotic decisions got *us* to the finish." She smiled at her man. "And I came out of it with the ideal fiancé. Something money can't buy."

Dominic burst out laughing. "Yeah, *ideal*," he said before cringing and holding his hand to his chest.

Chelsea jumped off the couch and rushed to his side, her features lined with stress.

"Take it easy, man," Easton cautioned. "The surgery's only days away. Don't push it."

Dominic drew in a shallow breath. "See, Coop *is* the ideal guy."

Amity glanced at Easton, beaming. "Turns out he is ideal—ideal for me."

Easton chuckled. "Keep telling yourself that, Princess, and I might have a chance."

~

LESS THAN TWO MONTHS LATER, just after the final episode aired across America, Amity and Easton sat hand in hand, lined up on benches with the other contestants. On a large stage in Hollywood, they were being filmed for the live reunion show, intrusive cameras surrounding them for what Amity hoped was the last time.

Overwhelmed, Amity teared up as she stared at several members of the audience holding up signs that stated, 'Amity, she's why you'll win!' Apparently, she'd become a fan favorite, and the multiple times contestants had told Easton, 'She's why you'll lose,' had generated a counteractive supporting phrase on social media and beyond.

Squeezing her hand, Easton kissed her cheek.

After discussing key scenes from the season with each contestant, Alex announced, "Just as we'd hoped, throwing several single individuals on a show under intense circumstances generated natural, organic romantic relationships. Amity and Cooper, Becky and Liam, and Jade and Isaac are all still together to this day."

Alex replayed romantic scenes from the season, causing Amity to blush into Easton's shoulder countless times, and began to ask probing questions about the current status of each relationship.

"We'll ask our couples more questions in a few minutes, but now, it's time for a special announcement," Alex broadcasted to the cameras. "So audiences at home, listen up, please. For the past two months, we've been telling you we'd like your vote. This is it, America! Please vote via the text instructions on the screen for your favorite couple from this season. The winning couple will take home a two-hundred-thousand-dollar bonus."

Amity's hand flew over her mouth. No way! It wasn't a million dollars, but it was more money than she'd ever had.

Easton tensed beside her before whispering in her ear, "It's just money, Princess. If we don't win, it's fine."

She nodded.

A few minutes later, the host opened a large gold envelope. "Thanks, America, for voting. So, Amity, can you really win it all—Riches *and* Romance?"

Why was he asking her? Alex had already fired so many questions at her this evening that she wanted to climb inside a hole and hide, but fortunately, this one was easy to answer.

"I've already won," she said, flashing her fiancé a beaming smile because that's exactly how she felt.

"Well, Amity and Cooper, you're two-hundred-thousand dollars richer because you *are* America's favorite couple by a landslide."

The audience broke out with a loud cheer, and Amity's head spun as everything moved in slow motion. Bria added in a few audible whoops, and Justin clapped Easton's shoulder.

Alex motioned his hand out in front of him. "Becky and Liam, what are your thoughts?"

Becky smirked and said, "Amity deserves it," while Liam added, "Like I said after the balance challenge, Amity's pretty badass. And Cooper"—Liam made eye contact with him—"you're not so bad yourself. I had no idea during the race why you wanted the money. I'm glad to hear that friend of yours is on the road to full recovery."

Easton nodded. "Thanks, man."

Liam tipped his cowboy hat. He'd announced earlier in the show that he and Becky were living together interchangeably between his ranch in Montana and her family's homestead in Alaska. Amity was glad they'd worked out.

"So," Alex prompted, "Amity and Cooper, what's your plan for the money this time?"

Easton smiled warmly at Amity. "My fiancée is going to start her own trail-running business in Aspen. She wants to guide daytime trail runs. Daytime runs only, I'm told, no camping." He laughed along with everyone else in the studio. "That's what she said her dream is, so we're going to make it happen."

Excitement flooded through Amity. They'd discussed saving up for her business, but she'd thought it would take them a few years.

"And you, Cooper?" the host asked. "What are your plans for the future?"

"Besides having an incredible woman to share my life with?" Easton kissed Amity's lips, receiving more cheers from the audience. "Once Dominic gets the go-ahead from the doctor, we'll be back to our backpacking and climbing tours five days a week."

"That's good to hear, Cooper. But you might have to make room for another change in your life."

Easton's eyes popped wide open, and he turned, looking at Amity.

Amity shook her head and whispered, "No, I'm not pregnant. I swear. Not yet anyway. I have no idea what he's talking about."

Easton whipped his head back around and glared at the host. "What?"

Alex smirked, turned to the crowd, and made an animated gesture with his hands. "Join us for Season Two of *The Race for Riches or Romance, Tangle in the Tropics*—filming and airing soon. Let's meet some of the contestants for the upcoming season!"

The crowd went wild as five pre-chosen contestants walked onto the stage.

"Oh shit, no way!" Easton yelled, thrashing his head from side to side. "Not happening."

Amity started laughing, enjoying the shell-shocked look on her fiancé's face. "I kinda think it is, Caveman. Good luck stopping her."

Easton's sister, Hannah, stood on the stage, first in line. She shot her big brother an ornery glance.

Amity turned to Easton and whispered, "Who says reality TV relationships aren't real?"

Easton glanced between his fiancée and sister and smiled. "Whoever he is, I hope he has to fight like hell for her."

Tangle in the Tropics

Don't miss Hannah Cooper's adventure in *Tangle in the Tropics*, Book 2 of *The Race for Riches or Romance* series. Available April 2023! Read on for a sneak peek…

EXCERPT FROM TANGLE IN THE TROPICS

"The flu?"

Holy snowflakes! What was she supposed to do now?

"Hannah, I'm sorry, but I literally can't get out of bed." Her best friend's wet sniffles vibrated through the phone. "I'd throw up if I got on a plane. Not to mention, get you and everyone else sick."

Hannah paced in the foyer of her alpine-roof townhouse and eyed her already packed suitcase. "But it's male-female teams only, and filming starts in three days," she said, hating the whiny tone that slipped into her already panicked voice. "What am I supposed to do, Bren? This isn't fair. I *really, really* want to go on the show."

"Don't worry," Brendan said in a confident overtone as he sputtered out a few coughs. "I've made alternative plans for you. Logically, it's the best choice."

"Logically?" Hannah scowled at his dorky analytical view of things. Brendan was a computer and finance nerd, complete with the glasses and predictable desk job, but she loved their differences. It's what made their friendship work. "What alternative plans?"

"So," he began carefully, "with this short of notice, I contacted the one guy I thought might say yes. And, well, he —"

"He who?" she asked as the doorbell rang. "He what?"

"Is someone at the door?" Brendan asked, too chipper for her taste.

"Yes, probably my mom coming by to hug me again for the twentieth time. She seems to think I'll get sucked out into the ocean by dangerous rip currents or eaten alive by killer sharks. I mean, I know we're landlocked here and all, but come on."

Hannah pulled open the door, backing up to let her mom enter while continuing to rail at her best friend. "Who is he, Bren? Spit it out!"

Brendan sighed. "Listen, before you get mad, please understand that the directors were going to go with a backup team. I couldn't let that happen. He has the kind of ratings-worthy popularity where the show wouldn't replace you for being without a pre-filmed partner." Hannah noticed a movement to her side but wanted to hear the punchline before she reassured her mom *again* that she wouldn't get eaten alive. "I knew you'd be heartbroken if you couldn't go on the show," Brendan continued, "so I called— "

"Hi, Hannah," a deep voice interrupted from her side.

She froze, her pulse spiking while a thousand tiny tingles prickled across her skin.

With full confidence, he continued, "Sorry to interrupt your call, but it sounds like telling you I'm here will clear things up." His footsteps shuffled across the entryway. "Brendan told me the flight number. Our plane leaves soon, so," he drawled out, hanging on the word, "we need to get going. Can I help with your bags?"

Swiveling around, Hannah's breath caught. Andrew Meyers stood before her in a casual blue T-shirt and jeans, all two-hundred-plus pounds of thick, hard muscle, tattoo-covered forearms, broad shoulders, and short black hair. The trimmed hair and clean-shaven face were different than what she'd seen on TV a few months ago, and yes, she'd watched him. She couldn't help herself.

Our plane? Why would Andrew Meyers be going with *her* on a plane? And then it clicked.

"Brendan, what did you do?" she whispered into the receiver.

"He's so famous, Hannah, they didn't even think twice about casting him. Don't worry. I called Drew before I notified the directors. I knew it would be the only way you could still be prioritized over one of the backup teams. No producer on earth would turn down casting Andrew Meyers. They didn't even believe me until Drew put his agent on the phone. It took them all morning to verify the validity of my claim."

There went Brendan with his dorky analytical phrases, but there was nothing systematic about this. This was personal. She'd dated Andrew Meyers her senior year in high school and through most of college when he was the star quarterback for both schools. They were a hot item until he'd been a first-round draft pick for the NFL. Andrew's family home was just down the street from her parents' house in Aspen, as was Brendan's. They'd all grown up together.

Hannah had avoided speaking to Andrew for the last three years since he'd become a starting quarterback for the Denver Broncos. She didn't go to the neighborhood's holiday barbecues when she knew he'd be there. She didn't respond to group texts with friends from their childhood. And she didn't say more than hi when they accidentally crossed paths. Because Andrew Meyers was a danger to her overly loving, fragile heart. She liked him beyond all the hype and muscle. If she were being honest, she still loved him.

Hannah hung up on her best friend, looking her hunky ex in the eyes. "I don't know what Brendan told you, but this is a *terrible* idea. For your career. For your image." She pointed at his arm. "For your injury. Why would you do this?"

"Why not?" Andrew shrugged his left shoulder, holding his sling-encased right arm rigidly straight. "I doubt you follow NFL news—"

Oh, hell yes, she did. Especially news about Drew.

"—but I'm out with a torn rotator cuff. Just got done with surgery a couple of weeks ago. Don't know if I'll ever play again—"

Hannah's jaw dropped open. *That* hadn't been on the news. He'd probably kept it a secret from the hounding tabloids.

"—and Brendan said you needed me. He said you'd be heartbroken if you couldn't go on this show. Whatever it is. Some reality thing, right?"

She could *not* go on a romance show with the one guy she couldn't get out of her head—the one guy she could never touch again.

"Drew, this is a show about *romance*. And yes, money, but with the intention to create romantic drama between people. I'm guessing Bren didn't tell you that. I promise I will get over not being on a TV show, but you will *not* get over it. You're a football player, not a reality TV joke."

His eyebrows shot up in amusement. "Yeah?"

"Yeah," Hannah returned with a nod. She walked toward the door, expecting him to follow. "I'll have Bren call and cancel for you."

Not moving, Andrew folded his healthy arm across his sling. "So tell me, Hannah. It's been what? A couple of years since our last real conversation? You typically small talk me—and avoid me," he added pointedly. "Why are you going on this show? You lookin' for money?"

"No," she shot back, snapping him a look.

"Ah," smirking, he added, "then love?"

Hannah hesitated.

"Seems like an odd choice to choose Brendan for the show." Scratching his chin, his mouth dipped into a frown. "Thought the two of you didn't feel that way about each other."

"We don't," Hannah said, "but this season, they required teams to enter as a guy-girl pair. I thought the teams might get shuffled around like last season, and…"

Andrew pinched his lips together. "And what?"

Why hide her intentions? It was best if Andrew gave up and went home anyway. Letting out her breath, Hannah finished, "Maybe one of them would end up being the man of my dreams."

A look of concern crossed his face. "So we don't get to be partners then? What happened last season?"

"Why would you go on a show you know nothing about?"

He eyed her, dumbstruck. "It's obvious, isn't it? I have feelings for you. Always have, always will."

Hannah laughed in mock disbelief as a jolt of adrenaline shot through her system. "You expect me to believe that? You have a different woman on your arm every week."

"Paying attention to my press coverage, huh?" Andrew asked while his mouth lifted into a satisfied smile.

Ugh! Hannah hadn't meant to boost his ego—in fact, she'd intended exactly the opposite, hoping to protect herself from his charm. But naturally, he latched onto the one aspect of her statement that gave her away. Yes, she paid attention. Didn't everyone?

"I really don't know anything about you anymore," Hannah delivered as nonchalantly as possible. "What I do know is that this show is a bad idea for your career. I'm guessing your agent told you as much?"

"Yeah, well..." Beginning to pace, Andrew raked a hand through his cropped black hair. "I don't listen to crap advice from my *football* agent regarding my personal life. And I'm not about to listen to advice from you either. The last time I did that, I lost you."

Goosebumps lifted her wispy arm hairs on end. She looked away, hiding her face, and took a few much-needed breaths. After all this time, was it possible he still loved her? Surely not. There was nothing definitively special about her.

"You're my only passion besides football," Andrew

continued in a firm voice, "and since I can't play right now, you'll have to work harder than the last time to get rid of me. Fortunately, Brendan told me you *really* want to go on this damn show. So apart from you ordering me away, I'm going with you."

Hannah straightened her spine and turned to face him. "Drew—"

"I'm headed to the airport," he interrupted, rotating toward the door. "If this show is what you want, I suggest you grab your bags and come with me."

Hannah watched him retreat through her door and immediately felt the loss of his presence. Dammit, he had her. She did want to go on the show, and she didn't want to order him away either. Because as much as she didn't want to admit it, Hannah wished she'd never ordered him away in the first place.

About the Author

Lisa S. Gayle lives in the beautiful, mountainous Pacific Northwest. She enjoys traveling and all things outdoors, including hiking, camping, and s'mores. She's a soccer mom who loves to take her family on adventures while attempting to keep up with her energetic husband and children. She specializes in contemporary romance and believes in falling in love with a happily ever after.

facebook.com/LisaSGayle
twitter.com/LisaSGayle
instagram.com/LisaSGayle

Made in the USA
Monee, IL
14 March 2024